MW01124997

Last Dance Before Dawn

Also by Katharine Schellman

THE NIGHTINGALE MYSTERIES

Last Call at the Nightingale

The Last Drop of Hemlock

The Last Note of Warning

THE LILY ADLER MYSTERIES

The Body in the Garden

Silence in the Library

Death at the Manor

Murder at Midnight

A Scandal in Mayfair

Last Dance Before Dawn

Katharine Schellman

MINOTAUR BOOKS
NEW YORK

First published in the United States by Minotaur Books, an imprint of St. Martin's Publishing Group

www.minotaurbooks.com

Designed by Gabriel Guma

The Library of Congress Cataloging-in-Publication Data is available upon request.

ISBN 978-1-250-32582-2 (hardcover)
ISBN 978-1-250-32583-9 (ebook)

Our books may be purchased in bulk for promotional, educational, or business use. Please contact your local bookseller or the Macmillan Corporate and Premium Sales Department at 1-800-221-7945, extension 5442, or by email at MacmillanSpecialMarkets@macmillan.com.

First Edition: 2025

10 9 8 7 6 5 4 3 2 1

For those lunatics at the beach,
even though they probably wanted me to write
Laid to Rest instead. I love you guys.

ONE

Manhattan, 1925

Everyone came to the Nightingale looking for something.

They didn't have much else in common, the folks who snuck down the alley toward a single electric light that flickered like it had been forgotten for years and could burn out at any moment. You never knew who would whisper the password at the door under the light, who would make their way through the midnight velvet curtains that muffled loud laughter and louder jazz.

Maybe your family could have bought half of Fifth Avenue, or maybe you couldn't even buy new shoes. More likely, you lived somewhere in between, with work that paid your bills and the hope, one day, of something a little more. At the Nightingale, it didn't matter who you were in the daytime. If you could hold your booze and let loose on the dance floor and keep a secret for a stranger, you were in.

They came looking for excitement, for the thrill of breaking a law that no one liked anyway. They came to dance and drink and maybe find a new friend, the sort of friend who—after a glass or three of champagne—would meet them in a quiet corner to get a little bit friendlier.

They came because they loved the music, the way it curled through the air and carried them across the floor, the way the singer's voice filled the room and made their hearts ache.

They came for the party. They came to escape.

If they were lucky, they could pretend that whatever waited for them back at home didn't exist. They could lose themselves in the music and the arms of someone new. They could feel free, even if it would never last, because in that moment nothing mattered but the next dance, the next drink, the next hour.

If they were lucky, they found what they were looking for, and they left before trouble could find them.

But not everyone was lucky.

TWO

Vivian recognized the sound of danger before she even realized what she was hearing.

Twilight had settled on the city, humid and heavy and speckled with the glow of streetlamps. She and Beatrice Henry—Beatrice Bluebird, as she was known at the Nightingale, where she sang six nights a week—moved through it with the practiced carefulness of two women who were used to navigating New York's streets alone. Their steps were quick, but their eyes were quicker, always on the lookout for a man who might be trouble or a cop who might be trailing them.

The Nightingale paid off the police weekly, like any other dance hall or juice joint. But everyone who worked there knew to be wary just the same.

It was that wariness that sent a prickle of warning down Vivian's back when they were two blocks from the Nightingale's entrance.

"Bea—" Vivian tossed out a hand to stop her friend in the middle of the sidewalk. A few steps ahead of them, a cat yowled as it ran out of a narrow alley. "You hear that?"

For a moment, the only sound out of the ordinary was the distant grumble of thunder. Then Vivian heard it again.

"Look a little closer, pal." The voice was low and menacing, snaking out of the shadows and clearly not meant to be overheard. "I want to make sure you and me is on the same page."

"Viv—" Bea hissed, but Vivian couldn't help herself; she took a step forward, just enough to peek down the alley.

Halfway down the narrow stretch of filthy brick walls, two men were just visible in the fast-fading light. One had his back against a wall. He was the taller of the two, but he still shrank from the menacing bulk of the second figure. That one loomed toward him, his wide shoulders cutting off any escape as he shoved some kind of paper toward the nervous man's face.

"—told you, when I have something, I'll let you—"

The menacing man shoved him against the wall, the gesture nearly careless enough to hide the violence of it. The voice broke off with a grunt of pain, but it had been enough. Usually, Vivian would have stayed far away from anything that sounded like a beating and wasn't her business. But she recognized that voice.

"Don't interrupt," the menacing man snarled. "My boss don't take kindly to rude fu—"

"It's Spence," Vivian hissed.

Bea tried to pull her away. "It's not our business. We can tell Silence or Benny," she whispered, naming two of the bruisers who worked at the Nightingale keeping customers—and anyone else who needed it—in line. "They'll come handle it."

"That'll take too long." Vivian shook her head, pulling away from Bea's cautious hand and running down the alley toward trouble. "Hey! Leave him alone!"

The bruiser barely glanced over his shoulder at her, just cocked his fist back and drove it, almost casually, into the nervous man's stomach.

He doubled over, heaving and gasping for air, as his assailant tipped his hat mockingly. "We'll be seeing you soon, boyo. You can count on it."

He was gone before Vivian could reach them. She stood, panting and staring at the gap between buildings where he had disappeared. A drizzling rain began to fall, plastering her hair against her cheeks. She wasn't dumb enough to go after him.

"You okay, Spence?" she asked instead, turning toward the remaining man as he braced his hands on his knees.

"Swell," croaked the Nightingale's second bartender, a lanky, mouthy, handsome grump. "What the hell are you doing here?"

"Apparently chasing off the fella who was about to beat you to a pulp," she said, stung. Spence had been working at the Nightingale all summer and still hadn't managed to endear himself to any of the other staff. But Vivian had expected at least some gratitude. Instead, he scowled at her like she was the one who had just punched him in the stomach, not the one who had run the attacker off. "But no need to say thanks or anything."

He hauled himself upright, wincing. "I had it handled, you know," he said, still sounding resentful. "I didn't need a rescue."

"Sure you did, pal," Bea said, joining them at last. "That was a stupid thing to do, by the way," she added, glancing at Vivian as she opened her umbrella and held it over both their heads. "Be glad he didn't have a friend waiting to beat the stuffing out of you too."

"My stuffing's doing just fine," Spence groused, pushing his wet hair off his forehead and straightening his jacket and tie.

"What was that about?" Vivian asked, laying a hand on his arm. "Spence? Are you in trouble?"

He shook off her hand. "What makes you think he wasn't just trying to rob me?"

"I can tell when a fella like that wants something particular," Vivian said.

"And his suit was too nice," Bea added, glancing at Vivian, who nodded in agreement. "You owe him money or something?"

"It ain't any of your damn business who I owe what," Spence said, crossing his arms over his chest and glowering at them. But Vivian could hear the thrum of fear under his defensiveness. Goose bumps prickled across her skin that had nothing to do with the rain. "Now, I don't know about you," Spence continued, "but some of us gotta get to work. So if you could move out of my way?"

Bea sighed and started to step aside, then yelped in surprise as one of her feet went skidding out from under her. Vivian had to catch her arm to keep her from falling. Her heel had caught on a square of paper on the ground, its once-glossy surface now slippery with rain and alley muck.

Vivian would have bent to pick it up, but Spence pushed quickly past her, his own heel grinding it farther into the dirt. "You coming?" he asked, though he didn't look back over his shoulder as he did. He had disappeared from the alley before either of them could answer.

"You all right?" Vivian asked her friend.

Bea scowled as she gave her hair a pat to check that it was still in place. "Must be a photograph for it to be so slippery," she muttered. "Stupid thing. Nearly turned my ankle."

"Bet someone's going to miss it if it is," Vivian said, bending to pick it up. The bruiser had been holding some kind of paper, hadn't he? Or had she imagined that? "Photographs ain't cheap." There was a hole torn in the middle of it now, and the rest of it was soaked and muddy. If it had been a photograph, there was no telling what it had shown.

"Come on, Viv," Bea said, starting to sound impatient. "Rain's picking up."

Vivian dropped the paper and brushed her hands against each other to wipe off the muck. "He could have said thank you," she grumbled as she ducked back under the umbrella.

"Some folks got no manners," Bea said with a shrug. "Now let's shake a leg, or I'm going to look like such a drowned cat that they won't let me on the bandstand."

Bea, do you recognize those two fellas?" Vivian whispered as she gave her friend a hand down from the bandstand.

It was close to midnight, and the Nightingale's band had just pounded out the last bars of "Mack the Knife." Vivian was delivering a tray of drinks for thirsty musicians, and her ears were so filled with the music that she could barely hear anything happening in the rest of the dance hall. On the floor, couples—dressed to the nines and most of them two or three drinks into their night—applauded raucously. It was a lively crowd, playful and flirty, calling happily for the gin and rum that they knew was always waiting after a foxtrot or a quickstep.

Vivian longed to be on the dance floor with them. She always did, even when she was working. But the two men had caught her eye as soon as they sauntered down the steps into the main room, and they kept catching it as they lingered at the bar or coaxed a new partner onto the dance floor.

Bea gulped the glass of water that Vivian handed to her and snuck a sideways glance toward the men in question.

"No, should I?" she asked, wiping away a trickle of sweat from her collarbone. It wasn't midnight yet, but the Nightingale was already heating up from all the bodies on the dance floor, the air filled with the scents of smoke and cologne and each new bottle that the bartenders opened. The men hadn't started stripping off their jackets yet, but it was only a matter of time. Summer heat could linger well into October in New York. "They're not regulars."

"No," Vivian agreed. They'd both been coming to the Nightingale long enough to spot the familiar faces, including the years when

Vivian had been sneaking out there to dance before she was an employee. "But . . ."

She grimaced, not sure what to say. On the surface, they were exactly the sort who found their way to the Nightingale every night, friendly and well-dressed and halfway between plain and good-looking. It wasn't the clothes they wore, though those were swanky enough; after years spent hunched over her sewing in a dressmaker's shop, Vivian Kelly had an eye for fine stitching and suits cut to order. But plenty of men in the Nightingale were as well-dressed or better. And it wasn't just the flow of drinks they'd been buying, poured out with no more thought for the cost of each bottle than for the laws that made those bottles illegal.

It was . . .

Around her, the cheerful noise of the Nightingale took on a sultry murmur as the band played the opening bars of a tango. She spotted one of the two men on the dance floor, whispering in the ear of a waitress who was on her break. Vivian shivered.

That was the fourth waitress he'd cozied up to since he'd arrived. He was the charmer of the pair, his dark red hair slick with pomade. He had a smile like a Hollywood dreamboat and the sort of muscles that would come in handy in a back-alley brawl. His friend was taller, lankier, with a flashy pinstriped suit and what Vivian thought might be tattoos just barely visible where the cuffs of his jacket met the backs of his hands.

It all could have been a coincidence, of course. Anything could be a coincidence. But Vivian didn't think so. They were being careful about it, free with smiles and cash in equal measure, happy to sweet-talk a girl onto the dance floor or buy a fella a drink. But once Vivian saw the pattern, she couldn't make herself unsee it.

They were scoping the place out. She just didn't know why.

"Bluebird!" hollered Mr. Smith, the bandleader, as he counted in the bass. "We're waiting on you!"

Bea had every reason to roll her eyes and get back to work; the Nightingale was already crowded and rowdy that night. And plenty of people only showed up because they'd heard of Beatrice Bluebird and wanted to get lost in her smoke-and-honey voice.

But Bea and Vivian had known each other for years, two girls from tenement homes who came for an escape and stayed for the work, which was its own kind of escape, too. They might not trust the world, but they trusted each other.

"You jumpy because of what happened to Spence?" Bea asked, her forehead creased with concern. She waved one hand at Mr. Smith to show she'd heard, but her eyes were on Vivian. "Or is it something else?"

"I don't know." Vivian shook her head. "It's probably nothing. Here." She reached up to adjust the feathered headband that held back the careful wave of Bea's hair. "Now you're all fixed."

"Bluebird!"

Bea handed her glass over. "We know trouble when we spot it," she murmured. "I'll keep an eye from up there."

"It's probably—"

But Bea hadn't waited for her reply. The band had been vamping impatiently for over a minute by the time she reached the microphone, and the rich whisper of her voice filled the air as the music swelled around her. Vivian watched her for a moment, caught up in the magic of what her friend could do. Then her eyes drifted back over the dance floor, trying to spot the two men once more.

"Hey there, beautiful girl!" A cheerful, wobbly young man with a mustache that was still mostly peach fuzz caught her hand. "Tell me you're free for a dance, or I might perish of a broken heart right here at your feet."

Vivian was happy to push aside her jumpy thoughts. "Guess it'll be the broken heart then, Gus."

"Aw, c'mon, Viv," he said, giving her a mournful look. "I saw you gazing all longing-like at the dance floor not half a minute ago. Just one song?"

"Maybe we can catch a quickstep in a bit," she said, patting his cheek, even as she glanced toward the bar. "I don't have a break for another hour. In the meantime, there are plenty of girls waiting to go for a spin. Ask one of them."

Gus sighed but didn't protest any further as she retrieved her tray from where she had left it on an empty table. Blowing him a quick kiss over her shoulder—Gus was harmless, as far as men went, and she never minded being asked to dance—she hurried back toward the bar.

Standing at one end of it, greeting a well-dressed couple and gesturing for two coupes of champagne to be delivered to them, was Vivian's boss and the owner of the Nightingale.

Honor Huxley was dressed more like the man whose hand she was shaking than like his companion. Vivian had never seen Honor in a dress. Instead, the Nightingale's owner preferred tailored trousers, black suspenders, and crisp white shirts, worn open at the neck to reveal the curve of her collarbone. In contrast to her masculine attire, her hair and makeup were pristine, blond curls pinned back around her head and red lips curving up in response to something her guests said.

Honor moved through the world on her own terms. And when that world didn't welcome her, she had built her own in the small but thriving domain of the Nightingale, where a poor Irish orphan like Vivian could dance with the brother of a local alderman. A place where a Black girl like Bea was cheered every time she took the stage, where no one blinked an eye when two men danced a tango with their cheeks pressed close together.

And where two men with sharp suits and sharper eyes made the back of Vivian's neck prickle uneasily when she caught sight of one of them chatting with the bartender—not Spence, though; Spence was nowhere in sight. Had he been more hurt than he let on? Vivian tried to ignore them as she waited for a new round of drinks to land on her tray, hoping to sidle away through the crowd before Honor realized she was there.

She was too slow. Honor, turning away from the couple she was glad-handing to survey the dance floor, caught sight of Vivian; the polite smile that she had worn softened for a moment. "Everything all right with Beatrice?" she asked quietly as she stepped away from the bar, putting some distance between their conversation and the guests that crowded there.

Trust Honor to notice everything in her club. Vivian shrugged. "Nothing to worry about," she said, giving a quick wave to the bartender so he'd know she had an order for him. "Just chatting."

"You looked uneasy," Honor said quietly.

Vivian tried not to frown, wondering how closely Honor had been watching her. Or maybe she'd just been watching her songbird. Vivian was about to repeat that it was nothing, but the stranger at the bar caught her eye again. Her eyes slid from him to the dance floor. "Any chance you know the fella dancing with Ellie?"

"Ellie's dancing a tango?" Honor murmured, smiling. "Now there's something I never thought I'd see. She's usually all business, even on her breaks."

"Pretty Jimmy taught her the steps last week," Vivian said.

Honor's gaze flicked toward the dance floor, a bare movement of her lashes that Vivian never would have noticed if she hadn't been looking for it. "I don't recognize him. He making any trouble?"

"No, nothing like that," Vivian said quickly, her face hot with embarrassment. She shouldn't have said anything. "Just caught my eye, is all. Suit that fancy, I didn't know if he was someone important."

Another quick movement of Honor's eyes. "No one that I know, if he is." Her eyes narrowed. "And if he's a cop, he's playing it pretty cool."

"They don't look like cops," Vivian said, laughing. "He's got a friend with tattoos down to his hands. Never seen a cop marked like that before."

A frown flickered across Honor's face, so brief Vivian thought she might have imagined it. "Interesting. Well, I'd go out of business if I turned away paying customers just because I didn't recognize them. Maybe I'll say hello if I have the time."

A wave from behind the bar caught Vivian's eye. "I'm up," she said, but Honor laid a hand on her arm before she could leave.

"You're doing all right?" she asked, her voice dropping to a murmur that made Vivian shiver. "I've been getting the feeling like maybe you're avoiding me."

Vivian's dancing dress left her arms bare, the sleeves little more than beaded gauze that swooped over her shoulders. It was too hot in the Nightingale to wear much else, and she liked that her job gave her a reason to get dolled up. But for a moment, she wished there were a few more layers of fabric between her and Honor. The sweaty, smoky warmth of the air around them was nothing to the heat of Honor's hand where it rested on her skin. Half of her wanted to lean into that heat, close enough to smell the perfume that lingered on Honor's skin. And half of her wanted to put as much distance between them as possible.

Vivian took a step back, and Honor didn't stop her. "Danny's ready for me," Vivian said carefully. "And I've got a table full of your customers waiting on their cocktails."

They both knew what she was really saying. Being close to Honor Huxley was a risk Vivian longed to take. But Honor lived according to her own rules, and more than once, those rules had ended up getting Vivian hurt.

For a moment, Vivian thought Honor would reach for her again. But a heartbeat later, her cool smile was back in place. "Time for work then, pet," she said. "Still a lot of night left ahead of us."

Vivian watched as she disappeared into the crowd, then turned back to the bar. "Three fizzes," she told the bartender waiting for her. "Extra gin and plenty of lime. Is Spence okay?"

"Took breaking a bottle of gin for him to finally tell us something about what happened," said the bartender, Danny Chin, his voice low. His hands moved as fast as the dancers' feet as he stirred up the cocktails, and he smiled over her shoulder at the customers who were waiting their turn. Vivian hid her own smirk. Danny's smiles were something close to legendary at the Nightingale. It was easier being short-staffed when the customers would wait in line just for a chance to flirt with the handsome bartender. "Honor's worried he hit his head too hard. She told him to lie down in the men's dressing room."

"He gonna be okay?" Vivian asked as Danny slid the tray of glasses back toward her.

"I'm sure he'll be bothering us all again in an hour. Now get back out there, night's not getting any less busy."

The next hour was a blur of shouted orders and weaving through the crowd, the band playing hot and fast as Bea belted her heart out into the microphone. When she finally hopped down from the bandstand, Vivian's break was just starting, and she was about to go join her friend in the staff dressing room when the band launched into a quickstep.

Gus materialized at her side, a sloppy grin on his face. "Ready?" he asked.

Vivian's feet were tired enough that she almost said no. But there were few things she liked more than racing across the dance floor with a good partner. "All right, you handsome thing, just because it's you," she said, holding out her hand.

Gus beamed, and after that they needed all their breath for dancing instead of talking. When the band finally flourished through the last few bars, Gus spun her in a tight circle, both of them laughing as they finally fell still.

"Golly, Viv, but you're a good time," Gus said, panting a little as he beamed at her. He lowered his voice. "Any chance we could slip out for—"

"Don't be like that, Gus." Usually, Vivian would be more careful with her words. But Gus was a regular, and regulars knew that Honor Huxley expected good manners if they didn't want to make a quick and painful exit. "Or I won't say yes next time you ask me to dance."

He shrugged. "Can't blame me for trying," he said, taking the rejection without too much disappointment. "Maybe—"

"Hope this little fella's not bothering you," a deep voice rumbled, while an accompanying hand landed on Gus's shoulder.

Vivian's eyes traveled up the arm attached to that hand, across the red hair slicked back from his forehead, the dreamboat eyes, the lazy smile that he flashed when he saw her sizing him up. This close, she could also see his scarred knuckles, could tell that his face would have been more handsome if it hadn't met the wrong end of someone's fist a time or two.

The man gave Gus a shake that only pretended to be friendly, and the smaller man winced in his grip. "Because if he is . . ."

"Not at all," Vivian said firmly. "Gus is a pal. And he was just about to go grab himself a drink. Weren't you?"

"Sure was," Gus said, sliding out of the man's grip and straightening his cuffs. He threw the redhead a belligerent look. "So there's no need to get so—"

"I'll see you around, Gus," Vivian said quickly, seeing the stranger square his shoulders as if readying for a fight.

Gus snapped his mouth shut and took the hint, heading for the bar without looking back.

Vivian didn't take her eyes from the man. "I'm sure you meant well," she said, not sure about it at all. "But Gus is a sweet kid. And if he wasn't, we've got our own muscle to take care of things."

The man smiled at her, and Vivian's stomach fluttered nervously. His expression was clearly meant to be friendly, even flirtatious, and he was good-looking enough that it might have worked. But with a scar cutting through one eyebrow and a nose that had been broken at least once, he looked like someone who made a living with his fists.

Vivian knew how much trouble that sort of fella could cause.

"I'll remember that," he said. "In the meantime, can I make it up by taking you for a spin?" When Vivian's eyes flicked to the hand he held out, then back to his face, he leaned closer. "I'm guessing you're the sort of girl who'd spend her whole life on the dance floor if she could. So what d'you say?"

It felt like a bad idea, but Vivian had gone along with plenty of bad ideas in her life. And if he and his friend had been scoping out the Nightingale, she wanted to know what they were looking for.

She laid her hand in his. "Why not, mister? Lead the way."

THREE

"You got a name, little bunny?" the man asked as they fell into the rhythm of the foxtrot.

She thought about giving him a fake one. But half the people there that night knew who she was, and one of them might have already told him. "Vivian," she said after only a moment of hesitation. "What—"

"Well, Miss Vivian, I have to be honest," he said before she could ask him for his own name. "I've been watching you half the night, thinking you'd be a dream to dance with. And you don't disappoint."

"Glad to hear it, mister . . ."

The hand on her back rose, and one of his fingers flicked playfully at the edge of her bobbed hair, which swung like a black curtain just below her ears. Vivian tucked her chin, but his hand had already slid away, returning to her back so he could guide her through the next turn. "Guessing a girl like you loves it here."

"Who doesn't?"

"Can't argue with that. You been working here long?"

"Depends on who you ask, I guess," she said, careful and trying not to sound like it. She saw a muscle clench in his jaw at her nonanswer before his lazy smile came back. He wanted something, that much was obvious; she just wasn't sure what. Not yet. "What about you?"

His brows rose just the slightest bit. "What about me?"

"What kind of work do you do?" She gave him her emptiest smile, just a girl chatting on the dance floor and nothing more.

"Oh, bit of this and that," he said, laughing. Before Vivian could stop herself, her eyes flickered down to their clasped hands, to the scars on his knuckles, before she pulled them back to his face. She hoped he hadn't noticed, but his hand tightened on hers for a moment, as though he was worried she might slip away, before he relaxed once more. "You're a swell dancer, sweetheart. Must be hard to spend your nights running drinks around instead of kicking up your heels."

"Sometimes, sure." Vivian smiled blandly. His voice had a polished, uptown lilt to it. But there was a hint of something rougher underneath that she couldn't quite place.

He laughed again, and it almost sounded natural. "You're a cheerful girl, aren't you?"

"Can be."

He glanced around the room, eyes lingering on the dancers before they returned to her once more. "Seems like a fun place to spend a night. Sort of place people come back to, yeah?"

"I suppose so."

This time, the twitch in his jaw was sharper. "You know, sweetheart," he said, and she could hear the undercurrent of irritation in his voice, though he was doing his best to still appear playful, "I'd almost think you're not having fun out here. What's the matter?" He flashed her another dreamboat smile. "I promise I'm a nice fella."

He was older than she'd first thought—older than Honor, probably. Vivian wished he were younger. Usually, the green boys were easier to handle, to send on their way with no trouble.

The man guiding her around the dance floor was trouble; they both knew it, and she was getting tired of pretending otherwise.

"Nice fellas don't have as many scars as you do, mister," she said, smiling at him. "And they give you a name, even if it is a fake one, when they take you for a spin."

His brows rose, but the look he gave her was amused, rather than openly angry. "You know a lot about men, little bunny?"

Again, Vivian could hear that hint of roughness in his voice, as if he couldn't quite hold on to his ritzy accent when he was distracted.

"I'd know when they want something from me," she said. She was still smiling at him, the sort of look that said maybe she wasn't so bright, maybe she had a high opinion of herself. "So if you're thinking I'll follow you somewhere more private, think again. I already told Gus no, and I know him a hell of a lot better than I know you."

"He's not nearly as good-looking," the man suggested, but his heart clearly wasn't in it. She could see his irritation still simmering below the surface before he seemed to make up his mind about something. "All right, then, if you like a fella to lay all his cards on the table. I'm not looking for company tonight. I'm looking for an . . ." He paused, his smile twisting to one side. "Old friend."

That smile made Vivian's stomach drop. That smile meant someone was in trouble. She couldn't tell whether he thought she was too dumb to notice, or whether he wanted her to know. "Don't know if I can help you there, mister," she said, wishing the song would end.

"You're a friendly girl," he said. "I've been watching you tonight. Got a smile for everyone. If my friend's been here, I bet you've met him. Maybe even danced with him. Fella liked to dance, and he loved having a pretty girl on his arm."

Vivian rolled her eyes. "That could be half the folks here."

"Calls himself Hugh Brown," the man said softly. "Ring any bells, little bunny?"

Vivian gave him a narrow-eyed stare. She could guess easily enough that the man wasn't looking for Hugh Brown, whoever he was, to throw him a party. "If he's a friend of yours, how come you don't know where to find him?"

"We lost touch," the man said, smiling.

That smile made Vivian want to shiver. Instead she shrugged. "Not a name I know. Sorry, mister."

"You sure about that?" he asked. "White fella, dark hair. Smooth talker. Bigger nose than mine, though he's better-looking since it ain't been broken. Might know a bit of Yiddish, though he doesn't use it much." He tapped his temple. "Little birthmark, right here."

"And *that* could describe half the fellas in this city," Vivian said. "Maybe if you had a picture of him, I could help you."

The man's jaw clenched. "I don't," he said, his voice short and irritated.

Vivian would have shrugged if they hadn't been dancing. "Well, then what makes you think you can find him here?"

"Because I know he came to New York when I lost track of him," the man said. His smile never faded, but his grip on her hand grew tighter. "And this is exactly the sort of sordid little place he'd like to come. So think hard before you lie to me." For a moment, his playful mask dropped, and he let his eyes wander over her, his lip curling. He added, his voice soft and dangerous, "I don't like it when tenement trash lies to me."

Anger curled in Vivian's stomach. "And here I thought you had some manners," she said, tossing her head and pouting, an empty-headed girl who wasn't having fun anymore. "In the second place, it'd be worth my job if I was gossiping about customers."

The man, about to open his mouth, frowned at her. "In the second place?"

"Yes. The second place." Vivian scowled at him. "Because the first place is the fact that I have no idea who you're talking about, and that's the God's honest truth." She put her chin in the air. "And I go to church on Sundays, which I doubt you do, mister. So either learn some manners or don't come back to the Nightingale. We don't like rude fellas here." As the song came to an end and applause filled the dance hall, she tried to step away from him.

His grip on her hand tightened again, and his mouth took on that same ugly, angry twist. But then he glanced over her shoulder and, his movements careful and deliberate, let her go.

"Everything all right here, Viv?" a deep voice rumbled.

Vivian didn't take her eyes off the man in front of her. "Swell, Benny," she said with a smile that didn't reach her eyes. "This fella was just thanking me for the dance." She took a step back so she was standing next to the hulking bouncer.

Benny, who looked exactly like the professional tough guy that he was, nodded. "You heading out for the night, pal?"

The man's jaw tightened. "I was thinking of grabbing one more drink. Unless there's a reason I shouldn't?"

Benny's expression didn't change. "I hope not." He glanced at Viv. "Boss says to tell you that your break's done."

"Sure thing," Vivian said, her empty-headed smile back in place. Honor didn't send the muscle to tell her employees to get back to work—not unless she thought someone might be in trouble. "Thanks for the dance, I suppose, mister."

"Vivian, right?" The man reached out as if he'd grab her arm, then, with another glance at Benny, seemed to think better of it. He dropped his hand. "I'll be around for a little longer if you got anything else to say to me. Anything you remember."

"Can't remember what I never knew," Vivian said with a shrug. "Enjoy the rest of your night."

She could see the muscle twitch in his jaw once more, but he gave her a friendly-seeming nod. Neither she nor Benny moved until he had disappeared into the crowd.

"He get ugly with you?"

"He thought about it," Vivian said as they stepped off the dance floor. She didn't bother to hide the way her voice shook, not with Benny—he needed to know that she was shaken so that he could do his job. But she kept her expression cheerful in case any of the other customers were watching them. "I don't think he's stupid enough to do it, though. Not in the middle of the dance floor. You going to keep an eye on him?" she added, glancing at Benny, glad for the comforting bulk of him walking beside her.

"Saul's on it," he said, terse as always. "Boss wants to talk to you."

He tipped his head toward the bar, where Honor was waiting, her elbows resting on the counter's surface. She was listening to something Danny was telling her, nodding along. But her eyes were on Vivian before a crowd of giggling women on their way back from the ladies' powder room came between them, the scent of fresh lipstick and Shalimar filling the air as they tumbled toward the bar.

Vivian glanced over her shoulder. "He's got a friend—"

"Saul's on it," Benny repeated. He was a man of few words. Most of the muscle who worked for Honor were. But they were kind enough in spite of their rough profession—at least to the people they liked, which was most of the Nightingale's staff. And the clipped rumble of his voice was familiar enough to quiet Vivian's jumpy nerves. "Let's go."

Honor leaned back against the bar as they reached her, fingers tapping the sides of a glass of amber liquor. Vivian could feel sweat prickling along her own back and arms, but Honor seemed fresh and relaxed as always, not a curl out of place in spite of the heat. She looked Vivian over, an unreadable head-to-toe glance. "All right, pet?" she asked quietly.

Vivian swallowed, her smile firmly in place. "As rain, boss," she said, too aware of the customers crowding around the bar only a few feet from them.

Honor looked over her head toward Benny. "Thanks, Ben. Back

to work for now. No getting rough unless they do, but if they make trouble, toss 'em out, same as you would with anyone else. I'll let you know if there's anything more."

"Yes, boss," Benny rumbled, nodding. He turned away to return to his place by the dance floor, a glowering mountain in a dark suit.

Honor looked Vivian over. "You look a little shaken up."

"I'm fine," Vivian said too quickly. They both knew it wasn't true. "He's looking for someone."

Honor's eyes drifted past Vivian, scanning the crowd, then surveyed the crowded bar. "Dressing room's not empty," she murmured, then held out her hand. "Dance with me?"

The band had just started a waltz, and Vivian knew how much Honor loved a waltz. But more importantly, they could stand close and whisper on the dance floor in a way that wouldn't attract too much attention. Without thinking whether it was a good idea or not, Vivian nodded. "All right."

Each couple on the dance floor swayed as if they were in their own world, as if nothing but the music could touch them. Vivian slid into Honor's arms, wishing it were true. Honor danced like poetry, her shoulders strong, her steps confident, her hand so gentle against the small of Vivian's back it might not have been there at all if it weren't for the electric feeling that it sent through her entire body.

"I've missed you, pet," Honor murmured.

"I haven't gone anywhere," Vivian pointed out. She felt giddy, as if every light in the room were passing by in a blur. She couldn't remember the last time she had been in Honor's arms.

Honor spun her in a gentle turn, and when they came back together, the breath of her laugh brushed Vivian's ear. "You know what I meant, though."

She did. Once, Vivian had trusted Honor too freely. She had known better, even as she did it. But longing and hope could cloud even the best judgment, and Vivian would be the first to admit that her judgment in the past had been far from the best.

But that electric current still jumped every time they touched, and the longing and hope were still there. It was still easy to fall into Honor's rhythm, easy to follow her lead. Vivian wished everything, between them and around them, were that easy, too.

Against her better judgment—there was no such thing, not when it came to this—Vivian laid her head against Honor's shoulder. There was just enough difference in their heights that they fit together.

"I missed you too," Vivian whispered.

Vivian had never been a girl who loved a waltz; her feet wanted to move fast, until she was dizzy and breathless and couldn't think about anything except keeping up with the music. But in that moment, she would have happily waltzed forever.

But even as they swayed and turned, she could feel the tension in Honor's body. The rest of the world was there, and it wouldn't wait long before it demanded their attention.

"Looked like an interesting dance you were having," Honor said quietly.

Vivian laughed hoarsely. "And then some."

"Who was he looking for?"

A gentle backward motion; Honor's hand slid from her back and down her arm, catching her hand and guiding her into a smooth, sideways cross of their feet. It was as easy to follow as the rest of it, but it put enough distance between them that Vivian could think a little more clearly.

"Someone named Hugh Brown," she said as they came back together. "Not a name I know. Do you?"

"Never heard it before," Honor said, the words brushing against the curve of Vivian's ear. "Can't say I much like the idea of them looking for someone at my place, but . . ." Vivian could feel the ripple move across Honor's shoulders as she shrugged.

Another turn; Vivian waited until the music carried them together again. She wanted her next words to be for Honor's ears alone. "He looked like the sort of fella who was good at making trouble. But that doesn't mean he will."

The music ended, gentle and sweet, and they drew to a halt. Around them, the other dancers applauded politely, and the trumpet swung immediately into a lively Charleston rhythm, the rest of the musicians catching him a moment later. The room filled with music and laughter.

At least half of Vivian wanted to stay in Honor's arms. But she knew it wasn't a good idea, so she stepped back. "Anyway, I don't see them anymore, so I guess they took off. And my break is past done. I should get back to work unless you need anything else?"

Honor shook her head, but she still looked thoughtful, and Vivian wasn't entirely surprised when her boss followed her to the bar.

"Took you long enough," Spence growled, back behind the bar when Vivian reached it. He was just lining up a set of lowball glasses on a tray and filling them with ice. "These'll be for the table by the stairs, wait half a tick and I'll have 'em ready."

"Looks like we're going to need more gin soon," Vivian said, eyeing the bottles behind the bar. "Thirsty crowd tonight."

"I know," Spence snapped, looking harried. His elbow caught a jar of just-squeezed lime juice; he cursed, catching it before it fell to the ground but not before it spilled half its contents across the bar. "You handle the customers, Viv, I'll handle the booze, all right?"

"Spence," Honor broke in as he began wiping up the lime juice. "You heard the name Hugh Brown before?"

"Danny said two tough guys were in here asking about someone. That him?" Spence asked, his eyes fixed on his work. "Who is he?"

"No idea," Honor said, but she was leaning forward as she said it. "You thought they looked rough, then?"

"I didn't see 'em," Spence said, shrugging. "But plenty of tough folks end up here, right? Danny said the fella he talked to was friendly enough."

Friendly wasn't anywhere close to how Vivian would have described the redheaded man, but she nodded anyway. "See? Probably nothing to worry about."

"Hmm." Honor's lips pressed together. "Still. When you have a sec, Vivian, skip on up to Silence and tell him to keep an eye out for those two."

"Will do, boss."

"Spence." Honor nodded at him. "Looking good tonight. Keep it up."

He stared at her. "Did you just give me a compliment?" he demanded, but Honor was already walking away. He turned to Vivian. "Did she just give me a compliment?"

"You say it like it's never happened before."

He scowled at her. "It hasn't, not for me. We can't all be pretty girls that the boss has a sweet tooth for."

Vivian bit the inside of her cheek. She could have told him exactly why Honor didn't usually compliment his work—he was slow and sloppy, and he got impatient with customers when he was feeling overwhelmed. But it wasn't worth starting a fight. "I'll be back for those drinks as soon as I deliver Honor's message to Silence," she said instead, pasting a smile on her face. "Works for you?"

His smile was as insincere as her own. "Sounds swell, doll."

The band was playing "Ain't We Got Fun" now, Bea's voice pattering out a duet with the trumpet while the rest of the musicians took a welcome breather. On the dance floor, Vivian caught a flash of red out of the corner of her eye: two girls in bright dresses, young enough that Vivian could guess their parents had no idea they were out. Bangles clashed on their wrists as they threw their hands in the air and kicked toward each other like mirror images, feet moving almost too fast to follow and their mouths wide with laughter, the other dancers cheering them on until they fell into each other's arms, exhausted and smiling and too breathless to keep going.

There was no sign of the two men looking for Hugh Brown.

Vivian slipped through the crowd like smoke. The stairs swept her up from the dance floor and through the velvet curtains that looked black but were really a deep, rich blue. As they fell closed again behind her, they blocked most of the noise and the heat.

The door was closed at the end of the hall, like always, and Silence waited next to it, perched on a tipped-back stool so he could lean against the wall, arms crossed as he waited for the next knock.

He nodded to her as she came toward him, the heavy carpet that ran along the hall muffling the sounds of her feet.

"Evening, pal," she said cheerfully. "Busy night, isn't it?"

Silence nodded without speaking. Vivian wasn't offended; there was a reason no one called him Silas. A half-full glass sat on the floor next to the stool, but she knew it would have only water in it. If it had been any other employee, she probably would have snagged a drink at the bar for him. But Silence never touched a drop of hooch when he was working. A doorman at a place like the Nightingale needed to stay alert, and Silence took his job seriously.

"Message for you from Honor."

Silence nodded at her description of the two men. "They left," he said. "Maybe ten minutes ago."

"No sign of them coming back?"

This time Silence shook his head. "Not at this door."

If the men knew about any other doors into the Nightingale, that was a whole different kind of trouble. But Vivian wasn't going to borrow that unless she had to. "Honor says to keep an eye out for them," she said. "Wants to know if they come back tonight or any other night."

"Got it."

Behind her, Vivian could barely hear the band starting a new song. Slower, this time, and sweet. A song to get couples on the floor, cheeks pressed together while they caught their breath. It must be getting late. Vivian paused, half turned to head back. "By the way, that suit looks real handsome on you. Is it new?"

That cracked the marble of his face; Vivian was shocked to see him offer her the ghost of a smile. "Custom-made," he rumbled, one hand rising to smooth down the charcoal-gray lapels before he seemed to realize what he was doing and dropped his hand. "First time I had the dough for it."

"You look swell," Vivian said sincerely. She had worked as a dressmaker for years; she knew what stitching like that cost. And what it meant to folks like them to be able to pay for custom tailoring instead of ordering clothes from a catalog or buying them secondhand and already in need of repair. "Like a Fifth Avenue fella for sure."

It was hard to tell in the dim light, but she thought she could see a hint of red in his cheeks, and the image of the gruff, glowering doorman blushing made her smile as turned back to the dance hall.

FOUR

"Table by the stairs is getting rowdy," Vivian said, letting out a breath as she slid her tray onto the counter. Her hair was clinging damply to the back of her neck, and she was desperate for a breath of fresh air. Even the Charleston the band was playing wouldn't have tempted her onto the floor. "Might be time to cut them off for the night."

Danny, his hands busy with a bottle of champagne, glanced toward the crowd of boys she was talking about. They were a sort that showed up at the Nightingale most nights, looking for an adventure that they could buy with their parents' money before slinking home at dawn. As long as they stayed cheerful—and didn't get handsy—they were fun to have around. But when the mood of one turned, the rest of them usually followed, and then you had a group of drunk boys trying to prove how important they were. If things got rough, Benny or Saul would have to show them to the door. No one wanted to reach that point if they could help it.

Danny looked relaxed, with the cuffs of his shirt rolled up and the knot of his tie loose, but the glance he gave the crowd of boys was shrewd. Few of the patrons who crowded around the bar knew that Danny was the Nightingale's unofficial second-in-command. He had been at the Nightingale longer than anyone except Honor, and he knew how to manage things.

"Spence," he called cheerfully. The bartender—his shirt stuck to his back and his brow furrowed in concentration—glanced up. Danny made a few quick gestures with his hands, keeping them low so the guests on the other side of the bar wouldn't be likely to notice: two fingers making a crawling motion through the air, both hands flipping over with a brushing flick. *Stair, done.* Spence glanced at the table in question, then gestured back, two quick bobs of his fist like a nodding head. *Yes, yes.*

Most of the Nightingale's employees learned and used the signs Honor taught them without wondering where they came from. Vivian was one of the few people who knew Honor had learned them as a child to talk with her nearly deaf sister. She often wondered whether Danny knew, too, but she had never asked. Honor didn't like people talking about her private life.

Danny turned back to Vivian, already pulling a new bottle from under the bar. This one held only soda water. A knife and a lime followed, a cluster of lowball glasses lined up next. "You doing all right, Viv?" he asked, hands busy slicing wedges for each glass.

Friendly and relaxed, and far more approachable than his boss, Danny was usually the one the staff came to with troubles or concerns. And if any of them balked at taking orders from a Chinese man, they didn't last at the Nightingale more than one shift. That didn't happen often, though, once they'd already shown that they were willing to work for Honor herself.

But Vivian found herself confiding in him less these days, for one particular reason. "I'm swell," she said. "What about you, Danny-boy? I hear a baby's hard work."

Danny pushed his hair off his forehead. "Can't wait for you to take a shift tonight and find out, kitten," he teased, grinning at her.

"You say that like I haven't been around every week since she was born," Vivian protested. "I'd have taken nights, too, if Florence hadn't needed to feed her."

That made Danny sigh. "Thank God Ma said Florence could ease off nursing at night some," he said, more seriously. "Your sister *is* looking ragged these days. I know she'll like waking up to have you there."

"I'll like it too," Vivian said quietly, studying herself for a little pang of envy and pleased when she didn't find one. Three months of a whirlwind romance had seen Danny and her sister Florence married the year before, and the new baby had followed quickly after. Vivian was happy for them—how could she not be, when they met because of her, because of the Nightingale? But so much of her life before their wedding had been her and Florence against the world. It had been impossible, at first, not to feel like the one left behind.

Vivian glanced around the dance hall. Florence had managed to build the life she wanted. And Vivian, in her own way, had done the same. The Nightingale was as much her home, her family, as Florence's life with the Chins. And if some of the things she once dreamed of were still missing . . . she could live with that.

Her eyes fell on Honor, greeting a pair of men in expensive silk suits at the bottom of the steps. Didn't everyone live with that, in their own way?

"Ellie!" Danny's shout pulled Vivian out of her drifting thoughts. Danny slid the tray of soda waters across the bar to the young waitress, less wide-eyed than she had once been but still puppy-dog eager to please, who appeared in response to his call. "Take these to the table by the stairs, flash that sweet smile of yours, and tell 'em that everyone drinks one if they want to stay. Got it?"

"On it," Ellie said with a little salute. "All right, Viv?"

"Vivian's about to take a break," Danny said, giving her a wry smile. "Her head's so high up in the clouds she didn't hear me say her name three times."

Vivian felt her cheeks heat. "Sorry," she muttered.

"It happens. Bea's just finishing her set," Danny said as Ellie headed toward the rowdy table. "Why don't the two of you go get some fresh air?"

Vivian sighed. "Thanks, Danny-boy."

The alley behind the Nightingale was dim and crowded, half filled with stacks of empty crates and surrounded by brick walls that got slimy when it rained. But you could catch a breath of air there, even if it was often perfumed with the garbage-and-motor-oil smell of New York's streets or filled with the noise of distant shouts and fighting cats.

The alley wasn't quite a dead end, but it led into a warren of back streets and narrow fences. Few people who didn't work at the Nightingale knew how to find it from the street, so it was usually left unlocked while the club was open. But someone—probably Benny or Saul, on Honor's orders—had flipped the lock so it only opened from the inside.

The light from inside the hall zigzagged across the bricks like lightning when Vivian pushed the door open. She and Bea tumbled into the night, and Bea snagged a brick with one foot, sliding it in front of the doorjamb so it wouldn't close behind them. When they turned around, just enough light still came through it to catch the shadows of two fellas getting cozy in one corner. One of them sprang back with a gasp.

"Didn't see nothing," Bea called cheerfully, one hand rising to the side of her face like a blinder. Anyone who worked for Honor knew better than to blink an eye at that sort of thing. But the man still scrambled away, disappearing into the warren of alleyways.

A moment later, the other fella sauntered toward them, straightening his tie and cuffs before shoving his hands in his pockets and whistling a jaunty little rhythm.

"Evening, ladies," he said, winking.

"Evening, Jimmy," Vivian said, smiling at him. "Your friend a little shy?"

Pretty Jimmy Allen glanced over his shoulder, and Vivian caught the look of regret on his face before his smile reappeared. He shrugged. "That's just how it goes, most of the time. You know the deal, sweetheart," he said, meeting her eyes. "He's probably hightailing his way home already."

"And you?" Bea asked, lighting a cigarette and blowing out a stream of smoke, her chin tilted up so it went over their heads. She held the case out to Jimmy, but he shook his head.

"No thanks, Bluebird. Dance floor's still calling my name."

"You're lucky we came out, then," Vivian said. "They've locked the door tonight. Only opens from the inside right now."

Pretty Jimmy's expression grew wary. "Trouble in the air?"

"Nothing you need to worry about," Vivian said, hoping it was true. "Just a precaution. But maybe take your next friend to a different dark corner."

Jimmy glanced over his shoulder again. "Not going to be a next friend for a while," he said, almost too softly for them to hear. Then his cheerful smile was back in place. "See you girls back in there."

"Saw you talking to Honor," Bea said to Vivian once he had disappeared inside. She hopped up to sit on a stack of crates and stretched out her legs. "And now the door's locked like we're waiting for a raid even though there's not a cop in sight. Slide on up here and tell me what's going on?"

The back of Vivian's neck itched, and she paced around the alley instead of settling next to her friend. The light from the door caught on her dress, bouncing around the walls of the alley like the fabric was sewn with real diamonds instead of cheap spangles. She tapped one hand nervously against her thigh. "I think Honor's feeling cautious because of those two fellas."

Bea took a long drag from her cigarette. "The ones you had your eye on?" When Vivian nodded, she let out a relieved breath. "Well, thank the Lord it's just that. I think I might kill someone if we got raided this week."

"Something going on I should know about?" Vivian asked, surprised.

Bea shrugged, though she couldn't quite hide her jittery excitement. "There might be—it's not a sure thing—there might be someone from Paramount Records coming by this week."

Vivian stared at her friend in shock. A record producer coming to hear Bea sing was exactly the sort of break her friend had always dreamed of. "How did that happen?" she demanded. "And why didn't you say anything before?"

Bea flicked the ash from her cigarette, smiling nervously. "You know Abraham takes late shifts now, so that neither of us are working during the day?" she said. Vivian nodded; the young man Bea was involved with—who Vivian was pretty sure was going to ask her friend to marry him one day soon—was a cabdriver. "Well, a couple nights ago, he picked up two fellas who were complaining about the singer they'd gone to hear that night. Turns out they were scouts from Paramount."

"And he talked you up, of course."

Bea smiled. "Of course," she said, not quite modestly. Vivian didn't blame her for that; there was nothing to be modest about when it came to Bea's talent. "And they'd heard of me! Can you believe it? He told me where they could find me this week."

"Bea, that's amazing," Vivian said, her excitement pushing away any thoughts of the two strangers looking for Hugh Brown, whoever he was. "They're going to love you, absolutely no doubt about it."

"It's not a sure thing that they'll even come," Bea cautioned her.

"Of course it is," Vivian said loyally. "They'd already heard of you, hadn't they? Can you just imagine, a record by Beatrice Bluebird?"

Even in the dim light, she could see the dreamy look in Bea's eyes. But a moment later, those eyes had gone wide, fixed on something over her shoulder. She didn't have a chance to turn around before she was grabbed from behind, a strong hand locking around her arm.

"Caught you," a low voice growled in her ear.

Bea's mouth opened to yell—a warning or a call for help, Vivian wasn't sure which—as Vivian spun around, her free hand balled into a fist and swinging.

At the last moment, the light from the door caught the man's face, and she pulled back her punch, colliding with his shoulder instead.

"Jesus, Mary, and Joseph," she gasped, yanking her arm away as he let out a grunt of pain. "Leo, what the hell do you think you're doing?"

He rubbed his shoulder and glared at her. "Trying to keep a low profile," he grumbled. "Cops like to fill the drunk tank at the end of the month to make a little extra cash. I figured I wouldn't lead them straight to the Nightingale's front door. Didn't expect I'd get sucker punched for my trouble."

"Wouldn't have mattered," Bea said, taking another drag from her cigarette and smiling in amusement at his discomfort. "The amount Honor pays in bribes, they're not visiting here unless she upsets someone pretty high up."

Vivian barely heard her; she was too busy glaring at Leo. "You scared the hell out of me."

He grimaced, still rubbing his shoulder. "My mistake. Where'd you learn to throw a punch?"

"Danny's been teaching me," Vivian snapped. She was still shaking and resented it. "I'd've asked you, but . . ."

"But I haven't been around much." Leo sighed, pulling the hat off his head so that he could run his fingers through the loose, wavy curls of his dark hair. He reached out as though he might touch her arm, then dropped his hand, thinking better of the gesture. "I thought it was better that way. Thought you'd like some space, after . . ."

For a moment, the alley was silent except for the sound of two cats fighting in the distance. Vivian shivered. She still had nightmares, sometimes, about the days when she thought she was headed to prison for murder, when the city's police commissioner needed a scapegoat for a crime that was getting too much public attention.

Leo cleared his throat, as though he were about to say something else, then seemed to think better of it. The commissioner was his uncle, though the man would never admit it; he and the rest of his family had disowned Leo's mother for marrying a Jewish man. And for all Leo had wanted to help Vivian—for all he had wanted to love her, and she had once hoped she loved him—nothing had been the same between them since, even after the commissioner caught the person responsible for the crime.

Vivian, not wanting to meet Leo's eyes, turned away. Bea, who had slid back onto her seat on the crates, was watching them warily, her arms crossed over her chest.

"Don't you go looking at me to smooth this over," she said, brows rising. "You two deal with your own selves, I got no interest in being in the middle."

Vivian glanced back at Leo to see a reluctant grin pulling at his lips. "Evening, Beatrice," he said, nodding to her.

Bea's cigarette had burned down to a faint ember; she ground it out against the alley wall and tossed what was left to the ground. "How's tricks?"

He chuckled, unoffended by the question. "Quiet, luckily." He cut his eyes back to Vivian, brows rising. "Don't go for the face next time, by the way. It was a good hook, but skulls are hard, and you'd've hurt yourself as bad as you hurt me. If you use your knee—"

"Leo," Vivian said, her voice sharp. "I don't need a lecture, I need an apology for scaring the living daylights out of me. You should know better than to grab a girl in the dark."

"All right, that was dumb, and I'm sorry. I could see you just fine, I guess I thought you'd recognize my voice and . . ." He trailed off, shaking his head. "Doesn't matter. I'm sorry. Can I take you for a spin to make up for it?"

Vivian gave him a narrow-eyed glance, still not entirely placated. "We'll see how I'm feeling by my next break," she said.

Bea smirked as she hopped down from the crate. "Good luck, tough guy."

Vivian had to get back to work once they were inside; Leo shrugged good-naturedly and went to the bar. As she fetched drinks and empty glasses, Vivian kept an eye on him. Leo, for his part, seemed happy to pick up a drink from Spence and then settle in to chat with Danny, who he had known since they were two kids growing up downtown, running wild and occasionally throwing punches at each other when they ended up on opposite sides of various street brawls.

By the time her last break of the night rolled around, Vivian's irritation had mellowed along with the crowd. It would be last call in less than an hour, and some of the staff had been sent home. The bar wasn't too crowded when Vivian finally dropped onto a stool next to Leo. He had a drink in front of him—something with plenty of ice that smelled of rum—and she didn't ask before she slid it out from between his fingers and took a sip.

"Not sore at me anymore, then?" he asked. He was grinning as he said it, but Vivian didn't miss that he was spinning his hat in circles on the top of the bar. Leo always fidgeted with his hat when something was on his mind.

"I've decided not to be," Vivian said, putting her chin in the air. "What's eating you, pal?"

Leo's hand fell still, and his smile grew a little rueful. "Just worried about you. Danny said there was a fella in here giving you trouble earlier?"

Vivian glanced down the bar to where Danny was leaning on his elbows, a towel tossed over one shoulder and a smile on his face while he chatted with a handful of regulars. "Not really, no. Just two tough guys looking for someone."

"Hugh Brown, the other bartender said."

"Spence?" Vivian asked, a little surprised. Spence wasn't usually chatty with customers, and mentioning Hugh Brown wasn't much of a conversation starter. But maybe he'd overheard Leo and Danny talking and wanted to chime in.

"That's the one." The hat took another spin on the bar before Leo caught himself and pulled his hand away. "Those tough guys hassle you any?"

Vivian shrugged, not wanting to think about it. "The one fella looked like the type to get nasty if he caught you alone, but I'm not dumb enough to let that happen."

"And it's not like you know the guy they're looking for," Leo put in.

"I'd never rat out someone at the Nightingale, even if I did," Vivian said, stealing another sip of Leo's drink. "But I doubt they'll be back."

"Probably not." Leo smiled at her as he stood, holding out his hand. "Well, what do you say? This song's pretty sappy, but we could still kick up our heels a little."

It had been a long time since they had danced together, and Vivian was surprised to realize she'd missed it. Things might have changed between her and Leo, but maybe they could still have that.

She took his hand. "All right, pal. Let's see if you still know how to show a girl a good time."

Leo smiled as he caught her around the waist, and a moment later they were off, all thoughts of troublemaking strangers lost in the pull of the music, the sway of two bodies that still, in spite of everything, fit together when they were on the dance floor.

Less than an hour later, the final notes of the trumpet drifted through the air like drops of rain, chasing the last of the guests up the stairs and through the curtains. For a moment, everyone left in the Nightingale seemed to hold their breaths. Then, a collective sigh, almost a groan, and the lights began flickering on.

Vivian slumped against the bar, eyes half-closed and cheek pillowed on her hand as her jaw cracked in a yawn.

"Not yet, kitten," Danny said, tossing a towel at her. She straightened just in time to catch it. "Closing shift is a bear, but we're stuck with it. Come on."

There were glasses to wash and tables to wipe down, empty bottles to pack in crates that would be discreetly picked up when the next round of inventory was dropped off. Vivian kicked off her shoes as soon as the floor was mopped, to make it easier on her feet. Not everyone was stuck with closing; Honor was smart enough to rotate them through, and smart enough to stay at least half the nights herself. Those who were left got it done fast, eager to stumble home to their beds for the few hours they had left before sunrise—and eager to see what careless guests had left behind, because whatever cash they found, they got to keep. Honor was smart about that too.

Vivian was dragging her feet by the time she emerged from the ladies' powder room, hands smelling of Borax and triumphantly clutching the three quarters she had found behind the powder room's bench. In the dance hall—bright now, smelling of lemons and soap, the empty space echoing with sleepy footsteps and sleepier voices—Honor was having a quiet word with each of her employees before they left for the night. Vivian sidled over when she saw Bea shaking her head.

"No, Viv's going to see her sister tonight. I'll be on my lonesome walking home," the Nightingale's songbird was saying. She wore catalog shoes now, practical and flat, the red velvet heels that she kept for singing tucked back in their box in the dressing room.

Honor frowned. "What about your fella, Abraham? He's not going to pick you up?"

Bea shrugged. Driving a cab was good work in the city since Prohibition became the law of the land, though dangerous, sometimes, for a Black man to pick up strangers. He had to be careful about which neighborhoods he chose to wait in for fares. "He's up in Harlem tonight."

Honor sighed. "All right, don't go anywhere yet. I'll get you cash for a cab home."

"I've walked home plenty of times, boss," Bea said. "You put Spence in a cab when he left too. Are we worried tonight?"

Honor's mouth drew into a tight line. She wasn't the sort to tell people anything they didn't need to know. But anyone who worked at the Nightingale was hers, and she took protecting her people seriously. "Just take the cab, Beatrice. And let's leave it at that for tonight."

Bea nodded. She knew better than to argue or press for more information. "Got it, boss. And thanks." She glanced at Vivian. "See you around?"

"Count on it," Vivian said as she slipped the quarters into her jacket pocket. Over Bea's shoulder, she could see Danny giving the bar one final wipe before he grabbed his hat and jacket from the hook on the wall.

"Give that baby a squeeze for me," Bea added as she turned to follow Honor toward the door. "And tell Flo my mama wants to see her soon."

That made Vivian smile. "I'll let her know," she said as Danny came to stand next to her.

He nodded at Bea, already shrugging his jacket over his shoulders. "Ready, Viv?" he asked, settling his hat on his head and giving the brim a tweak so it sat at a jaunty angle.

Vivian wanted to talk to Honor, to ask about the cabs and whether there was something to worry about. But her boss was busy talking to Benny and Saul, and it was already past two in the morning.

Vivian yawned. Whatever it was, it could wait.

"Ready," she said at last, turning back to Danny.

FIVE

Vivian had heard plenty of people say that the city never slept, with its subways running until the small hours of the morning and electric streetlights on nearly every corner. There were too many people living on top of each other, fighting and loving and sharing what little they had, for there to be any real quiet. People with too many children and too little space, too many dreams and too much hope that things would get better, this time, next time, if only—if only—if only.

Babies cried in the early hours of the morning, hushed and rocked by parents who were only hours away from their dawn shift at the Palmolive factory. Couples swayed into the night after last call with their arms around each other, still laughing and singing snatches of music like there was no one else in the world. On the widest streets, the ones with stone mansions that smelled of generations of money, the parties would continue, no need for a last call and no worry that the cops might come by if the music grew too loud. The revelers would stumble home eventually, but even then, the houses were awake and alive, servants rising from their beds or arriving for the day with tired eyes and callused hands and hours of work stretching ahead of them.

There was no moment when the city slept. But sometimes, when her feet traced the path home after a late shift, Vivian thought it might be dreaming, or maybe holding its breath. When a breeze blew off the river, lifting goose bumps on her arms and filling her lungs with air that was almost fresh. When the noise of late-night parties had faded but the clang of the factory bells hadn't yet begun. When Vivian turned her face toward the sky and glimpsed—or maybe she was imagining it—the glitter of stars through the clouds that smudged the night sky.

Then she would hold her breath too, feeling, just for a moment, as free as she did on the dance floor, feeling that she was exactly where she was meant to be, until the distant wail of a siren or the shout of a drunk broke the spell and sent her heart tumbling back into her chest.

Vivian tucked away that feeling of freedom, of belonging, of everything being, for one cold clear moment, *exactly right.* She buried it deep, wanting to keep it safe, knowing that it could be a long time before it came again.

Danny was holding open the door of the cab he had just flagged down, waiting for her, a puzzled look on his face. "You all right?" he asked.

"Just fine," she said. "Let's head on home, I'm beat."

SIX

The restaurant was quiet and dark when Danny let them in through the kitchen door; his parents didn't like him coming and going through the front after his shifts at the Nightingale, in case a neighbor happened to be awake and wondered where he had been so late at night. In a few hours one of his cousins, or maybe his mother, would be up to receive deliveries of eggs and vegetables, and the kitchen would thrum slowly to life while the streets around them did the same.

But for now, the only light came through the wide windows at the front, the empty tables lined up in neat rows and casting shadows across the floor, their chairs pushed in and red tablecloths pristine. At one end of the room, a folding screen half blocked the staircase up, the rope that was usually strung across it absent while the restaurant was closed. The whole building was quiet as they made their way upstairs.

A thin whimper startled Vivian in the middle of a yawn as they opened the door to the family's parlor room. Florence sat in one corner, her eyes half-closed as she nudged her rocking chair back and forth with one foot, the sleepy smile on her face barely visible in the dim, ever-present streetlight glow that came through the window. Her nightgown was pulled down over one shoulder so she could hold the tiny bundle that was her daughter to her breast.

"Why'd you bring her out here?" Danny whispered as he slipped off his shoes, padding across the room on silent feet.

"Wanted to see my sister," Florence murmured, sounding half-asleep as she lifted her face for a kiss. Danny brushed one against her lips, then bent to brush a second against his daughter's head. Florence glanced past him and smiled. "Hi, Vivi."

Vivian toed off her own shoes and left them with the others by the door. "Hi, Flo," she whispered. "How's the little bird doing?"

"Hungry," Florence said, her voice quiet as she smoothed down the black hair that stuck up around her daughter's head like tufts of feathers.

Vivian felt the familiar ache in her chest that seeing Florence in her new life always brought, half pleasure and half loneliness. Florence had been married for over a year, but Vivian still woke up some mornings expecting her sister to be at the stove, cooking breakfast for them both and scowling at Vivian for sleeping too late when they were supposed to be getting ready for work.

"Aren't you, Mei, my love?" Florence murmured. "But I think she's finishing up."

Mei chose that moment to let out a burp that seemed far too loud for her tiny body.

Vivian smothered a laugh. "Will she need to eat again?" Florence, resettling her nightgown on both shoulders, shook her head. "Then why don't you bring her basket out here? Put it next to the sofa so I can get up with her, and you two can get a little extra shut-eye."

"Won't argue with that," Danny said, yawning as he disappeared into the room that he, Florence, and Mei shared. There were two more doors leading off the parlor room, one to the room where three of

Danny's cousins slept, one to the washroom. His parents slept on the next floor up.

Vivian took the opportunity to wriggle out of her dancing dress and duck into the washroom to clean away as much of the smoke and sweat of the night as she could without a proper bath. When she came out, Florence was holding up a nightgown, which Vivian pulled hastily over her head.

"Did you just want to see me?" Vivian asked as she yanked it down. "Or was there something particular you wanted to say?"

"Something particular," Florence said. She still spoke quietly, not wanting to disturb either the baby curled against her shoulder or the relatives in the next room. But she couldn't hide the way her voice trembled. "Vivi, I got a response to my letter. The one I sent in the spring."

Vivian paused in the middle of brushing her hair. "You mean the one you sent to our . . . whoever it was?"

Florence nodded. She looked wide awake now, her expression torn between eagerness and worry. "That one, yes."

Vivian took a deep breath and slowly, deliberately, began brushing her hair again, just to have something to do with her hands. Their mother, Mae Kelly, had died when they were both barely old enough to remember her. The Kelly sisters had spent the rest of their childhood in one of New York's orphan homes before being taught a trade and set loose into the world to fend for themselves. And they had, clinging to each other, sometimes as much through stubbornness as love, knowing that in the entire world, they only had each other.

Until the day they had decided to visit their mother's grave on Hart Island, where the city's poor and unclaimed were buried, and discovered that perhaps they weren't as alone in the world as they had always assumed. Because their mother's body hadn't been left unclaimed. And Vivian had eventually called in enough favors—and promised plenty more—at the city coroner's office to track down the person who had claimed it. There was no name, but there was an address. And Florence, in a moment of bravery, had written to that address.

She had sent the letter months before, and both sisters had given up on ever getting a response. People moved away, after all, or died, or maybe just didn't want to know the strange girls who had written to them out of the blue, desperate to find out whether, somewhere in the world, they had a family.

Vivian had told herself she didn't care. That she had Florence, and baby Mei, and Danny and Bea and everyone else at the Nightingale. She didn't need the strangers who hadn't cared enough to find Mae Kelly's children and bring them home.

But then Florence nodded and said, *That one, yes.* And Vivian knew she still cared—so much—too much—because her whole body felt like it might split open with hope and longing and fear.

She clutched the brush so hard it hurt. "What did it say?"

Florence shook her head. "I haven't opened it yet. I thought . . ." She swallowed, and Vivian was relieved to see that Florence was as scared as she was. "I wanted to wait until we could do it together."

Danny chose that moment to reemerge with the basket and tiny cotton mattress that served as Mei's bed, and the baby herself slumped to one side in her sleep and cried in protest as she lost her cozy spot against her mother's shoulder. Vivian held out her arms for her niece, rocking her back to sleep while Florence helped Danny get the basket settled and tossed another blanket on the couch for Vivian. When they were done, and Vivian had settled the now-quiet baby in her bed, Danny glanced between the sisters.

"I interrupted something, didn't I?"

Florence rose up on her toes to kiss his cheek. "Only a little," she murmured, glancing at Vivian. "Vivi, what do you think we should . . ." She trailed off, shrugging a little helplessly.

Vivian made a shooing motion with her hands. "We're not dealing with it until the sun's up," she said firmly, grateful for the excuse to put off opening the letter—whatever it might say—a little longer. "And that'll happen way before any of us are ready. Both of you go get some sleep while you can."

Vivian sank onto the edge of the couch once she was alone, pulling her knees close to her chest and wrapping her arms around them while she stared at the shadows. Now that she was alone, her thoughts wanted to race but felt as though they kept running into a brick wall in her mind. It had been too much all for one day. The bruiser in the alley threatening Spence. The men at the Nightingale. Florence's letter and the aching possibilities it might bring. The tight corners of Honor's mouth as she sent them all home for the night.

Vivian rubbed her hands over her face as she lay down, trying to find a comfortable position. That thought, more than anything else, was hard to push out of her mind, even as her eyes struggled to stay open. Honor never showed worry openly like that. But it had been plain as day, at least to Vivian.

Beside her, Mei grumbled in her sleep, her fingers stretching forward as though reaching for something before she settled back down. Vivian tossed restlessly for another moment before she stood up and grabbed her purse from where she had left it on the table. It was a pretty little beaded bag, but it was heavier than it looked. At least until she pulled the revolver from it.

The undersized Fitz Special caught the edge of the light coming through the window as Vivian slid it out of the bag. She didn't like it. She wasn't even supposed to have it. The snub-nosed gun had been designed for undercover officers, and it had come into Vivian's possession sideways after a crooked cop had dropped it on the street. Vivian had never used it, but she still kept it close. Sometimes. Just in case.

She stared at it for a moment, remembering again the worry on

Honor's face, the ugly twist in the redheaded man's mouth as he snarled at her. Then she slid it under her pillow and lay down, half-asleep before she even closed her eyes.

She didn't stay that way long. The clock on the wall had ticked forward only half an hour when she woke up to Mei whimpering, the sound clearly only moments from becoming a full-throated wail of outrage.

Vivian sighed. She had volunteered for this. Groaning, she hauled herself up as Mei's cries grew in volume, half dragging her pillow and blanket with her before she tossed them back onto the couch. Her head felt fuzzy with fatigue, but she managed to scoop Mei up just before the baby began to really wail.

By the time Vivian had changed Mei's diaper and wrestled her squirming body back into clothes, the baby was wide awake, one fist pressed against her mouth while she slurped absently at it, her eyes fixed on the other hand she was holding above her head, still unsure who was controlling her waving fingers. Vivian shook her head, smiling in the dark.

"You're a little tyrant," she whispered, kissing her niece's sweaty forehead. Juggling the baby into one arm, she held Mei curled against her chest while she swept up a baby blanket to drape over her tiny form. "Let's go for a walk, little one, shall we? That way if you start yelling your head off again, at least you won't wake anyone else up. Shh shh, there we are. There we are. How do you manage to be so loud, hmm? When you're so little . . ."

Keeping up a soft, soothing murmur of words, Vivian slipped out of the parlor and headed downstairs, not bothering with any lights. She'd been there enough that her feet knew the way, even in the near-dark, and anyway, she didn't want to risk Mei waking up any more than she already had. Swaying gently back and forth, Vivian walked around the shadowy restaurant, weaving between the tables and humming quiet snatches of her favorite songs. The baby's babbles and yelps gradually turned to murmurs, and finally, as they paced around the kitchen, faded to no more than squeaky breaths as her eyes began to drift closed.

Vivian let out a relieved breath—*finally*—and turned back toward the dining room, hoping she could get Mei back upstairs and in her bed before the baby was fully asleep. She had just reached the doorway when a shivering crack echoed through the silent kitchen, followed by the sound of something falling. Vivian frowned, her sleepy mind not recognizing the noise, and looked around in confusion, even as she continued the gentle, rocking motion. Then she froze, her eyes on the kitchen's back door. One of the windowpanes—the one closest to the handle—was broken, a cloth-covered hand pushed through the glass. As she watched, the owner of the hand smashed through the remaining glass, the slivers falling to the floor with that same shivering sound.

The cloth dropped to the floor, and the hand reached for the doorknob. The click of the door unlocking was too loud in the silent room.

SEVEN

Are you sure it's the right place?" a gruff voice demanded in a whisper as the back door swung open.

"Shut it, or someone's going to hear you." The second voice was barely more than a nasal hiss.

Vivian slipped behind the door into the dining room, holding Mei against her chest and praying the baby would stay quiet. The restaurant was dark, and whoever the men were, they weren't expecting anyone to be downstairs, not at this time of night. If they stayed quiet . . . Still swaying, she crouched in the shadows behind a table, her heart pounding.

"We saw him go this way, didn't we?" the nasally voice continued.

"Yeah, but there's a bunch of doors back there, how do we know it's the right building?"

Two shadows slunk into the dining room, footsteps careful and silent in spite of their hulking silhouettes. Vivian swallowed, pressing her back against the wall and trying not to whimper. *Him,* they had said. Were they looking for Danny? One of his cousins? Young men could get into all kinds of trouble in the city, the sort of trouble that might see you heading home without your wallet and shoes, or jumped in an alley . . . or on the receiving end of a late-night visit from someone's bruisers.

Mei wiggled against her, and Vivian couldn't tell whether the baby was waking up or just shifting in her sleep. *Stay asleep,* she prayed silently. Even if they weren't in the right place, even if they wouldn't otherwise care about her or anyone else there, the two men wouldn't want any witnesses to a break-in. *Stay asleep, stay quiet, stay asleep . . .*

"Did he say it was a restaurant?" the gruff voice grumbled.

"He didn't say nothing," the second voice sighed. "Not that it was, and not that it wasn't. Now shut it and help me find—"

"We should come back when we know for sure."

"They'll see the back door, idiot, and we won't be able to—"

Vivian's arms ached from keeping up the gentle bouncing motion. Mei shifted again, squirming, and Vivian could feel her breathing change. She held Mei more tightly, lips against the baby's forehead in the desperate hope of soothing her with the soft touch. Mei hauled in a squeaky breath. She felt the baby haul in a squeaky breath.

"But if he didn't say nothing about it being a restaurant—"

"All right, fine," the second voice snapped, loud with irritation. "You win. We'll come back when we know for sure. But if the boss gets mad, I'm telling him it was your—"

Mei let out a wail.

Vivian flinched, huddling back against the wall, the baby pressed against her chest, as two shadows loomed over her hiding place.

"Stand up," gruff voice ordered, still speaking quietly. "And make that baby be quiet."

Mei was now fully crying, eyes screwed up and mouth wide open. "I can't," Vivian whispered as she rose to her feet. She inched to one side, trying to keep as much distance as possible between herself and the two men. They didn't look like they had weapons, but even in the faint glow the streetlights cast through the window, she could see the size of their fists. "She's just a baby, she doesn't understand—"

"For God's sake," nasal voice snapped, pushing the table out of the way and taking a step toward her. "Then I'll shut it up for you."

As soon as she saw his hands reaching for her niece, Vivian kicked out, her foot hitting his knee by luck more than aim. She heard him grunt in pain, saw him stumble. She knew she should yell for help, but she couldn't seem to catch her breath. She was already dodging around the tables, Mei held tight with one hand as she used the other to fling chairs behind her, anything to slow them down as she dashed toward the stairs. She heard another grunt of pain, a half-muffled shout, the thump of heavy feet.

And then a shadow appeared on the stairs above her, something glinting in its hand. The two men saw it at the same time and froze, suddenly wary. The click of a gun's hammer was loud in the silence.

"You might want to rethink whatever you're about to do." Danny's voice, normally so cheerful, was sharp and cold as ice. He held Vivian's snub-nosed revolver pointed steadily at one of the men. His other hand rested white-knuckled on the banister, as though he were moments away from vaulting over it. "Viv, bring the baby up here."

Vivian didn't need to be told twice; she dashed up the steps, Mei still crying in her arms, until Danny's body was between her and the men.

The two men both had their hands raised by their jaws, palms out to show they weren't planning to make trouble.

"Look, fella, there's been some mistake," the nasally voiced one said. His eyes darted toward his companion, who hadn't looked away from the gun pointed at them, then back to Danny. "We got bad information, see. Showed up in the wrong place. Our apologies for the inconvenience."

"We're on our way out, all right?" the gruff-voiced one said, already inching back toward the kitchen with awkward, shuffling steps as he tried not to bump into any of the overturned furniture. "No need for trouble."

Danny raised the pistol a threatening inch. He didn't move from his place on the stairs, which gave him a clear view—and a clear shot—of both of them. "Who are you looking for?"

"Don't know his name," the nasally man said quickly. "Bad debts, you know how it goes. Not something you want to stick your nose in." He gave them a sickly smile. "For your sake and ours, you see?"

There was no way to know if they were telling the truth, and it was a risk to try to find out more. Danny was used to using his fists in a fight, not a gun. And he had Mei to worry about.

"Get out then," he said, his voice shaking with anger. Vivian suspected with fear, too, but he hid it well. "Before I change my mind. And if you ever show your faces here again, I will fill you full of so many holes you'll look like—"

"We got it, fella," the gruff one said. They were both nearly at the kitchen now. "We're outta here, okay?"

"You got seven seconds," Danny snapped. "One. Two. Three—"

The two men took off, and Vivian heard the back door slam before Danny finished counting. He glanced at her, and she could see now that his eyes were wide and scared as he reached for his daughter. Vivian handed Mei to him, taking the gun from his hand and holding it raised in front of her as she made her careful way toward the kitchen to check that the men were really gone.

They were. Vivian ran to the door to throw the locks. She couldn't do anything about the broken windowpane, so she dragged a chair over and shoved it under the handle. Then she slammed the door between the kitchen and dining room closed and put a chair under that handle for good measure.

When she finally looked up, Danny was at the bottom of the stairs. He raised his eyes to meet Vivian's, and for a moment, neither of them spoke.

"I thought you were going to shoot them," Vivian said at last, her voice barely above a whisper. Her hands were shaking now, and she set the gun abruptly down on the nearest table.

Danny stared down at his daughter. "I nearly did," he said. Vivian had never heard that kind of rage in his voice, and it made her shiver. She had seen Danny in a fight before, and she knew more than she liked about what it took to survive in their world. But she still usually thought of him as her cheerful, flirting friend, the giddy new father, the man who loved her sister. She didn't want to see that darkness on his face. He cuddled Mei close to his chest, and her cries faded into whimpers now that she was in her father's arms. "But I don't know who they're working for, and I won't risk making an enemy if I don't have to."

"Do you think they were telling the truth, then?" Vivian asked. "They weren't here for any of us?"

"No telling in this neighborhood," Danny said, shaking his head. The darkness seemed to fade with the gesture, and he pressed a kiss against Mei's feathery hair. "I'm just glad I saw that gun peeking out from your pillow when I came out to see what the noise was."

"Me too." Vivian glanced uneasily around the room. She didn't want to think about what would have happened if Danny hadn't heard his daughter crying. "What now?"

Danny handed Mei gently back to Vivian before he picked up the Fitz Special once more. "You get that little lady back upstairs to Florence, then shake Lucky awake and tell him to get down here and help me keep watch. If they were here on purpose, they might wait until they think we've gone back to bed and try again."

Vivian shivered. "I'm not going to be able to sleep with that thought in my head," she said, her voice coming out barely more than a croak.

Danny gave her a lopsided smile. "Me neither, kitten. But one of us should at least try."

"Should I tell Florence?"

Danny hesitated, then shook his head. "Not yet. I'll tell her and my folks in the morning. But someone around here should get a decent sleep." He reached out to brush a wisp of hair back from Mei's sweaty forehead. She was asleep now, her miniature fist pressed in her mouth once more. "Go on. Makes me nervous having you two down here now."

"You'll be okay?" Vivian asked.

"Go on," he repeated, grabbing her shoulders to turn her gently toward the stairs. He didn't answer her question.

Vivian still did what he asked. Florence woke up just enough to issue a sleepy query of "Does she need to eat?" as Vivian moved Mei's basket bed back into her parents' room, slumping back down against her pillow as soon as she heard Vivian's quiet "Not yet." Lucky woke up more quickly, and to Vivian's relief, he didn't ask any questions after her whispered explanation, just pulled on the trousers that had been tossed across the foot of his bed and went to join his cousin downstairs.

Alone once more, Vivian hesitated, staring at the bed that had been made up for her on the couch. Then she went to Florence and Danny's room and lay down next to her sister. Florence murmured a sleepy hello, still not really awake, and Vivian at last pulled up the blanket, shivering in spite of the warm fall air. She stared into the darkness for a long time, ears straining for sounds from downstairs that never came.

Danny's family was grim-faced in the morning when they heard what had happened. Florence, who had known something was wrong when she woke to feed the baby and found her sister next to her instead of her husband, held Mei tightly. Her eyes stayed fixed on Vivian as if demanding more answers while Danny laid out the bare bones of the late-night encounter over breakfast.

There was silence when he finished speaking, then his father asked, "But there was no more trouble?"

Lucky shook his head. "We took it in shifts for the rest of the night, especially with the back door busted like that. Not a peep more from anyone."

Danny's parents exchanged a glance that seemed to speak volumes. This was the second restaurant they had opened—the first, farther downtown, was now run by Danny's uncle—and they had lived in New York so long that nothing seemed to surprise them much anymore. But anyone would be unnerved by a break-in like that, even if it had ended with no harm done.

"Well, I suppose all we can do is hope it was a misunderstanding," Mr. Chin said at last. "And repair the window so our door is not wide open to anyone who walks down that alley."

"We nailed a board over it for now," Lucky said quickly. "And I'll stop by Ye Li's later today to ask how soon he can fix the glass."

"Then there is no point sitting around worrying," Mrs. Chin said briskly. "We have a business to run. And these boys need to go back to bed. You'll be no help today if you are asleep on your feet." She fixed Danny with a stern eye. "Especially you, Yu-Chen. I see you yawning."

"I'm fine, Ma, I'll just—"

"Bed," she said firmly, turning just enough to include Lucky in the order as well. "Now."

They didn't argue further; Danny stopped only to kiss both Florence and Mei before he and Lucky disappeared upstairs. One of the other cousins began to clear the breakfast dishes, and Vivian rose to help while the rest of the family prepared for the restaurant to open.

"See you upstairs?" Florence asked as she rose with the baby in her arms. "And then we can read . . ." She trailed off, looking anxious.

Vivian, her hands full of teacups and plates, nodded. With everything that had happened, she had almost forgotten Florence's letter. "Be up soon."

When she made it to the kitchen with her load of dishes, Mrs. Chin was already cooking, ingredients spread across the counter before her. One of the cousins was at the sink washing dishes; when Vivian went to join him, Mrs. Chin stopped her.

"And you?" she asked. "You were not too shaken by what happened last night?"

Vivian felt gratitude rise like a lump into her throat. Danny's mother, with her cheerful sternness and blunt way of speaking to her family, could be intimidating, especially to a pair of girls who had grown up without a mother of their own. But she was kind, and when Florence and Danny had married, she had begun treating Vivian as part of the family as well.

"I'm all right, Auntie," Vivian said quietly. "It could have been much worse."

Mrs. Chin sighed. "Isn't that always the way we think? It could have been much worse." She shook her head. "You are working at the dressmaker today?"

"Not until this afternoon."

"Good." She nodded firmly. "Then you have time to help wash those dishes. And get some more sleep if you can." She looked Vivian over with a critical eye and shook her head. "Tired eyes make you look sickly, and I don't want you making my customers worry."

Vivian bit the inside of her cheek against a smile, and she heard a quiet snort from the dishwashing cousin. Once, she had resented such pronouncements. But she had eventually realized it was the way Danny's parents showed their care for the many young people who ended up in their home. "Yes, Auntie."

Mrs. Chin patted her cheek. "You're a good girl, Vivian Kelly." Her sharp glance cut toward the sink. "And I heard that, Wei Wei."

When Vivian finally made it upstairs, Florence was dressed and washed for the day, sewing up a hole in one of Lucky's shirts while Mei lay on a blanket, kicking her feet and cooing as she stared at the ceiling.

"I know there's probably more you could tell me about last night," Florence said softly, not looking up. "But I haven't decided whether I want to hear it or not."

Vivian thought about the men at the Nightingale. What were the odds of unexpected, threatening visitors in both places on the same night? "Nothing I know for sure."

Florence sighed, setting aside her mending. "Let's distract ourselves for now, then. Are you ready?"

Vivian settled on the floor next to Mei, tickling the baby's palms and trying to pretend she didn't feel like she was about to be sick. "What does it say?"

EIGHT

Vivian stared at the house in front of them, curtains fluttering in its windows and pots of flowers and ivy on either side of the door. It was a typical row house, one of thousands in the city. But the neighborhood where they stood might as well have been a different world from the one where Vivian lived.

"Are we sure this is a good idea?" she whispered, panic sitting in her stomach like a weight. "She sent the letter weeks ago. What if she's not here?"

"She said she was generally home in the morning, and she invited us to come visit." Florence spoke calmly enough, but she kept bending down to the baby carriage to fuss with Mei's blanket, tucking it tighter around her napping daughter and smoothing it down unnecessarily. "I shouldn't have brought Mei, should I? We don't know how she'll feel about a baby. But I couldn't just leave her at home, not after last night, and—"

"It's not like you can be apart from her for hours, anyway," Vivian pointed out for what felt like the tenth time since they had left the restaurant. "She'll need to eat when she wakes up, and we don't know how long we'll be."

She smoothed down the skirt of the day dress she had borrowed from Florence and resisted the urge to fidget with her hat, too. Eager to make a good impression, they had both dressed as respectably as possible. Even Mei, asleep in the baby carriage, had on a bonnet with lace trim around the edge instead of the plain cap usually tied under her chin.

"Which one of us is doing the reassuring here?" Florence asked, reaching out to tuck in the blanket once more before she caught herself and curled her hands deliberately around the baby carriage's handle.

"We both are," Vivian admitted.

They stared at the door for another minute before Florence blew out a sharp breath. "Come on. Either we're doing this, or we aren't."

"Maybe we should decide we aren't," Vivian whispered, but Florence was already marching up to the front door. She hesitated, then raised one hand and knocked. She was shaking, and Vivian sidled up next to her, weaving her fingers through her sister's as they waited to see if someone was home.

The sound of footsteps on the other side of the door made Vivian want to run away, and Florence's hand tightened on hers as if she could tell exactly what Vivian was thinking. Or maybe she felt the same and was trying to keep herself from running too. The door swung open before either of them were ready, and Vivian found herself staring at the puzzled face of a stranger.

The middle-aged woman in front of them was short and narrow; her graying brown hair and bright black eyes made Vivian think of the birds that crowded in the public parks, especially when she cocked her head sideways and frowned at them. "Yes? Can I help—" The woman broke off, her already pale face draining of color, and she stared at them as if she had seen a ghost. "Dear God in heaven," she whispered. When

Vivian glanced down at her hand, she was clutching the handle of the door so tightly her knuckles were white. "What are you doing here?"

"Miss Quinn?" Florence asked, stepping forward. With her curly brown hair pinned low around her head, she was the picture of a young, respectable mother. Vivian fought the urge to hide behind her. "Ruth Quinn? My name is Florence, and this is my sister Vivian. We wrote you a letter a few months ago, and you were kind enough to— I mean, I think we might be—" Florence took a deep breath. "Our mother was Mae Kelly."

Ruth Quinn stared at them. "Of course she was. You look exactly like . . ." Her eyes lingered on Florence, and she pressed her lips together as though she needed to stop herself from saying more. "I see. Yes. I'm a bit surprised to see you, though. I thought— That is, I didn't expect to see you so suddenly."

"Your letter took a little while to arrive," Vivian explained. "Florence just got it yesterday, and we thought . . . Well, to be honest, we didn't want to lose our nerve. You wrote that we could visit and, well . . ." She offered the woman a smile, unsure how much to say and unnerved by the way she was still staring at them.

Ruth looked past them, as though she were searching the street for someone, then nodded, a sharp jerk of her chin that made Vivian think of a bird once again. "Yes. I did say that, didn't I? And I'm certainly not going to . . . Well, I mean, you should come in instead of just standing there." She stepped backward, out of the doorway, and motioned them inside.

Vivian and Florence exchanged a quick glance, and Vivian saw her own wide, nervous eyes reflected in her sister's face. Something was strange. Ruth's letter had been so eager, it was unnerving to find her so hesitant and distant in person. But they had turned up on her doorstep unexpectedly. And at least she wasn't turning them away.

She did, however, look a little startled when Florence began to maneuver the baby carriage up the stairs and through the door. "Oh! I didn't see— You have a baby?"

"My daughter," Florence said quietly, lifting Mei out of the carriage. The baby was sound asleep, tufty hair sticking out from under the yellow lace cap, and she slumped bonelessly against her mother's shoulder, burbling without opening her eyes. "She's just three months old."

Ruth pressed a hand against her mouth as she stepped around Florence to get a look at the baby's face. "So little," she murmured, reaching out to touch a finger to the miniature fist curled under Mei's chin. Vivian wondered if there were tears in the woman's eyes or if it was just a trick of the light. It was dim in the hall. Startled by the touch, Mei opened her eyes, and Ruth snatched her hand back, staring at her as if in shock. But a moment later, the baby had settled, eyes drifting closed and head lolling sideways once more.

Ruth turned away abruptly. "Come through, then. The sitting room is just this way."

Her voice was distant once more, almost cold, with any hint of eagerness or emotion gone. Maybe it had been a trick of the light after all. Vivian glanced nervously at her sister and found Florence biting her lip, her brows drawn together in a frown, as they followed Ruth Quinn from the hall.

The sitting room seemed a bit like Ruth herself, tidy but faded, with plump armchairs, a couch crowded with embroidered cushions, and framed paintings on the walls that showed the sort of rolling country hills and forests that Vivian had never seen in person. The chair under the window had a depression worn in the middle from years of someone sitting in the same spot; the other furniture looked like it was rarely sat in. Vivian wondered if Ruth lived alone. A heavy, floral scent hung in the air, and the clock on the mantelpiece ticked too loudly in the quiet room. Vivian thought longingly of the Chins' parlor, where everything was overused and cozy, and the side tables were crowded with photographs of family members who were still in China.

The sisters settled gingerly on the couch, perched on the edge so as not to disturb the cushions, while Ruth settled into what was clearly her usual spot by the window. For a moment, none of them spoke. Ruth glanced out the window, then at the clock, though Vivian couldn't tell whether the gesture was caused by nerves or impatience. There was a coffee service on the table next to her, but she didn't offer them anything.

Vivian took a deep breath. Might as well be straightforward. It wasn't as though things could feel any more uncertain than they already did. "If you knew our mother, then, Miss Quinn, does that mean it's true?" Florence's hand found hers again, gripping it tightly. Vivian felt as though her heart was trying to escape from her chest, it was beating so hard, but she pressed on. "Are you our aunt?"

Ruth's mouth trembled, and her gaze settled on Florence once more. She swallowed visibly before nodding. "Yes," she said, her breath coming out in a rush as she spoke. "Yes, I'm your father's sister. So I suppose . . ." She hesitated, then said, very quickly, "I suppose you could call me Aunt Ruth, then." She pressed her lips together as soon as the words were out, as though she were already regretting them, and stared down at her hands. "If you want to," she added. "It doesn't matter much, I suppose. What's your daughter's name?"

Vivian stared at her, not sure whether she was more startled by the unexpected invitation, the immediate attempt to withdraw it, or the abrupt change of topic. Something was definitely strange, and she didn't know how to ask what it was. But beside her Florence was already smiling eagerly.

"Mei," she said softly, shifting the sleeping baby so that her face was a little more visible.

Ruth sucked in a sharp breath, her hands tight on the arms of her chair. "She's named after your mother, then?"

Florence laughed nervously. "She is, but it's . . ." She hesitated, glancing at Vivian. When she spoke again, her words came out as quickly and nervously as Ruth's had a moment ago. "It's spelled a little differently. Her father—my husband—his family is Chinese." She lifted her chin defiantly as she said it, but Vivian was sitting close enough to feel her trembling, waiting to see how Ruth—their *aunt,* Vivian thought wildly, still barely able to believe it—would react.

Ruth raised her eyes to Florence's face. Her eyes shifted sideways, glancing at the window once more, before settling on the baby again. "Pretty little thing," she said.

Before silence could fall again, Vivian jumped in. "Do you sew?" she asked, nodding toward the mending basket that sat by the foot of Ruth's chair. When her aunt nodded, she said eagerly, "We both do, too. We were trained as seamstresses in the orphan home. The nuns make sure all the children there are taught a trade before we turn eighteen. Both of us started working as dressmakers as soon as we left."

Vivian didn't add that she had always hated dressmaking; it was respectable work, and she had been grateful for the roof it put over their heads. But she had always been miserable bent over a tray of beads or sewing rows of tiny stitches in a dress she would never be able to afford for herself.

"Florence doesn't work there anymore, not since she married," Vivian continued. "And I do the deliveries now. But we both sewed for years. Beautiful dresses, too. The kinds that end up at Fifth Avenue parties."

"Never been to any of those myself," Ruth said with a faint smile.

Vivian laughed. "Us neither," she said, feeling a little giddy at having broken through the other woman's reserve.

But a moment later Ruth's smile faded. "The orphan home, you said? That's where you ended up after Mae . . ." She swallowed. "After your mother passed away?"

"It wasn't too bad," Florence said softly, swaying a little without seeming to realize it as Mei murmured in her sleep. "They were as kind as they could be."

"That's good," Ruth said. She sighed. "I suppose you want to know about . . ." She glanced between them. "Of course you do. Well, and I suppose you have the right. To know where you came from, I mean."

She shook her head, and Vivian and Florence exchanged a nervous glance.

"You said your brother is our father?" Florence asked carefully. "Where is . . . Is he still . . ."

Vivian held her breath, waiting to see what Ruth would say. But their aunt looked past them, her gaze drifting toward the window once more. And when she spoke, she didn't quite answer the question.

"My brother Clyde—Clyde Quinn, same last name, of course, I never married—Clyde met Mae at Coney Island." Ruth's words were jumbled, as if she wasn't sure how much to share or how to say it. She watched them nervously as she spoke, her fingers fidgeting in her lap. "He was smitten and, well, who could blame him? Mae was a sweet thing. We got along too. They were married only a few months after, and you"—she nodded at Florence—"came along less than a year later." Her eyes drifted over both of them then, taking in their features in a way that made Vivian's chest tighten. "You both look like her," Ruth murmured. "You said she called herself Mae Kelly when you were little?" Both sisters nodded, and Ruth sighed. "Well, I can't blame her for changing it. Kelly wasn't her family name, though. I wish I could remember what it was. But we never saw any of them after she and Clyde were married. I don't think they approved of him."

Vivian had a dozen questions pushing up inside her, but she bit the inside of her cheek and stayed quiet. Ruth was already so hesitant; Vivian was afraid that any interruption might make her retreat into silence.

But Florence asked, quiet but determined, "Why did she leave and change her name?"

Ruth sighed. "Things soured between them after you were born.

Clyde was wild about her, and I think she loved him too, but they began arguing."

Vivian felt her stomach plummet. "What about?" she asked, needing to know the answer and dreading it all the same. She had always wanted to imagine her parents in love but forced apart by some tragedy, like the characters in a story. But the thin walls of the tenement building where she lived meant she had overheard plenty of couples arguing. Those fights were never tragic, just sad and squalid and desperate.

Ruth's eyes darted between them before shifting toward the window once more. "I don't know," she said, shrugging. "Money, maybe. Isn't that always the hardest thing for folks?"

Vivian nodded. She hated that answer, but she believed it.

"Eventually, Mae disappeared," Ruth continued. "She was expecting again at the time, and that was you, of course," she said, meeting Vivian's eyes at last. "I know it was because you've got Clyde's coloring. You both could practically be your mother's twins, but you got your coloring from your father, and Vivian, yours is almost exactly like his."

Vivian's hand found her sister's again, resting on the seat between them, and they clutched at each other like a lifeline. "Did our father look for us?" she whispered. "For them, I mean?" She almost asked, *Did you?* but held the question back.

Ruth sighed again. "He did. We never heard from Mae again, and Clyde was furious, of course. Furious and heartbroken. He spent ages looking for her, and for Florence, but there was no trace."

For a moment there was a look like wonder in her eyes, and Vivian's heart beat painfully hard against her ribs. Here was everything she'd ever wanted. A father who *had* wanted them, who had tried to find them. He must have found their mother, eventually, in those records at Hart Island. And if he had paid to have her buried, then he must have still loved her, even though she had left and taken their children with her.

And if he had still loved her, maybe that meant he would still want those children.

"Where's our father now?" she asked. She wanted to sound calm, to pretend the answer didn't matter after so many years. But she could hear the desperation in her voice and knew her aunt could too. "Is he still in the city? Can we see him?"

Ruth's lips pressed together, her eyes going flat. She was only silent for a moment, but it seemed to last forever. "No," she said. "He died a few years ago. Influenza."

Beside her, Vivian could hear Florence haul in a sharp breath, and tears pricked at her own eyes, though she held them back. She wouldn't let a stranger see her cry. And she could tell, from Ruth's closed-off expression, that the woman in front of her was a stranger and, for whatever reason, intended to stay that way.

So Vivian wasn't surprised as Ruth continued, "But maybe that's for the best. We don't really know each other, do we? When I replied to that letter, things were very different. I thought perhaps . . . But it's best not to pretend like we can catch up on all those years. I'm glad to know you're both doing well, of course," she added quickly, a pained smile on her face. "You were a sweet baby, Florence, and I remember rocking—" She broke off, swallowing quickly. "Well, it was a long time ago. And you've got a baby and a family of your own to manage these days." Her eyes darted quickly to Mei, then away, and she looked almost embarrassed by her own words. "And now you know what happened to your parents, you can get on with your own lives."

Vivian wasn't surprised, but it still hurt, like a punch to the stomach that she had seen coming but hadn't been able to dodge. "And what about you?" she asked, willing the words to come out strong and easy. Anything to fool this woman into thinking she didn't care.

Again, that pained smile. "Well, I've got a busy life of my own," Ruth said briskly, standing. "In fact, I have to head to church in just a few minutes. We're preparing for a ladies' social tomorrow, and they're expecting me soon."

It was a dismissal, plain as day. Beside her, Florence looked frozen, her eyes wide and hurt, her lips parted as if she wanted to argue but didn't know how. In her arms, Mei began to fuss and squirm. Vivian wanted to argue, too, to grab Ruth Quinn by the shoulders and shake her, to yell in her face that they were *family,* and didn't that mean something?

Instead, she stood, the same breezy smile on her face that she wore whenever she was having a rough shift at the Nightingale. The sort of smile that said good news or bad, nothing could touch her, and nothing really mattered beyond having a fun time. "Thanks for talking with us, anyway," she said, trying to give Florence a chance to pull herself together. "We've always wondered what happened to our father, and—" The words got caught against the lump in her throat, and she broke off, smiling even more broadly. "Well, now we know," she finished, holding out her hand. "We appreciate it."

Ruth stared at Vivian's hand for too long, as if she had forgotten what to do with it, before she gave it a quick shake. "Of course," she said. "I'll show you out."

At the front door, she stopped on the threshold while they stepped into the fall sunshine. When Vivian looked back at their aunt. Ruth was staring at them, an almost hungry look in her eyes as she watched Florence tuck the now loudly protesting Mei into the baby carriage. When she saw Vivian watching her, she took a step back, shrinking farther into the shadows of the hall. "Good-bye," she called.

Before Vivian could reply, the door was closed, and Ruth Quinn had disappeared.

NINE

She didn't want us," Vivian said flatly, staring straight ahead as she spoke. There was no chance of hiding how upset she was—Florence always seemed to know how Vivian was feeling—but she still didn't want to cry. Instead, she clenched her fists in her lap, focusing on her anger. That was easier than feeling hurt.

Florence, who had just settled Mei at her breast after checking to make sure no one else was around, sighed. "I think I know why she changed her mind."

That made Vivian glance at her sister. "What?"

"She was so encouraging in her letter," Florence said, sounding more resigned than sad. "But did you see the way she kept looking at Mei? She didn't say it outright, but once I said my husband was Chinese, I don't think we stood a chance." She dropped her chin to kiss her daughter's forehead.

"Well, I'd rather have Mei and Danny than her," Vivian snapped. "And we don't need her anyway, stupid, useless—"

"Don't," Florence said quietly. "It's okay to be sad, Vivian. I am."

Vivian scowled. "I'd still rather have Mei and Danny."

That made Florence smile. "Me too," she said softly. "I just wish we'd had a chance to know our father."

Vivian slumped against the tree where they had settled, the bark scratching at her back, and tipped her head up toward the cloudy-bright sky. She felt restless and jittery. Maybe if the visit with Ruth Quinn had gone differently it would have been enough to distract her, but the anger and hurt simmering in her belly were too close to the fear that was still left from the night before, and looking at Mei took her straight back to the confrontation with those dangerous visitors.

"Come on," Florence said, tucking her sweater back down and standing up. She brushed the grass from her skirt. "There's nothing we can do about it. And you need to get to work."

"Vivian, are you paying attention?"

The sour voice snapped Vivian out of her exhausted, drifting thoughts. At least she hadn't needed to arrive when Miss Ethel's dress shop opened promptly at eight, the seamstresses and shopgirls filing dutifully in and taking their places. Now that Vivian wasn't one of them anymore, Miss Ethel rarely let her work full days, and she only paid for the hours Vivian was actually making deliveries, even when she had to be in the shop waiting. It was Miss Ethel's way of punishing Vivian for finagling herself into the position of delivery girl.

The stack of dress boxes that she pushed across the table to Vivian might have been part of the punishment too. She knew Vivian couldn't afford to take a cab, and Miss Ethel was too tight-fisted to ever pay for it herself, no matter how many orders there were to deliver.

The shop owner sniffed. "Or do you plan to daydream while our customers are waiting for their clothing? Clothing which, I might remind you, puts money in your own pocket and food on your own table? You might show them a little respect, even if you are too ill-bred to show any to me."

Vivian gritted her teeth. Behind Miss Ethel, she could see the seamstresses with their heads down as they worked, their sewing tables lined up in two neat rows. Some shops tucked their workers out of sight. Miss Ethel wanted everyone who came in to see the well-behaved, grateful girls who made their silk day dresses and beaded evening gowns. And she wanted those same well-behaved, grateful girls to know that she was watching them at every moment.

"I'll need to do two rounds," Vivian pointed out, stifling a yawn. "That's too many for me to carry all at once."

Miss Ethel sniffed again. "Then you will do two rounds, Vivian. Or do you have somewhere else to be? Somewhere more important than the work I pay you for?"

"Not at all," Vivian said, trying to sound as cheerful as possible. It was some satisfaction to see Miss Ethel's jaw twitch in irritation at her bright tone. "But are there any I should take first? Any that need to be delivered earlier than the others?"

Miss Ethel scowled at her, then pulled the stack of flat boxes back toward herself. She sorted through them briefly, then pushed four back toward Vivian. "These ones. Before two o'clock, if you please. Ladies may be willing to wait for quality, but they aren't pleased to wait on a lazy girl."

Vivian was barely listening to her anymore. The name written across the top box, and the Fifth Avenue address it came with, was so familiar that it nearly wiped the sunny expression from her face. She bit the inside of her cheek.

Of course—of *course*—this would be a day Mrs. Wilson wanted to see her.

"Do you order from Miss Ethel's just because you like making me trek up here and wait on you?" Vivian demanded as soon as the housekeeper showed her into Mrs. Wilson's office.

When Vivian had first seen the room, it was still oppressively masculine, decorated in the taste of Hattie Wilson's late husband, who had died only days before. That had been the same week that she met Mrs. Wilson herself, china-doll pretty and skillfully playing the part of a grieving widow. Even in that first meeting, she had made Vivian nervous; anyone that glittering and hard, that carefully in control of herself, had to be hiding something.

But Hattie Wilson hid in plain sight, still every inch the perfect society widow, apparently content to spend her time on charity work and caring for her son and her younger sister with the money she had inherited upon her husband's death. She had, in fact, inherited a great deal more than money from him, including a rapidly growing criminal empire that she ruled with a smile and a ruthless hand.

Hattie's laugh was barely more than an amused *hmm* in the back of her throat. "Maybe I like the quality of the dresses," she suggested. She tapped away the ash of the cigarette held delicately between two fingers as she lounged behind her desk, now a lighter and prettier piece of furniture than the one that had outlived her husband.

"Or my sparkling company," Vivian said, not bothering to hide her sarcasm. She stood just barely inside the door and glared at the woman who had summoned her. There was only one dress box clutched in her arms now, along with the neat black satchel that held her sewing kit; it had been spite as much as convenience that made her leave Mrs. Wilson's delivery for last, determined to make the other woman wait as long as she could. "But I can't help wondering if I'm really here because you want something from me. Isn't that usually how this goes?"

"I've no need of you for business, Miss Kelly. It's been a quiet time around here. Though I suppose I have used your work to summon you in the past," Mrs. Wilson conceded, rising leisurely to her feet.

She was impeccably dressed, as always, this time in a day dress of pale pink cotton. Hattie Wilson never stinted when it came to keeping up appearances. Though the pure prettiness of her face had hardened some in the time Vivian had known her—becoming a crime boss would do that—she still gave the impression of a sweet young society matron.

Until she turned that sharp gaze directly on you. Vivian had seen hardened criminals cower when faced with Hattie Wilson's displeasure. The woman was a force of nature: beautiful, terrifying, and remorseless.

"You suppose?" Vivian let out a short laugh. "I seem to remember you ordering a delivery just so you could put me in the next room to eavesdrop on you and a guest."

"That was a favor to you," Hattie reminded her, eyes glittering with what Vivian hoped was amusement. "But speaking of favors, I don't suppose you'd like to get the one currently on the books between us out of the way?"

This time it was Vivian's turn to be amused. "Don't like having a debt hanging over your head?"

Hattie Wilson pursed her lips. "No one does, Miss Kelly."

It was good for her to remember that they were on, if not equal footing, then at least far less unequal than in the past. Because Hattie Wilson could be ruthless, but she was meticulous about paying her debts. Vivian smiled. "Not just yet."

Mrs. Wilson sighed. "Pity," she said, shrugging as though she didn't particularly care. But Vivian had caught the moment of irritation in her expression before she turned away. "Well, I think you'll be pleased to know, then, that this time the dresses aren't for me. My sister is waiting for us upstairs."

Vivian stared at her, not bothering to hide her surprise. "Your sister?"

Mrs. Wilson's expression grew hard. "Surely you remember that I have one?"

Beryl, Mrs. Wilson's younger sister, was rarely seen by anyone outside the family; she never appeared on the society pages of the newspapers or at the charity events that Hattie Wilson attended. Vivian had seen Beryl only once before, and her memory was of a wild-haired, angry girl, fiercely protected by her older sister.

Vivian swallowed. "Does she need me to check the fit?" she asked, polite and careful, back to being a seamstress and not whatever irritation or challenge or ally she sometimes was to Mrs. Wilson.

Hattie considered the offer, her expression wary, then nodded. "I suppose she'd appreciate it. Don't dawdle, Miss Kelly. I have a busy day."

On most of her previous visits, Vivian had been taken to what was known in the house as the ladies' parlor, a comfortable upstairs sitting room decorated to the height of fashion with velvet drapes, plush couches, gilded mirrors, and walls of bookshelves. Vivian loved the luxury of the room, though she always suspected that the servants who brought her there were eyeing her suspiciously, worried she would pocket some of the crystal knickknacks scattered carefully across the shelves and tables.

Vivian expected Beryl to be waiting for them there. But when she and Hattie Wilson reached the parlor, they found that Beryl wasn't alone.

She looked more grown-up than she had the last time Vivian saw her, with her dark hair pinned back and the childish roundness of her cheeks grown leaner. But more than that, she looked happier, less brittle, as she sat on the floor building towers of wooden blocks with a chubby-cheeked little boy, her shoes kicked off and a contented smile on her face.

That contentment faded as soon as they walked in, her smile replaced by wide-eyed wariness as she scrambled to her feet. Then she saw the dress box in her visitor's hands and relaxed. "I'm sorry, Hattie, I should have already sent him upstairs, but he was having so much fun, and—"

"It's all right," Mrs. Wilson said, but her eyes were on Vivian as she said it, as wary as her sister had been a moment ago. "Miss Kelly, you might remember my younger sister, but I don't think you've met my son Johnny before."

Vivian shook her head. She could guess, now that she saw them together, why Beryl went out and about so rarely. The resemblance between her and Johnny was obvious—and much stronger than the resemblance between him and Hattie, the woman everyone knew as his mother. Maybe that would change as he grew up. Or maybe by then, everyone would be so used to thinking of Johnny as Hattie's son that they would find it sweet but unremarkable that he looked so much like his aunt.

Vivian crouched down next to Johnny. "Hello," she said gently, giving him a smile. He stared at her uncertainly. "Do you like building towers best, or knocking them down?" He looked startled by the question, then gave her a big smile and swung one chubby fist, knocking the blocks down with a clatter. He laughed loudly.

Vivian stood up, rubbing her sweaty palms against her dress. She tried not to look nervous or to glance too much at Beryl. "He's a handsome little fella," was all she said, waiting to find out what consequences she would face for seeing this hidden corner of Mrs. Wilson's life.

Hattie regarded her without speaking, then turned to a maid who was seated in the corner mending a little boy's shirt. "Close the curtains so Miss Beryl can have her dress fitting, then take Johnny upstairs to his playroom."

When they were alone once more, both sisters regarded her without speaking, standing side by side, allies against whatever she might say or do or threaten them with now.

Vivian swallowed. If it had just been Hattie . . . But there was Beryl staring at her with wide, fearful eyes. Vivian had squirreled away plenty of information in the past, ready to use it without hesitation when it gave her a leg up or a bit of leverage against folks who had more than their fair share. But this time all she did was set the dress box and her bag on the table. "Shall we check the fit of your new dresses?"

She watched them out of the corner of her eyes, and a moment later, Hattie nodded. "Let's get on with it, then. We've plenty of other things to do with our day."

Beryl began the fitting tense and nervous, but she seemed to relax as the appointment went on, and even smiled once or twice in response to Vivian's careful chatter. But she still left the room quickly when they were done, saying she wanted to spend some time with Johnny before his nap.

Mrs. Wilson was still seated, one elbow propped on the arm of her chair and her chin resting lightly on her hand as she regarded Vivian. She was silent for what felt like ages, the fingernails of her other hand tapping slowly against the marbled table next to her chair. At last, she raised her brows. "Do you need my driver to take you home, Miss Kelly?"

It sounded like a kind offer. It wasn't. It was a reminder that Mrs. Wilson knew where Vivian lived, that she still held most of the cards in whatever game they might end up playing. It was a reminder that even if Vivian knew a secret or two about Mrs. Wilson's family, she'd never really have the upper hand between them.

Any other time, Vivian would have hated her for it. But she had to admit, just to herself, that she admired Mrs. Wilson's commitment to protecting her family above all else.

"I've told you before," she said softly. "I got nothing against your sister. She's been through enough, and I'm not interested in adding to that."

Hattie Wilson's eyes narrowed, and it was impossible to guess what thoughts might be moving behind them. But at last she nodded, a regal dip of her chin. "Then I believe we're done here, Miss Kelly," she said, placing her palm down on the table and sliding something toward Vivian. She stood. "For your trouble today. You can show yourself out."

Vivian waited until Mrs. Wilson left the room before going to see what was on the table. She found herself staring at a tauntingly crisp five-dollar bill.

A usual tip for the work she did was twenty-five cents. Many clients didn't bother to tip at all. For Hattie Wilson to have left five dollars meant . . . something. Vivian just wasn't sure what. It could have been a payoff for her silence or a thank-you for her discretion. It could have been another warning, a reminder that Mrs. Wilson had money and the power that came with it.

Vivian wanted to leave it there, along with whatever strings or meaning were attached to it. But she had spent too many nights in her life hungry to let caution triumph over practicality. She pocketed the five dollars before anyone else could come along and see it, then packed up her sewing kit and hurried out of the room.

But she was still distracted as she made her way down the stairs, her mind trying to make sense of the last hour. She didn't see the man lurking at the bottom of the stairs until he spoke to her.

"Heard there was a little dressmaker hanging around today," he said, his grin like an oil slick across his weaselly face, like fingers creeping across the back of Vivian's neck. "What are you up to, little dressmaker?"

It took all her willpower not to step back. "Working, George," she snapped, not bothering to hide the curl of her lip. "Some of us have jobs that don't involve our fists, though I don't suppose you ever heard of them."

Bruiser George only grinned bigger, sprawling across the bench where he was waiting. "I heard of 'em," he said. With a wiry build and a narrow face, George was shorter and thinner than many men in his particular profession. He made up for that with extra aggression and no small bit of cruelty. "Those are the folks always bleating like scared little sheep when I cross their paths."

"I think you know I don't bleat," Vivian said softly. She refused to let him see how nervous he made her. But she was glad he was seated and she was standing.

Every time she thought she might sympathize with Hattie Wilson a little, Vivian remembered that the woman kept people like Bruiser George on her payroll, men whose job it was to scare people, warn them, sometimes hurt them, whenever it suited Mrs. Wilson's business. Vivian had never been on the business end of George's fists but she knew folks who had, and she had come close herself. He was good at his work, and he enjoyed it.

Down the hallway, two maids appeared, one with a stack of linens in her arms, the other holding a bouquet of fresh-cut flowers. They took one look at Bruiser George, and Vivian stuck there with him, and turned right back around. Vivian couldn't blame them. George was living up to his nickname, with busted-up knuckles on one hand and a bruise around one eye. Vivian had always wondered what the servants knew about Mrs. Wilson's business; clearly, they knew enough to look away when they needed to and keep themselves out of it.

Vivian knew she should do the same. "Well, enjoy your day, George," she said, as though he wasn't worth her notice anymore. "I'm sure Mrs. Wilson will need you eventually. And in the meantime, you can sit there waiting like a good puppy dog."

As soon as the words were out of her mouth, she knew they were a mistake; he surged to his feet, blocking her way.

"I'm no one's dog, girlie," he snarled, shoving her backward against the wall. Vivian hadn't expected him to move so fast, and her neck snapped back, her head striking the wood paneling. She gasped in surprise; it didn't hurt too much, but it caught her off guard. George kept one hand pressed against her shoulder, pinning her there, while he loomed in her face. "And you'll watch that smart mouth if you know what's good for you. There's things shaking up around this city. I'd hate to see your pretty face end up on the wrong side of them."

Vivian felt a chill settle in her stomach. "Your boss said things have been quiet recently," she said, her eyes lingering on his bandaged knuckles. "But clearly you're keeping busy with something. What might that be?"

George's mouth tightened, then stretched into a cruel smile. He stepped carefully back, straightening the cuffs of his sleeves and jacket. "You got a pretty high opinion of yourself if you think the boss lady's gonna spill her business to someone like you," he said. When he saw Vivian bristle, he laughed. "Besides, her definition of quiet might be a little different from yours."

"George, are you wasting your time with the delivery girl?"

The amused voice made them both start; when Vivian turned—not completely away, she'd never turn her back on Bruiser George—she saw Mrs. Wilson watching them from the stairs, a smile on her face. "I know you like to entertain yourself, but there really are better uses for your talents. Up you come. The dressmaker needs to be on her way."

George gave an oily smile as he took another step away from Vivian. "On it, boss," he said. Bruiser George might be the sort of man that smart folks avoided, but even he knew better than to keep Mrs. Wilson waiting. He winked at Vivian. "I'm sure I'll see you around, girlie," he said as he started up the steps.

"Woof," Vivian said under her breath. But she knew he heard; his shoulder stiffened, and she saw his hand clench on the banister. He turned around to glare at her.

"George," Mrs. Wilson said, her voice like the crack of a whip, before he could say or do anything else. "Upstairs. I won't say it again."

She waited until he had gone past her, disappearing toward her office, before her gaze settled on Vivian. She shook her head. "And here I thought you were a smart girl, Miss Kelly."

Vivian could admit to herself that it had been a stupid taunt to make, but she'd never say so out loud. "I don't like it when folks try to intimidate me."

The amused smile was back on Mrs. Wilson's face. "I'd have thought you'd be used to it by now," she murmured. She didn't wait for Vivian's response before she turned away.

Vivian shivered. She wanted to know what sort of things Mrs. Wilson was *shaking up* and what might put Vivian on the wrong side of it. But she pushed the thought away. For once in her life, she would keep her head down and stay out of it.

She had enough to worry about without looking for more trouble.

TEN

Vivian collapsed into her bed as soon as she was home, planning just to shut her eyes for a few minutes. But by the time she woke, the evening was already slipping into night, and she stumbled out of bed groggy and hungry. The streetlights were coming on, leaving shadows on the sidewalks that, from the safety of her window, looked like excitement and temptation instead of danger.

She wasn't scheduled to work. No one was expecting her, at the Nightingale or anywhere else. She could have stayed home where it was safe and quiet. But nighttime was calling, and Vivian had realized long ago that she didn't have it in her to resist.

There was a little hot water left in the shared hall washroom. Vivian cleaned up, smoothing down her bob and brushing it until the dark hair fell like a silk curtain to her chin. Her best dancing dress had six inches of beaded fringe around the bottom; it had taken her over a month of sewing, squeezed in during her rare free hours, to string all of them onto the amethyst-colored gown she had bought secondhand and hemmed to just the right length. Silk stockings, which she had to baby because she couldn't afford to replace them.

A feathered headband across her forehead and pinned in place. Vivian tied the ribbons of her shoes and slid her arms into the sleeves of her coat—it wouldn't do to look too much like she was heading to a party where any cop on a corner might see. The fabric was growing threadbare at the elbows and would need to be patched soon, but she wasn't planning to wear it for long.

There were clouds overhead when she closed the door behind her, billowing across the sky like a spreading bruise but silvered around the edges with hidden moonlight. The subways and streetcars still ran like clockwork, but Vivian rarely took those when she was alone at night. Better to be out in the open, in whatever passed for fresh air, the city spread around her like a promise of escape. Escape to or escape from, whichever she needed.

Vivian waited until there was no one around before ducking into the alley that hid the Nightingale's front door, a single light flickering overhead as if it had been forgotten years ago and left to illuminate nothing. She knocked, a quick syncopated rhythm that all the club's employees used. It was still early enough that they weren't open yet, but it wouldn't be long before the night's revelers began to appear. Someone would be at the door to let her in.

The door swung open. "In you get," Benny growled. "No lingering outside tonight."

Vivian frowned as the door closed behind her. "Something happen?"

"You could say that." Benny's voice was a tense rumble that made the hair on the back of her neck stand up.

If anyone had asked, Vivian wouldn't have been sure whether she was thinking of the man who cornered Spence in the alley or the one with the dreamboat smile and the dangerous eyes. Maybe it was the memory of glass shattering from the Chins' back door. Maybe it was all three. Either way, she was only halfway surprised when Benny said quietly,

"Silence is dead."

ELEVEN

"Does anyone know what happened?" Vivian demanded, leaning across the bar as she watched Danny stack glasses and check his ingredients for the night. Around her, the Nightingale thrummed with whispered conversation as the staff finished their preparations. There were a few worried glances and whispers, but mostly folks just looked sad. Everyone had liked Silence, even if he barely talked.

"Robbery gone wrong, far as anyone can tell," Danny said, his hands never slowing even as he spoke. "Got jumped in an alley on his way home. Just the sort of bad luck that happens all the time in this city." He nodded toward the bandstand, where Honor was talking through the set list with Mr. Smith. "His wife called Hux this morning."

"I didn't know he had a wife," Vivian said quietly, guilt twisting her stomach. Most people at the Nightingale kept their personal lives to themselves. It felt safer that way. Usually.

"He did," Danny said, shrugging. "No kids. Hux'll help her out for a few months. Probably pay for a funeral. But mostly she needs to find a new doorman soon. No good being short-staffed, especially when it comes to muscle."

The band chose that moment to launch into the cheerful, bouncy tune they generally used to warm up, and Vivian could feel the mood in the dance hall relax. She caught a glimpse of smiles on more than one face as the staff finished setting up, and she even heard someone laughing in the back hall.

"Doesn't anyone here care?" Vivian said, scowling around the room. She tried not to picture Silence as she had last seen him, looking proud of his new suit. "Isn't Honor going to do anything? Look into it at all? Isn't there something—"

Danny flicked her arm with the back of his fingers, not bothering to look up from his work. "Of course we care," he said. "But we've got work to do, and there isn't anything we can do right now. Folks are going to show up at that door any moment expecting a good time. The party goes on."

"Do you think . . ." Vivian hesitated. But now that she was thinking it, she couldn't keep it to herself. "There was the break-in last night at your place . . ."

Danny gave her a sharp look. Clearly, he had thought of it too. And just as clearly, he didn't want to talk about it. "It's a dangerous city, Viv," he said firmly. "There's no reason to think they had anything to do with each other. Now, hop back here and help me out."

"I'm not working tonight," Vivian said automatically. Danny was right. It was a dangerous city. Anyone who took the wrong street home could end up facing someone desperate enough for a little cash that it made them dangerous. Even someone as tough as Silence.

"No, you're sitting there looking pretty while I try to do the work of two people," Danny said, scowling at her. "Lend a hand, kitten. And then we'll have our toast."

"Where's Spence?" Vivian asked, already sliding off her barstool to do what he asked.

"Late," Danny grumbled. "Not the first time it's happened. That kid needs to get his act together."

Vivian kept her eyes on her hands as she began to slice limes. "Do you think—"

"No." Danny sighed. "He's been late before, plenty of times. No reason to borrow trouble we don't have to buy."

Vivian nodded, happy to push the thought from her mind. They worked quickly, easily dodging around each other while the band warmed up, and once the bar was ready, Danny popped open two bottles of champagne. Together, they began to fill glasses, just a splash in each, and lined them up on the bar. One by one, the staff members finished their work and drifted over, each taking a glass and gathering in front of the bandstand. At a nod from Danny, Vivian joined them, her own glass clutched between palms damp with unease. Someone had taken drinks to the bandstand, and Danny joined Honor in front of it, handing her a glass of her own.

She lifted it in a toast. "Silas Abernathy," Honor said simply, her words carrying through the quiet room. "He was a hell of a guy, and we were lucky to know him. To Silence."

"To Silence." The words echoed around the room as everyone lifted their glasses in reply. Vivian caught Bea's eye through the crowd, and her friend smiled sadly as she drained her glass. Vivian drank with the rest of them, tears pricking her eyes. She hadn't even known Silence's last name before that toast.

The glasses made their way back to the bar, the staff dispersed to finish their prep work or get a last smoke in before the night began in earnest. The musicians took up their instruments again, and Bea returned to the bandstand as Mr. Smith counted her into a quiet rendition of "Three O'Clock in the Morning."

But Vivian couldn't shake her feeling of unease. When she saw Honor finish talking with Danny, Vivian hurried across the empty dance floor to meet her at the foot of the stairs.

A flicker of surprise crossed Honor's face, melting into a softer smile than Vivian had ever seen her boss wear, though that was gone just as quick. "Vivian," she said. "You doing all right?"

"Bit shook up," Vivian said, feeling her cheeks heat. The expression on Honor's face might have been cool, but the concern in her voice was plain as day. "Gonna miss him."

"We all are." Honor sighed. She reached out to tuck a strand of Vivian's hair behind her ear, and her palm lingered for a moment, warm against Vivian's cheek, before she dropped it back to her side. "What were you doing behind the bar? I didn't think you were working tonight."

Vivian shrugged. It was confusing to see Honor being so unguarded. "Helped Danny get set for the night since Spence is running late."

Honor shook her head. "Not sure I made a smart call with that one. Well, I'm sure our Danny-boy appreciated the help." She gave Vivian a sideways glance. "I do too. Maybe you can save a dance for me later so I can thank you properly."

Honor's smile was barely there, only the slightest lift of the corners of her mouth, but it was enough to make heat pool at the base of Vivian's spine. She wasn't sure how she felt about this new Honor, whether or not to believe that she had moved beyond flirtation into something more. Whether or not to trust her.

Honor was standing only inches away, close enough to smell her perfume. Close enough that Vivian wanted to lean toward her, though she wouldn't let herself. Not here. Maybe not anywhere. She still hadn't decided.

And she couldn't, not now. Not when there was something more important tickling at the back of her mind. "Did Danny tell you about last night?"

A hint of a frown, though it was smoothed away quickly enough. "He mentioned having a rough night," Honor said. "A bit of trouble, he said. We haven't had much chance to talk, though, with—well, with everything. Was there more to it than that?"

Without thinking it through, Vivian drew closer to Honor. "There was a break-in at his parents' restaurant after we got back last night."

Her voice shook as she described the two men, their whispered words to each other, the excuses they gave when Danny scared them off. She left out her own fear, but she knew Honor heard it anyway.

"I'm glad everyone was okay," Honor murmured, but Vivian could see the thoughts behind her eyes, the swift consideration as she turned over the odds she'd been presented with. Honor was wondering, just like her, whether it was really a coincidence.

"And Bea and I caught that fella hassling Spence yesterday before we opened," Vivian pointed out. "Three makes a pattern, boss."

"I don't disagree," Honor said, her voice so steady it was impossible to know what she was really thinking.

"But it doesn't make sense," Vivian said, not bothering to hide her frustration. Or her fear. "If they're trying to send some message to Nightingale folks, what is it?"

"I don't know," Honor said, her eyes fixed on the bandstand, where Bea was starting the first song of the night.

Guests were starting to slip in, trickling down the stairs in ones and twos, heading for the bar and the dance floor. Vivian caught sight of Spence hurrying through the back door, looking flustered and nervous as he ducked under the bar flap. She let out a heavy breath. At least he was one less person to worry about.

Honor was silent for a moment. "Not yet. But the last thing I'm going to do is let someone mess with my people." Her eyes were fixed on Vivian's, and she looked as if she wanted to say something else. But she only shook her head. "Enjoy your night off, pet." Honor's cool smile slid back into place as she spoke, but her words were still soft as she turned away. "And keep your eyes open."

Vivian threw herself into the music after that, bouncing from partner to partner, the faster the song the better. She wasn't sure which she was more desperate to put from her head: the shivery, uncertain weight of that moment with Honor or her sense that something dangerous—some*one* dangerous—was lurking just out of sight. But if she kept her feet moving, if she laughed and flirted, if she let an old friend buy her a drink and swapped lipstick with a girl who had forgotten hers in the ladies' powder room, then she could ignore the shadows under Danny's eyes and the empty spot where Silence usually stood.

If the two men from last night were the ones behind the trouble, they'd be back. No one made half a point and then left you to wonder what it was. Not when they wanted something from you.

She didn't have to wait long.

He appeared on the stairs before the night was halfway done. His suit was as elegantly cut as the one he had worn the night before, silk tie at his neck and the shoes on his feet so polished they would probably reflect Vivian like a mirror if she got close. His red hair gleamed too, heavy with pomade and not a strand out of place, and he smiled like he knew a secret as he surveyed the dance floor and sauntered over to a table by the bandstand.

Vivian, seated on a stool at the bar, watched as he raised one hand, catching the attention of Alba Diaz, one of the waitresses. She had to bend close to hear his order. Watching them, Vivian had the feeling that she was watching a bird bend its neck toward a feral alley cat. She shivered and looked around for Honor, but her boss was nowhere to be seen.

"Cool customer out there," Alba said when she returned to the bar. She had been working at the Nightingale for years and looked bored or irritated most of the time. Now, the scowl on her face said she was nervous. "His smile gave me the heebie-jeebies. I wouldn't keep him waiting if I were you."

"What's his order?" Vivian asked, not taking her eyes from the red-headed man.

"Whiskey and soda," Alba said to Spence, who was washing glasses with his back to the dance floor. She glanced at Vivian impatiently. "Why do you care?"

"We need a new bottle," Spence said, sighing. "I'll be right back."

"Mind if I take it over?" Vivian asked instead of answering, as Spence disappeared into the cellar where the stock was stored.

"You're not even working," Alba pointed out. But she shrugged, clearly not too bothered. "Suit yourself. Danny?" She raised her voice to call down the bar. "Mind if I take an early break? My poor little puppies are barking something fierce."

"Sure thing," he replied, glancing their way and nodding.

Vivian caught his eye before he could turn away again, and the look on her face was enough to snag his attention. He caught the motion of her hands down by her waist, too, held flat and gesturing briefly toward each other at an angle: *trouble*. Danny followed the flick of her eyes to where the redheaded man was sitting, surveying the dance hall and waiting with a smile on his face. He saw them watching and his smile grew.

"Alba, Honor's in the back hall," Danny said, his voice careful and calm. "Will you first poke your head out and tell her there's a fella who needs to speak to her?"

Alba glanced between him and Vivian. "Everything all right?"

"Swell," Danny said, giving her a broad smile before Vivian could answer. "Go take a load off once you tell her." Once she was gone, he glanced at Vivian. "Don't take his drink over until she gets here. What did Alba say it was?"

"Whiskey and soda. Spence went to get a new bottle."

Danny glanced at the shelf. "There's enough left for one more."

Vivian waited while Danny mixed the drink slowly, watching out of the corner of her eyes. It didn't take long for Honor to reappear; she exchanged a brief look with Danny, nodded, and strolled toward the red-haired man.

Danny slid the drink across the table toward Vivian. "Don't get in the middle. Whatever it is, Honor will handle it."

Vivian tried to pretend like her hands weren't shaking as she carried the drink over.

"Well, I suppose you're right, I didn't introduce myself," the man was saying as she approached the table. He smiled at Honor. "Harlan O'Keefe."

Vivian didn't know the name. But the moment of stillness that came over Honor—so brief Vivian might have missed it if she hadn't been watching so closely—said that she did. O'Keefe noticed it too, and he looked pleased about it.

"And you, I understand, are the owner of this fine establishment?" he continued.

"That's the shape of it," Honor replied, taking a seat at his table and leaning back in her chair as if perfectly at ease.

"And this sweet little thing is Vivian," O'Keefe said, looking her up and down as she set his drink on the table. The uptown polish was strong in his voice tonight, broad and smooth, the sound of money and power. Vivian tried not to shiver. It might have been an act, but it was a damn good one. "I was lucky enough to meet her last night."

If it was meant to be bait, Honor didn't rise to it. "I'd say it's a pleasure, O'Keefe, but I suspect it's not."

"Well, now, little lady, that depends," O'Keefe said, sipping his drink and clearly enjoying himself. "You might have heard I stopped by yesterday looking for a friend. Do you remember his name, little bunny?" he added, glancing at Vivian.

She had been about to head back to the bar; when he spoke to her, she hesitated, glancing at Honor before she answered. "Hugh Brown," she said softly when her boss nodded.

"Not a great look to show up at a place like this asking too many questions," Honor said, still calm and unbothered. "Fella like you ought to know that's not how we do things."

"You keeping secrets, little lady?" O'Keefe said coldly. Vivian could hear the rasp of a Bowery-raised street tough creeping into his voice as his irritation grew.

Honor smiled. "I'm a whisper sister, O'Keefe. That's part of the job. But I'll level with you: even if I wanted to help, I couldn't. I don't have any idea who that is."

O'Keefe made a *tsk*ing sound in the back of his throat, like a disappointed father. "Think carefully, little lady, before you lie to me," he said. His voice was still pleasant, but its softness made Vivian shiver. "I always make sure people regret lying to me. And my information says different. In fact, I hear that not only does he come here often, he was here last night, and he looked pretty cozy with some of your folks. What do you have to say to that?"

Honor shrugged. "Plenty of people come through my door, O'Keefe. It's my job to make sure they have a good time, not to be their pal. If he was here, I don't know him."

"But I hear you know all your regulars so very well. Keep track of 'em, even." He glanced at Vivian and smiled. "Do your employees know how closely you keep tabs on them, Miss Huxley? Do they know about your little files full of secrets, the ones you keep under lock and key?"

Vivian didn't say anything. She knew about those files, but she wasn't sure if everyone who worked there did. She wished O'Keefe would look away from her so she could leave. She suddenly realized Honor hadn't corrected him when he addressed her, even though Honor hated for anyone to call her "miss." She was just watching him warily, her mouth pulled into a tight line and her eyes flat.

"Now, I gave you a taste of what might happen to your folks here last night," O'Keefe continued. "A little warning. I'm sure you noticed." His smile grew. "I'd say I'm sorry about the missing face but, well, that's just business, isn't it?"

Vivian's stomach felt like it had dropped straight toward the floor; for a moment, she thought she would be sick. *Silence.*

She didn't realize she had said his name out loud until Honor and O'Keefe both looked in her direction. O'Keefe shook his head, still smiling. "Now, now, little bunny, he wasn't supposed to end up dead. How was I to know he'd get so unpleasant just because we asked him to share a little information? Really, he had no one to blame but himself."

One of Honor's hands clenched into a fist where it rested on the table. "You've got a hell of a nerve, walking into my place and talking like that. I ought to shoot you where you're sitting."

"Ah, that's why I came during business hours." O'Keefe leaned back in his chair and took a satisfied sip of his drink. "That and your excellent bar, of course. But you've got a reputation for being a businesswoman, Miss Huxley. We both know that kind of unpleasantness would spoil all the fun your lovely customers are having."

"Fine." Honor stood. Her voice was soft and controlled, but Vivian could see the rigid tension in her spine. She had never seen Honor so shaken before, and it terrified her as much as the smiling man sitting in front of them. "Then I'll have some of my boys escort you out back for a little chat."

"You think I was dumb enough to come alone?" That rough edge was back in O'Keefe's voice, and for a moment his smile looked more like bared teeth. "I didn't get to be who I am by playing games I can't win, Miss Huxley. And you know who I am, don't you?"

"Yes," Honor bit off.

"Good. And *I* know you don't want anything worse to happen around here. So let's try this again: Where can I find Hugh Brown?"

"I can't tell you what I don't know," Honor said softly. "And we don't like rats around here."

O'Keefe sighed. "I don't deny that I admire the principle, little lady. But you might need to make your peace with it anyway. One way or another, I get what I want, and I don't appreciate it when folks stand in my way." He glanced at Vivian. "Don't look at me like that, little bunny. I'm not a monster. You and your pals here are safe from me."

He bared his teeth. "For now. But I'll be back in two days, Miss Huxley"—he turned back to Honor as he stood—"and I hope you'll have a different answer for me then." He sounded almost regretful. "My thanks for the drink."

Vivian didn't move as she and Honor watched him saunter across the floor. Around them, the dance hall still buzzed with careless energy, with the stomp of feet and the laughter from the bar, the voice of the trumpet rising over it all as the band slid through the notes of "Ain't Misbehavin'." No one seemed to notice the redheaded man making his way toward the stairs, two other men falling in behind him. Vivian couldn't see their faces; she wondered if they were the same men who had found their way to Danny's home last night. Either way, O'Keefe hadn't been lying about not being alone.

Neither of them spoke until he was out of sight.

"Plenty of fellas are all talk," Vivian said at last. But Silence was still gone, and she knew the words were meaningless. She swallowed and glanced sideways at Honor. "What do we do now?"

"Nothing. You do nothing," Honor said sharply. It was impossible to tell what she was thinking. "Not yet. But no one leaves tonight without telling me. Not even you, all right?"

"Honor—" Vivian caught her arm as she was about to turn away. "How scared do we need to be?"

It took Honor longer to answer than Vivian liked. "We've got two days," she said at last. "I hope we don't need to be scared until they're over."

TWELVE

Honor was careful not to say too much; she played her cards close to her chest as a general rule. But she made her way around the dance hall after O'Keefe left, checking in with each of her employees.

Vivian tried not to watch her. Honor clearly didn't want to make anyone panic, and Vivian was afraid she would give something away. So she stayed on the dance floor as much as she could, glad for the distraction, until Bea finished a set and caught Vivian's eye, gesturing toward the bar with her chin.

"He's not here," Bea sighed as Vivian slid into a seat next to her.

"Who?" Vivian asked, her mind immediately going to O'Keefe. At the end of the bar, Honor paused to talk to Danny, their heads bent close together and faces serious.

"The record producer," Bea said as Spence placed a glass of water in front of her. "Thanks, pal. I've been keeping an eye out. No sign of him yet."

"Well, there's still plenty of night left," Vivian said, bumping her friend's shoulder with her own. "And you sound amazing up there, you really do. Don't you think so, Spence?"

"Hmm?" He had been watching Danny and Honor, too, a frown on his face. "Sorry, wasn't listening. What was the question?"

"Doesn't Bea sound like an absolute dream tonight?"

"Oh yeah, killing it up there for sure," Spence said, still not looking at them.

"Not a great choice of words tonight," Bea said sharply.

That got Spence's attention. "Well, 'scuse me for trying to give you a compliment," he said, scowling. "I'll leave you to your moping." He turned back to mixing drinks for a couple that needed theirs refreshed just as Honor appeared next to them.

"Why are we moping, Bluebird?" she asked quietly.

"Nothing, boss. Just looking for someone who's not here." Bea sighed and took a long gulp of water.

"But he might get here any moment," Vivian said, still trying to sound encouraging. "Or tomorrow night. There's no telling. Just sing your heart out, pal. Like you always do. Folks show up every night just to hear you, and you never disappoint. You won't when he shows up either."

"Thanks." Bea smiled, but the expression faded as she turned to Honor. "What are all the whispers about tonight, boss?"

Honor glanced at Danny, who was pulling bottles from the shelf and lining up glasses. "Nothing to worry about, Bluebird. Not yet, anyway. Danny-boy, I'm going to talk to Benny. Keep an eye on the dance floor?"

"You got it, Hux."

"And remember, no one who works here leaves without letting me know." Honor glanced at Vivian, looking for a moment as though she would say something else. Then her cool mask slid back into place and she strode off toward the stairs.

"Hey, Danny, mind if I take a quick smoke break?" Spence called as he slid the couple's drinks toward them. "We're in a bit of a lull."

"Fine. But don't make it too long."

Bea sighed, sliding off her stool. "And I've gotta get back to the bandstand. You sticking around, Viv?"

Vivian tried not to think about O'Keefe and shivered. "Yeah, I'll be here."

Danny and Bea went back to their work, and Vivian watched Spence head toward the back hallway, tapping the pack of cigarettes against his palm. But at the doorway, he paused, looking quickly left and right before ducking out.

She frowned, remembering the man who had cornered Spence in the alley and slipped away before she or Bea could see his face. Had it been one of O'Keefe's men? Or someone else entirely? Either way, with what had happened to Silence, none of them should be going out alone. Honor seemed to think that O'Keefe—whoever he was, Vivian still didn't really know—had meant what he said about two more days. Vivian wasn't so sure. Quietly, without drawing Danny's attention, she slipped off her stool and followed Spence out.

The hallway was empty when she reached it; Vivian hurried toward the door to the back alley and found it shut tight. That was no good—Spence would get himself locked out if he wasn't careful. Vivian shoved it open.

The alley was empty.

Vivian stared around the dank space. "Spence?" she called softly. There was no response, just the sound of some small, fast creature scuttling through the shadows. Vivian shivered. "Spence?" she called, a little louder, but there was still no reply. She let the door fall shut.

Slowly, Vivian made her way back down the hall, sweat starting to prickle along her neck and spine. Everything felt too loud all of a sudden, as if her nerves had sharpened her hearing. She needed to tell Danny or Honor—

The band finished their song just as Vivian reached the bottom of the stairs. In the brief seconds of silence before the dancers applauded and the next tune began, she heard the creaking shuffle of footsteps upstairs.

Halfway up, the staircase opened onto a landing with two doors. Behind one, always locked during working hours, the staircase continued up to the apartment where Honor usually lived. Behind the other was Honor's office, a spot off-limits to anyone not accompanied by the Nightingale's owner or, from time to time, by Danny.

With both of them downstairs, no one should have been up there.

The band launched into a hot, fast Charleston and the sound disappeared into the music, but Vivian was certain someone was on the landing. She only hesitated a moment before she followed her hunch up, the wail of the brass masking the click of her heels against the stairs.

She stopped just a few steps shy of the landing. "Spence?"

He yelped in surprise and scrambled to his feet from where he had been crouched in front of the keyhole.

"What are you doing?" Vivian asked before he could say anything.

He shoved his hands in his pockets, but Vivian could see them shaking before they disappeared. "Looking for Honor," he said. "I knocked, but there was no answer. I was trying to see if she was there."

"She went to talk to Benny, remember?"

"Oh. Right, of course." Spence shrugged. "Should have remembered that. Brain's a bit of a jumble tonight," he added with a grimace. "Guessing I'm not the only one, after what happened. Why are you here?"

"Looking for you," Vivian said. "You said you were going out for a smoke, but you shouldn't be out there by yourself right now. Not after what happened to Silence." She climbed a few more steps closer to him. "Or what happened to you."

He pushed his hands farther into his pockets and looked away. "Nothing happened to me."

"It could have, though," Vivian said. "Spence, are you in trouble?"

"I'm fine," he said. "Nothing I can't handle, see?"

"Because if you are, you can ask for help. Anyone here would—"

"I said I'm fine," he snapped. "You got a problem with your hearing?" He pushed roughly past her.

"Spence, don't be an idiot—" Vivian tried to lay a hand on his arm, but he shook her off.

"That's what everyone here thinks of me, isn't it?" he said, wheeling around to glare at her. "Spence the idiot, just because I'm not as fast behind the bar as Danny."

"That's not what I meant," Vivian said sharply. "Everyone here's been in a jam before. You owe someone money? They got you running scared? Just ask for some damn help. Doesn't have to be from me. But let *someone* help you."

"I don't need any help," Spence said, lifting his chin. "I told you, I'm fine. I'm swell. I'm the dandiest fella there ever was." He gave her a broad smile that was as fake as it was beaming. "Now if you'll excuse me, some of us are working tonight."

Vivian rolled her eyes. "Fine," she said, biting off the word. "You handle your own mess, then. We got plenty else to deal with around here."

She left him there before he could say anything else, stomping down the stairs and heading straight for the dance floor.

Honor paid for cabs again at the end of the night.

Vivian had stayed on the dance floor. Every time she thought about leaving, she remembered the smile on O'Keefe's face, and the idea of walking out into the night alone made her shiver. So she found another partner, another distraction, until last call had passed and the electric lights were flickering back on and she was cursing herself for how tired she would be in the morning.

Danny had drawn the early shift and already headed home to Florence and Mei. Vivian could have caught a ride home with Bea, whose fella Abraham was picking her up, but she could tell from the way they were smiling at each other that they wanted some time to themselves. Before Vivian could convince herself that it was fine to head out alone, there was nothing to worry about, Honor materialized at her side.

"Come on, pet," she said quietly. "Let's lock up."

The air outside wasn't fresh, but the cold of it was welcome in Vivian's lungs after the stifling, nervous energy of the night. She hauled in a deep breath as soon as her feet hit the alley pavement, tipping her face up toward the sky.

"You look ready to take off for the stars," Honor murmured. When Vivian turned toward her, she thought she saw—just for a moment—pure, naked longing in Honor's eyes. But it was gone so fast she might have just imagined it. Instead, Honor smiled at her, one corner of her red lips tilted up, sleek and sly as always.

Vivian wasn't imagining the heat in that smile, though. That was still there, and it chased across her arms, even as they prickled with goose bumps in the midnight chill.

"Since when do you think like a romantic?" Vivian said, trying to shrug off the moment, to return to their usual meaningless flirtation instead of whatever serious thoughts were behind Honor's eyes.

But Honor didn't look away. "Since always," she said quietly. "I just never said it out loud before."

They stood there, staring at each other, for too long, neither one wanting to take a step forward, to bridge the uncertainty that still stretched between them, but neither willing to break the moment either. It was broken at last, though, by the clatter of a trash bin. Probably just a stray cat, Vivian told herself. But it still made her jump.

"Come on," Honor said, sighing. "We shouldn't linger. Let's find a cab."

It never took long to find a cab, even after midnight, not in a city that couldn't stop dancing long enough to sleep. But when Honor gave the driver the intersection where they were heading, Vivian frowned.

"That's not where I live," she pointed out as the cab pulled away from the curb.

Honor gave her a sideways look. "I know."

She was so close, Vivian could have slid a few inches over and pressed against the warmth of her body, inhaled the smell of her starched shirt and wool suit. Instead, she pressed her back against the closed door and crossed her arms. She hadn't agreed to go anywhere, and she didn't like anyone making assumptions about her. Not even Honor. "Are we dropping you off first, then?"

Honor sighed. Streetlights flickered through the cab's windows, illuminating her face in flashes, and Vivian couldn't tell whether she was irritated or not. "No. You're not going home by yourself tonight." It was irritation, but it softened—and since when was anything about Honor soft?—as she added, "Until we know more, just in case."

"What about everyone else?" Vivian asked. She didn't mention the Nightingale by name, not with the cabbie up front listening who knew how closely. "They've got as much reason to be careful."

"They weren't the ones O'Keefe was watching like a vulture tonight," Honor replied. "No one's walking home alone, and everyone knows to be on alert. But I didn't like that he made a point of telling me he knew your name. And you live alone."

Vivian couldn't argue with that, but it made her feel suddenly lonely to have it said out loud. Most everyone she knew had someone—a mother, a brother, a sweetheart. Maybe an entire damn family depending on them. She had Florence, of course. She had friends that were like family. And most of the time, she was proud of making it on her own. God knew it wasn't easy.

But sometimes none of that mattered, especially when she went home at the end of her long days or longer nights and no one was there to notice. On those nights, when she fell asleep to the sound of her own breathing, it felt like more than just walls and city blocks were separating her from everyone she loved.

But she wouldn't say any of that out loud. She would barely say it in her own head. So instead she nodded like Honor's words hadn't hurt. "Guess that's true. And Danny's still got my . . ." She was too conscious of the cabbie to say the word *gun*.

But Honor seemed to know anyway. "The one you stole from me?" she asked.

Vivian glanced sideways at her, but Honor only looked amused. "It wasn't yours anyway," Vivian pointed out.

To her surprise, Honor laughed, a quiet *hmm* of sound that Vivian could feel down to her toes. "I've been glad to know you have it, pet. A woman alone should always be able to look out for herself." She glanced out the window as the cab slowed. "Looks like we're here."

Vivian climbed out slowly while Honor paid the cabbie, her eyes fixed on the building in front of her. She had been there once before, what felt like a lifetime ago. Her shoulders tensed as Honor came to stand beside her. "I guess I'm spending the night with you, then?" Vivian asked.

They were at the edge of a puddle of streetlight, half their faces golden, the other in dense shadow. Vivian couldn't read Honor's expression. "You have somewhere else to be?"

Vivian swallowed and lifted her chin. "Nope," she said, as carelessly as she could manage. Her heart was hammering as she added, "But only because there's trouble, and only until it blows over."

A moment of hesitation before Honor answered. Was it disappointment? Surprise? Vivian didn't think she'd ever be brave enough to ask.

"Of course," Honor replied at last. "Whatever you like, pet. Whatever you need."

Vivian's heart was still hammering as she followed Honor inside.

Honor usually lived in her rooms above the Nightingale. But she kept a second spot for when things around there got a little too hot for safety, when she needed to sleep somewhere anonymous. And maybe, Vivian thought for the first time, when she just wanted to be alone with her thoughts.

Vivian was one of the few people who knew that Honor had two other houses, inherited after her father died. Sometimes she wondered whether Honor would ever leave the world of the Nightingale for the world of those houses. She could have asked, and she was pretty sure Honor would have answered. But Vivian hadn't wanted to ask, like she was a friend or a lover, like she was anything more than someone who watched Honor with wary, hungry eyes and pretended she wasn't looking at all.

But this place, Vivian knew. She'd been here once before, on another night filled with trouble that meant she needed to lay low, and the safest place to do that had been with Honor. It was barely more than a bed and a door with a lock, with only steps between them and an old, rickety-legged stove with its pipe snaking into the wall. Certainly not a home.

Except that, this time, it was more than that. Vivian stared around as Honor closed the door behind them. There were curtains at the windows, a quilt on the bed, a teakettle sitting on top of the stove. There was even a print hanging on one wall, the same sort of misty landscape that Vivian remembered seeing in Honor's home above the Nightingale.

Vivian took a step forward. "You spending more time here now?"

she asked before she remembered she should pretend like she hadn't noticed, like how Honor lived meant nothing to her.

Honor flipped the locks. Her eyes were fixed on Vivian's face, as though waiting to see what she would think. "Not much," she said, as if it didn't matter. "Just thought it might be worth making the place a little more comfortable. In case—" She broke off, turning toward the coatrack as she shrugged off her jacket and hat.

"In case what?" Vivian asked, her voice hoarse. She should have been thinking about O'Keefe, should have been insisting that Honor tell her what they were going to do. But all she could think about was the woman in front of her.

Honor paused in the middle of hanging up her things. She didn't look at Vivian as she answered, "Thought it might be more comfortable if I had a visitor again."

Vivian swallowed, the backs of her eyes burning like there were tears hiding there. "Who were you hoping would visit, Honor?"

Honor took a careful step toward her. "There was a time, not long ago, when I thought you'd never let me this close to you again," she said. Her voice was hoarse too. "I couldn't blame you for that, you know. For not trusting me."

Vivian swallowed. "You'd given me plenty of reasons not to," she whispered, her heart beating a Charleston against her ribs. She tried to remind herself that she was there to stay safe. Nothing more. But it was hard to lie to herself with Honor watching her like she was the only person in the world.

"And now?"

There were only inches between them. Vivian knew that if she took a step back, if she looked away, Honor wouldn't push. She'd let the walls go back up between them, polite and distant and respectful. Vivian lifted her chin, as reckless as if she had half a bottle of champagne in her. She didn't move.

"I don't know," she said, her voice shaking. Standing this close to

Honor felt like reaching for a fire, like she was desperate for its warmth and terrified of getting burned all at the same time. "I don't know what to think, Honor. And I don't know what I want."

"I don't think that's quite true," Honor murmured. She took a step forward, and when Vivian didn't back up or turn away, she took another. "I think we both know. The question is . . ."

She raised one hand, slowly, and ran her fingers across the edge of Vivian's hair, letting it fall across them like a curtain of black silk. They were close enough now that Vivian could see her hesitation, and it helped that Honor felt uncertain too. Vivian closed her eyes as one of Honor's palms curled around the curve of her cheek.

"The question is," Honor whispered, "do you trust me enough?"

Vivian wanted to say that it didn't matter—that none of it mattered. All the lies and hurt and stolen moments that speckled their history together. Her ache to belong with someone, to be wanted. The threat lurking outside the door that had pushed them together, tonight, when Vivian would never have chosen it for herself.

She wanted to believe that none of it mattered. But it did.

"I don't know," Vivian replied, her eyes still closed. "I want to. But I don't know, Honor." It was the most she could offer.

"Then I'll just have to keep earning it," Honor whispered, and her lips were only a breath away from Vivian's now. They brushed across them lightly, once, twice.

It wasn't enough. Not after the fear and sorrow of the night. Not after everything that had pushed them together and pulled them apart for so long.

Vivian's hands fisted into the fabric of Honor's shirt, trying to pull her closer. Honor was strong and tall and always in control, and Vivian couldn't have said which she wanted more, the heat like an electric charge that flowed between them or the feeling of safety that wrapped around her with Honor's arms. They fit together so easily, in spite of everything they knew about each other, or maybe because of it.

Vivian knew the bed was just behind her, but she couldn't have said who got them there. She just knew that the scent of Honor was filling her head and leaving her dizzy with longing, that the feel of her was almost perfect enough to make Vivian forget everything that waited for them outside that door.

She whimpered when she felt the chill of air between their bodies as Honor pulled back. Vivian's eyes flew open, all the uncertainty and wariness rushing back like a punch to the gut. Her face flooded with heat as she realized what had nearly happened, and she scooted away quickly, until her back was pressed against the headboard. Honor was watching her, a smile on her face that might have been surprise or curiosity, but was certainly nothing like how Vivian was feeling.

Vivian looked away. She couldn't hide that her breathing was coming too fast, but she could try to look as cool and composed as Honor. "That was unexpected," she said, giving her hair a little toss.

"Was it?" Honor said, her voice telling Vivian nothing she needed to know. "I thought it had been a long time coming." When Vivian sneaked a look at her, Honor was watching her closely. "But I thought maybe we shouldn't let things go any farther. Not tonight, anyway."

"Not—" Hurt and confusion were too painful to show, so Vivian settled on anger. "Make up your mind, Honor. Just one damn time, make up your mind."

Honor was staring at her now. "I thought I made it pretty clear that I did, pet," she said. "A long time ago."

"Then stop looking so damn calm," Vivian snapped, her heart still racing.

"Looking so—" Honor tipped her chin up, staring at the ceiling for a moment. Then she reached for Vivian's hand. Before Vivian could pull away, Honor had pressed it flat against her own chest, just below the curve of her collarbone. Beneath her palm, Vivian could feel Honor's heart pounding. "Calm is the last thing I feel right now, Vivian. Do you know how long—" She broke off.

"Then why did you stop?" Vivian said. It sounded like a plea again, and she hated how vulnerable she felt in that moment. But she couldn't have held the question in.

Again, that wry smile. "The timing is hell," Honor said.

It was a simple enough answer that Vivian choked out a laugh before she could stop herself. Honor slid closer, until she was sitting against the headboard too, their hips and arms pressed together. Vivian hesitated, then laid her head against Honor's shoulder. She felt Honor go still, and then one arm slid around her waist, pulling her close, as Honor leaned against her too.

"The timing is hell," she repeated. "And both our emotions are running a little too high for us to think clearly."

"I didn't know your emotions could do that," Vivian said, her voice shaking a little.

"They always do," Honor murmured, running her fingers down Vivian's arm so lightly that it made her shiver, "when it comes to you. And I think it would be a big decision for you if—" For the first time Vivian heard the nervousness in her voice, nervousness that had maybe always been there but that she had ignored because it hadn't seemed possible for someone like Honor to be that uncertain. "You and your sister both go to church, don't you?" Honor asked quietly.

Vivian was suddenly glad that they were side by side, that she didn't have to look Honor in the face as she realized what she was asking. It was one thing to make a bad decision at the Nightingale, where folks would turn a blind eye to all kinds of things. But in the daylight, the world wouldn't be so kind to them. Not if this was something real.

Did she want it to be something real? "I think you know that wouldn't stop me from going for what I wanted," she said, a cautious answer but a true one.

"There's not much that stops you from going for what you want, is there, pet?" Honor murmured. "You've got no idea how much I love that about you." Vivian sucked in a breath at that, but Honor was still talking. "But would it stop your sister?"

Vivian tensed. She didn't know the answer to that question. She had hoped she would never have to ask.

"I know she's all you've got," Honor said quietly, and Vivian could feel equal tension thrumming through her body. "And I would never want to—" She broke off, but Vivian could hear what she wasn't saying.

Honor didn't want just one night. She wouldn't have asked, wouldn't have been so cautious, if that was all there was to it. Vivian wasn't sure whether the heat that filled her was elation or panic. Probably equal parts both.

She wasn't ready for this conversation, not ready to think through what it might look like to say yes to Honor, yes to more, whatever that meant. Not ready to decide whether she could trust herself enough, trust Honor enough, to do that. Not when Harlan O'Keefe was lurking out there. Not until they knew they were safe.

She knew she had been silent too long when Honor sighed. But she didn't pull away; instead, she leaned over to press a kiss against Vivian's temple.

"The timing is hell," she said again, as if she could read Vivian's thoughts. "And we're not in the clear yet."

Vivian couldn't stop herself from shivering, then, remembering the look in Honor's eyes when she realized who the red-haired man was.

"Who is Harlan O'Keefe?" Vivian asked quietly.

She could feel the hesitation as Honor decided how much to say.

It made Vivian pull away, just a little, a reminder that there was still plenty they kept from each other.

"Bootlegger, mostly," Honor said at last. "Started out as a small-time criminal, from what I heard, but he built a nasty reputation for himself in the city a few years ago. I thought he was long gone."

"Arrested?"

"No, I heard he took his operation to Chicago. Good pickings for a bootlegger there."

"Wonder why he seems so certain that the Nightingale is how he's going to find this Hugh Brown fella," Vivian said, glancing at Honor out of the corner of her eye. "Seems like an odd place to fixate on, unless . . ."

"Unless he's got someone particular tipping him off," Honor said quietly. She glanced at Vivian and added, more wryly, "You got any suspicions in that busy mind of yours, pet?"

Vivian sighed. "No, and I don't want to. All I want is to keep my head down. That's how girls like me get through life, right?"

Honor smiled. "Vivian, you might be worse at keeping your head down than just about anyone I know."

Vivian wanted to laugh at that, but she couldn't quite bring herself to. Honor was right, and there had been plenty of times it had gotten her in a world of trouble.

Honor pulled her closer. "Let's try to get some sleep," she suggested.

There was only one bed, the same bed they had shared last time Vivian was there, just wide enough for the two of them. Honor waited for Vivian to kick off her shoes, then pulled the quilt over both of them. Vivian couldn't have said which was making her more tense, the thought of O'Keefe or the feel of Honor pressed against her back, one arm resting lightly over her waist. Either way, she didn't expect to get much sleep. She stared at the door, lit by the dim glow of the streetlights that filtered through the curtains.

But all she heard was the sound of Honor's breathing, the soft rustle of the sheets every time one of them shifted. And at last, her tired eyes were too heavy to stay open.

Are you hungry?" Honor asked through a yawn the next morning, both of them still in their rumpled clothes from the night before. "I don't really keep any food around since I'm not here often. But we could grab a cab back to your home so you can change and then find some breakfast." Her expression was carefully neutral as she added, "My treat."

"I don't think I could eat anything," Vivian said, eyeing her reflection sideways in the mirror as she tried to smooth down her hair, glad she had a hat and coat to cover up her dancing clothes from the night before. "My nerves are still too jumpy."

In the mirror, she saw Honor's reflection shake her head. "It's going to be okay, pet. I promise."

"You got a plan, then?" Vivian asked.

Honor's mouth twisted to the side. "Not much of one," she said at last. "Not yet."

She hesitated a moment, then, stepping forward, wrapped her arms around Vivian's waist. Vivian stared at their reflections, not sure whether she was elated or terrified by how well they fit together.

"We need to get him off our backs," Honor continued, leaning her cheek against Vivian's temple. "He gave us two days, so I have to use them. I don't care if that means bumping off O'Keefe or finding this Hugh Brown fella and handing him over. Whichever is going to keep the Nightingale safe." Her expression was serious as she met Vivian's eyes in the mirror. "Whichever is going to keep you safe."

"He's got no reason to come after me," Vivian said, hoping it was true.

Honor turned Vivian to face her. "He's not the sort who needs a reason," she said quietly. "He's got a nasty reputation, pet."

"But you'd hand this Hugh Brown fella over to him anyway?" Vivian asked, shivering a little as she remembered the way O'Keefe had shrugged off Silence's death. "Nasty reputation and all? Not knowing anything about who he is or why O'Keefe wants him?"

"In a heartbeat," Honor said without hesitating. "If it would keep everyone at the Nightingale safe? Keep *you* safe? In a heartbeat." She sighed. "Shame I don't know who he is."

Vivian shivered again. Honor's ruthless streak was something she usually admired; without it, the Nightingale wouldn't have existed. But this morning, it was making her nervous. She took a step back, suddenly wanting some space between them. "Not like you to be so comfortable with the idea of someone ending up dead," she said quietly.

"You got another idea?" Honor snapped. "I'm all ears, pet."

Vivian flinched at her sharp tone, then lifted her chin. "I do, actually." She had woken up with the idea in her mind, as though she had been thinking it through all night while she slept. It scared her, and she knew Honor wouldn't like it. But it was the best she could come up with. "What if we get the police to help us out?"

"The police?" Honor's eyebrows shot up, then immediately drew into a frown. "You want to go talk to the commissioner."

Vivian swallowed nervously. "Yes."

"No."

"You can't stop me," Vivian pointed out.

Honor grabbed Vivian's shoulders, her fingers flexing as though she wanted to shake her but was holding herself back. "Vivian, the last time you talked to that man, he was trying to throw you in jail for murder."

"Well really, the last time I talked to him, he told me he *wasn't* going to throw me in jail for murder. So that's not too bad, right?" Vivian said, smiling weakly. When Honor didn't say anything, Vivian's smile dropped. "If O'Keefe has the kind of reputation you say, the commissioner should jump at the chance to get him. It's the best way to get him off our backs with no one else ending up dead, and you know it."

Honor's fingers tightened once more before she let her hands fall. "Fine," she bit off, turning away. "Guess you'll be going to see your Mr. Green now."

Vivian's stomach dropped. Honor and Leo had worked together plenty when they needed to, but they had never trusted each other. Not really. "Don't do that, Honor."

Honor let out a heavy breath, then nodded. "You're right. It's the best option. But that doesn't mean I have to like it." She turned back around. "We'll get a cab, and I'll drop you at his place so you can ask for your favor."

"What will you be doing?" Vivian asked, glad it hadn't turned into a fight.

Honor's mouth pulled into a tight line. "Checking in on everyone else," she said, and the chill in her voice made Vivian shiver.

She looked away, wishing she hadn't asked.

THIRTEEN

Are you sure about this?" Leo asked, laying one hand on Vivian's arm to pull them both to a stop. Around them, the city was quieter than usual, the bustle faded into Sunday-morning stillness. Especially here, where the elegant stone houses—not mansions, it wasn't quite that part of town—were set off by trees still changing color and drivers waiting in gleaming cars for their employers to emerge for church.

Vivian grimaced. She and Florence usually attended mass together on Sunday mornings. But God would have to give her a pass today—she had other things to worry about.

"There's still time to change your mind," Leo said quietly, pulling her back to the present.

Vivian swallowed. "I'm sure," she whispered, trying to ignore the knot of nerves in her stomach. "It's the only way to keep Honor from doing something too dangerous. Or from handing over some fella we don't know for O'Keefe to bump off."

"You think she'd do that?" Leo asked. "Find this Hugh Brown fella and hand him over? Seems cold, even for her."

"I hope not," Vivian said, staring at the house in front of them without really seeing it, trying not to picture Honor's face when Vivian accused her of being too comfortable with the thought of murder. "And who knows if she'd even be able to. She's just as likely to go after O'Keefe, and that—" Vivian broke off.

"That's a good way to end up dead," Leo said. He gave Vivian a quick glance, as if he immediately regretted saying it. "From what I hear about the fella."

Vivian shivered. "Anyway, she agreed that I should talk to your uncle first. So that's what I'm going to do. But you don't have to come in, too."

At that, Leo laughed. "Like hell, Viv. "I'm not letting you walk into the lion's den alone." He gave her a curious glance. "You sound pretty worried about Honor. Protective, even. Are you and she—" He broke off, grimacing. "Sorry. None of my business, right?"

Vivian felt her face growing hot as she remembered Honor's kisses the night before. But those memories were all tangled up now with her fear of what Honor might do to keep the Nightingale safe—to keep *her* safe. "I don't know," she whispered. "I want—" She shook her head. "But I still don't know if I can trust her. Not after everything that's happened."

Leo nodded. He knew more than he probably wanted to about Vivian's checkered history with Honor. "Well." He blew out a breath. "If we're going to do it, better do it."

Both of them knew the front door was reserved for actual guests, not those who were there on business. Leo led the way around to the back entrance, the one used by servants and delivery boys and the cops who were occasionally summoned to their boss's home. The servant who opened it at his knock looked surprised to see them.

"Mr. Green." He glanced over Leo's shoulder at Vivian. "And a guest. I'm not aware that the commissioner is expecting you."

"He's not, Davis," Leo said, all trace of his earlier hesitation gone in a show of smiling confidence. "But if you'd tell him I'm here anyway, I'd appreciate it."

The man, Davis, frowned. "I'm not sure—"

"Trust me, pal," Leo said, leaning on the doorframe and dropping his voice confidentially. "He'll want to hear this."

Davis considered that for a moment, then nodded and stepped back to allow them through the door. There was no hint on his face of what he was thinking. "I'll show you to the study."

Vivian paced nervously around the commissioner's study while they waited, barely seeing the walls lined with books or the massive wooden desk, its surface empty except for a stand of pens and an inlaid wooden box that she would have bet all her rent money held a stash of cigars. She had been there before, and never for good reasons. Each time, she hoped she would never come back. Maybe this time really would be the last.

Leo didn't pace. But he leaned against one wall, his face expressionless. Only the hat making endless circles around one finger gave away his thoughts.

Leo probably hated being there even more than she did. But he hadn't hesitated when she told him what she wanted to do. Danny had already told him what happened to Silence. And Leo wasn't the sort of fella to leave his friends in danger when he could do something about it.

"I was enjoying a particularly marvelous cup of coffee."

The commissioner didn't bother with a greeting as he strode into the room. Vivian and Leo both snapped to attention, their eyes fixed on him as he took his seat behind the desk. In spite of the brocade dressing gown he was wearing, the commissioner looked like he could have been ready for a day at the office, his hair smoothed down with pomade and his luxurious silver mustaches already trimmed and brushed for the day.

Vivian glanced between him and Leo. There had never been much family resemblance. She had wondered, more than once, whether either of them looked like the commissioner's sister, Leo's mother. But she had never asked, and she never would.

"So this had better be worth my time, Mr. Green. I don't appreciate interruptions." The commissioner glanced at his nephew and sniffed. "And I thought I had made it clear that I have no work for you at present."

Leo's jaw tightened, and the fingers that had been spinning his hat now clutched the brim tightly enough to dent it. He worked for his uncle from time to time, whenever the commissioner needed the connections that a skilled bootlegger would have in New York's criminal underworld or someone who could operate outside the strict bounds of the law. But that work was always on his uncle's terms, and it never came with any acknowledgment that they were family.

"You did, sir," Leo said, his voice cold and polite. "But I thought you'd want to hear this."

The commissioner looked Vivian up and down, as though she were something unpleasant that had stuck to his polished shoes. "Miss Kelly. I hope these are more favorable circumstances than the last time we met."

Vivian wanted to shrink into herself. The commissioner could make her feel more insignificant than anyone else she had ever met. "Thank you for seeing us, sir," she said, relieved when her voice wavered only a little.

The commissioner sighed. "All right. What is this about?"

Vivian took a deep breath. "Do you know the name Harlan O'Keefe?"

The commissioner stared at her, and Vivian realized that, for possibly the first time, she had genuinely surprised him. "I do indeed." A curious smile spread over his face. "All right, you've piqued my interest. Harlan O'Keefe. Petty crook turned public menace. Ruthless, vicious, and a suspected murderer who manages to never get his own hands dirty and so has never been caught." He glanced at Leo. "Does that sound about right, Mr. Green?"

"Sounds about right, sir," Leo said, his voice tight.

Vivian wasn't surprised by that, or by the way his eyes were fixed like knives on his uncle. Being around the commissioner always made Leo, normally so easygoing, tense and belligerent. But the question caught her off guard. "You know much about O'Keefe?" she asked, unable to hide her surprise even though she knew it would be better to present an entirely unified front. "You didn't say."

"Fella had quite a reputation before he left New York a few years back," Leo said, glancing at her only briefly before his eyes returned to his uncle. "Hard not to hear about him. Isn't that right, Commissioner?"

The commissioner was silent for a moment, then inclined his chin in a stately nod. "Indeed, Mr. Green. Are you telling me he's back in New York?"

"Back and . . ." Vivian swallowed, trying not to remember O'Keefe's cruel smile during their dance, his feigned regret as he told Honor she had two days to give him what he wanted. "Yes, sir. He's back."

"Then I'm curious, Miss Kelly, what brought him into *your* orbit," the commissioner said, steepling his fingers together. "I wouldn't have thought your sort of petty criminal activity would take you into contact with a man like O'Keefe."

Vivian wanted to protest that she wasn't a criminal, but of course she was to a man like him. The Nightingale was hardly a legal establishment, even if the cops from their local precinct stopped by regularly to take their share of Honor's bribe money—and of her bar, too. Even if the commissioner had been there before. "He brought himself," she said quietly. "Seems to have taken a dislike to the Nightingale."

"And why is that?" The commissioner leaned forward as he spoke. Having his full attention for the first time unnerved Vivian, and she glanced at Leo in a panic.

"Seems like he wants something from the owner," Leo said, coming to stand next to her. "And he's willing to make trouble to get it."

Having him there was a comfort, and Vivian found her voice again. "He says he's looking for someone," she added. "And he seems to think he can find that person through the Nightingale. A man—"

"And he's already killed a man," Leo put in, cutting her off. She felt his hand find hers and squeeze. She could guess what he meant: sharing more information than they had to with the commissioner was never a good idea. There was no knowing what he would do with it. She squeezed back. "Or at least, had him killed. Like you said, he rarely gets his own hands dirty."

The commissioner stared at Leo, his eyes narrowing, before he shifted his gaze to Vivian. "Who was the man that died?" he asked.

"Silas Abernathy," she whispered, feeling as though a knot had tightened in her chest at the thought of Silence.

"And O'Keefe claimed responsibility for his death?"

Vivian glanced at Leo out of the corner of her eye. "Indirectly," she admitted. "Called it an accident. He wasn't too broken up about it, though."

"I see." The commissioner sighed and leaned back in his chair. "And what are you hoping I will do?"

Vivian stared at him. "Take care of O'Keefe," she said at last, sputtering a little. "He's a menace and a criminal, you said so yourself. And you're the commissioner of police, aren't you? So put your boys on him. Catch him and lock him up for good."

"On what grounds, Miss Kelly?" he asked. "If we had something to pin on O'Keefe, we'd have done it five years ago before he left New York. Now you're telling us he's back, but can you tell me where he might be hiding out this time? Who his associates are and where to find them? What crimes he might be involved in?"

The knot in Vivian's chest tightened with each question. "No," she whispered.

"Mr. Green?" the commissioner turned to his nephew, brows rising. "Do you have any information to share that might illuminate what O'Keefe is doing here?"

Vivian could see Leo's jaw clench. "No, sir," he bit off. "I don't."

The commissioner shrugged. "Then there isn't much I can do just yet aside from tell my detectives to keep their ears to the ground. But to take any action against O'Keefe, I need a reason to arrest him, not to mention I need to know where to find him." He settled back in his chair. "If either of you can give me those, we're in business. Until then . . ." He shrugged and picked up the silver bell at the corner of his desk, giving it a deliberate ring.

"Yes, sir?" Davis asked, reappearing at the door only moments later.

"Show Miss Kelly out." The commissioner gave Leo a cold smile. "Mr. Green and I need to have a further chat."

Vivian glanced at Leo. She would rather have waited for him, but arguing with the commissioner didn't seem like the best idea.

Leo gave her an encouraging smile. "It's all right," he said. "You got enough on you for cab fare? I don't like the thought of you walking around alone."

"Yeah, I'll be fine," Vivian said, with no idea whether it was true or not. But Honor seemed to think O'Keefe would give them the two days he had promised, and she wanted to believe Honor was right. Besides, it was broad daylight outside, and not exactly his part of the city. "See you later?"

"Count on it," Leo said, but his eyes were already back on his uncle, who was watching the exchange with increasing impatience.

"Miss Kelly?" Davis gestured toward the door.

Vivian wanted to grab the commissioner and shake him, to insist that he help, but she had no choice except to follow Davis out. She hated it. Hated feeling helpless, hated waiting to see what would happen.

Hated not knowing what to do next.

By the time she emerged back into the sunlight, she was spoiling for a fight, helplessness and worry bubbling inside her with nowhere to go. If she didn't start moving, she wasn't sure what she might say or do.

It wasn't until she had started walking, taking deep breaths to try to calm herself down, that she realized she wasn't far from Ruth Quinn's house. At the thought of her aunt, she felt hot and angry all over again, all of it mixing up inside her heart. She couldn't keep people she cared about safe from O'Keefe. She couldn't even decide how she felt about Honor. But she could go tell Ruth Quinn how wrong she was.

Before Vivian could talk herself out of it, she had changed direction. Maybe it hadn't been Danny; maybe Ruth just hadn't liked the thought of two poor dressmakers as her nieces. Either way, they deserved better, and Vivian was going to tell her so to her face. And wouldn't it be satisfying to tell Florence that she had? Florence would never stand up for herself like that. But Vivian could do it for both of them. She had to stand up to someone, soon, or she was going to lose her mind.

It didn't occur to her until she was standing at Ruth Quinn's door, the flower-patterned curtains still fluttering at the windows, that her aunt might not even be home. Maybe she went to church on Sundays. Maybe there was no point in being there at all. Vivian couldn't tell whether she actually believed that or whether she was just looking for an excuse to leave; just in case it was the second, she hammered on the door before she could lose her nerve.

It only took a moment for her to hear footsteps in the hall, and she frowned. They thumped toward the door, heavy and careless, not at all what she remembered from her previous visit. They sounded like a man's footsteps—but Ruth had said she had no husband.

Before Vivian had more than a moment to wonder, the door opened, and she found herself staring wide-eyed at the owner of the footsteps.

He was tall—much taller than her—and dressed casually only in his trousers and shirtsleeves, with a glass of something amber in one hand. Clearly, wherever Ruth was, he was the sort to spend Sunday relaxing at home rather than making his devotions. His black hair and eyes made Vivian catch her breath, but not as much as he did at the sight of her. The glass fell from his hand as though it had gone suddenly nerveless, landing on the carpet with a muffled *thunk,* the liquor beginning to pool around his shoes.

"God in Heaven," he whispered. "You look just like Mae."

Vivian stared at his eyes, so like her own, barely able to breathe. "Dad?"

FOURTEEN

"What?" The word dropped out of him as he stared at her, as if his mind had frozen when he opened the door and he wasn't sure how to thaw it again.

Vivian felt the same. "Are you Clyde Quinn?" she whispered, amazed that she could get out any words at all.

"Yes, that's me. Who are you? You can't be Mae's . . ." He was still staring at her. "You look just like her," he repeated.

"Vivian. Vivian Kelly. Mae was my mother. Are you—" Vivian couldn't seem to organize her scattered thoughts into anything that made sense when they came out of her mouth. "I think you're my father."

He stared at her for a moment that felt like a hundred years. And then, before Vivian knew what was happening, he had grabbed her shoulders and hauled her to him, his arms wrapped around her so tightly she could barely breathe. She didn't care. Her father—*her father*—was holding her, like she was the most precious thing in the world, like he never wanted to let her go. She felt tears pressing against her eyelids, and for once she didn't need to be stronger than tears. She hugged him back, praying that she wasn't dreaming. *Her father.*

When Clyde finally let her go, his hands stayed on her shoulders as he stepped back to get a better look at her. He shook his head, a wide smile on his face. "Well, damn me. Vivian? Vivian. I can barely believe it. You look like someone took me and your mother and fit the prettiest parts of both of us together." He cupped his hands around her face, lifting her chin and beaming at her. "My little girl. I can barely believe it. Last time I saw you, you weren't more than a bump under your mother's apron."

Vivian looked him over as greedily as he was taking her in. With his sharp eyes and thick hair, it was easy to picture the handsome young man that her mother must have known when she married him. He had no jacket on, so Vivian could see that he had broad shoulders and muscled arms, though neither could quite hide the hint of a paunch around his midsection or the way the skin was beginning to droop around his cheeks. His hair, the same black as hers, was shot through with threads of silver. *Her father.* It still didn't seem real.

"And your—" Clyde hesitated. "We had a little girl. She would have been your big sister."

"Florence," Vivian said quickly, and his face broke into a broad, beaming smile that was so much like her sister's it made Vivian's heart ache. "She's doing so well, she has—"

"Wait just a moment," Clyde broke in. "Ruth should hear this too. You have an aunt, did you know? Ruth!"

His sudden bellow was so loud that it made Vivian jump. She had forgotten about Ruth, forgotten that the woman had said her father—her father who was standing right in front of her—was dead. She felt a surge of rage replace the happy ache in her chest and opened her mouth to tell him exactly what Ruth had tried to do. But Clyde was still bellowing.

"Ruth, get down here! You'll never guess who showed up at our door!" He turned back to Vivian, beaming as he grabbed her hand a little roughly. "This way, come inside. No, never mind that," he added impatiently when she bent to pick up the glass he had dropped. "That's Ruth's job, she'll take care of it. Ruth! Where are you?"

"I'm coming, Clyde." That was Ruth's voice, sounding harried and worried both. As Clyde pulled her out of the hall, Vivian saw her aunt rushing down the stairs so quickly she nearly tripped at the bottom. "What on earth—"

She broke off as she caught sight of Vivian, all the color draining from her cheeks. "Clyde, who is that?" Ruth asked in a small voice. Her eyes were wide and pleading, her narrow chest jumping with short, quick breaths.

Clyde laughed. "You blind? Can't you see she looks just like Mae? It's my little girl, Vivian. Mae named her Vivian. My little girl found us. Her and Florence! Out there all this time and we never knew!" When Ruth didn't respond with instant elation, still staring at Vivian in shock, his beaming smile drew into a scowl. "What in God's name is the matter with you, Ruth?" he demanded. "Say something! My girl's come back to us, after all these years."

"I'm just in shock," Ruth squeaked out. "She looks just like Mae, it's like . . . it's like seeing a ghost." She smiled tremulously at Vivian, her eyes still begging. "Except you have your father's coloring. Vivian, was it?"

A slow, cold trickle of doubt began to drip through Vivian's elation. She was sure that the man holding her arm was her father. But with him scowling at her aunt, she was suddenly conscious of the size of the hand wrapped around her wrist, the broad shoulders that loomed over her in the hall. There was more than just surprise in the way Ruth was watching her. Vivian knew what fear looked like, and it was coming off Ruth in waves, real enough that whatever she had planned to say about Ruth's lies stayed stuck in her throat.

Her father was overjoyed to meet her, she believed that much. But she didn't know him, not yet, not well enough to say anything else for sure.

Vivian held out her hand. "Vivian, yes. Nice to meet you, Aunt Ruth."

Ruth didn't slump with relief, not with Clyde's eyes on them, but Vivian had a feeling she wanted to. Ruth took her hand, but instead of shaking it, she pulled Vivian into a tight embrace. "I am so happy to meet you," she whispered fiercely in Vivian's ear, before letting go. She turned a smile toward her brother. "Shall we invite Vivian into the parlor?"

Clyde chuckled. "That's more like it. Let's sit down and have a chat. And pour me another drink, will you? I was so surprised when I saw my girl here that I dropped mine in the hall."

Vivian found herself ushered once again into Ruth's parlor. Clyde seemed out of place there, a bear surrounded by china knickknacks and too many floral patterns, but that didn't stop him from settling into the largest chair and accepting the drink Ruth brought him with complete inattention, his eyes still fixed on Vivian and his smile stretching across his whole face. He didn't offer either woman a drink, and Ruth didn't suggest it, just settled into another chair as Vivian found herself on the sofa again, looking around the room and hoping she gave the impression that she was seeing it for the first time. Her hands were suddenly clammy, as though she had been thrust on stage in the middle of a vaudeville show and didn't know what the act was. She could feel sweat trickling between her shoulder blades.

"Now, Vivian, tell us all about yourself," Clyde said, leaning forward. "You've no idea how long I looked for your mother and sister. How did you find me? Or, I guess," he said, chuckling, "how did you find your aunt?"

So the house was Ruth's then, and not his. Vivian tucked that bit of information away. "My mother's burial," she said, watching Clyde eagerly.

But he only stared at her, waiting. "What about it?"

Vivian wasn't sure whether her thoughts froze at his words or whether they started racing at double speed. Had he not been the one to arrange her mother's burial? She had assumed he found a record of Mae's death but hadn't been able to track down her children.

But the address associated with the burial had been this house—the house that she had just learned was Ruth's. Which meant that Ruth had been the one to arrange the burial, and she hadn't told her brother about it.

Ruth's wide-eyed panic was back, so intent and focused this time that Vivian was amazed Clyde didn't see it. But he never glanced at his sister.

"After my mother's burial," Vivian said, thinking quickly, "a neighbor kept some papers that she had. Because Florence and I were so young. She was worried that we would lose them." When Clyde nodded with interest, Vivian tried not to look too relieved. "The neighbor tracked us down and returned them. After we left the orphan home, I mean. And we found Aunt Ruth's name in them." She was glad when he just nodded instead of asking what kind of papers they might have been. Better to say as little as possible when she was lying so much already. "It took a while to find where she lived. But I did, eventually. So here I am."

Clyde shook his head. "That can't have been easy, going on so little information. I'm amazed you found us at all."

"I had a few favors I could call in," Vivian said without thinking, before remembering that it wasn't the sort of thing a good girl, a respectable dressmaker, might say.

But her father only laughed loudly. "Got a few tricks up your sleeve, hey? Might have guessed it with that hair." When Vivian put a hand up to her bob, he laughed again. "Don't fret, little one. I'd be disappointed if a daughter of mine didn't have some spunk." He winked. "I've always got a few tricks up my sleeve too."

In spite of her nervousness, Vivian found herself sitting up straighter, almost basking in the praise. Maybe she did have something in common with the man in front of her. Maybe she could be a daughter he wanted.

"Now." Clyde settled back in his chair and took a sip of his drink. "Tell me all about yourself."

So Vivian told her story again. If it hadn't been for Ruth's eyes fixed on her like a warning, it would have been easy to forget to be careful. Clyde smiled at her the whole time, looking exactly like Vivian had always imagined a proud father would. It had felt like coming home, when he had held her, when he had said without hesitation that she was his. She had been yearning for that her whole life.

But Ruth was there, and her wariness hadn't faded. And Vivian had seen plenty of ways men could get unpleasant when they had the upper hand with the women who lived with them. As much as she might want to, she wasn't going to throw herself in his lap and start calling him Pops until she knew more. So she stuck to the simple things: her mother's death and the orphan home, her work as a dressmaker, Florence's marriage.

"And did Florence stay in the city, like you?" Ruth broke in. "Or did she move away after she married?"

Maybe it wasn't Ruth's feelings about Florence's marriage and her half-Chinese daughter that they needed to worry about—maybe it was Clyde's. Either way, Vivian could take a hint. "She and her husband wanted to be close to his family," Vivian said carefully, sticking to as much of the truth as she could.

"My Florence," Clyde murmured, shaking his head. "She was the sweetest little thing. Smiles and sunshine all day long." He gave Vivian a pleading look. "Is she close enough to come back to the city? Or for me to visit her? She didn't head out west or anything, did she?"

Vivian laughed at the puppy-dog sad look on his face, though she could hear the nervous edge in the sound. She hoped no one else could. "No, she's not too far. And she'll want to know I found you too. I didn't . . ." She bit her lip, trying not to glance at Ruth. "I didn't tell her I was coming here today. I didn't want to upset her if nothing came out of it."

"My little girls. All grown up and looking out for each other. I'm so . . ." Clyde let out a gusty sigh. "Tell her I want to meet her, will you? I can pay for a train ticket or whatever she needs to get here."

Vivian felt herself softening toward him again; the pleading was back in his voice, and he was still staring at her like he was afraid she wasn't real, like he would blink and she would disappear. She could tell herself to be wary all she wanted—and she would be, she wasn't dumb—but the ache was back. Vivian had been waiting her whole life for a father who would look at her like that. "She'll want to meet you too," she said quietly. "I'm sure she will."

Clyde beamed at her. "I just had a telephone installed here," he said, giving Ruth an indulgent smile. "Ruthie never would have gone to the expense on her own, but that's what big brothers are for, right? So you can let me know when you hear from Florence and what she says. The number is Archer three-six-three-five."

"That's swell," Vivian said, not having to pretend her excitement.

"And how can I reach you?"

That made her pause; her excitement didn't dim, but she knew better than to give a near-stranger her address, even if he was her father. "I don't have a telephone," she said, hoping she didn't sound too cautious. "There's a drugstore not far from my place that takes messages for folks. Krakowski's General. The number is Palmer eighteen-twenty-five."

She could have given him the number for the Chins' restaurant, or even Leo's, and just not explained how she knew the person on the other end. But Mrs. Krakowski was safer; she took messages for lots of people. Besides, what were the odds that a man who lived on this cozy, ritzy street would venture into her run-down little neighborhood?

Vivian smiled at her father, hoping none of her careful thoughts were on her face. "Can you tell me a bit about you, then? I've told you all about my life, not that it's very exciting. What about you and Aunt Ruth?" She glanced at her aunt then, who was sitting with her hands folded in her lap. "Have you always lived here?"

"Grew up in this very house," Clyde said easily, taking a drink and leaning back in his chair. "Belonged to our father. And it was where I brought your mother when we married." His expression softened as he stared around the room. "Doesn't look much like it did then. But Florence used to have a little chair in that corner . . ." He cleared his throat, blinking rapidly a few times. Vivian wanted to go to him, to take his hand and tell him how long she and Florence had been searching for him. She clenched her fists in her lap and stayed where she was. Clyde cleared his throat again. "But I was gone from the city for a while, so it's been Ruth's place these last few years."

"Where were you?" Vivian asked, not bothering to hide her curiosity.

Clyde waved a hand. "Here and there. I work for a businessman—smart son of a bitch, much smarter than me—so I've been all over. Not much to tell about it, though." He gave his sister a sideways glance. "We're pretty boring people, aren't we, Ruthie?"

"Not much interesting about us," she agreed, a polite smile on her face now that their eyes were turned toward her. "Clyde has his work, I keep busy with the church and the Ladies Aid."

"Speaking of which," Clyde said, glancing at the clock, "ain't it nearly time for that charity dinner you've been talking about all week?" He gave Vivian a regretful smile as he stood. "Not that I wouldn't like to spend all day with you, Vivian. But it's a widows of war benefit, you see. And Ruth and her gals have worked so hard to get it ready."

"Oh—sure, of course," Vivian agreed, climbing to her feet, a little disoriented at the quick dismissal. But how could she argue with a charity dinner? And she had shown up on their doorstep so unexpectedly. "But maybe I can come back another day this week, and we could—"

Before she could even finish, Clyde had pulled her into another massive hug. She squeaked a little, but she didn't really mind. It didn't even feel like being embraced by a stranger, not when she kept seeing her sister's smile on his face. Not when she had his eyes.

"Yes, yes, for certain," he agreed, resting his hands on her shoulders as he beamed down at her. "Tuesday, yes? You come by around lunchtime. Ruth will prepare something grand for us, and we'll talk more." She felt warm all the way through as he added, "I'm so glad you found us, Vivian. So glad."

It wasn't until Vivian was back on the sidewalk, the door between them once more and her steps already turning toward home, that she realized how neatly he had avoided telling her anything about himself.

FIFTEEN

He was there? And you saw him? You talked to him, and he was happy about it?"

Florence had asked the same questions at least five times already, and after an hour of astonishment, she finally seemed to believe that Vivian was telling the truth.

Vivian nodded. "And Ruth was acting completely different. The whole thing was . . ." She bit her lip, and Florence's face fell.

They were talking after dinner, which Vivian joined the Chin family for every Sunday evening once the restaurant had closed—the only night it wasn't open late. Vivian had pulled Florence aside to tell her what had happened as soon as she could, but they had to wait until the meal was over and the dishes were washed before they could discuss it in private. Or nearly in private; Danny was there too, bouncing a grumpy Mei on his knees and making faces at her. Vivian could tell by the tight line of his jaw that he was listening closely, but he hadn't yet offered an opinion.

"Do you think it's safe?" Florence asked, pausing in her pacing to glance at her daughter and husband. "Maybe it wasn't Ruth who would have reacted badly to . . . She might have been trying to give us a sign that we should stay away."

"I thought of that too," Vivian said, the familiar ache tugging deep in her chest. She sat cross-legged on the floor, watching her sister's restless progress from one side of the little room to the other. "He's our dad. I don't want to just walk away without at least trying. But you're the one with a family now. I think you get to decide."

"I don't know if I can." Florence stopped in front of Danny, who was watching her without speaking. "What do you think?"

"It's not my pop," he said, not looking up. "It's not me who's been longing for a family my whole life."

"But it's not just me and Vivi now," Florence said.

"Might as well be, for this," Danny said. "You've already made up your mind, haven't you?" He glanced at Vivian. "I know Vivian has."

"And I know you have an opinion, even if you don't want to say it," Florence said, her voice growing sharp. "So spit it out."

"And folks think you're just a sweet little thing who'd never give an order in her life." Danny shook his head, meeting his wife's eyes at last. "All right, then, I think it's a risk."

Florence's face fell. "So that's you saying no, then?"

"It's me saying you don't know a thing about this fella, and you're just going to bring him into your lives? Into our lives? If you want to introduce him to our daughter and try to play happy family, then do it." Danny's voice had risen with each word, but he sighed when Mei began to fuss. "You don't need to ask my permission," he continued in a quieter voice, rocking the baby gently until she calmed down again. "Like I said, it's not me that's been looking for a family for years. Just be honest with yourself that it's a risk before you do it."

Florence held out her arms, and Danny stood to hand over the baby. Florence cuddled Mei under her chin. "Fine, then. I want to know my father," she said. "I can't give up the chance to know our family any more than you can, Vivi. Not without at least trying."

Vivian couldn't tell whether her heart sank or jumped. Maybe both at the same time, everything felt so mixed up inside her. But she knew she agreed. "Then I'll go call—"

"Wait 'til tomorrow," Danny suggested. When Vivian looked at him, he tried to smile at her, but she could see the nervousness hiding under the expression. "You might not have lied to him about where Florence was, but if you tell him you talked to her already, he'll know you fed him some kind of line. And you probably don't want that, not yet. Not until you know him better. In fact . . ." He glanced between the sisters. "In fact, you should probably talk to that aunt of yours again, find out what's really going on."

"Can't do that so easily with him there," Vivian pointed out.

"There's ways around that," Danny said quietly.

"But we're not going to get that figured out tonight," Florence said. Vivian could see her sister shiver and hold her daughter a little closer. "You have to get to work—"

There was a quick *rat-a-tat* knock at the door, and Lucky stuck his head around it. "Danny? Everything all right up here? Thought I heard you getting riled up."

"None of your damn business, pal," Danny said, though his smile took the edge off his words.

Lucky shook his head. "Married folks' stuff," he said, sounding disgusted. "Anyway, there's a girl downstairs asking for you or Vivian, though she looks like she's settled in for a good long chat with Auntie. Beatrice, I think she said her name was?"

"I'm coming." Vivian stood quickly, eager to get away. Florence and her husband clearly needed to talk privately.

"Ask her up if she's staying," Danny said, wrapping his arms around Florence. He sighed. "I just hope there hasn't been any more trouble," he muttered.

Florence's head jerked up. "What does that mean?" she demanded.

Vivian couldn't close the door fast enough behind her. On the stairs, Lucky shook his head. "I'm never gonna get married," he said with feeling before disappearing toward the upper floor.

Downstairs, Vivian found Bea in the kitchen, sitting on a stool and chatting while Danny's mother prepared dough for the morning. When she saw Vivian, Bea hopped up.

"Thanks for the chat, Mrs. Chin," she said. "Good to see you again."

Before Vivian could ask why she was there, Bea had grabbed her arm and hustled her out of the kitchen, back into the empty restaurant.

"Okay, spill," she whispered, guiding them to a table in the corner where they were far away from both the kitchen and the stairs. "What the hell is going on?"

"What do you mean?" Vivian asked, her thoughts still on her father and the conversation upstairs.

Bea smacked her arm. "Don't you dare, Vivian Kelly. Honor being tight-lipped I'm used to. But you don't get to keep secrets from me. What's going on? Who was that man last night?" Her voice, already quiet, dropped even lower, and Vivian could hear it tremble. "What really happened to Silence?"

Vivian braced her elbows on the table and dropped her face into her hands. "Bea, you remember in the spring when we thought I was going to get hauled off for murder?" she said, her voice muffled.

She could almost hear her friend frown, even without seeing it. "Not likely to forget that, Viv."

Vivian lifted her face. "I think this might be just as bad. You ever heard the name Harlan O'Keefe?" Bea shook her head, and Vivian leaned forward. "All right then. Here's what I know."

Vivian didn't hold anything back: not the conversation with O'Keefe or his smiling dismissal of Silence's death, not her worry about what Honor might do or her conversation with Leo and the commissioner. It took less time to tell than she expected—her dance with O'Keefe felt like a lifetime ago, but it had barely been two days. Bea's expression grew more worried as Vivian spoke, until she was gripping the edge of the table with both hands.

"So he just said no?" she demanded when Vivian finished repeating what the commissioner had said. "That's it?"

"That's about the shape of it," Vivian said. She rubbed at her temples, which had begun to ache hours ago. When had she last gotten a full night of sleep? "I don't know what I do now, Bea. I can't tell Honor I came up empty-handed. I don't—" Vivian glanced up at her friend. "I don't know what she'll do next."

"Either you trust her, or you don't." Bea said quietly. "One day you'll have to make up your mind." She took a deep breath and stood. "In the meantime, I know what we do next."

Vivian lifted her head in surprise. "What?"

"We try to shake something useful out of whatever tree we can find," Bea said. "It's Sunday, so I'm not singing. And you've got the night off, right?"

"Yeah, but—"

"No buts," Bea said firmly. "I'm not sitting around doing nothing and waiting for more bad news, and neither are you. We're going to find out where else O'Keefe has been and why he's so certain he'll find this Hugh Brown joker at the Nightingale."

"And how are we going to do that?"

Bea smiled. "Get your glad rags on, Viv. We're going dancing."

SIXTEEN

The photographers near Salon Doré weren't difficult to spot: they lounged against their cars, cameras hanging around their necks, smoke curling up from the cigarettes that they tossed aside each time a Rolls pulled up to the curb. Sometimes the photographers sank back in disappointment, fishing in their pockets for a new cigarette. Other times, the shutters began clicking like a swarm of insects as they crowded toward the women in diamonds and fur, the men in perfectly tailored suits and silk ties.

"Jesus, Mary, and Joseph," Vivian muttered as she and Bea watched from the shadows. "It's one thing to see it in the gossip sheets, but in person?"

Bea shrugged. "Some folks really don't care where their face ends up," she said. "Nothing bad's going to happen to them because of it. And places like this one love the press. Folks who don't want their picture taken go to the other door."

"World away from the Nightingale," Vivian said, shaking her head. "You really think O'Keefe would be looking for someone in a place like this?"

"Probably not," Bea conceded. "But a fella named Sweet Georgie works here on Sundays, and he tends bar at three different places. The others aren't nearly so ritzy, so he hears gossip from all corners of the city. If he doesn't know anything, no one does."

"Will he talk to us?" Vivian asked doubtfully.

"He better. My mama brought his mama chicken soup three times last month when his sister was sick. He doesn't play nice, he'll be getting an earful from both of them."

That made Vivian smile, in spite of her nerves. Bea's mother was a force of nature. "Okay, but how're we gonna get in? We're clearly not society girls." She gave Bea an apologetic glance. "And this place doesn't look much like a black-and-tan joint. I only saw white folks getting out of those cars."

"Black folks can get in around back, if we look fancy enough," Bea said, her voice very even. "I've never tried, but Abraham's got a pal who works the door. He's a big softie; he'll let us in if I ask."

"You sure?" Vivian asked quietly, not wanting to put her friend in a tough spot.

Bea glanced at her. "Nothing's ever sure, Viv. But it's worth trying. Come on."

The upstairs of Salon Doré pretended to be just another classy restaurant with good entertainment, so the front door was hardly hidden. If you wanted to get where the real party happened, you had to know the right people or the right password. But the back door went straight to the cellar, so it was around the corner and tucked into the shadows of the building. Vivian wouldn't have even noticed it if Bea hadn't led her straight there. *Deliveries Only,* the sign above it declared. Bea didn't hesitate, walking straight up and knocking slowly three times.

The door swung open, revealing a small room lined with shelves, half of them full of the sort of things a restaurant would, in fact, have delivered. Another door led farther into the building, and the one they had just entered through was being held open by a broad-shouldered young Black man with close-cropped hair and a neatly trimmed beard. His eyes lit up when he saw them.

"Well, looky what the cat dragged in," he said as he closed and locked the door behind them. He swept Bea into a hug, chuckling. "What are you doing here, girl? You're looking swell tonight."

"Thanks, Claude. You're looking pretty sharp yourself. I don't think you've met my pal Vivian before?"

Claude's enthusiasm faded a little as he stepped back to look Vivian over. "Heard Abraham mention her name a time or two. Took your old job when you started singing, ain't that right?"

"About the shape of it, yeah." Bea nudged his arm. "As for what we're doing here . . . We're *looking for something that glitters*."

Claude's face fell as Bea gave the password with a wink. "Bea, you know I'd wave you through in a heartbeat if it were up to me. But the boss has a way he likes to do things, and—" His gaze swept over them.

Bea's clothes were always stylish and new—Mrs. Henry insisted on her children being well-dressed, and Honor made a point of paying her enough that she could afford the latest fashions when she was up on the Nightingale's stage. But no one would have mistaken her for someone from a wealthy family. And Vivian . . .

She felt her face grow hot under Claude's scrutiny. She had always taken pride in fixing up the secondhand clothing she found, adding her own fashionable flourishes. But she had worked in Miss Ethel's shop long enough to know that her best efforts would never be mistaken for the clothing that wealthy women ordered there. And even if they were, one look at her catalog shoes and glass pearls would give her away. It had never really mattered to her before; at places like the Nightingale, she still fit right in, and anyway, the folks there cared more about how well she danced than how well she dressed.

But here it mattered. She wished she could sink through the floor.

Bea lifted her chin. "Tell your boss that Beatrice Bluebird is here, and she'd like to sing a song for his guests. In exchange for a little visit to his fine establishment."

Claude's eyebrows climbed toward his hairline. "Well," he said, a smile creeping across his face once more. "Well then. I have a feeling he's going to be interested in that. Wait here, girls. I'll be right back."

He disappeared through the other door; Vivian briefly glimpsed the bustle of a kitchen behind him, though the door was heavy enough that it cut off the sounds of the restaurant when it swung closed.

"Bea, you sure?" Vivian whispered once they were alone.

Bea rolled her eyes. "Singing a song or two is far from the worst thing I've had to do to help you out," she said.

Claude's boss turned out to be a short, plump man with a bald head and huge mustaches, his expensive waistcoat straining over his paunch and thick gold rings on each of his pinkie fingers. He looked, Vivian thought nervously, exactly like the sort of man who made his money in ways you didn't want to ask about and had friends you didn't want to know. But his eyes glittered eagerly as he looked them over.

"Beatrice Bluebird, is it?" he said, rubbing his hands together. "Heard you sing at the Nightingale once, and of course, you've built a bit of a reputation. But I thought you didn't sing anywhere else."

Bea ducked her head as she smiled eagerly at him. "I've heard you have the best entertainment at Salon Doré, mister. I know it's a little irregular, but I'd love to see inside, and I don't mind trading a song or two to do it. What do you think?"

When he hesitated, Vivian put in, "It'd sure be a fun surprise for your guests. Be the talk of the night, maybe even make it into a few papers this week."

The man looked her over, his lips pursing. "And you are?"

"My manager," Bea said smoothly. "She comes too."

Vivian held her breath; to her relief, the owner chuckled and rubbed his hands together again. "Well, why not, why not?" he said. "Like you said, it would certainly get some attention! Let's do it. Claude, if you would?"

Claude fiddled with something Vivian couldn't see. There was a click, and one entire section of shelves swung out, a doorway that blended seamlessly with the rest of the wall and let out a burst of light and heat and music as it opened. Behind it, a dimly lit stairway descended underground.

The owner chuckled again at their surprise. "After you."

The cellar of Salon Doré was amazing, and Vivian didn't even try to pretend she wasn't staring. Multiple crystal chandeliers hung from the ceiling, all filled with electric lights and turned down low, creating a warm glow throughout the room. The walls were dripping with swags of silver and gold cloth, all of it shimmering and reflecting the light. The crowd gathered there was even more fashionable and glittering, and a low hum of conversation and laughter filled the room.

The owner seemed pleased with her admiration. "I like to think it's an elegant establishment," he said with obviously false modesty. "I hope you'll enjoy your glimpse of it, Miss . . . ?"

"Kelly," Vivian said without thinking, then immediately wondered if she should have given a fake name. But Bea had needed to give her real name, and anyone who knew them would guess who the black-haired white girl with her was.

"Well, then, Miss Kelly, why don't you take a seat at the bar while I introduce our Bluebird to the bandleader?"

It was phrased as a request but clearly more of an order. "Sure thing, mister," Vivian said, not interested in arguing but not sitting down just yet either. "Beatrice, I'll be here when you've finished."

Bea, on the other hand, stayed where she was, even as the owner took her arm and tried to move her toward the bandstand. "What should I sing, Miss Kelly?" Bea asked, her smile eager and guileless.

Vivian wanted to laugh; trust Bea to look as sweet as possible while refusing to let anyone push her around. "Start with 'What'll I Do,'" she suggested. "Then give 'em something fast and fun, like 'Somebody Loves Me.'"

"You got it." Bea turned away and strode toward the bandstand before the owner realized they were done, and he had to hurry to catch up with her.

Vivian smiled to herself as she slid onto a stool at the bar. The atmosphere at Salon Doré was less raucous than the Nightingale; most of the space was filled with small tables that sat two people at a time, though some of them had larger groups squeezed around them. There was a small dance floor in front of the bandstand, and a few couples were up there, but most people seemed content to talk and flirt and watch the entertainment. At the moment, four girls in skimpy costumes were tap dancing while a six-piece band played. There were no cocktail glasses on the tables, which made Vivian frown. Instead, everyone had coffee cups in front of them.

The bartender, a young Black man, smiled at her as he came over. He was slim, wiry, and handsome, wearing the same white coat, black bow tie, and dark pants that she saw on the waiters taking orders at the tables. "What can I get you, miss?" he asked politely.

"What are you serving?"

"That depends." He leaned his elbows on the bar. "Do you like your coffee strong, smooth, or sweet?"

"Coffee?" Vivian didn't bother to hide her surprise. "Seems pretty tame."

That made him grin. "First time at the Salon, I'm guessing? I'll start you off with smooth."

"Thanks." Vivian watched as he filled a delicate porcelain cup with coffee, then added a generous pour from a second bottle.

"It's how the boss likes to do it around here," the bartender said, still smiling. "No one orders anything illegal at Salon Doré."

"Got it," Vivian said with a huff of laughter. "Rich folks always like to pretend they're not up to no good."

That made the bartender chuckle. Up on the stage, the song wrapped up, and the dancers tapped their way offstage to polite applause. The bandleader stepped forward and introduced a "surprise guest—Beatrice Bluebird!"

The applause got more enthusiastic as Bea stepped up to the microphone. Vivian noticed the bartender's eyes were on her friend, a smile on his face as he watched her.

"Look at that," he murmured to himself as Bea began to sing. "She wasn't bragging about those pipes."

Vivian took a careful sip of her coffee. It was, indeed, smooth. It was also at least half liquor. "So, if you know Bea, I'm guessing you must be Sweet Georgie?"

That made him give her a wary look. "Who's asking?"

"Vivian. I'm a friend of Bea's." She glanced around, but the bar wasn't crowded, and most of the eyes in the room were on Beatrice. Vivian leaned forward. "She said you're a fella who tends to hear things. I was hoping you might be able to answer a question or two." When she saw him hesitate, Vivian smiled ruefully. "I know, strangers coming around asking questions rarely goes well. Bea would have been the one asking, but she had to trade a couple of tunes to get us in the door."

"Did she?" Georgie glanced at the stage and smirked. "Smart girl. Well, Vivian-friend-of-Bea's—" He poured a little more coffee into her cup and picked up a white cloth, carefully wiping down the bar so it didn't look like they were in deep conversation. "I won't promise any answers, but go ahead and ask your questions."

She dropped her voice. "We've had a bit of trouble at the Nightingale. A fella named O'Keefe—red hair, slick sort of smile, nose been busted up a few times—he's been sending his boys out looking for a man named Hugh Brown. You heard anything about that?"

Sweet Georgie took his time answering, swiping the cloth slowly over the bar top while he thought about how to respond. "I ain't seen anyone looks like that around," he said at last. Vivian's heart sank, but he wasn't done. "But I've heard the name Hugh Brown."

Vivian sucked in a breath and leaned forward. "You know the fella?"

"I've met him a time or two. I work at the Blue Room a couple days a week, and he did a job or two for them a while back. Didn't know that was his name, though, until a few boys came there asking about him." Two waiters converged on the bar, and Georgie nodded at them. "'Scuse me a moment."

Vivian's mind raced while Georgie went to talk to the waiters, one of her legs bouncing in time to the music as she tried to keep her nerves under control. She needed to stay calm; if she seemed too anxious, odds were Sweet Georgie wouldn't tell her anything else. And she needed him to tell her more.

She stared around the room to distract herself. There was plenty to look at. The band wasn't as good as the one at the Nightingale, but Vivian had the feeling folks didn't come here for the music. They came to see and be seen. Looking around, she spotted more than one face that she recognized from the society pages. There was another set of stairs opposite the way she and Bea had come down; Vivian could guess that way led to the restaurant. No surprise there—a place like this would have more than one way in and out. Likely it had more than two.

While she watched, a man with wings of gray in his hair and a slick suit came down with a much younger woman on his arm, beaming at him as he led her to a table. Vivian shook her head, turning back to the bandstand as Bea finished her first song. Before the enthusiastic applause could die down, the band swung into the next number.

"Was that all?"

Vivian jumped a little as Sweet Georgie reappeared next to her, pretending to refill the drink she had barely touched. He glanced up at her through dark lashes, his expression wary.

"Not quite," Vivian said quietly. "What did you tell the fellas doing the asking? About where to find Hugh Brown?"

Sweet Georgie shrugged. "Couldn't tell them much, I hadn't seen him in almost a year at any of the places I work. But I recognized him in the photograph pretty quick."

"Photograph?"

"Sure, they were showing a picture of him around, seeing if anyone recognized the fella."

"They didn't have that when they came to the Nightingale," Vivian said slowly, her mind racing through half a dozen conversations from the past two days. Dark hair, O'Keefe had said. A bigger nose than his, that had never been broken. Had he mentioned anything else? "Could you tell them anything about where to find him?"

Georgie shrugged again. "He knows his way around a liquor bottle, I could tell them that much. I suggested they hit up the other juice joints south of Forty-Ninth. And not the fanciest ones, I don't think that was his style." He grinned. "No offense to your Nightingale."

"Not taking any," Vivian said. But she wasn't really paying attention anymore, because at Georgie's mention of someone who knew his way around a liquor bottle, her thoughts had jumped to Spence. And to the man who had cornered him in the alley. The bartender had been jumpy as an alley cat ever since, even for him. And she'd caught him sneaking around too. Maybe he knew about Honor's files and was trying to find out what she knew about Hugh Brown. Because if *he* was Brown—

But that didn't make sense. He'd been working the past two nights. Surely O'Keefe would have—

Vivian sucked in a breath, not noticing the wary look that Sweet Georgie gave her at the sound. O'Keefe wouldn't have seen him, because somehow, Spence had managed to be out of the dance hall each time he was there. The bartender had ducked out that first night, claiming his head was bothering him. And then when O'Keefe showed up to talk to Honor, Spence had disappeared into the cellar to grab a new bottle of whiskey. Danny had even said he thought there was plenty still at the bar. There had been—he had made O'Keefe's drink himself and sent her over with it. Which meant Spence had just wanted to get out of the room.

He'd needed to make himself scarce so that O'Keefe wouldn't recognize him.

"Huh. Well, speak of the devil."

The surprise in Sweet Georgie's voice pulled Vivian out of her thoughts just as Bea finished her song and applause echoed through the room.

"You want to know more, you can just ask him yourself."

Vivian stared at the bartender, not sure she was hearing him right. "He's here? Hugh Brown is here tonight?"

Georgie chuckled. Up on the bandstand, Bea took a bow, beaming at the whistles and cheers. "Not likely. No, the fella who was asking me about him is here. At the table in the corner." He shook his head. "Wouldn't have pegged him as the type to get into a place like this. But money always talks, don't it? Guess he has some."

Vivian followed the direction of Georgie's nod, suddenly cold with fear that O'Keefe had followed them. But the man at the corner table wasn't a redhead. Instead, he was a short, beef-shouldered bruiser in a slick suit. He watched as Bea hopped off the bandstand and made her way over to the bar. As soon as he turned her way, Vivian recognized him.

It was the nasally voiced man who had broken into the Chins' restaurant two nights before.

Vivian spun around fast, hoping he hadn't had a chance to see her face. Her heart was pounding. If the man in the corner had been asking about Hugh Brown, that meant O'Keefe had been behind that break-in. Her hands shook so hard she didn't want to try picking up the delicate coffee cup. How close had she and Danny come to ending up like Silence?

"Well, that was a smashing success, Bluebird," Sweet Georgie said cheerfully. "Good to see you."

"You too, pal," Bea said, breathing a little heavily and beaming. "I see you've been getting to know my girl here— Oh, hell."

The soft curse made Vivian's head shoot up. "What is it?"

"I should have done one more number." Bea was watching the stairs from the restaurant, a look of shock on her face. "Do you think they'll let me back up on the bandstand?"

"Why—" Vivian followed her gaze and saw a smartly dressed couple coming downstairs. The woman was all too familiar. "What the hell is Hattie Wilson doing here?"

The elegant mob boss was coolly surveying her surroundings as one of the waiters led her and her friend to a table. When her eyes fell on the bar, her brows climbed in surprise to see them there.

"Never mind her," Bea hissed. "Do you see the fella with her? That's Ralph Peer."

"Who?" Vivian realized too late that she had turned too far to look at Hattie Wilson when the bruiser in the corner came back into view. He had been frowning after Bea, as though trying to place her. But when he saw Vivian sitting beside her, his heavy brows snapped into a scowl. "Oh damn."

"Ralph Peer. He's a record producer at—"

"Bea, we've gotta scram," Vivian hissed. The bruiser had stood up and was making his way through the crowd of tables toward them, earning more than one complaint from the other guests. "Come on, quick."

"What? No, Viv, if he hears me sing, he might—"

Vivian grabbed her hand. "Sorry, pal, but trouble's headed our way."

Bea spotted the man coming toward them. "Who is— Never mind. Georgie, can you stall him?"

"I'll do what I can," the bartender said, looking less surprised than Vivian had expected. But maybe he was used to this kind of trouble at the other places he worked. "Get out of here, girls. Back door."

They slipped out the way they had come, dashing up the stairs toward the hidden door. Behind them, they could hear Georgie talking to the man, cajoling him to stop for a drink, and the gruff, irritated response.

"He's not going to be able to distract him," Vivian panted as they reached the top of the stairs and pushed at the hidden door. "And I don't like our chances of outrunning him."

The door swung open, and they both stumbled a little as they emerged in the delivery room and shoved it closed behind them.

Claude, who had been lounging on a stool tipped back against the wall, shot to his feet. "What happened?" he demanded.

"No time," Bea said quickly. "Fella coming after us that we don't want to meet up with. Is there somewhere we can hide?"

To Vivian's relief, Claude didn't ask any questions. "Duck in here," he said, swinging the other door open. The noise and heat of the restaurant's kitchen was a shock after the elegant bar downstairs. "Just stay out of the way. Hurry."

They did as he said, crouching behind one of the counters as the door closed behind them. Some of the kitchen staff gave them frowning looks, but they were out of the way, so no one stopped their work to ask what they were doing there. Apparently, folks at Salon Doré knew to keep their heads down and their mouths shut when something strange was going on.

Vivian could have kissed them all with gratitude. Instead, she clutched Bea's hand. They leaned against the wall and waited, breathing heavily and straining to hear what might be happening, even though the door was too thick for any noise to make its way through.

When the door did finally open again, Vivian had to swallow back a yelp of surprise. Bea's hand tightened painfully on hers before Claude stuck his head through and they both slumped with relief.

"All clear, girls," he said cheerfully. "Come on out."

"What happened?" Bea asked as they joined him in the delivery room once more. It felt cold after the heat of the kitchen, and Vivian rubbed her hands over her arms to warm them up.

"I told him you'd run out and looked like you were heading uptown." Claude shrugged. "No idea if he bought it, but he's gone. I checked before I came to get you."

Vivian let out the breath she had been holding and heard the sigh mirrored from Bea.

"Thanks, pal," she said. "I owe you one."

"Anytime," Claude said, grinning cheerfully. "Nice to have a little excitement every once in a while. But maybe take a cab home. Just in case."

They did, though the minutes it took them to find one felt like hours. Vivian jumped at every noise from the dark streets, wondering if O'Keefe's bruiser had circled back to find them. But no one was waiting in the shadows, and they managed to get back to the Henry family's home without any more trouble.

"You should stay here tonight," Bea suggested. "Just, you know. Just in case. So you're not by yourself."

Vivian didn't argue.

Della Henry, Beatrice's mother, was waiting up, as she always did when one of her children was out late. She only looked surprised for a moment to see Vivian at her door. Then she folded her into a hug that almost made Vivian want to cry as her tense body finally relaxed.

"You okay, sugar?" Della asked, looking her over as she cupped one hand around Vivian's cheek.

Vivian nodded. "Yes, ma'am," she whispered. Della Henry looked after everyone she knew, and Vivian and Florence had been no different. She had been there almost from the first moment they arrived in the neighborhood, fresh out of the orphan home, two scared girls who had no idea how to survive on their own. "Just didn't want to be alone tonight."

Della gave her a tight-lipped look that said she knew there were things Vivian wasn't saying. But she had been through enough trouble in her own life that she knew when to pry and when to nod along. Tonight, she nodded. "All right, you girls get washed up. I'll make you two a bed out here." She patted Vivian's cheek. "And in the morning you can tell me all about what that little baby niece of yours is up to."

When they were finally alone again, wrapped in blankets on the thin carpet of the living room floor, Vivian could hear Bea roll over in the dark.

"Well?" she whispered expectantly. There was just enough streetlight coming through the window for Vivian to see the outline of her face. "Was it worth it?"

Vivian swallowed. "I think I know who Hugh Brown is," she whispered.

"Who?"

Vivian hesitated. Once the words were out, there was no taking them back. But if she couldn't trust Bea, she couldn't trust anyone. "I think it's Spence."

Quietly, her voice barely louder than a breath—there were too many other people asleep in the Henrys' three-room tenement home for her to risk being any louder—Vivian repeated what Sweet Georgie had told her and what she had pieced together.

"And that has to be why O'Keefe's looking at the Nightingale," she finished. They were both sitting up now, their backs against the wall and arms wrapped around their knees, shivering a little in their thin blankets. "The fella who cornered Spence must have been one of his boys, and that was only a few blocks away."

"Easy enough to put two and two together," Bea said in quiet agreement.

Vivian nodded. "He had that photograph with him, remember? He'd have recognized Spence from it. And when we chased him off, O'Keefe came back himself a few hours later to check the place out."

"Spence might've even destroyed that photograph on purpose," Bea said slowly, nodding. "So that none of us would recognize him in it when O'Keefe's boys came showing it around." She let out a slow breath. "Damn. Always thought that boy was trouble."

"If what folks are saying about O'Keefe is true, then he's the one that's trouble," Vivian said, feeling the need to defend Spence, even if she didn't like him. "Spence is just in it."

"Not much difference between the two for the rest of us, though. Especially Silence," Bea said. They were both quiet for a moment. "So Spence is this Hugh Brown that everyone's looking for. We should tell Honor."

"No," Vivian said quickly. "Not yet."

She could feel Bea staring at her. "Wasn't the whole point of doing this to find some way to help? Some way to deal with O'Keefe? We've got that now. Why bother if we're just going to keep it a secret?"

Vivian pulled her knees tighter underneath her chin. "I wanted to find something that would lead us to O'Keefe. Turn him over to the commissioner. If we tell Honor about Spence, she's just going to . . ." Vivian tried to read her friend's face, but there wasn't enough light in the room. "I'm worried he'll be the one getting turned over, and not to the police. I don't want that."

"Why not?" Bea asked, practical as always. "She's right that it's the fastest way to get O'Keefe off our backs. Everyone at the Nightingale safe in exchange for one fella. Could you blame her for taking that deal?"

"*If* she trusted O'Keefe to leave us alone after she handed him over, which Honor might be too smart to do."

"She might be desperate enough to take the risk."

"But then what happens to Spence? I don't much like the fella, but if you'd talked to O'Keefe up close . . ." Vivian shuddered. "I couldn't do that, even to someone I don't like. And I'm not going to risk Honor doing it either. Please, Bea. Don't tell her. Not yet."

At last Bea sighed. "Fine."

Vivian slumped with relief. "Thank you."

"But O'Keefe's going to be back soon," Bea warned, "and there's going to be trouble when he is. I'm not going to wait forever."

"You don't have to," Vivian said. "I just want to talk to Spence first, see what he has to say. See if he can point us toward O'Keefe."

"You know where he lives?"

"No," Vivian admitted. "But he'll be working tomorrow. We'll see him at the Nightingale."

"I hope you know what you're doing, Viv," Bea said, settling back down and rolling over. "Or a lot of people could get hurt."

Vivian lay in the near-dark, staring at the ceiling, and hoped she did too. It took her a long time to relax enough to get to sleep.

SEVENTEEN

Vivian could feel the tension humming through the staff that night. Even the people who didn't really know what had been happening—and Vivian knew Honor well enough to guess that she hadn't shared any more information than she had to—were laughing too loud and jumping every time they were startled.

She had spent the day running deliveries around Manhattan, but her feet were aching less than usual. Still nervous and jumpy from the past few days, she had used half of the five-dollar tip from Hattie Wilson to pay for cabs. It was an expense that she normally would have avoided: cabs weren't cheap, and living on her own, she needed to save everything she could. But after nearly swinging her fist at a stranger who bumped into her on the streetcar, she decided the cost was worth it.

And she had called her father, trotting down the street to use the phone at Mrs. Krakowski's store. Clyde had been overjoyed to hear from her, and his excitement when she said Florence wanted to meet him was almost enough to distract her from her worry. She had suggested meeting for breakfast the next morning—just the three of them, without Ruth—and he immediately agreed.

"My treat," he added eagerly. "I can't wait to see you both."

It had felt jarring to talk about breakfast with her father—her father!—with what she knew about Spence and O'Keefe hanging over her. And more, what she didn't know. But after so long waiting to find her family, Vivian wasn't willing to wait any longer, even if it was hard to keep her mind on her part of the phone call.

There had been no word from O'Keefe, no other threats. Honor had spent the day visiting her staff, and Vivian spent the night trying to avoid Honor, worried she would give away what she knew before she had a chance to talk to Spence. He was running late again, and Vivian was jumpy with nerves, trying to tell herself that he was often late and it probably didn't mean anything.

"You all right, Vivian?" Honor asked when they finally crossed paths, Vivian with a tray of empty glasses in her hands, Honor just ducking under the bar flap after checking in with Danny. "You're on edge tonight."

"Aren't we all?" Vivian said, meeting Honor's eyes and then looking away quickly. "Do you think O'Keefe will be back tonight?"

Honor surveyed the dance floor, crowded with smiling couples gliding through a slow, elegant foxtrot. "Let's hope not. Any good news from the commissioner?" She glanced at Vivian, who reluctantly shook her head. Honor didn't look surprised. "Didn't think so."

"It was worth a try," Vivian said softly. It might still be worth it, if Spence could tell her anything. But she couldn't say that to Honor. Not yet.

"Don't suppose it hurt, anyway," Honor said. "But I've got nothing for O'Keefe, so you can bet I'm hoping he won't be back tonight. Best case for us, he found a more promising lead and moved on." When she realized Vivian was staring at her, Honor raised her brows. "What's that look for?"

"I think that might be the most information you've ever shared with me that I didn't have to pry out of you with a crowbar," Vivian said. "When did you become so chatty?"

Honor had turned back toward the dance floor, but her sideways glance lingered on Vivian. "I think I've made it pretty clear that I want to know what you're thinking," she murmured. She didn't move, didn't try to reach out, but the look in her eyes was like a physical touch that Vivian could feel drifting across her cheek, along her lips. "It seems only fair that I tell you what I'm thinking in exchange. Don't you agree?"

"You're planning to sweet-talk me with your inner thoughts, is that it?" Vivian said, trying to sound playful and not like her heart was hammering in her chest. "I think we both know you're not the type to share those."

"I can share my secrets, pet," Honor said. "Just ask Danny."

"That's different," Vivian pointed out. "You and Danny are basically partners. He might not own this place with you, but you run it together."

Honor glanced at her star bartender, and Vivian was surprised to see a hint of regret in her expression. "We do," she said agreed softly. "I'll miss that when it ends."

Vivian stared at her, too startled at first to say anything. By the time she found her voice to ask what that meant, Honor was changing the subject.

"Are you picking up another round?" she asked, nodding at Vivian's empty tray as the foxtrot came to an end. "Or do you have a break coming up?" She cocked her head toward the bandstand just as they picked up the tempo, swinging into the opening bars of a Charleston.

Vivian loved a Charleston, and everyone who worked at the Nightingale knew it. Any other night, her feet would be itching to get on the dance floor. But she suddenly found herself panicking at the thought of dancing with Honor. Things between them had changed too much, too many times. And she didn't want to risk letting anything slip before she talked to Spence.

"Not time for my break yet," she said, keeping her voice light as she turned away, waving at Danny to get his attention. "I'll have to leave the Charleston to everyone else."

There was a moment of silence behind her. Vivian wasn't brave enough to turn around and see what Honor might be thinking.

"Be careful tonight, Vivian," she said, her voice low. It was impossible to read any emotion in it. Vivian wasn't sure whether that was a good thing or not. "Things still aren't safe out there. No one should go home alone."

"I'm planning to stay at Bea's," Vivian said as Danny sauntered over, sleeves rolled up to his elbows and a sheen of sweat visible on his forehead. "Don't worry."

"Wish I could promise that," Honor murmured behind her.

The dance floor was crowded, the band was swinging, and Danny was fully in the weeds behind the bar by the time it became clear Spence wasn't arriving for work that night.

"He and Honor never got along," Bea pointed out as she gulped a glass of water in the shadow of the bandstand. The piano was playing a pretty, delicate version of "It Had to Be You" while the rest of the musicians took a breather. "Maybe he just quit without telling anyone. He wouldn't be the first bartender who did."

"Maybe," Vivian agreed, nervous goose bumps prickling along her spine as she watched the door.

Bea wasn't wrong; it had become a running joke among the staff, the small parade of forgettably handsome, nearly interchangeable bartenders who could never quite keep up with Danny or the demands of the Nightingale's eager clientele.

It had never really been a problem; Honor pulled a few strings and found them a job somewhere else so they wouldn't try to make a buck by reporting her business to the cops, and she paid enough in bribes that even if one of them had, it wouldn't have gone anywhere.

"Bet you that's it," Bea said, but the declaration lacked her usual confidence.

"Probably," agreed Vivian, though she didn't think she sounded any more convincing than her friend. "Do you have another set before your break, or are you off for a little?"

"Another set." Bea gulped down the last of her water, then handed the glass back to Vivian. "Look, Honor's over by the bar. Go talk to her, will you? She'll know what's going on."

But Honor, when Vivian reached her, was distracted, and not because of Spence. "Alba, a round of the best Canadian whisky we have to the gentlemen at that middle table," she was saying as Vivian slid her tray onto the bar. Honor didn't look nervous—she never did—but she was focused. "The best we have, got it, Danny? And a bottle of champagne with glasses for the ladies."

Vivian looked toward the table Honor was talking about, where four men in some of the sharpest suits she'd ever seen sat with two women in spangled silk dresses and pouty red lips. "I know one of them's an Astor," she murmured to Danny, leaning her elbows on the bar so she didn't have to raise her voice. "Who are the others?"

"The one on the left has a brother who's going to run for mayor next year," Honor said, replying before Danny could. She put the last of the champagne coupes on Alba's tray and shooed her toward the table. "Good job spotting the Astor, though." She gave Vivian a quick smile as Alba hurried across the dance hall, a wide, welcoming smile on her face as she greeted the table where the potential mayor's brother and his friends waited for the drinks they hadn't needed to order. "We'll make a criminal of you yet," Honor added.

It passed for a compliment in the Nightingale, and Vivian would have smiled if she hadn't felt so on edge. "Honor, we need to talk."

But Honor was already shaking her head. "I can't right now, pet," she said, taking the champagne from Danny. It was hot enough in the dance hall that Vivian could see the sides of the bottle sweating. "I have to go make nice with the money before they get restless and decide to make trouble."

"But Spence—"

Honor laid a finger against Vivian's lips, and Vivian was so surprised that she fell silent. "That's the job, pet," Honor said, shaking her head. "We'll know more about Spence when we know. Right now I've got hands to shake and egos to stroke. But I could use your help," she added, sliding her finger away.

Vivian resisted the urge to touch her tingling lips. "With them?" she asked, nodding toward the table.

Honor shook her head. "Danny needs another set of hands," she said, nodding toward the crowd still jostling and laughing around the bar. "Hop on back there, will you?"

Vivian wanted to argue that there were more important things than glad-handing a few society darlings. But Honor had a business to manage—one that ran on favors and cash and goodwill in just the right places. If she said she needed to go make nice first, then she knew what she was talking about.

"On it, boss," Vivian said quietly. She understood, but that didn't mean she liked it.

"Thank you." Honor looked for a moment like she wanted to say something more. But there was a loud laugh from the table where Alba was entertaining their important guests, and the bottle of champagne was warming by the second. Honor settled for giving Vivian a quick smile that could have meant anything at all before returning to her work.

Vivian ducked behind the bar flap without bothering to open it. "All right, Danny-boy, what do you need me to do?"

It wasn't the first time Vivian had ended up behind the bar when Danny needed an extra set of hands, so the regulars who crowded around weren't too surprised. Vivian still received startled or skeptical looks from folks who didn't expect to see a woman serving them, but she had picked up a few tricks from years of listening to Danny mix drinks and charm customers.

She wasn't as fast as he was, and she needed a few reminders as the orders flew around her—"Don't use that gin unless you're adding something real sweet," Danny hissed in her ear at one point. "It tastes like gasoline if you serve it on its own." But she could tease and flirt with the best of them, sharing her smiles equally with preening fellas and blushing girls, moving as fast as she could manage while she poured bourbon and lime juice, gin and champagne, sliding drinks across the bar into waiting hands. With two bartenders working, the crowd began to thin, and Vivian thought she'd be able to catch her breath in a moment or two.

Until she looked up and found her father staring at her. Vivian was so shocked that for a moment she felt numb all over, and the drink she was just about to hand to Ellie slid from her nerveless fingers, crashing to the floor and splattering her shoes.

"All right there, Viv?" Danny asked without turning around, while a few of the customers around the bar whistled and applauded her clumsiness.

Vivian's cheeks burned with embarrassment, but she didn't let her smile fade as she took a bow. "Just trying to keep these lovely folks on their toes so they're ready for the quickstep," she said, earning a round of laughter. She added, "One moment, if you please," to her father, not quite ready to face the shocked look on his face, as she grabbed a towel and bent to clean up the mess. Dropping the broken glass in the trash, she wiped off her hands and turned to him, plastering on as normal a smile as she could manage. "What's your poison, sir?"

Clyde Quinn narrowed his eyes, mouth twisting to one side. "Corpse Reviver," he said at last. "If you can."

It wasn't the most complicated cocktail that he could have asked for, but it took a sight more skill to make well than a rickey or a fizz would have. And given the slight lift to his brows, Vivian had the distinct sense that he was testing her. Vivian tossed her hair and smiled brightly. "Coming right up, sir," she said, before calling out cheerfully, "Anyone else need a little reviving while I'm at it?"

A couple of men perched on barstools, with gray in their hair and smiles only for each other, called out that they'd take a pair as well. Vivian grabbed three glasses and the four different bottles of liquor that she'd need, never letting the smile fade from her face. Clyde tossed his hat on the bar and settled in to watch her. Vivian hoped he couldn't see her hands shaking as she added the final squeeze of lemon juice to the pitcher and grabbed a long spoon to stir it up, straining the cocktail into the three glasses and placing them on the bar.

"Enjoy," she said to the two men, who barely glanced her way as they tossed a wad of cash onto the bar. Vivian pocketed it—she'd tuck it in the cash box later—before turning to her father.

"Well, I guess we've got even more in common than I thought," he said as he took a sip of his drink. "No wonder you knew folks who could help you track me down." There was an edge to his voice as he demanded, "What's a daughter of mine doing in a place like this?"

"Working," Vivian said defiantly. He might have technically been her father, but he had no say in how she ran her life.

"Better hope you don't keep making messes like that if you want to keep your job, then."

Vivian hoped he was teasing. "I'm usually serving drinks, not making them," she admitted. "They were shorthanded tonight."

"Well, that's a relief," Clyde chuckled, and Vivian tried not to bristle. "Women got no place behind a bar. Though this is pretty good," he added, lifting his glass in a toast before Vivian had a chance to snap out the argument on the tip of her tongue. "Top shelf, just like I heard."

"Where'd you hear?" Vivian asked curiously, leaning her elbows on the bar. There was no one waiting for a drink for the moment, other than a pair of beautifully dressed women making eyes at Danny, and she was glad for the break.

"An old friend mentioned where I might find the door, but this is my first chance to pay a visit. I have to sneak out so Ruth doesn't catch me," Clyde admitted with a crooked grin. "She's been a temperance girl for years."

Vivian wanted to be annoyed by his earlier dismissiveness. But she couldn't help the fizz of pleasure in her chest at the thought that she and her father had something else in common, even if that something was just a longing for a little adventure and the disapproving sister to go with it. She beamed back at him. "Florence didn't used to be a fan of me going out either," she said. "She mostly got over it, but I had to sneak out with my dancing shoes plenty of times."

"You got a nose for trouble, little girl," he said sternly, though the twinkle in his eye made it clear he was being playful. "Just like your pop." He glanced around the dance floor. "Does that mean Florence is here tonight too?"

"Not likely," Vivian laughed. "She doesn't fuss about it anymore, but she's never had a taste for drinking or dancing with strangers. And she—" Vivian caught herself just in time. She wouldn't tell him about Mei until they knew how he'd feel about a half-Chinese baby. "She got married a little while ago," she finished, almost as smoothly as if that was what she always intended to say.

"So you said." Clyde shook his head, looking almost sad. His voice was softer when he spoke again. "Can't believe my little girl is so grown up. Never thought I'd see her again, much less that she'd be married when I did. Where did you say she was these days?"

"She's looking forward to meeting you," Vivian said, swiping at the bar with a towel and pretending she hadn't heard the question. He had spoken quietly, and the dance hall was loud with the wail of the trumpet and the stomp of feet. "Anyway, can you imagine if you'd come by here some other time?"

Clyde chuckled again. "I'd have had no idea who you were. But now . . ." He frowned. "But I thought you said you worked for a dressmaker?"

"Dressmaker's not open at night," she pointed out. "And I've got rent to pay. Besides." She couldn't keep the smile from her face as she glanced around. "I like it better here than just about anywhere else."

Clyde nodded. "You've been coming here a while, then? You must know a lot of folks."

"Oh, ages, since—"

"Viv!" The holler from Danny made her jump; when she turned toward him, he was standing only a few feet away, looking impatient. "I'm glad you made a new friend, kitten, but I've said your name three times now. There's folks waiting for a drink, so maybe get back to it?"

Vivian felt her face heating again; when she looked where he was pointing, she saw Alba waiting by the bar flap and holding an empty tray.

"Sorry," Vivian mumbled. "Got distracted. What am I making?"

"Three South Side fizzes, if you got time in your busy social schedule," Danny said with a grin, shaking his head. "And a little more attention, if you can manage it. Talk with the customers all you like, but keep your hands busy, yeah?"

Before Vivian could apologize again, Clyde jumped in. "You saying I can't have a chat with my own daughter?" he demanded, drawing himself up to his full height and scowling as he looked Danny up and down. His lip curled. "Don't know that I like a fella like you bossing her around."

Danny's manner changed in less time than it took to blink; his shoulders tensed, and Vivian could see his feet planted wide on the floor, ready for trouble. His voice was still perfectly polite as he spoke, but the playfulness of a moment before was gone. "Viv's father, is it?" he asked, giving her a sideways look. She nodded, her mouth gone suddenly dry. "Well, welcome to the Nightingale. Like I said, mister, I don't mind her having a chat as long as the job gets done, and I'm sure you two have a lot to talk about. But I *am* her boss, and she's on the clock, so if you'll excuse her for just—"

"Well, that's a funny thing to claim, because I don't remember hearing that this place was run by a Chinese fella," Clyde rumbled. "And if I want to talk to Vivian, or to anyone else here, then I figure I'll just go ahead and—"

"Clyde," Vivian snapped. "Cut it out."

He turned his scowl on her, and she nearly took a step back. No wonder Ruth had looked so nervous around him, if he had a temper like his glare said. "He's got no right to talk to you like that."

"He's got every right when I'm supposed to be working," she said. She gave him a smile, trying to calm him down; if he made any trouble, one of Honor's bruisers might be called over to toss him out, and she didn't want that. "Besides, don't you want to see how I do with this one? How 'bout I mix up an extra fizz and you can tell me how it is?"

She held her breath, waiting for his answer and hating the feeling. But a moment later, he barked out a laugh, slouching back onto his stool and shaking his head. "Sure, kid. Mix your pop up a drink. I like 'em with plenty of lime. What about you?"

"Not a fan of drinks with mint, actually," Vivian said as she gathered her ingredients. "I'm more of a champagne girl."

Clyde chuckled again. "Guessing you've had to make a few friends around here, with expensive taste like that."

"Got a pal or two, but nothing serious," she said without paying much attention to what she was saying. "Someone's always happy to buy a round here."

She shouldn't have been so unnerved by his exchange with Danny; it was the sort of thing that happened all the time outside the Nightingale, and it wasn't exactly rare inside it, either. Discouraging that kind of ugliness was one of the reasons Honor kept her muscle on hand and visible. But this time, with her father the one making the trouble, it had landed different.

She glanced at Danny out of the corner of her eye and saw him watching her; Vivian could see the lines of tension around his mouth and eyes. When he caught her looking, he gave her a humorless smile and looked away, turning his attention—playful once more—back to a new round of customers. But she could guess that he was thinking about Florence too.

Maybe it wasn't such a good idea for Florence to meet their father after all. But Vivian knew even as she thought it that neither she nor her sister was ready to give up the chance to know their family. If they had to, if they knew for sure that it wouldn't work, they'd walk away and wouldn't look back. But not yet.

Vivian gave the cocktail a final stir and poured it into four glasses; three went down the bar and onto Alba's tray, and the other she placed in front of Clyde with a flourish.

Then there was the fact—impossible to ignore—that he knew where she worked now. Honor would help her out if she needed to send him packing. But unless she quit her job, he'd be able to track her down if she tried to disappear on him. And that might lead him to Florence and her new family anyway.

"Happy days, kid," Clyde Quinn said, grinning as he lifted it in a toast to her. He took a drink, then smacked his lips. "Not bad, I have to say. Not bad at all. Maybe you've got a future back there if you don't find a fella." He winked at her and downed the rest of the drink.

She kept her thoughts carefully hidden behind a bright smile. "Just wait 'til you see me on the dance floor."

Clyde shook his head. "Always heard daughters would give a man a heart attack," he grumbled. "Seems like it might be true." He slid his glass back across the bar to her. "Let's get another. Plenty of lime, remember."

Vivian nodded. She could still feel Danny's eyes on her, wary and watchful and waiting for trouble. "Coming right up."

EIGHTEEN

Vivian half thought her father was going to keep her talking and mixing drinks for the rest of the night. But after one more fizz and a little more time watching the dance floor—though he never went for a spin himself—he slapped his cash down on the bar and grabbed his hat.

"You're a swell kid, Vivian," he said with a smile. "I'm glad I ran into you tonight."

"Really?" she asked. "Because you looked horrified when you first saw me."

"Well." He rubbed the back of his neck, smiling sheepishly. "Surprise'll do that to a fella. But you mix a mean drink, and you don't stint on the good hooch, that's for sure."

"Company policy," she said, shrugging. "Keeps folks coming back."

He laughed. "I'll bet it does." He nodded down the bar toward where Danny was chatting with a customer while he filled glasses. "That's your boss, then? Thought this place was run by a whisper sister."

"It is," Vivian said, a challenging note creeping into her voice. "But Danny runs the bar. And if I make a good drink, it's because he taught me how to do it."

"Hmm." Clyde's expression could have meant anything as he surveyed the bar for another moment, then he turned back to her with a smile. "I guess I'll see you and your sister tomorrow?"

Vivian kept her hands busy wiping down the bar as she nodded. "Eight o'clock, right?" She had chosen the time because it was only half an hour before she'd need to head to work, giving them a good enough excuse to leave if they needed it.

"Eight o'clock. Can't believe I'm going to see my Florence again," he said, shaking his head and smiling. Vivian found her nervousness fading a little in the face of his obvious excitement. Clyde slapped his hat on his head and winked at her. "Night, kid."

Vivian watched him weave through the crowd and disappear up the stairs. When she turned back around, she wasn't surprised to find Danny watching her.

"You're going to do it, then," he said, his voice low enough that no one else would be able to hear him. It wasn't a question, but Vivian nodded anyway. Danny sighed. "Just . . . be careful, okay? I get it, I do. But Florence doesn't understand how . . ." He rubbed the back of his neck, his happy-go-lucky façade gone for the moment. "People can get ugly. Real ugly, when they don't like who you decided to make your life with."

Vivian caught a glimpse of Honor just then, striding past the bar from the direction of the stairs. "I know," Vivian said, her eyes tracking Honor as she moved across the room.

Danny smiled sadly when he saw where she was looking. "He might not like that either," he said softly. "Plenty of people don't."

"I know," Vivian said again. She didn't want to talk about it anymore. They'd see what happened tomorrow. There were half a dozen liquor bottles on the bar in front of her; she tossed the empties in the bin and turned to replace the others on the shelves where they belonged. "Any word on Spence yet?"

Danny grimaced. "Nothing. But it wouldn't be the first time he's been unreliable. Doesn't mean we need to worry yet." He sounded like he was trying to convince himself as much as her.

"Doesn't mean we don't need to either," Vivian pointed out. She took her time lining up the liquor bottles as straight as possible, not wanting to risk anyone else overhearing.

Danny was silent for so long that she thought he might have walked away. But when she turned back, he was staring at the dance floor.

"Hux'll tell us if we need to worry," he said. "And in the meantime, we've got work to do. You're up, kitten." He gave her shoulder a quick, encouraging bump with his fist before striding back to his end of the bar.

Vivian wished she could believe him. Over the heads of the crowd, she caught Bea watching her from the bandstand. If Vivian didn't figure out where Spence was, she'd have to tell Honor what she knew, or Bea would beat her to it. And Vivian didn't like to think what would happen if Honor found out she'd been keeping secrets.

Maybe he'd show up. There was still time.

A trio of bob-haired college girls giggled their way up to the bar, and Vivian gave them her best dance hall smile. "Evening, girls. How adventurous are we feeling tonight?"

"Very," one of them laughed as the other two shoved her forward. "What do you recommend?"

The band kept playing and Bea kept singing, bright and hot and fast. Honor sent a round of drinks to an alderman's table and had words with a fella who was getting too handsy with the staff. Vivian and Danny hauled more bottles of champagne and whiskey up from the cellar while the waitresses ran their feet off. As the clock ticked past midnight, Vivian made herself stop watching the door. Instead, she met Bea at the end of a set, carrying a drink for each of them. They collapsed in the dressing room, shoes kicked off and legs in a tangle on the sofa. Neither of them spoke, but Vivian could feel Bea watching her, waiting.

It wasn't quite last call yet, though the crowd was dying down, when Honor leaned her elbows on the bar. Vivian, who was lining up clean glassware, didn't catch sight of her until she turned around.

"How long have you been standing there?" she demanded, wiping her damp hands on a towel.

"Feeling jumpy tonight, pet?" Honor asked quietly, but she didn't smile. Honor would never show it, but Vivian could guess that she was feeling jumpy herself—or whatever her version of that was. "Came to tell you that we don't need both of you behind the bar anymore. Get a dance in if you want, or a drink, while you wait for Beatrice. She's on her last set."

Vivian glanced at her friend, who was pattering through an extra-fast rendition of "Yes Sir, That's My Baby." When she looked back, Honor was already walking away.

"Wait!" Vivian ducked under the bar flap and caught her arm. When Honor turned back to her, brows raised in surprise, Vivian dropped her hand quickly. No call to be making a scene. She dropped her voice too. "Honor, what about Spence?"

She could see the muscles clench in Honor's jaw. "No word yet," she said quietly. "But that doesn't mean anything's wrong. People have quit without notice before."

"And he'd be the type to do it, sure," Vivian said impatiently. "But shouldn't someone check on him?"

"No," Honor said, shaking her head. "Not tonight. Maybe tomorrow."

"But if I'm cut, couldn't I just—"

"No." Honor didn't raise her voice, but the word came out so sharp it made Vivian flinch. Honor cleared her throat, looking surprised by her own intensity. "No, pet," she said, more gently. She lifted a hand to cup Vivian's cheek, her thumb brushing back and forth. "I've already told you, I don't want anyone wandering around alone, not at night. Danny'll handle it in the morning if we still haven't heard anything from him."

The shivery touch was almost enough to distract Vivian. Almost. "But—"

"Vivian." Honor closed her eyes briefly, dragging in a slow, deliberately patient breath through her nose as she dropped her hand. She let it out on a sigh. "If nothing is wrong, you don't need to be taking the risk. And if something is wrong, I'm not putting anyone in the middle of it. So have a dance. Wait for Bea. Go home. All right?"

Before Vivian could say anything, the crash of glass and breaking wood echoed through the room, even over the sound of the band. There were shouts from one side of the dance floor, and between the bodies suddenly craning to look, Vivian could see that two young men in suits were shoving at each other's shoulders, a table overturned next to them.

"Jesus, Mary, and Joseph." Honor sighed, though you'd never know looking at her face that she was anything but calm and self-assured. "People have no manners sometimes." Vivian could already see Benny making a beeline for the troublemakers, his mountain-like shoulders parting the crowd with almost no effort.

"Honor?" Vivian stepped closer and reached out, laid her hand on Honor's arm, trying to get her attention.

Honor gave her a wry look as she shook her head. She was already pulling away, and Vivian let her hand fall. "Sorry, but that's my cue," she said, before heading across the dance hall, an icy smile on her face and her long legs eating up the distance in no time. Vivian knew it would only be a matter of minutes before the two rowdy boys were either forking over the cash to pay for the damage or tossed out in the alley.

She also knew that, for the moment, everyone's attention would be on the small scene, a headache for Honor and her staff but a bit of entertainment for the customers on an otherwise normal night. No one would be watching the girl who had spent the night behind the bar as she slipped into the back hall and up the stairs toward Honor's office.

Any dancer at the Nightingale would have feet as light as hers, but dressmakers had light fingers too. Vivian held the keys she had slipped from her boss's pocket—in the moment when Honor's attention was split between the brewing fight and Vivian's hand on her arm—tightly in one fist so they wouldn't jingle as she headed up the stairs.

There were only three keys on the ring, and it didn't take half a minute to try them all and find the right one. Vivian closed the door carefully behind her, muffling the brassy wail and the stomp of feet from downstairs. She didn't let herself think about what would happen if Honor checked her pocket and found her keys missing. She didn't waste time thinking that it was stupid and reckless. She knew all that. There was no use repeating it, even to herself.

Vivian headed straight toward the heavy wooden desk under the window.

The locked bottom drawer took the smallest of the keys on the ring. That was where Honor hoarded information, in careful files about her important guests and many regulars and those whose pockets took the bribes that kept the Nightingale open. Who they were, who they knew. What kind of favors she might be able to ask from them. Honor teased out information about everyone she could. There was no telling what might end up useful, down the road.

She also kept careful records on the people who worked for her, and that was what Vivian needed. Any other night, she would have been tempted to read through them all, to see what Honor thought it was worth noting about Bea, or Benny, or Vivian herself. But she didn't want to waste time. And more importantly, she didn't want to get caught.

Vivian flipped through the papers until she found the one she was looking for. There was only a single sheet of paper on Spence—*used to gamble, parents in Newark* noted next to his name. It would have been risky to take the paper with her, but she didn't need to. The many days Vivian had spent running deliveries around the city meant she was used to keeping track of addresses; it took only a moment to commit Spence's to memory. She shoved the papers back where she had found them, ignoring her shaking hands as she locked the drawer once more.

Vivian pressed her ear against the wood of the door, listening for the sound of someone on the stairs. No one was there; she slipped out, locking the door behind her before heading back down.

"Viv!"

Vivian nearly jumped out of her skin as she reached the bottom of the steps and heard someone call her name.

"I was wondering where you'd got to," Bea said, frowning as she glanced up the stairs past Vivian. "What were you doing up there?"

"Nothing," Vivian said quickly, squeezing her hand into a fist so tightly that she could feel the teeth of the keys biting into her palm. "How is it in there? Calmed down at all?"

"Back to normal," Bea said, shaking her head. "They were fighting over a bird, of course. Stupid fellas. Lucky it's already slowing down, so there weren't too many people to get in the way. But one of them fell onto the bandstand."

"Lord almighty." Vivian could hear the band playing a lively quick-step, so she could guess that the fallout hadn't been too bad. But she still asked, "Everyone okay?"

"Everyone except my microphone. Got knocked over and broken, so Honor said they'd finish up without a singer tonight. You sticking around a bit, or should we head off?"

"I—" Vivian broke off as a cluster of women bustled into the hall, heading to the powder room to freshen up for the last few dances of the night. They pushed carelessly past, one bumping into Vivian hard enough to knock the keys out of her hand. They went clattering to the floor.

Bea scooped them up before Vivian could, raising her eyes to Vivian's. For a moment, they were both silent.

Bea spoke first. "These aren't yours" was all she said, but it was plain she knew whose they were.

"There still hasn't been any word about Spence," Vivian said, dropping her voice as she pulled Bea farther into the shadow of the staircase. "I wanted to look up his address. I'm going to go check on him."

"That's a dumb idea," Bea pointed out. Before Vivian could do more than bristle, she added, "I'm coming with you."

"Thought you just said it was dumb?"

"To go alone, sure." Bea shook her head. "But I'm worried about that stupid grump too, even if he is a lousy bartender. If he *is* in trouble, someone should get there sooner instead of later. And if he's just holed up with a head cold feeling sorry for himself—"

"He would," Vivian said with a laugh, though the sound was forced.

"—then I won't have any problem chewing him out for making everyone worry. When do you want to go?"

"Now's good," Vivian said, not admitting to herself that she wanted to go before she lost her nerve. "I need to give Honor's keys to Danny—he won't know that I took them without asking until he hands them back to her—"

"Not quite as sneaky as you think, kitten."

The quiet voice made them both jump, and Vivian squeaked in surprise as she spun around to find Danny leaning against the doorframe and watching them, stone-faced, his arms crossed against his chest.

"What are you doing lurking there?" Vivian demanded.

"Eavesdropping," Danny said, straightening. "You don't make it hard. I wanted to catch you before you took off and tell you to come to Spring Street tonight." He glanced at Bea. "But it sounds like you two have other plans."

"Someone should go check on him," Vivian said defensively. "And you know it."

"Doesn't mean it has to be you," Danny snapped. "You girls can't—"

"We can," Bea said, lifting her chin. "And you can't stop us, you know."

Danny's mouth drew into an unhappy line. But he didn't argue.

"We take care of our people here, Danny-boy," Vivian said, "Honor can't do it herself. But we can, so we should."

Danny glared at her for a moment longer, then he sighed, the fight seeming to go out of him. "Wait here," he said, turning away.

"You going to get Honor?" Bea demanded.

"No," he said without turning around, and disappeared into the dance hall.

Vivian glanced nervously at Bea, wondering if they should take off before he got back. But Bea shook her head. "Don't make more trouble than we need to," she said, and Vivian knew she was right.

Danny was back faster than she expected, and he tossed something to Vivian as he came through the door. She caught it by reflex, grimacing in discomfort as the sharp, metallic object hit her palm. When she glanced down to see what she held, she found a ring of keys—weird ones, that looked like narrow metal sticks with most of their teeth missing.

"What are they?"

Danny sighed and had to step closer to answer; the band had gotten even louder, pulling out all the stops for the end of the night, and the dancers were whooping along in time with the music and the stomp of their own feet. "Skeleton keys," he said, glancing over his shoulder to make sure that they were alone in the hall. "One of them will probably get you in his building," he said. "Please don't do anything stupid. First sign of trouble, you run the hell away."

"Okay," Vivian agreed quietly. She didn't miss the look of relief on his face.

"I've got to get back behind the bar," Danny said. "Be careful out there." He glanced between them and added, "Both of you."

"We've been around the block before, Danny," Bea said. Dropping Honor's keys into his waiting hand, she added, "We know how to keep our heads down."

"I know," he said. "Good luck, girls. I hope it's a boring visit."

Spence didn't live far from the Nightingale. Vivian and Bea stuck to the main streets, the kind that still had cabs cruising past and people heading home for the night. Not that many, not this late—not this early—but enough that they didn't feel alone.

That didn't stop Vivian from glancing over her shoulder every time they turned down a new street. There was a man in a hat half a block behind them on one, though he disappeared on the next. But was that the same fella two streets later, the collar of his coat now turned up around his chin? It was almost impossible to tell in the fitful darkness.

Vivian grabbed Bea's hand and yanked her into a side street, barely more than a gap between buildings, after they rounded the next corner and were briefly out of sight of anyone behind them.

"What's the idea?" Bea demanded, though she kept her voice down. "I'm not walking down there, not if you pay me."

"Quiet for a sec," Vivian hissed, trying to watch the main street without sticking her head out. "I think someone might have been following us."

"You're jumpy as an alley cat," Bea whispered. "There's no one there." But Vivian could hear the worry in her voice.

"Just give it a minute, okay? Just to be sure."

"Fine. You watch the street. I'm keeping an eye on this garbage heap."

They were both silent. A couple lurched past Vivian's line of sight with their arms around each other's waists, and she winced at the man's sloppy, off-key singing. Someone stuck their head out the window and yelled at him to pipe down, and he shouted back but didn't stop to argue. After they had stumbled past, the street was quiet, with no man in a hat and turned-up collar to be seen.

"Can we get a move on?" Bea demanded after a few more minutes. "I'm standing in a puddle, and I don't even want to think about what it's getting on my shoes."

"Yeah, let's go," Vivian muttered. But she still couldn't shake the twitchy, prickly feeling between her shoulder blades that someone was watching them.

Spence's building was nicer than Vivian expected: it looked like it could stand up on its own, instead of slumping into one of the other buildings next to it like a drunk that needed a shoulder to lean on. There was no washing hanging out the windows, at least not on the front side, and someone had even planted a pot of scraggly flowers by the front door.

"Ain't that charming," Bea said, glancing at the blooms as they climbed the stairs. "Wonder what those are called?"

Flowers were one of those hopeful things, along with poetry and novels, that Bea loved and Vivian thought it would be nice to care about one day. They all had their ways of escaping, but the things Vivian longed for had always been more visceral: a dance without fear, a drink she bought herself. A pair of silk stockings that she didn't have to worry about ripping because there was another in the drawer. Someone who would look at her like she was the only thing that mattered in the world. She stared at the flowers, gray in the too-late, too-early light, then turned abruptly toward the door.

"Let's see if one of these works," she whispered. Bea nodded, leaning against the railing with the sort of posture that looked casual but carefully blocked what Vivian was doing from view of the street.

Vivian had never used a skeleton key before, though she had a decent idea of how they worked. Both Honor and Danny knew how to pick locks—Honor because she'd occasionally been dragged into criminal activity as a child, Danny because Honor had thought it would be useful to teach him. Vivian knew that skeleton keys were missing most of their teeth so they could bypass all the wards that kept a lock safe, and that certain ones could be paired with different sets of manufactured locks. She hadn't known that Honor and Danny kept any around, though it didn't surprise her. They were always prepared for emergencies. Some of the keys on the ring looked professionally made, the sort that a locksmith would keep around. Others had clearly been filed down from normal keys.

But there was no guarantee that they had the right one for the lock on Spence's building, so she had to try them one by one, holding her breath and praying that something would work.

Or maybe she was praying that they wouldn't, and she'd be off the hook and could go home without guilt. She didn't let herself examine that thought, just stuck another key in the lock and tried to turn it.

There were only two skeleton keys left when she heard the telltale click and the door shifted against its frame.

"Was that it?" Bea whispered as she straightened.

"He's on the fifth floor," Vivian said by way of answer as she pushed the heavy door open. It creaked, but the people who lived there were probably used to it. She doubted it would wake anyone up. "Quiet as we go up."

"Thanks for the advice," Bea said, dry and impatient. It was almost enough to make Vivian smile, in spite of her nerves, as she pulled the door shut behind them.

They made their way upstairs, quickstep-light on their toes, both of them keeping to the edges of the stairs because old buildings were all the same, whether they had flowers outside or not, and they knew the boards in the middle would creak the most. It was late enough that there wasn't much to hear: the occasional fuss of a sleepless baby on the other side of a door, the muffled sound of someone snoring, a late-night argument in hushed voices. The fifth floor, when they reached it, was quiet.

"Which one's his?" Bea whispered.

"Number twenty, I think," Vivian said. "Do they have numbers on them?"

They did, painted directly onto the wood by a steady hand. Twenty was at the end of the hall. But Vivian realized, her stomach dropping like her foot had missed a stair in the dark, that she would have been able to guess which one was Spence's, even if the number had been missing.

She and Bea both stood too still for too long, staring at the busted lock and broken handle of the door. Vivian's heart slammed against her rib cage. The door was closed. They could turn around and leave. They didn't have to know what was on the other side.

"Are we going to open it?" Bea asked hoarsely. "Or are we hightailing it out of here?"

Vivian didn't answer. She pushed the door open.

There was no sign of Spence inside, and no place that he could have hidden in the one-room apartment.

There was also no hiding the blood that was streaked across the carpet and the wooden floorboards—so much, too much—as though something had been dragged toward the door. Vivian stared down at the floor beneath her shoes. She was standing on blood, too, though someone had clearly tried to clean it up at the threshold.

"Jesus, Mary, and Joseph," she whispered. Beside her, Bea was frozen in shock.

Hesitantly, Vivian reached out the toes of her shoes, one by one, just far enough to wipe the bottoms of them against the edge of the carpet. Then she stepped backward, back into the hall that felt like safety now, her eyes still fixed on the floor of Spence's home. She tried to move, tried to decide what to do, but her mind was blank. She couldn't stop staring at the blood.

"Come on." That was Bea, stepping between Vivian and the view inside, reaching out to pull the door of the apartment as closed as it would go. Vivian could see that she was shaking. "We're getting out of here as fast as we can."

Vivian knew she was right. Even with no sign of a body, anyone in their right mind would take one look inside that door and conclude that someone had died there, and not of natural causes. Vivian knew they didn't want to be there when someone showed up to do just that.

The thought of running away made her feel almost as sick as the thought of staying. But she had been found at a murder scene once before. She still had nightmares about that time. She couldn't take that risk again.

"Viv," Bea hissed. "Come *on*."

She couldn't make Bea take that risk, either.

Vivian had to force her feet to move, and once they did, she had to force them to go slowly. They didn't run; running attracted attention, and they didn't want any of that. They still stuck to the outside of the stairs, still went down four flights on their toes. Still eased the heavy front door closed behind them. As far as they knew, no one had heard them come, and no one saw them go.

Until they turned toward the stairs and discovered that they weren't alone.

"Seen enough, girls?" the man blocking the foot of the stairs asked, almost pleasantly. His hat was pulled low over his brow, leaving his face in shadow. Vivian thought she recognized his voice, but it didn't matter. She could guess who he worked for.

"What happened up there?" she asked, her voice shaking.

The man shrugged. "Shame about your pal," he said, and she could hear the smile in his voice. "Squealed like a pig when the boss got a knife in him."

Vivian felt like she was going to be sick. Bea's hand closed tightly around hers.

"What do you want?" Bea demanded.

Vivian expected the man to reach for a weapon, or for them, but all he did was step out of their way. "Tell your boss O'Keefe is waiting. He wants Hugh Brown. And she's going to hand him over." He tipped his hat mockingly and, while they stared, disappeared into the shadows that lined the narrow street.

Vivian hauled in a breath of the cold night air, trying and failing to settle her churning stomach. "What do we do now?"

"We get the hell out of here," Bea said. She glanced over her shoulder at the building and shuddered. "Come on."

They didn't make it more than a block before they were running.

NINETEEN

Eventually, their steps slowed. You could only run in the city so long before you started attracting the sort of attention they wanted to avoid. And it didn't take them long after that to flag down a cab. They ignored the sidelong glances the cabbie gave them, too, wild-eyed girls out too late to be respectable, never mind that they were an odd pair to see climbing into a cab together.

"He wasn't Hugh Brown," Bea said, too low for the cabbie to hear. Her voice was shaking. Bea never shook. "If they're still looking . . . He wasn't Hugh Brown."

"I know," Vivian whispered, wondering when her heart was going to stop pounding. There was fear there, no question. But under that, she could feel a hot, blooming anger. At O'Keefe and his goons. At the commissioner, for leaving them to handle this threat on their own.

But more than just them. Because if Spence wasn't Hugh Brown . . . She had a sudden, terrible suspicion that the man everyone was looking for had been under her nose this entire time, lying to her face every time he saw her. She could have killed him herself for keeping her in the dark.

Still breathing heavily, she gave the cabbie the Henry family's address, earning a scowl from Bea.

"We need to go tell Honor," she said. "She needs to know what happened. *All* of it."

"I'll go and tell her, after we make sure that your family is okay," Vivian said, pushing the anger down. If Bea saw it, she'd get suspicious, and Vivian couldn't let that happen. "We know what these bastards are willing to do. I want to make sure they're safe."

Bea flinched, and she didn't argue anymore.

The cabbie didn't look pleased when Vivian told him to stick around, that she'd be back down in just a minute. "Fare first," he snapped. "I been hearing you two birds whispering back there. You think I'm an idiot?"

Vivian's jaw tightened, but she couldn't blame him for his caution. She handed over her quarter, then flashed another at him. "Twice the usual fare for the next leg, if you're still here when I get back down. Deal?"

He grumbled, but they hadn't actually caused any trouble, so he took her money and said he'd wait five minutes. "But there's plenty more action in this city, even this time of night, so don't think I won't leave if you're too slow."

Vivian had to be content with that; she didn't want to send Bea up alone, and she didn't want to hunt down another cab. She shut her jaw on a sharp retort and nodded. "Back in a jiffy, then, mister."

By the time they reached the second floor, Bea was taking the steps two and three at a time, and she burst into the door to her home with Vivian only seconds behind. Della Henry, dozing in the rocking chair by the window, sprang to her feet.

"Honey Bea, what's the matter? What happened?"

Bea stared, not moving, then flung herself into her mother's arms. "Nothing," she said, her voice muffled. "Nothing is wrong at all."

Vivian backed out the door and closed it quietly behind her. Part of her felt awful for making Bea worry, though she didn't think she'd been wrong to say they should check on her family. But she had also needed to make sure Bea stayed behind. She didn't want her practical, cautious friend to know what she was planning to do.

The Nightingale was next—Honor *did* need to know, Bea hadn't been wrong about that.

Vivian sent the cab on its way two blocks east of the Nightingale's basement entrance; the cabbie was still grumbling about girls being out when they shouldn't, but he took her money anyway and drove off without another word. Vivian glanced over her shoulder once, then told herself she wasn't going to do it again. Either someone was there or they weren't; jumping at her shadow wouldn't change anything.

The door to the basement opened in a narrow street, just large enough for a truck with wooden crates hidden in its back to pull up two afternoons a week. It was usually the last door to be locked; if someone was still awake and working at the Nightingale, the basement would be open; the trapdoor that led to it was right behind the bar, and it made for a quick getaway in emergencies.

Vivian breathed a sigh of relief when she found it unlocked. It was dark inside, but she knew her way by touch. When she got close enough to the second door—the one that opened into the basement storage room itself—there was still light shining around it. And when Vivian made her way to the top of the steps, the trapdoor had been propped open, as if it was waiting for her.

Honor was sitting at the bar, alone in the empty room. A glass of amber liquor sat in front of her, but it didn't look like she had touched it yet. Instead, she was watching the trapdoor, and she didn't look surprised when Vivian emerged.

"Bit late to be up, isn't it?" Vivian whispered, waiting to see what kind of reception she was about to get.

Honor stared at her for a long moment, her mouth tight, then slammed her hand down on the bar. Vivian didn't need to hear the rattle of metal to guess what would be left behind when Honor pulled her hand away. She looked at the keys, then at Honor.

"Would you have let me in if I'd asked instead?"

"I guess we'll never know, will we?" Honor said, her voice shaking. Vivian couldn't tell if it was anger or hurt—both, likely. "You trying to get back at me for all the times I did it to you?"

"No," Vivian said quietly. "If I wanted to get back at you, I'd quit and never talk to you again." Honor flinched, and Vivian would have felt bad if there hadn't been such a storm of anger inside her chest, bright and burning and driving her forward. "Someone needed to find out what happened, Honor, and I get that you couldn't go. But I won't apologize for being the one who did."

Anyone else might have kept going, insisting on more of an explanation, more honesty, an admission of guilt. Vivian herself probably would have, at least at one time. But Honor was too much the practical business owner. And she knew the world she lived in too well not to catch the edge in Vivian's voice.

"Was Spence at home?" she asked.

Vivian swallowed. It was impossible not to picture those streaks of blood on the floor, but she shoved the memories into that burning spot of anger that coiled tight in her chest. She needed to make them fuel for something other than fear.

"No. No, he wasn't there anymore."

Vivian could see Honor's jaw clench as she described what she and Bea had suspected, and what they had found. What the man who was waiting for them on the street had said. Honor's hands balled into fists, and she leaned heavily on them, staring at the battered wood of the bar top as she listened. When Vivian finished, Honor was still for a long minute.

"Why didn't you tell me you thought it was Spence?" she asked, her voice coming out strained, as though she were fighting to keep it even. "After what happened to Silence, how could you not tell me?"

Vivian swallowed. "I wasn't sure what you would do." She still wasn't sure, but she couldn't say that out loud. Not now. Not yet. "I thought . . . I wanted to hear his side of it first."

Honor's head snapped up, but whatever she saw in Vivian's face made the fight go out of her. She nodded slowly. "Come here."

Vivian hesitated. "What are you going to do?" But she took a tentative step forward anyway.

Honor reached out and yanked her closer, folding Vivian into her arms and pressing her cheek against Vivian's forehead. Vivian was stiff with shock for a moment; this wasn't how Honor acted, had never been how things were between them. But it didn't stop her from holding Honor back just as tightly, unable to pretend any longer that her shaking was just from anger.

"You're not angry at me?" Vivian asked.

"Furious," Honor said. "But that doesn't really matter, does it? Unless you wanted it to," she added suddenly, easing away to see Vivian's face. Her eyes narrowed. "Unless you were trying to make me—"

"No," Vivian said quickly, pulling Honor back to her. She was pretty sure she was telling the truth. "No, I wasn't trying to make you angry. I was trying to help."

"You didn't have to do it such a stupid way," Honor said, a hint of sharpness in her voice.

Vivian bristled, though she didn't pull away. "You didn't leave me much choice."

"You aren't the one responsible for—"

"I am," Vivian broke in. Her voice grew softer. "We're all responsible for each other, aren't we? Otherwise what are we doing here?"

Honor's arms tightened around her. "You scared me," she said, sounding like the words had been dragged out of her. Her voice was muffled against Vivian's hair.

"Scared?" Vivian burrowed deeper against her chest, breathing her in. "When did you become human like the rest of us?"

Honor said quietly, as though it were a painful admission, "I get angry when I'm scared."

Vivian felt the hot rage inside her chest again, the tight ball of fear at its center. "Me too."

She had thought she understood how things were handled in this world. Honor paid her bribes to powerful people in high places, and she traded favors with the powerful people in low ones. She stayed out of the way of people like Hattie Wilson, and if someone in all that mess had a problem with another, they solved it with fists or cash or a carefully timed police raid. It wasn't anything like safe, but there was a certain logic to it. It was, in its own way, almost civilized.

O'Keefe was playing by different rules, and Vivian had no idea what they were. She wondered if Honor did, or if she was making it up as she went, too.

Honor pulled away at last. "So. Seems like O'Keefe still thinks we know more than we've admitted." Her sigh was deep and exhausted. "I need to find some more muscle. Party's going to be closed down until I do."

Vivian gaped at her, wondering if she had heard correctly. The Nightingale was never closed. "Are you sure?"

"I'm not putting my people in that kind of danger. Nightingale's going to sleep until we come out the other side of this. For now, I've got some calls to make. And you . . ."

"I'm going to stay with Bea tonight," Vivian said quickly. "Not alone."

Honor nodded, looking relieved. It was strange to look at her face and be able to tell what she was thinking; maybe she was keeping less hidden, or maybe Vivian had just finally learned to read her. Either way, it made Vivian want to squirm with guilt for the lie. But that ball of anger was still there, burning as hot as ever. Her night wasn't done yet.

Honor went with her outside, put her into a cab and handed the driver a roll of bills as she told him the address; Vivian wasn't surprised she had it memorized. Honor probably knew exactly where most of her employees lived, especially the ones who had been there the longest. There was no real good-bye, not with someone else there. But there was heat in her eyes as she held the door for Vivian.

"Be careful," Honor said, just before Vivian climbed into the car. "I don't know what's going to happen. So just . . ."

"You too." Vivian wanted to reach for her but kept her hands clutched into fists at her sides. She slid into the back seat, but her eyes stayed fixed on Honor. "You tell me if you learn anything?"

There was enough of a glow from the streetlamp and the cab's headlights that Vivian could see Honor's mouth pull to one side. "You're going to keep asking the world of me if I keep you around, aren't you?"

"Most folks wouldn't consider that such a big ask," Vivian pointed out.

"But we do," Honor said softly, and Vivian wondered how much Honor guessed about what she was planning to do. If Honor was becoming less opaque to her, how transparent was she to Honor?

"I'll tell you what I can, when I can. That's all I can promise." Honor shut the door, then tapped on the roof of the cab as she stepped back to let the driver know he was good to go.

Vivian watched her through the window as they pulled away from the curb. She waited until they were a few blocks away before leaning forward. "Change of address, if you don't mind, mister. I've got another few stops to make."

The first stop was a hotel, a shabby place that catered to gentlemen who had found a new friend for the night and needed somewhere to take her before heading home to their wives and families in the morning. Vivian didn't like to walk in there alone, and she didn't like the way the cabbie smirked as she did, lighting a cigarette while he waited and blowing smoke out the window as he snickered after her.

But the place was open all night, and there were telephones in the lobby. Vivian ignored the slippery looks sent her way by the two men lounging there, cigars dribbling smoke into the air, and the narrow-eyed suspicion from the desk clerk as she hurried to the telephone booths that lined one wall. She breathed a sigh of relief that one was unoccupied and slipped inside, pulling the door closed firmly behind her and flipping the latch in case any of the men out there decided to see if she wanted company.

"Circle two-four-four-one," she told the operator on the other end, and then held her breath, waiting to see if it would connect.

She let out a sigh of relief when she heard the click of a receiver being picked up. "Bit late for a call," said the sleepy, husky voice on the other end.

"Leo, it's me," she said quickly. "I need to see you."

"Viv." He was instantly more alert. "What happened? Are you in trouble?"

"I'm fine. Mostly fine. But something happened—" She glanced through the glass door of the booth uneasily. "I don't want to hang around this rat house any longer than I have to. Can you let me in, maybe ten minutes from now?"

The silence on the other end was enough to make the back of her neck prickle, but it didn't last long. "Anything for you, sweetheart. But this had better be good."

"It's not," she whispered. "It's bad."

"I know," he said on a sigh. "See you soon."

It was a tense, silent ride to Leo's, and an even more tense and silent three minutes sneaking upstairs, past his sharp-eared landlady's door and through the dark building. The first time she had ever visited him there, Vivian had been pleasantly tipsy after an evening at the pictures, and she had clung to Leo's back, shaking with laughter, while he walked upstairs in case his landlady was listening for more than one set of footsteps.

That felt like a long time ago.

Now, he took her hand to guide her up the steps in the dark. There was none of the electric heat that used to jump between them. But her fingers still knew the shape of his as they crept up the stairs together, and she was grateful for the way that familiarity eased the frantic thumping of her heart.

It was dark inside his apartment, and she couldn't see his face as he unlocked the door and gestured her inside. Vivian didn't miss that he closed the door immediately behind them, or that he flipped the locks right away too.

There was only one room, but Leo had a knack for making the place feel homey. A wobbly little dining table and chairs, just big enough for two, sat near the icebox and stove; a checked quilt lay across the bed and a saggy sofa sat at its foot.

"All right," Leo said gently, once the door was locked and he had flicked on the lights. There had always been a gentleness to Leo, underneath it all, that never quite fit the world he lived in or the life he had chosen. He had once told her that his father—a quiet, bookish cobbler raising his son in a rough neighborhood west of Bowery—had hoped he'd grow up to be something more than a street tough. In that moment, Vivian wished he had too.

"All right," he repeated. "Tell me."

Vivian took a deep breath.

"It's not quite a social call," she said softly, not moving from her spot by the door. "But I'm guessing you figured that out, as careful as you're being."

Leo pulled a chair out from the table but didn't take a seat, too busy watching her with wary eyes. "I guessed as much."

They stared at each other in silence. Vivian could hear a car go by in the street below. Dawn was only a few hours off.

"Just say it, Viv," Leo said at last, shaking his head. His dark, curly hair was a tousled mess around his head, as if he'd rolled out of bed to come meet her. He probably had; it was late enough. "We both know you figured it out."

Vivian's hands clenched into fists by her sides. "I know you're Hugh Brown."

TWENTY

Leo sighed as he dropped into the chair at last. "Didn't think I'd ever be using that name again," he said, shaking his head. "What gave it away?"

"Not much," Vivian admitted. She didn't move from her spot by the door. "I didn't put it together until tonight. But you were all kinds of jittery that first night O'Keefe came to the Nightingale. I thought it was because you were worried about me."

"I was," Leo said quietly.

"Maybe. But you were worried about you more. You heard the name Hugh Brown, and you knew who was looking for you."

"That was all it took?" Leo said, shaking his head. "Must be losing my edge."

Vivian laughed shortly. "Not quite all. I didn't realize until later how careful you were not to let me say 'Hugh Brown' in front of your uncle. He knows the name, doesn't he?" Leo nodded, and she laughed again, though there was nothing funny about it. "And that's why he kept looking so amused when I mentioned O'Keefe. And asking you if you had anything you wanted to say about it. And then I met someone who had met Hugh Brown and said the fella knew his way around a liquor bottle. I thought at first that he meant a bartender. But he was talking about a bootlegger." Vivian didn't take her eyes from him. "I can put two and two together. Eventually, anyway."

"Did you tell her?" Leo asked, half standing.

Vivian didn't have to ask who he meant. She shook her head slowly. "No. Not yet."

Leo let out a relieved sigh. "She's never liked me, you know. Puts up with me. But the two of you . . ." He looked up. "I know you love her."

Something like panic clenched around Vivian's heart. "I never said that."

He shook his head, smiling sadly. "You don't need to. But you see why I couldn't say anything to you, don't you? I couldn't take the risk that you might tell Honor."

"I didn't, though."

"Why not?"

"Because—" Vivian couldn't meet his eyes. She pressed her hands backward, flat against the wood of the door, to stop them from shaking. "I wanted to hear your side of it first."

He sank back into his chair, dropping his head into his hands. "You said first night," he said, his voice muffled. "The first night O'Keefe came to the Nightingale. He came back?"

"He did," Vivian replied softly.

She could see Leo's jaw clench as he looked up. "Tell me."

He flinched as she told him, but he didn't look away, even when she described what she and Bea had found in Spence's apartment. "That's how he does business," Leo said. "I thought if I kept my head down . . ." His smile was bleaker than she had ever seen before. "Guess I was wrong."

"He'd been showing a photo of you around," Vivian said, crossing her arms tightly against her chest, as though she could hold herself together through sheer force of will. "Someone must have recognized you and realized you hung out at the Nightingale. Tipped him off that you knew the owner pretty well. I wish I knew who."

"You and me both, sweetheart," Leo said grimly.

"And I wish I knew why he was after you," she said, meeting his eyes.

Leo shook his head. "It's not a nice story."

"I didn't figure it was," Vivian said. She wanted to be cold, but she could see the pain at the edge of his eyes. "Tell me anyway."

Leo leaned on the spindly-legged table, weight resting heavily on his hands and his head bowed. Slowly, he reached to the back of his waistband and pulled out the gun that he kept there. Vivian flinched at the sight; she knew Leo usually kept some heat on him. She had never wondered about it, until now.

He laid it carefully on the table. "About five years ago, before I took off for Chicago, my father moved to Long Island," he said, still not looking up. "I always figured I'd go with him eventually, but there was someone in the city I wanted to stay close to. Her name was Nora. Nora Murphy."

Vivian stared. It was the first time Leo had ever mentioned a girl from his past.

If he noticed her surprise, Leo didn't say anything. He was looking past her now, talking softly. "Nora lived down near Bowery, close to where I grew up. Prettiest girl I had ever seen. Dark hair. Sweet—too sweet for that rough place—but a real spitfire, too. She'd stand up to any dumb kid who thought he was a tough guy, even if it would have been smarter to back down."

Vivian shivered. It sounded an awful lot like what Leo had said to her about herself, back when they had first met.

"Her father worked for some second-class criminal or other. I didn't pay much attention at the time. I was more concerned about him catching us." A wry smile kicked up one corner of his mouth. "He was a big fella, and he lived up to those jokes about Irish tempers like you wouldn't believe."

"I know the type," Vivian said, her thoughts jumping to Clyde Quinn for a moment before returning to the man in front of her.

"He was also very Catholic and didn't like it when boys came sniffing around. I didn't even want to think about what he'd do if he knew his daughter was sneaking out with someone like me. But we were pretty careful for two kids. I don't think he even knew I existed. Which luckily meant—" Leo broke off. His voice, when he spoke again, was so carefully empty of all emotion that it made the hair on the back of Vivian's neck stand up. "Which luckily meant his boss didn't either."

"What happened?" she asked, though part of her didn't want to know the answer.

Leo pushed away from the table abruptly, his steps jerky as he paced from one end of the room to the other. "Best I was able to piece it together after the fact, her father stole from his boss. Maybe a bunch of times." He stopped by the window, staring out at the darkness. Vivian could see his hands shaking before he shoved them in his pockets. He turned to look at her. "So his boss had the whole family killed, as a warning to anyone else working for him."

The silence in the room pressed against Vivian's ears. She couldn't take her eyes from him. She had seen Leo face plenty of hard, sad, or scary things without blinking. But maybe that was just because the worst thing he could have imagined had already happened to him.

"Were you the one who found them?" she asked at last.

"I almost wish I had been," Leo said. "Maybe then I could have figured out . . . No, I didn't find them. I read about it in the goddamn *papers*."

His face was blank and calm as he spoke, his street-tough face that didn't let any hint of emotion show through. Vivian felt her heart breaking for him, for the boy she'd never had a chance to know. She reached for him, but Leo took a step away from her, shaking his head. Vivian let her hand drop. She couldn't blame him for that. If it had been her story, she probably couldn't have gotten through it in the face of anyone's sympathy either.

"Husband and wife and son, all dead in their home, and the police with no idea who'd done it," Leo continued, his voice calm and careful. "Random violence, they called it, and no one brave enough—or stupid enough—to find out what really happened." He shook his head. "Some things don't change, do they?"

But Vivian heard what he hadn't said. "Husband and wife and son?"

Leo met her eyes at last, and his smile was a bitter, vicious slash across his handsome face. "All three of them," he said. "But not Nora."

"She was alive?"

Leo shook his head. "She was gone. I spent months here in New York trying to find out what had happened to her. But no one was talking. That second-class criminal her dad worked for was building a reputation that scared people. So when he moved his operation to Chicago, I packed up and followed. Started using the name Hugh Brown and set myself up as a bootlegger. And then I looked for every chance I could to get close to him."

Vivian hesitated, then asked, "Did you try to get your uncle to help you find out what happened to her? Before you left?"

She didn't think Leo was going to answer, but at last he nodded. "He wasn't the commissioner then, and I'd barely had any contact with him in my life. He agreed to help me find out who her dad's boss was. And then, when I decided to head to Chicago, he gave me money to set myself up there. I thought he wanted to help me out because we were *family*." Leo laughed bitterly. "It wasn't until I made a bit of a name for myself as a bootlegger and he got in touch, saying I owed him a favor with no questions asked, that I finally got wise to his real angle."

"What did you do?"

Leo shrugged. "He was right, I owed him. I did that favor, plus a few more, and we were square. But he kept track of me, and he'd pay when he needed something done off the books. That's how it's been ever since."

"And did you find her?" Vivian asked, though she could guess the answer. If he had found Nora—or at least, if he had found her alive—he wouldn't have come back to New York ready to flirt with the dark-haired girl he found on a speakeasy's dance floor.

Leo met her eyes. "I never heard a word about her. No sign of her in Chicago either. I held out hope for a long time, but . . ." He shrugged, looking away. "Eventually you have to be honest with yourself. She got offed too, same as the rest of her family. Just in a different spot, probably. Whoever did the job must have taken her with them, so they probably wanted to . . ."

He didn't say anything more. He didn't need to. They both knew why a group of bully-boys, set loose on that kind of ugly job, might have decided to take a girl with them for a little while before getting rid of her somewhere else.

Leo cleared his throat. "I figured if I wasn't able to save Nora, I could at least make the people who hurt her pay. I knew the fella her father worked for was named Harlan O'Keefe. He had a reputation as the sort of smart bastard that didn't let other people get close to him. Not easily, anyway. But eventually I got to know one of his deputies. The fella brought me on to help with a job that would've let me prove myself to O'Keefe, get in good with him at last."

"What went wrong?"

"I thought it was a normal liquor run," Leo said quietly. He was staring past her again; Vivian didn't want to know what he was seeing. "He didn't tell me until we were on our way that the plan was to rob a bank's cash transport."

Vivian sucked in a breath. Leo had once told her, open and unapologetic, that he'd spent his time in Chicago doing illegal things. But there was a hell of a difference between running liquor and robbing banks. Maybe a judge wouldn't agree, but she'd always thought of bootleggers and suppliers as practically businessmen, no more criminal than Danny serving drinks behind the Nightingale's bar. Robbery, though. That was something else entirely.

Leo smiled grimly at her shock. "That's exactly how I felt, too. It wasn't the sort of work I did. But you don't say no to a guy like that unless you want to end up floating in the river."

"What did you do?" Vivian asked. Her shoulders were so tense it felt like they were crawling up her neck.

Leo was silent so long that Vivian thought he wouldn't answer. "I decided getting close to O'Keefe was more important than anything else. Nora deserved that. So I'd have gone through with it. But it didn't matter in the end."

"Why not?" Vivian whispered.

"We were given our positions to wait for the truck to come. I took mine. And then the last thing I remember was hearing someone behind me." He stared past her. "When I woke up, everyone else was gone and the cash transport was nowhere to be seen."

"You were brought on as a patsy?"

"But not for the police to find." Leo shook his head. "It didn't take me long to learn that the cash was missing, and all the men who'd been there except O'Keefe's main deputy were dead."

"I'm guessing that deputy told everyone you double-crossed them?" Vivian asked.

"And Harlan O'Keefe was offering good money to anyone who could find Hugh Brown," Leo said, nodding. "I guess I could have tried to set the record straight. But I didn't like my chances of success."

"So you came back home?"

Leo shrugged. "Right about that time, my uncle let me know he could use a fella like me in New York, so I took him up on the offer. Hugh Brown had never really existed, so it was easy for him to disappear."

"Then how did they find you?" Vivian demanded. "If Hugh Brown disappeared when you left Chicago, how did O'Keefe show up at the Nightingale asking where to find him?"

Leo grimaced. "I used the name once, when I first came back to New York. I needed to set myself up as someone who could be trusted to do a job well. I hoped . . ." He let out a frustrated breath. "I hoped just once wasn't too much of a risk. And I figured that if I was working for my uncle, I'd hear whether O'Keefe and his fellas were back in New York. But I guess they slipped in real quiet."

"But that bank job had to be something like two years ago now," Vivian pointed out, remembering O'Keefe's smile as he watched her during their dance, his cold eyes as he talked with Honor. "Why's he coming after you all of a sudden?"

Leo was silent for a long moment, staring out the window. "Best I can guess, he was getting close to figuring out what really happened. His deputy probably needed to put him off the trail. Easiest way to do that would be tracking me down. O'Keefe would jump at the chance. He's known for holding a grudge."

"And you?" Vivian asked, her voice steadier than she expected. How many times had he looked at her and seen Nora instead?

It took Leo longer than she liked to answer. "I've held on to this one for a long time," he said at last.

"But this is the first time anyone else has been dragged into it," Vivian said. "Isn't it?"

"You want me to stop hiding, then," he said, his eyes hard. "You want me to turn myself over to O'Keefe before anyone else gets hurt."

It was what *he* wanted, she realized. Of course Leo hated hiding and waiting. He had never been someone who liked sitting still. And he had been waiting years to face down this man that he hated.

Vivian shook her head. "Don't be stupid," she said. Every muscle in her body was tight, ready to run or to fight, and she wasn't sure which impulse would win. "I don't want him to find you. Probably wouldn't stop the bastard from coming after the rest of us, anyway. Not anymore."

"Then what?" Leo demanded, and she could hear the desperation in his voice.

"You still want to know what happened to her, don't you?" Vivian said. "To Nora?" He didn't answer or nod, but he didn't deny it. "And I want to keep everyone from the Nightingale safe." Vivian leaned forward. "So we do what your uncle said. We find O'Keefe first. And he can't know that we're coming."

Leo lifted his head, and his eyes gleamed like a feral dog's hunting rats in an alley. He nodded. "I'm all ears, Viv. How do you suggest we start?"

It should have felt strange—too familiar, maybe—to spend the night at Leo's place. But Vivian had no intention of heading home alone, not after what had happened. And he wouldn't have allowed it, anyway. Dawn wasn't far away, and it hadn't taken them long to agree on a plan. By the time Leo offered her the bed and said he'd bunk on the couch, Vivian was too tired to feel awkward. She shed her dress and shoes and rolled herself in the blanket. She drifted off to sleep to the sound of Leo checking the locks and laying his revolver carefully on the table next to his head.

Leo wasn't the sort to own an alarm clock, but his next-door neighbor was. Vivian woke to the sound of it clanging through the walls and found Leo awake, already dressed and making coffee.

"Couldn't sleep," he said by way of explanation, holding out a steaming mug. Vivian, holding the blanket around her shoulders like a cape, climbed out of bed to take it. Leo nodded toward the basin next to the stove. "Left a towel and soap there for you. I'm heading next door for a few minutes. I'll knock three times when I come back."

Vivian clutched the blanket more closely to her as she nodded. Her head was fuzzy from fatigue, and in the shivery morning light, her awful discovery at Spence's place felt like a dream. Did they really need to be that careful? But Leo knew more about what was happening than she did; she wasn't going to argue with his caution.

The door closed behind him, and Vivian didn't waste any time before stripping off her clothes and scrubbing away the night's sweat and fear. By the time the three knocks came and Leo slipped into the room, locking the door behind him once more, Vivian was back in her step-in and stockings, holding up her dancing dress and frowning.

"I didn't think this part through," she admitted.

Leo grinned and held out the bundle he had tucked under his arm, though his cheeks were a little flushed as he turned his eyes away. "I did. Figured the missus next door was about your size, so I told them my sister was visiting and I'd spilled coffee on your dress. Got told off something fierce, but she was happy to lend you a spare."

The sweater and skirt weren't as fashionable as what Vivian would have normally worn—working for a dressmaker required looking the part—but they were pretty and well-made.

"Thanks, pal," she said as she tugged them on, relieved to find that the skirt was only a little too long and a little tight across the hips. As she buttoned up the sweater, she added, "So I'm your sister now?"

"Beats trying to sneak you out in your spangles without my landlady noticing," he said, giving her a small smile. "Just don't open your mouth on the way out; we don't sound like we were raised in anything like the same part of the city."

"No arguments here," Vivian agreed. She drained the last of her coffee. "Sticking with the plan from last night?"

"If you're still up for it," he said, his smile fading. "It could get dangerous, Viv."

Vivian set the cup down carefully. "It's dangerous now," she said. "And I'm not interested in sitting around, waiting for trouble to find me, thanks."

"You'd rather find it first?" Leo asked.

"Always," Vivian said, hoping her smile was convincing. "You ready?"

TWENTY-ONE

Leo's part of the plan was straightforward. He had a friend in the coroner's office who was usually willing to help out when he needed. If Spence's body had been found, that might give them some clue what part of the city O'Keefe was holed up in.

Vivian's part was just as straightforward in the telling, but she knew it could get complicated quickly. That was unavoidable when you tried to get help from a woman like Hattie Wilson. But the elegant criminal owed her a favor, and Vivian couldn't think of a better reason to collect.

Leo had wanted to come with her, but they eventually agreed that would be less safe, not more. Still, that didn't stop him from bringing it up again while they waited for the streetcar.

"I just don't like the idea of you marching in there alone," he said quietly, glancing around. His eyes hadn't stopped moving since they left the house.

"But there's no telling what she's heard, or what kind of description O'Keefe and his pals are sharing," Vivian pointed out. Leo's neighbor had included a scarf with the clothes she sent over; Vivian wore it wrapped around her head to hide her hair. Beside her, Leo had his hat tipped low to shade his eyes and the collar of his coat turned up. "Besides, early morning is probably the safest time to be going around by myself right now. Those big-six type of fellas tend to do their dirty work at night, not breakfast time."

Leo sighed as the streetcar screeched to a stop in front of them. "Okay, I suppose I can't argue with that."

"And you'll let me know what the medical examiner says?" Vivian asked as people began to push past them. "If anyone found . . ."

She couldn't quite say it, but Leo nodded. He reached out and squeezed her hand. "Give me a call after you finish work, okay? We'll swap news then."

"Sounds peachy." Vivian tried to smile like everything would be okay, like she believed they could do this. "We've been in some tough jams before, Leo, and we've come through them all right. This is just one more."

"Yeah," he agreed, leaning over to bump her shoulder with his. "And there's no one I'd rather have in my corner, pal. Now get up there. You go handle your business, and let's hope she's in a good mood."

Vivian watched through the window as the streetcar pulled away and Leo joined the throng of people streaming from the platform. He'd be heading east, now, toward Bellevue and the medical examiner's office. If Spence's body . . . Vivian swallowed, pressing her forehead against the cool glass, not wanting to finish that thought. If there was something to know, Leo would find it out.

That left Vivian with a task that looked cushier—it didn't involve any dead bodies—but was far more terrifying.

When she finally reached the house, she stood on the sidewalk in front of it for an uncomfortably long time, working up the nerve to go knock when she was just as likely to get thrown out as anything else. But this was one risk she was willing to take. Vivian marched up to the tradesman's entrance and knocked.

The maid who finally answered the door stared at her, baffled.

"You're the dressmaker's girl," she said at last, trying without success to hold back a yawn. She had probably been up for hours already. Behind her, Vivian could hear the clatter of people hard at work in the kitchen.

"Yes. Miss Ethel got a call asking that someone come by early today," Vivian said, lying with a smile on her face. "Would you send word up that Vivian Kelly is here and ask if she's ready to see me?"

"It's seven o'clock in the morning," the maid insisted, looking bewildered. "They haven't even had breakfast yet."

Vivian shrugged. "You know how she is. Likes things her way, and they'd better happen when she wants them."

The maid glanced over her shoulder, looking unsure what to do. But there didn't seem to be anyone with more authority around for her to ask, so at last she shrugged and opened the door. "Wait here, then," she said, covering another yawn. "I'll see if she's ready."

Vivian waited on a bench in the narrow hall, trying not to shift nervously from side to side. But the message must have worked, because it wasn't long before the sleepy maid returned and told her to follow her upstairs.

Vivian smiled when she was shown into the office. Good. She was there to discuss business, after all, not fit dresses. Everyone was on the same page. She settled into the chair in front of the desk to wait, turning just enough to keep her eyes on the open door.

She didn't have to wait long.

"Well, Miss Kelly," Hattie Wilson said, striding into the office with brisk steps. She was still in her dressing robe and her hair was down and loose. But even so, she radiated energy and control. She closed the door behind her, then stopped to look Vivian up and down. "It's a bit early for either a delivery or a social call, so I must assume that some other reason brought you here." She took a seat behind her desk and leaned her crossed arms on the polished wood. "Shall I make a guess?"

"No need," Vivian said. She wasn't there to play games. "You owe me a favor, Mrs. Wilson. I'm here to collect."

"I thought as much." Hattie Wilson leaned back in her chair. "Do tell."

"Harlan O'Keefe." Vivian was gratified to see Hattie's brows rise the barest fraction. "You've heard of him."

"I wouldn't be very good at my work if I hadn't," Hattie said. "What about him?"

"He's back in town," Vivian said, watching Hattie closely. But it was impossible to tell if she was surprised by the news. "I want to know where he's set up shop these days. I want to know what he's doing."

"I certainly haven't a clue."

"But you could find out," Vivian pressed. "Unless you've got a lot less pull than I thought."

"It's not a matter of pull," Hattie Wilson said, shaking her head, refusing to be baited. "I'm not stupid enough to cross a man like O'Keefe, especially when he's happy to leave me alone."

"How do you know he's happy to—" Vivian didn't need to finish the question. "Have the two of you been in touch, then?"

For a moment, Vivian thought Mrs. Wilson wouldn't reply. But then she shrugged. "He's not really a person you stay *in touch* with, Miss Kelly. But I have heard from him. And it was the sort of message that a smart woman pays attention to."

"Which was?"

"Not to get in his way," Hattie said, her smile like a knife's edge. "And in return, he wouldn't make a point of getting in mine. You'd do well to think about that. O'Keefe isn't a man that I, personally, would want to upset."

"You scared of him?" Vivian demanded.

Hattie Wilson's eyes snapped with anger at the taunt, but her voice stayed calm as ever. "I simply don't see any reason to make an enemy of him when he hasn't done anything to me. And to be honest, Miss

Kelly, I'd have thought you were smart enough not to either." Her expression took on a thoughtful edge. "Or have you already managed to irritate the man?"

Vivian drummed her fingers against the side of her chair, wondering how much to say, before she managed to quiet the nervous gesture. "I haven't," she said at last. "But he is . . . sending a message to someone. And some folks I know seem to be caught in the middle."

"No, that's not quite it." Hattie Wilson leaned forward once more, her fingers tapping together. "You're far too angry. It's personal, is it not? Involving someone you care about a great deal." She smiled. "Is it the delightful Ms. Huxley?"

Her eyes glittered as she said it; Hattie and Honor respected each other, as far as that went, and had made use of each other on occasion. But neither of them would have been sad to see the other out of the way.

"No," Vivian said sharply.

Too sharply. Hattie's smile grew; she could tell she had touched a nerve. Vivian gritted her teeth. She had to give Hattie something, if she wanted to convince her, and it was too much of a risk to mention Leo. But there were two people in the world that Hattie cared about, and one of them called her mama.

"My sister had a baby recently," Vivian said quietly, hoping she wasn't making a big mistake. It was dangerous to tell someone like Hattie too much. But Vivian had made it clear many times that she considered Hattie's sister and her son off-limits. She hoped Hattie would feel the same way. "Little girl. She's three months old now. Chubbiest cheeks you ever saw."

She watched Hattie's face closely as she spoke, and to her relief she could detect just a hint of softening around her mouth. But the mob boss's eyes stayed hard. "Charming. And?"

"Some of his goons were bashing around downtown, looking for someone. They ended up looking where my sister lives, and her baby was nearly . . ."

Vivian swallowed, remembering the fear she had felt when O'Keefe's bully-boy had reached for Mei, trying not to think about Nora Murphy and her family. He'd decided to use Spence to send his message this time. What if it had been Danny instead? What if Florence or Mei had been there too?

She met Hattie's eyes. "Next time they show up, she might not be so lucky. I can't let that happen."

"And how will knowing where O'Keefe is and what he's up to help you?"

Vivian took a deep breath. "That doesn't matter to you, does it? You owe me a favor, and I'm telling you what I want. Or are you the sort of person who doesn't pay her debts? Bad for business, you know."

"I don't need you to tell me how to run my operation, Miss Kelly," Hattie said, her voice even. She stood abruptly. "I always pay my debts, but that doesn't mean I'll agree to just anything. You'll have to come up with something else." Smiling coolly, she walked to the door. "Now, if you will—"

Hattie broke off as she swung the door open. Beryl was standing on the other side, Johnny on her hip and a scowl on her face. The two of them stared at each other.

"Beryl," Hattie said, and it was clearly a warning.

Her sister ignored her, striding into the room. "Close the door again, sis," she suggested. The little boy leaned against her shoulder, his hair still sleep-tousled as he chewed on the side of his fist and watched them with wide eyes.

"Beryl," Hattie said again. "I think you know that this isn't a house where it's safe to listen at doors."

Her voice was soft enough that it made Vivian want to shiver. But Beryl lifted her chin and met her sister's eyes. They stared at each other, then Hattie sighed. To Vivian's shock, she closed the door.

"Normally I keep my nose out of your business, Hattie," Beryl said, kissing the top of her nephew's—her son's—head. He smiled and cuddled even closer against her shoulder. "I'm not in it, and I don't want to be. But not this time."

"You don't know enough about it," Hattie said, and Vivian was surprised by how gentle her voice was as she reached out to stroke Johnny's hair. He giggled as she tickled him under the chin, and squirmed away. Vivian wondered whether they'd ever tell him the truth about who his mother was. There was no chance he knew now; they wouldn't risk him letting it slip once he started talking more.

"I know there's a baby in danger because of it," Beryl said. "And I know that you could help keep her safe."

"If I fell for every sob story someone tried to feed me—"

"And I know that she could have done plenty to hurt us," Beryl broke in, glancing at Vivian out of the corner of her eye. "To hurt Johnny. And she hasn't. Isn't that right?"

Hattie looked at Vivian, her lips pressed together. The words came reluctantly. "It is."

"Then there you go," Beryl said quietly. "It doesn't have to be a big thing, does it? Find this O'Keefe for her, and leave it at that."

Vivian watched them in fascination. This Mrs. Wilson was different from the steely, calculating manipulator that Vivian was used to dealing with, the one who made her hide her fear and choose her words like tiptoeing through shattered glass. Beryl didn't tiptoe. She didn't hesitate to face this Mrs. Wilson down, and Hattie was clearly wavering in the face of her insistence.

"Fine," Hattie said, the word dropping from her like a stone. "I'll see what I can find, Miss Kelly. And I'll be in touch."

Vivian tried not to let her relief show. "Peachy."

"But I'm not sticking my neck out beyond that," Hattie said, the warning as much for her sister as for Vivian. "I've got a business to run and my own family to take care of."

"Sounds fair to me." Vivian smiled as though the outcome had never been in doubt. "Thanks for making the time this morning, Mrs. Wilson. I appreciate it."

"Hmm." The soft noise in the back of Hattie's throat could have passed for a laugh if there had been any inkling of amusement on her face. But there wasn't. She opened the door again. "I certainly hope you do. You may leave now, Miss Kelly. My sister and I have a busy day ahead of us."

"Good luck," Beryl whispered as Vivian walked past, the words barely loud enough to hear. Vivian paused just long enough to nod at her, not wanting to provoke Mrs. Wilson any more than she already had. She could feel both their eyes on her as she left.

The morning bustle of the house had grown while she was talking with the sisters, and Vivian slipped out without anyone seeming to notice. Coming up the steps from the tradesman's entrance, Vivian blinked in the sunlight and took a deep breath, the cool air welcome against her nervous-hot skin as she glanced around out of habit, checking that no one was there, before she headed off.

And then she turned a corner and came face-to-face with Honor.

"Vivian." Honor stared at her, frozen in surprise. "What are you doing here?"

It took Vivian a moment to find her voice. "What am I— What are you doing here?"

Honor grabbed her arm and pulled her toward the shadowy corner of one cold, towering mansion, looking her up and down as if to check that she was unharmed. "You shouldn't be out wandering around, not even for work. Not alone, anyway. Isn't there someone you can bring with you?"

"I'm fine," Vivian said. "Really. I just needed to see Mrs. Wilson."

Honor's gaze sharpened. "For a delivery? Or for something else?" When Vivian hesitated, she sighed. "I don't think this is the time for secrets, Vivian."

"I had a favor to ask for," Vivian said quietly. "She owed me. I asked her to find out what she could about where O'Keefe might be holed up."

"Still hoping you can get the commissioner to help us out?" Honor shook her head, and her hand slid down Vivian's arm to squeeze her hand. "Always the optimist."

"You're going to see her too, aren't you?" Vivian asked. "That's why you're here."

"I am," Honor said, and once again, Vivian was taken aback by how easily she answered. "That woman hears a lot about what goes on in this city, and she keeps her information to herself until she can use it. But everyone's got a price. I'm hoping I can find hers."

What information? Vivian wanted to ask. But she was afraid she knew the answer. She had pieced together who Hugh Brown was. What were the odds Hattie Wilson could do it, too?

Maybe she should just say what she knew. Honor had been acting so different lately, sharing what she was thinking with more openness than Vivian ever would have expected of her. Maybe she meant everything she was saying, that she really had changed. Maybe, if Vivian asked her to, she'd keep Leo's secret, and they could find another way to get rid of O'Keefe.

Vivian wanted, so badly, to trust her. But did she?

"Vivian?" It took Vivian a moment to realize Honor had said her name more than once. "You still with me?"

"Sorry, thinking," Vivian said, shaking her head. "Don't know how she'll like back-to-back requests, but who knows? She probably respects you more than she does me. Money talks." She was babbling, she realized, and closed her mouth quickly.

Honor was frowning at her. "Is there something you're not telling me, pet?" she asked quietly. "About Mrs. Wilson or . . . anything else?"

"My father," Vivian said, blurting out the first thing that came to mind so she wouldn't let Leo's secret slip, right there in the middle of the street. She wanted to trust Honor, but there were still too many maybes. "There hasn't been a chance to tell you. I found my father."

"Your father?" Honor was staring at her. "Holy hell, Vivian."

"I know." Vivian smiled weakly. "There was a letter . . . It's too long a story to tell here. But I'm on my way to see him. Right now. Me and my sister both."

To her surprise, Honor pulled her into a tight embrace, there in the shadows of the Fifth Avenue mansions and with the city still waking up around them. "I hope he's everything you've been wishing for," Honor murmured in her ear. "Because you deserve it."

Vivian felt the brush of lips against her cheek, and then Honor had stepped back. "Good luck with Mrs. Wilson," she said, feeling dazed. Had she done the right thing? And would Honor forgive her when she finally found out?

Honor smiled. "Good luck to us all," she said, settling her hat on her head. "I'll see you soon, pet."

Vivian's thoughts were a mess as she turned her steps downtown once more, a tangle of Leo's story and Honor's gentle kiss and the fear she couldn't shake thrumming just below her skin. Her steps followed her usual route back without thinking, darting between cars and taking her normal shortcuts while she tried to convince herself that she'd made the right choice.

She had just turned into a narrow, empty side street when someone grabbed her arm and spun her around. Vivian stumbled against the brick wall of a building, her hair swinging into her face and blocking her vision for a moment. But as soon as he spoke, she knew who had grabbed her.

"All right, girlie," he snarled. "This is when you tell me exactly what you're playing at."

TWENTY-TWO

Vivian shoved Bruiser George away from her; she could hear him grunt as her fists collided with his chest. "Me?" she snapped, pushing her hair out of her eyes. "What are you playing at? Get the hell off me."

He let her go, but he still blocked her way, arms crossed as he scowled at her. "If you're trying to get my boss mixed up in something, that's my business as much as anyone else's. What were you doing at the house? What are you trying to drag us into?"

"What were *you* doing there, George?" Vivian countered. Her breath came too quickly, and her hands were shaking, but she was so tired of being scared. She took a step toward him. "Seems pretty early for a business call."

He smirked at her. "Shows what you know. Boss lady trusts me, girlie. I'm her right-hand man these days. So don't cross me."

"Well I guess if she wants you to know, she'll tell you. Until then, keep your mitts off me."

"What do you want with Harlan O'Keefe?"

Vivian didn't bother asking how he had overheard her. Bruiser

George had worked for Mrs. Wilson's late husband before she took over the business; Vivian wasn't surprised he'd found a way to listen in on his employers. She would have, too, in his line of work. "You know who he is, then?"

George narrowed his eyes at her. "I know that getting mixed up with a fella like him is bad for business," he snapped. "And I don't think—"

"And when Mrs. Wilson asks what you think, George, will you tell her?" Vivian taunted, knowing it was reckless and not caring. He was a bully-boy, through and through, but she suspected he had more ambition than talent. She was equally certain that, no matter how much she might depend on him, Mrs. Wilson would never show her hand to someone with his lack of subtlety.

Vivian could tell she had struck a sore spot. His cheeks grew red, and his hands clenched into fists. She braced herself, waiting for the blow.

It didn't come. He leaned forward, one hand planted on the wall next to her head, his body inches from hers. She could see the anger quivering through him, but he didn't do anything more than get in her space. "Girls like you end up bad places when they run off their mouths," he snarled. "Go ahead and cross O'Keefe. He'll take care of you. I just hope I'm there to see it happen."

One of his eyes was still ringed with bruises, and she could see the pink line of what would soon be a fresh scar on his jaw. Whatever Mrs. Wilson was having him do these days, it was rough for sure. Vivian tucked that thought into the back of her mind; she needed to remember that Hattie Wilson, for all they had reached something like an understanding, didn't mind dirty work if it got her what she wanted.

"Go meet with your boss, George," Vivian said, the fight and fury going out of her. She didn't relax—she'd let her guard down once that morning, and she wasn't about to make that mistake again. But she met his angry gaze without her usual challenge. "I'm not the problem you need to watch out for."

He looked her up and down. "We'll see about that," he said, stepping back. "You been nothing but trouble since you first crossed my path, and one of these days—" He broke off, mouth twisting. "One of these days," he said, more quietly, and this time Vivian knew it was a promise.

She shivered, but still made herself meet his eyes. "*Any* day, George," she said softly. "I'm not scared of you."

That made him chuckle. "Sure, girlie," he said. His hat had fallen to the ground in their scuffle; he swept it up, shook off the dirt, and settled it across his temples once more. "Keep telling yourself that."

Vivian stayed with her shoulders pressed against the wall for long minutes after he left, wanting to make sure he was really gone before she ventured into the sunlight once more. She could feel every one of her sleepless hours pressing down on her shoulders. But she needed to hurry. Florence was still waiting for her, and this breakfast would tell them what they needed to know about their father in more ways than one.

"What's wrong?" Florence asked as soon as Vivian slid into the seat next to her.

"Nothing," Vivian said quickly. When Florence gave her a skeptical look, she sighed. "Nothing that matters right now. Went to a client's house this morning and ran into a man who gave me the shivers." It was technically true.

Florence frowned. "Did he try to get fresh?"

Vivian couldn't help the short laugh that escaped her. "Nothing I can't handle," she said, which wasn't an answer, and Florence knew it. But before her sister could push further, Vivian asked, "Are you sure you're ready?"

Florence took a deep breath. "I think so. And anyway, I think we have to go through with it, now. Don't we?"

Vivian hesitated, glancing at the door to make sure their father hadn't appeared yet. They were still alone, but she dropped her voice anyway. "And Danny's on board?"

Florence nodded. Her fingers worried at her napkin, twisting it back and forth on the tabletop. "Can't say he likes it, but yes. He's on board."

"Can't say I blame him for being cautious," Vivian said, laying her hand on top of her sister's. Florence sighed and let go of the napkin. "Especially after Clyde showed up at the Nightingale last night." She closed her eyes. She could hardly believe it was only last night. Too much had happened since she served her father a cocktail and worried about how he was acting toward Danny.

Florence nodded. "Danny told me how he was."

"Well, whatever we find out, we'll be okay, right?" Vivian said. "We always are."

"We always are," Florence agreed softly. "And Danny will see what—"

"Shh," Vivian whispered. "That's him."

Florence's hand closed around hers, panic-tight. She took a deep breath, and both of them stood. "Whatever happens, Vivi, we've got each other, right?"

"We've got each other," Vivian repeated. Then she turned her smile toward Clyde Quinn, who had stopped in front of their table, hat in his hand as he stared at Florence. "Hey there, Clyde. Guessing that dopey smile on your face means you recognize Florence."

He swallowed hard, still staring. "You weren't even three years old last time I seen you," he whispered. One hand lifted as though he wanted to reach for her, but he hesitated. Vivian, remembering how he hadn't hesitated to embrace her at Ruth's house, frowned in surprise. But then she glanced at Florence and saw her sister's tense shoulders, the wide-eyed shock on her face as she stared at their father. "Never thought I'd lay eyes on you again. But I should have known you'd grow up to be as beautiful as your mother."

Florence just stared at him, still not speaking. Vivian glanced between them. "Let's sit down, maybe?" She gestured for a waitress to come over. "We can order some breakfast."

"Just coffee for me," Clyde said, his eyes still on Florence. "But you girls order whatever you like."

Vivian took him up on that; she never turned down a free meal. Florence was more cautious, which made Clyde chuckle. "I won't bite, baby girl," he said softly. "You don't need to be nervous."

"I'm not nervous," Florence said quickly. It was obviously a lie, and her red cheeks said she knew it. "I'm just . . ."

"I don't suppose you remember me?" Clyde asked, fidgeting with his hat. "I know kids that little don't remember much."

"I can't tell," Florence said, shaking her head. "I don't think I do, sorry. But you also . . ." Florence frowned. "I don't know. You sound familiar, Mr. Quinn."

"Clyde," he said, a little too quickly. He smiled nervously at her. "You should call me Clyde. And you sound familiar too. Like your mother."

"What was she like?" Florence asked. "I've got so few memories."

"She was the sweetest girl," Clyde said. He cleared his throat. "I brought pictures, actually, if you'd like to see?" He fumbled them out of his pocket. "Thought it might make this easier, you know. I'm sure you girls feel a little funny, meeting me. Guess you never expected to have a father."

It was more thoughtful than Vivian had expected him to be. And he looked more nervous than she expected, too, glancing between them as he asked about their life in the orphan home, their work as dressmakers.

"So it wasn't too awful a way to grow up," Clyde said. "I'm glad for that. But I still wish it hadn't happened."

Vivian didn't know what to say to that, and she was glad for the distraction of their breakfasts arriving. By that point, even she was feeling too jittery to eat much. But they still thanked the woman who brought their plates, and ate a few silent bites.

Beside her, Florence took a deep breath and set her fork down on her plate. "Will you tell us why?" she asked, looking at Clyde. Vivian stared at her sister, surprised by the direct question. She wasn't sure how long it would have taken her to work up the courage to ask. "What happened between you and our mother?"

Clyde frowned. "You mean, why did she leave?"

"I might remember only bits and pieces of her," Florence said, "but I know Mama was a good Catholic. It would have taken something particular for her to leave her husband."

Clyde's eyes narrowed as he looked from one of them to the other. "You girls been talking about this between yourselves?"

Vivian and Florence exchanged a look. "Can you blame us if we have?" Vivian asked. Under the table, she could feel Florence's knee shaking where it pressed against hers. "Wondering how we ended up orphans has kept us company for most of our lives."

She held her breath, waiting to see how he'd respond.

At last, the defensive look faded from Clyde's face. "I suppose that's fair enough," he said, staring into his coffee cup. "Don't feel good to say it, but I wasn't as good a husband as I could have been. I wasn't violent or nothing," he added quickly as the girls shared another look. "I'd never have laid a hand on her, God as my witness. But my family didn't approve. There were more of us than just me and Ruth then." He sighed. "It wasn't easy on her, and I didn't understand. I think . . ." He hesitated, not quite meeting their eyes. "I think my father might have paid her to disappear and to take you with her. He wouldn't admit it to the day he died, but he was a right bastard. And like you said, it would have taken a lot for her to leave." He shook his head. "I never forgave him for it. I looked for my girls, but I couldn't find any word about Florence or Mae." He smiled sadly, reaching out to tap Vivian's nose gently. "And I didn't even know if I should be looking for you."

Vivian knew all the reasons to be wary, to stop herself from expecting too much, but in that moment it didn't matter. She couldn't help smiling back at him. Out of the corner of her eye, she saw Florence blinking back tears.

"What happens now?" Vivian asked, trying not to sound too eager. "You're in New York, and so—" She broke off. She had been about to say *so are we,* but they still hadn't told him where Florence was living, and it wasn't Vivian's choice whether to give him that information or not. Beside her, she felt her sister stiffen, and she quickly cleared her throat, hoping Clyde would think it was emotion and not a slip of the tongue that had her choked up. "So where do we go from here?"

But Clyde glanced between the sisters and sighed. "I think where we go is that I tell you I already know."

Vivian and Florence exchanged a glance. "Already know what?" Florence asked. Vivian wished she hadn't sounded so wary. But they were both overwhelmed, and trying to hide what they were thinking was getting harder by the minute in the face of their father's cautious, hopeful affection.

Affection that was on full display as he smiled sadly at them. "I know about Florence's family. About the baby. About . . ." His mouth pulled to one side. "I know your husband's a Chinese fella, baby girl."

"Where did you hear something like that?" Vivian asked, trying not to give anything away. Under the table, Florence grabbed her hand and held it tightly.

"Ruth told me," Clyde said.

He said it with almost no emotion at all. Vivian didn't look at her sister, not sure what to do or say. Ruth had clearly been desperate to keep Clyde from finding out about their first visit to the house. Why would she have changed her mind and told him?

But Clyde was still watching them, waiting, and there was no point in denying it. Vivian didn't want to deny it anyway. That was Florence's family. *Her* family, now. And he was still there, sitting across from them. That had to count for something, didn't it?

Florence took a deep breath. "She doesn't approve, does she? Ruth, I mean."

Clyde was staring at his coffee again. "No," he said, his tone impossible to read.

The sisters glanced at each other, and Vivian was glad they were on the same side of the table, arrayed against him, for what she had to ask next. "What about you?"

His silence was painfully long. Vivian could feel Florence holding her breath.

"I never thought I'd see my daughter again," Clyde said at last, his eyes on the photographs scattered across the table. He ran his fingers over the image of his wedding day, their mother smiling next to him at the photographer's studio. Vivian couldn't decide if she wished she knew what he was thinking or if she was glad she didn't. "And since what's done is done, I won't make the same mistake my father made." His expression softened as he slid a photograph of Mae holding baby Florence toward himself. "Besides, I like babies real well."

Vivian let out her breath, squeezing Florence's hand even more tightly. It wasn't the answer they had hoped for, but it was better than it could have been.

"Maybe I could meet them sometime," Clyde added, looking up.

"You did," Florence said, glancing sideways at Vivian. "My husband, at least."

His gaze grew sharp. "Your boss at the bar, Vivian?"

"Yes," Vivian said, not quite hiding her nervousness. "He's a swell guy, you know. Sweet on Florence from the moment he laid eyes on her."

"If you say so," Clyde said reluctantly, glancing at Florence. "If he treats you good."

"Better than good," she said quietly. "The baby's a girl, by the way. We named her Mei. It's Chinese, but it's also—"

"After your mother," Clyde said. He took a deep breath. "She'd have liked that. And she'd have wanted me to meet my granddaughter, no matter who her father is." He hesitated, then slid the photographs across the table. "And she'd have wanted you to have these."

It was like being given a treasure. Vivian was almost scared to reach for them. "Are you sure?"

"Sure, I'm sure," Clyde said quietly. He stood, pulling a dollar and change from his wallet. "I have to get to work soon. But like I said, breakfast is on me, girls. You should stick around and finish yours." He dropped the money on the table, looking at each of them in turn. "I'm sure I'll see you again soon."

Vivian stared at the door as it swung closed behind him, feeling like she could suddenly breathe again now that he was gone. She didn't say anything for several minutes. Beside her, Florence silently gathered the photographs into a pile.

"Well?" Vivian said at last. "How much of that do you believe?"

"I want to believe it," Florence said. "I want to believe it so badly."

Vivian swallowed. "Me too," she whispered.

She could feel Florence's eyes on her. "But you don't?"

"Ruth was scared, that first time I met him. I've seen enough scared women in my life to recognize it," Vivian said, thinking of Bruiser George snarling in her face. She didn't want Clyde to be just one more man who liked to do his talking with his fists, but she'd met enough of them in her life that she couldn't shake her wariness. Not even for her father. "I want to know why."

"Well," Florence said, standing and tucking the photographs into her handbag, "we'll know soon enough. Come on, I have to get back to Mei. Unless you want to finish breakfast?"

Vivian glanced down at the plate in front of her. It felt wrong, to leave a meal someone else had paid for mostly untouched. But she couldn't have eaten another bite. She shook her head. "Let's go."

As they walked away from the restaurant, a lanky figure seemed to materialize beside them. Vivian jumped. "Holy Mother Mary, Lucky. Can't you give a girl any warning?"

Danny's cousin shrugged at her as he fell in step next to Florence. "Danny told me to stick close to his girl."

"His wife," Florence corrected him dryly. It had the sound of an exchange that had happened many times before.

"Sure, that's what I said," Lucky said. His eyes never stopped moving as they walked toward the subway.

"He doesn't want me going around the city alone right now," Florence said. "After what happened. And since he can't be here—"

"Makes sense," Vivian agreed. "I don't want you walking alone either."

"And what about you?" Florence pointed out. "Who's keeping an eye on you?"

"I keep an eye on myself," Vivian said, deliberately light. She didn't want her sister worrying about her. "And no reason to think I shouldn't."

Florence sighed. "But you'll come downtown after work today? So we can talk?"

"Yeah." They stopped outside the entrance to the subway, and Vivian gave her sister a quick hug. "And we'll see if Danny found out anything worth knowing." She looked at Lucky over Florence's shoulder. "Danny's not the only one counting on you."

"No pressure, I guess." He winked. Lucky never acted like anything was serious. But Danny wouldn't have trusted him if he didn't deserve it, and that was enough for Vivian to trust him, too. "See you around, Viv."

Vivian watched her sister disappear into the dark, and she tried not to look over her shoulder as she turned her own steps toward work. She managed to keep facing forward for all of half a minute before she gave in and glanced behind her. Two blocks later, she did it again, relieved not to see any of the same faces but knowing that feeling would be short-lived.

Vivian made it another two blocks before she gave in once more. She still had the remains of that five-dollar tip from Hattie Wilson in her pocket. There were smarter ways to spend it, but better a month of coffee for dinner than ending up . . .

Vivian pushed the image of Spence's home from her mind. She raised her hand and hailed a cab.

No matter what face she put on it, for Florence or anyone else, she couldn't stop thinking of Spence, or the dangerous game she and Leo were jumping into. But she didn't want to back out. Hattie Wilson, to her surprise, had said it best: she had her own family to look after.

Any girl with a spine would risk a lot to keep her family safe.

There were only two deliveries that day. Normally, Vivian would have regretted the lost income, but she felt only relief as she staggered home and up the stairs, worn out from too little sleep and too many fears. She'd pack a bag, then head downtown to meet Florence, who wouldn't complain if her little sister just wanted to crawl into bed and be unconscious until she had to rouse herself for her shift at the Nightingale—

Vivian's thoughts stopped as though they had slammed into a brick wall, and her steps slowed as she reached the top of the stairs. She wouldn't be working a shift at the Nightingale. No one would. Honor was closing her doors, for the first time Vivian had ever heard of. What would happen when folks showed up, ready to sneak down the alley and whisper their password, only to see that the flickering light was out, and no one was there to open the door?

Would they think the place had been shut down by the cops? Would they ever risk coming back?

Honor would be okay if the Nightingale closed for good—mad as hell, but okay. She had plenty of money now. But what about the rest of them?

Vivian realized she was staring down the hall at her own door. She rubbed her hands over her face, trying to wake herself up. Honor would have thought of all that. She'd have a plan in place. And if she didn't, she'd figure one out. There was no sense worrying about how many customers the Nightingale would lose. Not when there were so many other things to be worried about.

Vivian fished her keys out of her pocket. A few changes of clothing. That was all she needed. She had to get a move on.

Her key turned too easily in the lock. It took her half a heartbeat too long to realize what that meant. The door was already swinging open when she tried to grab it, knowing that someone was waiting for her on the other side. But she was too slow to stop it.

It was only one room, so there was nowhere for him to hide.

TWENTY-THREE

Vivian stared. "Clyde?" she demanded at last, her voice coming out in a squeak. She cleared her throat, pulling the door closed but not quite shut behind her. She'd had enough unexpected visitors in the past to be wary of closing it all the way. And if someone had messed with the lock, she didn't want to risk it getting jammed behind her. "What the hell are you doing here?"

He had been pacing around the table, but turned toward her quickly. "Lord almighty, you've got quiet feet," he said, laughing awkwardly. "Now, I ask, is that any way to greet your pop?" He smiled as he said it, but there was something unconvincing about his cheerfulness.

Vivian didn't move from her place by the door. "It is when you turn up at my place uninvited," she said, watching him carefully. "And without me ever telling you where I live."

His lips pressed together, a look that walked the edge between anger and irritation. Then he sighed and took his hat off. "Caught me, then," he said, shaking his head as he sat down at the table. He looked relaxed enough that Vivian's shoulders lowered, but only an inch. "All right, I'll come clean. I followed you when you left the Nightingale last night."

Vivian stared at him. She hadn't gone home last night. Had she? She rubbed her eyes, her brain feeling too fuzzy. "You did what?"

"I was worried about you, waltzing around the city like that by yourself," he said earnestly. "Haven't I got a right to be?"

"So it's your job to look out for me?"

"Well, I'm your dad, aren't I?" he asked, a defensive note creeping into his voice. "And there you were, standing behind the bar at a juice joint like it was nothing in the world. I never thought a daughter of mine would get mixed up in . . ." He waved one hand through the air. "All that sort of thing."

"It's not your business what I'm mixed up in," Vivian said, trying to piece through what he might have seen or heard if he had followed her. "I don't need you to worry over me."

He shook his head, the earnest look back. "Clearly you do," he said. He stood, reaching out to take her hands in his before she could stop him. His were like bear paws, and she stiffened, but he only drew her into the room and to a chair. When she sat, he did as well, leaning toward her. "You're mixed up in something, Vivian, it doesn't take a genius to figure that out. But whatever it is, you don't need to handle it alone. You come home with me, all right? Ruth won't mind. You lay low for a bit, until it all blows over, whatever it is."

She wanted to be touched at his concern, to believe in the life—the care—that he was offering. To believe that if she threw her arms around him, he would want her and hold her and keep her safe. But she had spent most of her life learning that if what you wanted came too easy, you couldn't trust it.

She hadn't gone home last night. And if he'd followed her like he said, he'd have known that. So however he had found out where she lived, it couldn't be good news.

She had to get out of there.

"If you're so concerned, why wait until now?" she asked, hoping she sounded more puzzled than wary. She didn't want him to know what she was thinking. Not yet. "Why not say something this morning?"

"I didn't want to mention it in front of your sister. She's got a new baby and all; it'd be cruel to make her worry. And"—Clyde's smile was the kind that invited her into the joke with him—"she seemed like the sort of girl who might fall to pieces at that sort of news."

Vivian could have told him that Florence was far less fragile than she seemed. That people often underestimated quiet girls like her; there had been a time when Vivian herself had, too.

Instead she asked, "Okay, so you knew which building was mine, but how did you get in?" She waved her hand at the door. "And how did you even know where to wait?"

He was still smiling. "You've got some good neighbors around here, for all it's a dank sort of place to live. That nice woman, Mrs. Thomas? She pointed me in the right direction. And you must have left your door unlocked when you went to work this morning." He shook his head at her. "You need to be more careful; that could get you in trouble if it was anyone other than your father coming around."

By the time he finished speaking, every hair was standing up on the back of Vivian's neck, and she could feel her palms growing clammy.

Not just because no one who had ever met Mrs. Thomas would describe her as a nice woman—she was angry, tired, and sour. But because Mrs. Thomas had once done exactly what Clyde described, pointing the way to Vivian's home when a well-dressed man showed up asking where she lived, making the easy assumption that Vivian was trading her company for his money. That night had ended with someone dead, and it had nearly been Vivian.

Mrs. Thomas wouldn't have made that same mistake twice. And after that night, Vivian had never forgotten to lock her door.

She knew for certain that she hadn't forgotten this time, either.

The man sitting in front of her wasn't just a liar. He was a criminal.

Vivian wanted to bolt for the stairs, but she didn't know if she could make it. She wished she had her gun, but that was still with Danny. She wished she could believe the earnest smile on her father's face, but she knew that ship had sailed and was never coming back.

"Well, good thing it was just you then," she said, giving a laugh that came out shakier than she wanted as she stood up. He was bigger than she was, but was he faster? If she could keep talking like everything was normal, maybe she could make it to the door before him. "It's nice of you to be so worried, but I'm really not mixed up in anything—"

"Don't be like that," he said, standing too. His tone hadn't changed, but she didn't miss that he was slowly moving between her and the door. "Don't be reckless. A father's got a right to be concerned. Those places can be dangerous, and I don't want anything to happen to you."

"Oh, don't worry, I don't want anything to happen to me either," Vivian said cheerfully. "In fact—"

She bolted for the door. But he got there first, his outstretched arm cutting across her path as he pushed it firmly closed.

Vivian could feel the rapid beat of her pulse, the shaky drag of breath in and out of her lungs, as she stared up at him. "Those places can get dangerous, huh?" she asked. "Guess you know something about that."

"I said don't be like that, Vivian." He sounded like he was scolding a child. "I told you I'm trying to look out for you. You don't have to make this difficult."

"Yeah?" Vivian took a careful step back into the room, away from the door. She kept her weight balanced under her, feet firmly planted on the floor with each step. She didn't take her eyes from her father. She needed to get him away from the door. "Ask anyone who knows me, Clyde. They'll tell you I'm a difficult bird all the way through. Guessing I got that from you."

His head turned to follow her progress. "Might have been better for you if you hadn't," he said. Vivian took another step away from him. "But you come with me easylike, baby girl, and there won't need to be any trouble." He dropped his arm as he stepped away from the door and walked toward her.

"Thanks, but—"

He moved faster than she expected. Vivian tried to get past him, but Clyde grabbed her arm, hauling her toward him. Vivian balled her hand into a fist, just like Leo had told her—was it only a few days before?—and slammed it into his face.

He bellowed with pain, and she gasped at the shock of the impact. He shoved her away, and she stumbled, catching herself against the table. When Vivian staggered back to her feet, her fist cradled against her chest, he was wiping blood from his nose and lip, looking stunned. But he was still between her and the door.

Clyde stared at her, his chest heaving. "Can't say I liked that," he growled, stalking toward her and grabbing her arm.

"Can't say I like any of this."

The words crashed through the air like a rock thrown through a window. Clyde spun around. His grip on Vivian didn't loosen, but she felt a grim satisfaction at his shock as he stared at the doorway where her sister stood, her eyes blazing with rage.

"But here we seem to be," Florence said. In her hand was a familiar short-barreled revolver, and it didn't shake as she lifted it to point at her father. "Let her go."

"You don't know what you're getting involved in," Clyde said sternly. Vivian could see the tight lines of anger around his mouth and eyes, could feel it in the fingers gripping her arm. "Be a smart girl and put that beanshooter down."

"No." No argument, no reasoning with him. Just no. Florence didn't waver.

"Look, you're making a big mess out of nothing." He stretched his lips into a smile. "Like I said to Vivian, a father's got a right to be concerned about his daughters."

"Doesn't look like she appreciates your concern," Florence snapped. "I'm guessing our mother didn't either, and maybe that had more to do with her running away than whatever your folks might have thought of her. Am I right?"

That struck a nerve; Clyde's grip on Vivian's arm grew tighter, and she winced in pain. Seeing that, Florence raised the gun another inch, and the click of the hammer was loud in the room. "Let her go."

Clyde shook his head. "You know, I'm not sure I buy that you're the ruthless one in the pair."

"Vivian's never killed a man before, *Dad*." Florence spat the word out like it was poison. "I have."

"Really?" he said, his surprise plain.

"Really," Florence said coldly. "Let her go, or I up that number to two."

His jaw tightened; then, to Vivian's surprise, he chuckled. "All right, all right. I know when to call it quits. For now." He dropped Vivian's arm and smiled. "I knew one of you had to take after me," he said, sounding almost pleased.

"She's nothing like you," Vivian snapped, pushing him away. He didn't fight or protest, just held up his hands and stepped back.

"Like enough," Florence said, moving out of the doorway and gesturing for him to go through it. She never took her eyes off him, and the gun never wavered. "Now get out."

His hat had fallen to the floor in the scuffle, and he bent to scoop it up, brushing off the brim as casually if there wasn't a gun pointed straight at him. He stopped just in the doorframe, though, and looked at them with a sad smile on his face. "I'd hoped it would go better than this, girls. I hope it still can. But business is business." He shook his head. "No getting around it sometimes. I'm sure I'll see you soon."

He wiped another trickle of blood from his lip and strolled away. Florence slammed the door shut and threw the locks with one hand. Vivian could see her sister shaking, but Florence slowly, carefully, de-cocked the hammer on the revolver. Then she sank to the floor and shoved it away from her. It skidded across the wood as Florence wrapped her arms around herself and put her head on her knees.

Vivian wanted to go to her, but she went to the window instead and waited. She hadn't counted to thirty before Clyde appeared on the street. He stood there for a moment, shoulders slumped and head bowed. Maybe he was regretting what had happened, or maybe his jaw just hurt. Vivian clenched her teeth together against the tears that wanted to come. She wouldn't cry over him. He didn't deserve it.

A moment later he straightened up. It only took a few steps until he was out of her sight.

Vivian staggered away from the window, the adrenaline suddenly going out of her. "Flo." Her legs didn't want to hold her up. She dropped down next to her sister. Her hand still throbbed, but that didn't stop her from pulling Florence into her arms. "Where the hell did you come from?"

Florence shuddered, and Vivian could feel tears against her neck. "Came to get you," she said, her voice muffled. "Pack a bag, Vivi. You're coming downtown with us."

"Danny got the scoop, then?" Vivian asked, dreading the answer.

Florence nodded as she sat up. Her eyes were red, but her voice was steady. "Pack a bag," she said again. "We're not hanging around here anymore."

Vivian didn't argue. She retrieved the gun and tucked it into the pocket of her coat. Then she grabbed Florence's hands and hauled them both to their feet. There would be time to fall to pieces later. For now, Florence was right. They couldn't afford to hang around.

Vivian squeezed her sister's hand. "Don't know what I'd do without you, Flo," she whispered.

Florence shuddered again. "Let's hurry."

Danny and Lucky were waiting for them around the corner in a gleaming Duesenberg, Lucky in the driver's seat. Florence climbed into the back, where Danny waited for her.

"Hop in, Viv," Lucky said impatiently. "Bad idea to wait around."

"How the hell did you afford this?" Vivian demanded, climbing into the front seat.

Lucky chuckled. "Borrowed it from a friend."

Vivian might have asked more, but she caught the lift of Lucky's eyebrows, the warning look in his eyes. More questions would be a bad idea, he was telling her. "Hell of a friend," she muttered, leaning back against the seat as the car pulled away from the curb.

"You okay?" Danny asked. Vivian twisted around in her seat and saw him looking Florence up and down as he pulled her into his arms. He knew something was wrong.

"We're fine," Florence said. She glanced at Vivian. "Clyde was there."

Danny swore. "I knew I shouldn't have stayed behind. What happened? Did he—"

"We're fine," Florence said again. "I think it would have gotten messy if you'd been there. He was trying . . ."

"He wanted me to go somewhere with him," Vivian said quietly. "And he didn't seem like he'd take no for an answer until Florence showed up. What did you find out, Danny? Did . . ."

Danny had suggested, back when Florence first agreed to meet their father, that he try to find out more about Clyde while he was busy with Vivian and Florence. Vivian had thought it was a risky plan, and she hadn't liked it, but she hadn't argued. Neither had Florence. They might have both longed for a father, but they knew better than to take anyone at face value—especially someone whose own sister watched him with wide, scared eyes. Someone whose sister tried to tell them he wasn't even alive.

"Did Ruth agree to talk to you?" Vivian made herself ask. "What did she say?"

"If you wait, she'll tell you herself," Danny replied, wrapping one arm around Florence's shoulders while she slumped against him. "She's at the restaurant now."

"She's that scared of him?" Vivian asked, her voice catching. She had been trying, in spite of everything, to hold on to her dream of a family, to think that maybe it was all a misunderstanding. But if Ruth was unwilling to stay in her own home after talking to Danny . . .

"Him," Danny said grimly. "But even more than that, his boss. She'd been feeling safe for a few years, she said. Thought she didn't have to worry anymore. Because until recently, they'd been out of New York."

Vivian felt herself go cold all over. "Where?" she whispered.

Danny met her eyes. "Chicago."

A feeling like ice and lead settled into Vivian's stomach. "What . . ." She couldn't bring herself to finish. Not yet.

"Wait 'til we get back to the restaurant," Danny said, kissing the top of Florence's head as he held her close. "There's more to it than I can tell you."

Vivian didn't ask any more questions as they headed downtown. She needed all that time to steel herself for the answers she knew were coming.

TWENTY-FOUR

It was a strange, tense gathering in the Chins' sitting room.

The restaurant was open this time of day, though not crowded; they came in through the kitchen and made their way upstairs, Danny and Florence first, followed by Vivian and Lucky a few minutes later, Vivian with a hastily assembled cold compress on her bruised and swollen hand. Danny's father, busy with customers, nodded gravely to them as they went past but didn't give them much attention. Vivian suspected that he was hoping the diners wouldn't pay much attention either.

Upstairs, Danny's mother sat with Ruth Quinn, making polite conversation while she rocked a droopy-eyed Mei on her lap. Ruth sat in a stiff-backed chair, sipping tea and staring openly around the room. She didn't look happy, but Vivian decided to give her the benefit of the doubt. Maybe it was because of why she was there, not where she was.

Ruth shot to her feet when she saw them. "Girls . . ." But she didn't seem to know what to say after that.

"Aunt Ruth," Florence said, not very warmly. She went to her mother-in-law, who handed over the baby. "She's still awake?"

"Just barely," Mrs. Chin said, standing. Mei yawned, grumbling and squirming into a more comfortable position against Florence's chest. Mrs. Chin smoothed back the baby's tufty hair, smiling, then gestured to the couch she had been sitting on. "You take my spot. I need to get back downstairs."

"You're not staying?" Danny asked. He went to the window and pulled the curtain aside, only a few inches, to glance outside. Vivian knew he was making sure they hadn't been followed. She tried not to picture her father's face as Florence pointed a gun at him.

Mrs. Chin was shaking her head. "You'll tell me what I need to know. But as for the rest of it . . ." She gave her son an unhappy look. "I'd rather not know more than I have to."

"Usually a good call, Auntie," Lucky put in.

She frowned at him but didn't argue. "Miss Quinn. It was a pleasure to meet you."

"Oh!" Ruth jumped a little at being addressed. "Thank you, yes, a pleasure to meet you too. Thank you for the . . ." She glanced down at her cup. "For the tea?"

Lucky muttered something under his breath, and it didn't sound complimentary. Mrs. Chin smacked the back of his head without looking at him as she left the room.

Another awkward silence fell. There were more teacups on the tray, but no one else seemed inclined to take one. Vivian settled on the floor by the window. Lucky lounged against the wall by the door, arms crossed over his chest.

"You sticking around?" Vivian asked, surprised. He normally wasn't interested in anything to do with the Nightingale. But nothing much had felt normal the past few days.

"In case you need me," Lucky said, shrugging. "If Danny wants."

"I do," Danny said before turning to Ruth. "Miss Quinn, thank you again for . . ." He trailed off, as uncertain as she had been what he wanted to say. He shrugged. "For coming."

She nodded, both hands wrapped around her teacup and her eyes fixed on her lap. "The girls should know," she said softly. Her eyes slid sideways until they found Vivian's. "I'm sorry I told you he was dead."

"Why did you?" Vivian asked.

Beside Danny, Florence made a small, pained sound, her arms curling protectively around Mei. But she didn't leave. As bad as knowing was, being in the dark would be worse.

Ruth sank into her chair. She didn't hunch, but she seemed to draw in on herself, and she chewed nervously on her lip. "I didn't know what else to do. If you knew he was alive, you'd want to know him."

"Tell us," Vivian said, her hands clenched into tight fists in her lap. She could guess that, however angry and heartbroken she was feeling now, it was about to get worse. "We have a right to know."

Ruth tapped her fingers nervously against the teacup as she tried to decide where to begin. "Clyde's always been involved in . . . unsavory things," she said at last. "Illegal things. He got a taste for it when he was younger, and, well." She looked around the room at everyone watching her, turned bright red, and fixed her eyes back on her hands.

Vivian wondered how long it had been since Ruth Quinn had an entire room full of people listening to what she had to say. Maybe it had never happened before.

"I don't know what our parents knew. I mostly just tried to stay out of his business, especially after our parents died. But Mae—" This time she looked at Florence, then Vivian. "Your mother didn't like it."

"Is that the real reason she left, then?" Vivian asked, meeting her sister's eyes for a moment before turning back to Ruth. "She didn't like what he was involved in?"

Ruth nodded, looking miserable. "They married so quick, I don't think she had any idea until Florence was already on the way. But she hated it. She kept asking him to give it up, to settle down in a respectable job, especially when some of his . . . his associates would come around. They were not nice men. And Clyde would tell her that he was done, that he'd give it up, but he never changed." She set the teacup aside and laced her fingers together. "When she found out another baby was on the way, I think she decided that was enough. We woke up one morning and she was gone."

"What about her family?" Florence asked, sitting forward.

"She didn't have much in the way of family of her own," Ruth said quietly. "Even if she had, she wouldn't have gone back to them. My brother looked there first for her."

"Did you help her leave?" Vivian demanded.

Ruth looked down again. "I hope I would have, if she had asked. But I didn't know she was planning to leave until she was already gone. That was a kindness on her part; Clyde could tell I was just as shocked as he was, so he never got rough with me over it. But I hope I would have helped."

"What did he do?" Florence whispered. Danny's arm tightened around her again.

"He looked for her," Ruth said, lifting her hands helplessly. "Whatever else I could say about him, he loved your mother something crazy. But when he couldn't find a trace, eventually he gave up." She gave them a tremulous smile. "I didn't, though."

"It was you, then?" Vivian demanded. Behind her, she heard Florence shift forward in her seat. "You're the reason she wasn't buried on Hart Island."

Ruth nodded. "It was pure luck. I'd check, every few months, for unclaimed bodies that matched her description. I was always afraid that . . . And then one day, there she was." She sniffed and gave her eyes a quick wipe. "I couldn't let her end up in a pauper's grave. But I had to do it quickly and secretly. I was terrified my brother would find out."

"Where is she?" Florence asked, her voice catching.

"Calvary Cemetery," Ruth said quietly. "In the Saint Agnes section."

Vivian swallowed back a sob. She'd think about her mother later. Right now, there were other things to worry about. "So you lied to us, and told us that he was dead, because you thought our mother wouldn't want us to know him?"

"I lied to you because I didn't want you to get hurt," Ruth said, starting to sound a little desperate. "If you'd found me when I first wrote that letter, I would have told you something different. Maybe I would have told you everything. Because you deserve to know, of course you do, and he wasn't here anymore, so what would it have mattered? But then he came back to New York, and I—and he—" She was wringing her hands and looking between them as though hoping someone else would tell her what to say.

Ruth fell silent as Lucky stepped away from the doorway—Vivian had almost forgotten that he was there—and watched him with nervous eyes. But he only refilled her teacup and handed it to her. Ruth took it, looking grateful. He poured cups for the others too—except Florence, who shook her head, her arms full of the dozing Mei—and handed them around.

"Hot drinks are good for hard talks," he said, shrugging in response to Vivian's surprised look, as he took up his post by the door again.

"Pretty sure you got that from Auntie," she said. Her smile as she said it felt forced, but she was still glad for the momentary distraction. She took a drink of tea. The warmth of it did help a little.

"Ma's a smart lady," Danny said, bending forward to kiss his daughter's forehead. Then he nodded at Ruth. "You okay to keep going?"

She nodded, both hands wrapped around the teacup, her shoulders rigid as she perched on the edge of her chair. She looked like a bird ready to flee at the slightest sign of movement, but her voice sounded a little stronger as she spoke. "A few years ago, Clyde started working for someone new. I don't think he'd been more than a petty criminal before that, but this man was . . ." Vivian could see the shudder that trembled through Ruth's shoulders. She took a drink of tea, then stared into the cup instead of meeting anyone's eyes. "He was a real businessman, for all he was a criminal one. And ruthless. He'd punish the people who worked for him as fiercely as his enemies. Clyde would never say his name, and I knew better than to ask. But the few times he came around . . ."

"What did he look like?" Vivian demanded, sitting forward. Her nerves felt like a plucked string on a bass, vibrating almost too low to hear. "Maybe tall, dark red hair? Handsome, if he didn't have a smashed-up nose? Scar through his eyebrow right about here?" She traced a line on her own face.

Ruth's eyes were wide as she watched the progress of Vivian's finger. "You know him, then. Do you know his name?"

"Harlan O'Keefe," Vivian said quietly, hoping that Ruth was telling them the truth—hoping that, after everything, she could at least trust her aunt. She looked at Danny. "Unless he uses a different one sometimes?"

He shook his head. "Hux said he's pretty proud of his reputation. Wants everyone to know he's coming for them."

"Coming for them," Ruth said, her eyes dropping to the cup in her hands. She took a drink and a steadying breath. "That sounds about right. But they left for Chicago a few years back. Clyde said there was better business there."

"Bootlegging," Lucky put in, as the others nodded. "Running liquor from Canada. Lot of money to be made."

"You sound like you know," Ruth said.

Lucky shrugged. "Doesn't everyone? But it's not my line of work, if that's what you're wondering."

"I don't suppose you know what he did for O'Keefe?" Danny put in.

Ruth shook her head emphatically. "I never even wanted to ask. I think . . . I think he was high up. His boss came by, more than once, before they left New York." She shivered. "I always tried to make myself scarce when that happened."

Something cold and heavy settled in Vivian's stomach, the icy feeling of a suspicion that she didn't want to have. She tried to push it from her mind.

"When they left, it seemed like it would be for good," Ruth continued. "I was so relieved. I thought that was the end of it all. But then Clyde came back, just showed up on my doorstep. And then you showed up, girls, and . . ."

"And you told us he was dead," Vivian said, wishing she was sitting with her sister. But Florence was cuddled up against Danny for comfort. Vivian felt a pang of loneliness, though she pushed it down. There were more important things to think about right now. "And you tried your best to send us away."

"You kept looking out the window that day," Florence added. "You were nervous he was going to come back and find us there, weren't you?"

Their aunt nodded, looking miserable. "I'm sorry. I'd have liked to know you. Your mother and I didn't have much in common, but she . . ." Ruth shrugged helplessly. "She was kind. And funny. And brave, to take her babies and run. It's more than I ever had the courage to do. I just settled for hoping that Clyde never got on anyone's bad side. I kept my head down and kept going as best I could."

"That's its own kind of courage," Vivian said quietly. "Sometimes, just managing to survive is a victory."

Ruth nodded, though she didn't look any less miserable as she stared into her now-empty teacup. "I just wish I knew why he came back to New York," she whispered. "Maybe then we could figure out how to make him leave."

"His boss is looking for someone," Danny said. "Someone named Hugh Brown. That name mean anything to you?"

Ruth shook her head. "No. No, not at all. I never tried to learn any of their names. I never wanted to know anything."

Danny growled in frustration. "If we could track down the guy, we might be able to get rid of O'Keefe." He turned his worried eyes toward Florence. "But until O'Keefe goes, I don't know how we get you and Viv away from your pop. And I think he's made it pretty clear he wants something. From Vivian, at least."

"But what?" Florence demanded. "Where was he going to take her?"

"What are you talking about?" Ruth demanded.

"To O'Keefe," Lucky put in. "He knows she works at the Nightingale now. Bet you anything he was going to take her to his boss. Get some leverage."

"We're not placing *bets,* Lucky," Florence snapped.

They were all talking over each other by now, Ruth still nervously trying to get someone to explain what had happened, Lucky and Florence sniping at each other, while Danny tried to calm everyone down. The noise woke Mei up, and she began fussing loudly.

Vivian wanted to press her hands over her ears to shut it all out. She wanted to run away. She wanted to tell them all that she knew exactly who Hugh Brown was. Any girl with a spine would do whatever it took to protect the people she cared about, wouldn't she?

Vivian clenched her jaw together, staring at the floorboards beneath her. She cared about Leo, too. And she didn't want to give him up, even to keep the rest of them safe.

"We can't do anything now." Danny's voice cut through the noise. "Hux is figuring it out, and we know to keep Florence and Vivian away from their pop. So for now, the best thing to do is keep our heads down, all right?"

"What about her?" Lucky asked, tipping his chin toward Ruth. "You send her home, there's no telling what she might spill to him."

"I wouldn't," Ruth insisted.

Danny and Lucky exchanged a glance, but it was Florence who spoke up. She was settling Mei at her breast to nurse, but she was watching Ruth, and there was nothing gentle about the look. "You lied to us before, Miss Quinn. You might have had your reasons, but that doesn't mean you won't do it again."

Ruth flinched. Vivian wondered if she should tell her sister to be kinder, that it wasn't Ruth's fault—any more than it was theirs—that their father was a criminal. But there was an icy feeling spreading through her chest and limbs, leaving her numb and focused in its wake. She had too many people to worry about already; she couldn't afford to add Ruth to that list.

Ruth shrank back into her chair. But to Vivian's surprise, her jaw was set. "I should stay, shouldn't I?" she said. "I know what kind of man he is. I'm tired of being scared."

The room was silent except for Mei murmuring and grumbling as she shifted in Florence's arms.

Danny cleared his throat at last. "Until we know more, all of you should stay here."

"Is that safe for us?" Vivian asked. "And for you?"

"Safe as anywhere else, and probably more than most places," Lucky said. When Vivian looked at him, he was examining his nails with studied casualness; he shrugged without quite meeting any of their eyes. "I've had a few pals keeping an eye on the place, ever since the break-in."

The careful way he said it—like it wasn't a big deal, like they shouldn't ask any more questions—told Vivian exactly what he meant. His friends were from one of the local tongs, the occasionally criminal societies that had parceled out the Chinese neighborhoods between them.

"You paying for protection, Lucky?" Vivian asked. "Or . . ." She trailed off, not quite wanting to say it out loud.

Every neighborhood had its gangs and crooks, petty or otherwise. This one was no different. Vivian just hadn't known Lucky was involved with them. But no one else looked surprised; Florence was even avoiding her eyes. Apparently, Vivian wasn't the only sister who could keep secrets.

"We look after our own here, same as anywhere in this city," Lucky said firmly. "Right now, that includes all of you." He looked around at the assembled company, most of whom weren't Chinese, and shook his head. "I didn't tell them that part. But I doubt O'Keefe wants to start that kind of fight if he doesn't have to. Or if he does, it'll at least take him a while to figure out the best way to do it."

"And I guess someone might owe your friends at the end of this?" Vivian asked.

"That might be the way it goes." Lucky shrugged. "But let's hope things stay quiet, so no one needs to owe anyone anything."

"Amen," Florence said fervently. She shook her head at Vivian as she stood. "And to think I used to complain when you'd leave me in the dark. I'm putting the baby down."

The Chins paid for a telephone line in the restaurant—not just for themselves, but for other families in the neighborhood to use. But it wasn't until after dinner that Vivian was able to sneak downstairs and duck behind the wooden privacy screen to use it.

She held her breath, waiting for the line to connect. What if Leo hadn't made it home safe after all?

"Hello?"

The wary voice at the other end made her sag against the wall in relief. "It's Vivian," she whispered, cupping her hand around her mouth to muffle the sound even further. "You okay?"

His sigh echoed in her ear. "I'm fine. Frustrated and jumpy as hell, but fine. Nothing from the coroner's office today, but Norris is going to keep his eyes open. What about you?"

Vivian closed her eyes. How was she supposed to answer that question?

"Viv?" Leo asked, a worried note entering his voice. "You still there?"

"Mrs. Wilson's going to see what she can find," she whispered at last. "We just have to wait. But . . ."

His voice was soft. "What happened?"

She could feel the dread in her stomach like ice. But the thought was in her head. She had to ask. "Leo, what was the name of . . ." She hesitated, knowing there might be an operator on the line listening to what they were saying. "Our redheaded friend's deputy? The one from the bank job?"

"Why?"

"Please just tell me," Vivian whispered. "What was his name?"

There was silence from the other end of the line. Vivian could feel her heart racing. "I never heard him use his first name," Leo said at last. "Everyone called him Mr. Quinn."

Vivian felt light-headed. If the cord had been long enough to allow it, she would have slid to the floor. Instead, she closed her eyes and leaned her forehead against the wall.

"Why?" Leo asked.

"Because he's my dad," Vivian whispered. "My dad was the one who set you up. And he's the one who brought them back to New York to look for you."

Another stretch of silence. Vivian squeezed her eyes shut, trying to hold off the tears that were pricking the backs of her eyelids. She wouldn't cry over Clyde Quinn. He was a stranger to her. He was a liar and a criminal. He didn't deserve it.

"Sounds like you got a few things to tell me," Leo said at last.

When Vivian finally stepped out from behind the screen, her hands were shaking. She wanted to curl up in a ball and sleep, to forget everything that had happened in the last day. She wanted to get into a fight. She wanted to cry.

The last thing she wanted was to find Danny waiting for her, arms crossed while he leaned against the wall with a casualness that didn't fool her for a moment. "What's going on, Viv?"

She stared back at him, chin lifted. "What do you mean?"

His eyes flicked toward the screen that hid the telephone, then back to her. "Who were you calling?"

She considered lying. But this was Danny; she didn't want to do that to him. "Leo."

That made his brows climb in surprise. "Why? What happened?"

She wouldn't lie to him. But she didn't have to tell him, either. "Nothing you need to worry about."

"We both know that's not true," he said softly.

"Nothing I need to share yet, then," she said. "Please don't ask for more right now, Danny."

She could practically see the thoughts flickering behind his eyes. "Viv, I don't like the idea of you keeping secrets right now."

"I don't like it much either," she said, wishing she could give him another answer. But Danny had a family, and she knew he'd do whatever was necessary to take care of them. She couldn't tell him. Not yet. "But we're both going to have to live with it for now."

"Viv—" He sighed and shook his head. "Come on. Florence set up a bed for you in our room. It's going to be a little crowded here tonight."

Vivian followed him back upstairs, but she could feel his unhappiness like another presence in the room. It jumbled up with her own fear, the memories she was trying not to think about, until she was lying on the floor of Danny and Florence's room, staring at the ceiling and feeling like she would suffocate in the darkness.

She told herself there was nothing she could do until morning. She told herself that she was safe, at least for tonight, at least as safe as she could be for now. But as soon as she closed her eyes, she saw her father's face as he stood, hand outstretched, between her and the door. She saw the mix of anger and heartbreak on Florence's face as she held the gun pointed at him. She saw the blood on Spence's floor.

Vivian tossed off the blanket, breathing heavily. She wanted the ice back, wanted to feel cold and numb again. But everything inside her now was heat and rage and fear, and if she didn't move, she was going to scream.

She rolled onto her knees, feeling in the darkness for her coat. The revolver was under her pillow once more; she slid it into the pocket and felt for her shoes. She didn't put them on, though, just held them in her hand as she crept toward the door.

"Don't."

The quiet voice nearly made Vivian jump out of her skin. When she turned around, she could just barely see the shadow sitting up in bed.

"Where are you going?" Florence whispered. Beside her, another shadow; Danny was awake and sitting up too, but he didn't say anything.

Vivian couldn't see her sister's face. "Out. I need to . . ." She swallowed. How could she explain to Florence, who had Danny there to keep her fear at bay? "I just need to go out."

"To see Leo?" Danny asked.

"No," Vivian said quickly. Leo's anger had been like a physical touch, even over the telephone line. She couldn't blame him for that, but she couldn't face it either. And Florence . . . Florence had made it clear that Clyde Quinn, and maybe his sister too, meant nothing to her now. She couldn't talk to either of them about the messy, ugly feelings that were burning in her chest. She needed someone else.

A pause. "Going to her, then."

"Yes," Vivian whispered.

"Who?" Florence demanded. Mei murmured in her sleep, and all of them fell silent for a moment, waiting to see if she would wake. But she only rolled over and sighed.

"Here." There was a shuffling sound, the clink of metal. Vivian could see Danny standing and holding out his hand. "You'll need these so you can lock up downstairs and let yourself back in." When Vivian reached for him, he fumbled a little, and then she felt cool metal in her palm. It was a set of keys. "And give her a call first," Danny added.

"She's at the Nightingale, but with all the heat right now, you don't want to risk catching her by surprise."

"I thought you'd tell me not to go," Vivian whispered.

She could hear the unhappiness in his voice as he answered. "My first responsibility is my family now. But that doesn't mean I want to leave Honor in the dark."

"Your boss?" Florence asked, confusion plain in her voice. "Now, of all times—" She broke off.

Vivian wondered what signal Danny had given her, how much Florence knew or guessed. She swallowed again. "I'll be back . . . sometime. Soon. I promise."

"Vivi." Florence's voice cracked. "Stay here. Please. Don't make any stupid decisions."

Vivian couldn't help herself. She laughed, though the sound came out as barely more than a gasp. "Haven't you noticed, Flo? I don't make any other kind." She folded her hand around the keys, feeling them bite into her palm. She wanted to say something else, wanted to explain. She wanted to have Florence all to herself again. She turned toward the door. "Soon," she said again. The words came out choked and painful. "I promise."

She tiptoed through the parlor, past Ruth sleeping on the couch, shoes in hand. When she got downstairs, Lucky was sitting up, spinning the chamber of a revolver around with a casualness that made Vivian shiver. He looked up in surprise when she arrived at the bottom of the stairs. "Going somewhere?"

Vivian sat down across from him to pull on her shoes. She nodded, not trusting herself to speak. Lucky watched her, then shrugged and stood up. "I'll tell my boys outside to whistle you up a cab."

"Thanks," Vivian whispered. "I need to make a call first."

TWENTY-FIVE

Honor met her at the door, looking like she had just been roused from bed. Her blond curls were loose around her shoulders, and instead of her usual starched shirt and trousers, she was wrapped in a silk robe that whispered as she moved.

They stared at each other in the dim light of the hallway. At last, Honor broke the silence. "Vivian. What—" She cleared her throat and pulled the robe a little more closely around herself. "What happened?"

It helped, some, that Honor was nervous. That she was human, in that moment, instead of aloof and unreadable as she had so often been. The cool night air whispered against them, sending the loose curls to tangle across her face until she brushed them away impatiently. Vivian felt goose bumps prickle across her skin, felt the angry heat that had been coursing through her start to fade. Her eyes prickled too, and she had to breathe deeply to find her voice.

"Can I come in?" she whispered, suddenly tired.

"Of course." Honor stepped back. "You shouldn't be out at night anyway. Especially not—" As Vivian stepped into the light, she broke off. Vivian wondered what her face must look like, for Honor to stare at her like that as she shut the door and locked it once more. "What happened?"

"My father is . . ." Vivian didn't know how to begin. "I told you, I found my father. And he . . . I thought he . . ."

"Wait."

Honor took Vivian's hand and drew her farther inside, down to the darkened dance hall, crowded with the shadows of tables, up the stairs and past the landing, and at last into her bedroom where the only light came from the streetlights outside. There was nowhere to sit, so Vivian settled on the bed. When Honor would have pulled away to switch on the lamp, Vivian didn't let go of her hand. She wanted darkness, or as close to darkness as she could get. She wanted to hide, to pretend that she didn't feel like she was lost and drowning.

Honor settled next to her. "Tell me," she said softly.

Vivian did. She hadn't known how to begin, but once she started talking she couldn't stop. Meeting Ruth, discovering her father, the cautious hopes that had been smashed to pieces when he appeared in her home. Ruth's story. Her realization that he worked for O'Keefe. Her thoughts tumbled over each other and out of her mouth as she jumped ahead and doubled back and tried to make it all make sense. She managed to keep herself from spilling Leo's secrets, but everything else came out in a torrent of heartbreak and anger, until there were tears on her cheeks—when had she started crying?—and Honor's arms were around her. They might have been the only thing holding her together, the only reason her heart wasn't shattering completely.

"I didn't lose anything, not really," Vivian said fiercely, trying to wipe the tears away. "I didn't have a father before, and I as good as don't have one now. So why . . ."

"Why does it hurt so much?" Honor asked softly. Her arms tightened around Vivian. "Because we're creatures of hope, pet. We live and breathe it. And it hurts when that hope is taken away."

"It hurts *so goddamn much,*" Vivian gasped, barely able to force the words out through the tears that had begun flowing again. "I still have Florence, I know that. And Danny's family . . . they're the nicest people, really. But he's my *father.* Isn't he supposed to . . ." She broke off, another sob shuddering out of her.

"I'm the wrong person to ask about parents, I'm afraid," Honor said.

That made Vivian choke on a laugh, though the humor had a bitter taste to it. She knew exactly what sort of misery Honor's parents had put their daughter through. "Guess I don't have much room to complain. Not to you," she said, trying to pull herself together.

"Vivian." Honor laid a gentle hand on each of Vivian's cheeks, her voice soft. "Just because something was a particular kind of shit for me doesn't mean it's not completely shit for you too."

That made Vivian laugh again, a hysterical edge to the sound after so many tears. "Such an elegant way to say it."

Honor smiled as she let her hands fall. "You know me. Always ladylike." She closed her eyes, taking a deep breath as though steeling herself before she opened them once more. "I have to know, Vivian: Why did you come here?" she asked. "To me. You could have talked to your sister. To Beatrice. To—" She broke off, and Vivian wondered if she had been about to name Leo. "Why me?"

"Because you were the only one I wanted to see," Vivian whispered. "Because I knew you would understand."

"Does that mean you've decided to trust me?"

The question hung between them. Vivian stared at her. Maybe, after everything, it did.

"Honor," she asked instead of answering. "If we found Hugh Brown . . . would you really hand him over to O'Keefe?"

"That depends."

"On what?" Vivian asked, her voice shaking.

"On what you wanted me to do. That's what it comes down to, Vivian. I'd do what you wanted me to do." The hand she cupped around Vivian's cheek was gentle. "Do you believe me?"

Vivian felt like she was drowning, and that touch was the only thing keeping her afloat. She couldn't speak, but she nodded.

"You know who he is, don't you?"

Slowly, Vivian nodded again.

Honor let out a slow breath. "All right. You don't have to tell me. We'll figure it out, some other way, if that's what you want."

They were both still, eyes on each other. Vivian couldn't find her voice. Before she fully thought it through, she leaned forward and brushed a kiss—so light and short it could hardly be called that—against Honor's lips.

It was as though an electric current had jumped between them.

Honor pulled back, but not away—just far enough that they could stare at each other. "What was that for?" she asked, and the words themselves felt like a kiss against Vivian's lips. It was too dark to see Honor's eyes clearly, but Vivian could tell they were fixed on her, and the intensity of that stare made her feel giddy and drunk.

"For being here," Vivian whispered back. "For knowing me. For—" She broke off. She had almost said *for loving me,* but she didn't know if that was true, and her heart was still too fragile to find out if it wasn't. So she kissed Honor again.

"Vivian—*Vivian*." Honor scooted away, breathing heavily. "You shouldn't— *Wait,*" she insisted as Vivian tried to pull her back.

Vivian stared at her, surprised and confused as she tried to read Honor's expression in the dim light, panting a little as they stared at each other. "Why not?" she asked, the words coming out like a plea. Wasn't this what they both wanted?

Honor's hands drifted down her arms, then dropped away. She shook her head. "It's not any different than before. You've had a hell of a day, and—"

"My emotions are running high?" Vivian asked. Her heart was pounding like it wanted to escape her chest, like what she wanted to say, to feel, was too big for her body to hold. "That's what you said before, wasn't it? But they're never not running high, especially not around you." Her fingers trailed over the curve of Honor's hip, sliding over the silk. She could feel Honor shiver under her hands, could feel the yearning in her own body. "You said . . ." Vivian hesitated, gathering her courage. "You said once that you chose me. That no matter what happened, even if we could never be together, you would choose me, again and again." Vivian couldn't make her next words come out louder than a whisper, longing for the answer and dreading it at the same time. "Is that still true?"

"I'm older than you are," Honor said, sounding as if she were forcing the words out through gritted teeth. She captured Vivian's hands in hers, held them away from her body. "And we both know you've had plenty of reasons not to trust me, so—"

"Is that still true?" Vivian pleaded.

"And I *know* you're not thinking things through tonight," Honor said. Vivian could hear the regret in her voice, her cool mask sliding back into place. "You're hurt and angry and—"

"Honor." Vivian cut her off. She pulled her hands free and cupped them against Honor's face, fingers brushing over her cheekbones. She didn't look away. "Do you still choose me?" she whispered.

The raggedness of their breathing was loud in the silence. Vivian waited.

"Always," Honor said fiercely, and there was nothing but heat in her voice now. *"Always."*

Vivian could have sworn that her heart leaped straight into her throat, like it could rise even farther and lift her out of all the pain and anger that had been filling her. She wasn't sure whether she wanted to cry or laugh. "Then why won't you let me choose you too?"

Instead of answering, Honor kissed her. It was like drowning, or maybe like coming up for air. All their careful control, her fear and Honor's hesitation, melted away into heat, into desperation, as though they were still both afraid that something would pull them apart. But it was just them, and the dark, and a silence barely broken by the outside world.

Vivian shifted to kneel on the bed, one knee on either side of Honor's thighs, and she shuddered at the feel of Honor's hands as they drifted up her legs. They slid under the edge of her dress, running along the tops of her stockings and freeing each garter with a flick. Honor wrapped her arms around her, and Vivian gasped in surprise as the world shifted. She landed on her back, and Honor smiled at her. She rolled each stocking down, inch by inch, then bent to follow their path with her mouth, and Vivian whimpered for more until Honor found her lips for another kiss.

Honor's breath came more quickly as Vivian slid the silk robe out of the way to find Honor's shoulder, her collarbone, the feel of her heart beating under her skin. Soon even that wasn't enough, and when Honor cupped her hands around Vivian's cheeks, looking at her with a question in her eyes, Vivian didn't answer with words. She stood slowly, never looking away, as she undid the buttons down the front of her dress. She could feel her own pulse leap as it fell to the floor.

And eventually it was all gone, and Vivian could pretend that the rest of the world and everyone in it didn't exist. It was just the two of them, and nothing mattered but the feel of Honor's body, the salt of her skin and the ragged sound of her breath and the way, at the end, that they lay next to each other, hearts pounding and the darkness wrapping around them like an embrace.

They were silent together. Honor rolled onto her side, one hand traveling over the curve of Vivian's hip. Vivian shivered, and Honor scooted closer, so that Vivian's back fit against the curve of her front.

"You're already asleep, aren't you?" Honor murmured, fingertips tracing a gentle path over Vivian's neck and shoulder.

Vivian closed her eyes, nodding as she let her body settle back against Honor's. For the moment, she was safe.

For the moment, she thought she might even be loved.

She tried to stay awake, to hold on to that feeling, that moment, like a lifeline that she could cling to against whatever was coming for them. But she was already drifting off as she felt a featherlight kiss against her jaw.

"Don't regret this, pet," Honor whispered. "Don't regret me."

Vivian wanted to answer, to promise that she wouldn't. But her eyes were too heavy to open, and she couldn't drag herself awake enough to form the words. Her hand managed to find Honor's, and she twined their fingers together before she sank down into sleep.

She woke when Honor moved beside her, suddenly sitting up in bed. Vivian rolled over, groggy and confused and still half-asleep. "What—"

Honor clapped a hand across her mouth. Vivian froze, panic flooding her in a wave, as her eyes and ears strained into the darkness, trying to understand what was happening.

In the silence, she heard it: the creak of steps, the sound of a door opening and closing. Before she could react, Honor's mouth was against her ear, her voice barely loud enough to be heard.

"It's someone downstairs," Honor breathed. "Get dressed, quick and quiet as you can."

Vivian didn't waste time arguing or asking questions as she yanked her clothes back on. She slid her feet into her shoes without worrying about her stockings; those went into the pocket of her coat, which she tugged on, not sure if they were planning to confront the intruder or run. They might need to do both.

The weight of the revolver in her coat pocket bumped against her thigh, and Vivian hesitated only a moment before she pulled it out. But her hands were trembling, and she felt sick at the thought of using it. Instead, she grabbed Honor's hands and pressed it silently into them.

Honor was already dressed, shirttails hastily tucked into her trousers, her movements as light and silent as Vivian's own. Vivian could see her surprise in the set of her shoulders, but she didn't stop for questions. There was a quick metallic burr as she checked the chambers of the gun, then held it ready at her side. "Stay here," Honor said, her lips close to Vivian's ear once more. "I'm going to try to surprise whoever it is."

"Not a chance," Vivian retorted in a whisper. "There might be more than one, and I'm not letting you—"

She was cut off by the crush of Honor's mouth against hers, quick and frantic. Honor didn't waste time arguing. "Stay behind me," she murmured. "And run like hell if it goes south."

"I—"

"And stop talking." Another kiss, even briefer than the first, and then Honor was heading toward the door. Vivian, her breath coming too fast, followed, wondering whether whoever was downstairs was listening as carefully as Honor had been.

They weren't. Honor and Vivian made it down to the landing, where the office door had been left open a careless crack, light shining around it. They could hear someone moving around, bumping into furniture, a man's voice cursing softly. It sounded like there was only one person in there, and whoever he was, he was sloppy. Vivian would have been grateful for it if she wasn't so terrified.

Honor put her hand out, holding Vivian back. Vivian nodded, hoping Honor could see, as Honor lifted the revolver and carefully cocked the hammer back. Then, without warning, before Vivian was even ready, she kicked the door open and strode in. Vivian hesitated only the barest moment before she followed.

"Don't! Don't shoot, please!"

The man stood behind the desk, his hands raised in front of him and a desperate look on his face. Honor stood in the middle of the room, eyes blazing and the Fitz Special held steady in front of her.

But Vivian couldn't move. She stared, her mouth dry with surprise and confusion, her mind scrambling to catch up with what she was seeing. "What— How—"

Honor didn't look at her, didn't take her eyes from the man in front of them. "Hello, Spence," she said, her voice soft and dangerous. "I can't wait to find out what a fella like you is doing in a place like this."

TWENTY-SIX

"Don't shoot, please," Spence begged again, his eyes darting to Vivian, then around the room, as if he were looking for an escape. There wasn't any, not with Honor between him and the door. Vivian could see his chest heaving as he realized how trapped he was. "Vivian, tell her. You don't need any—I promise, I'm not—"

"Not dead?" Vivian demanded, stepping forward until she stood just behind Honor's shoulder. "You sure gave a good impression of it. What the hell happened to you?"

"Nothing!" Spence said quickly, his voice cracking. Then he seemed to change his mind just as quickly. "I mean, something, something bad, I barely got away with my life, and I had to lie low, you know. You know?" he pleaded, looking between the two women.

"And sneaking in here to go through my things is part of lying low, is it?" Honor asked, her voice cold.

That made Vivian look for the first time at what the bartender had actually been doing. The drawers on Honor's desk were all open, but he had ignored anything obviously valuable in them, or anywhere else in the room. Instead, there were papers scattered around: Honor's carefully gathered files of information. Vivian felt a chill go through her. She suddenly understood.

Honor took a step forward. "Who were you looking for, Spence?" she asked softly.

"No one—"

"He's not going to protect you now, you know," Honor continued, almost conversationally. "Not now that I've seen your face and know I'm not the only one paying you. You're no use to him anymore."

Spence whimpered, the fight going out of him. He dropped into the chair behind the desk. "I needed the cash," he muttered.

"You wanted the cash," Honor corrected him, unmoved. "I'm not offering you my sympathy; I'm asking for information. I know who you were looking for. I want to hear you say it."

Spence slumped even farther into his seat. "Hugh Brown. O'Keefe is paying me to help him track down Hugh Brown."

Honor gestured with the gun. "Take off your jacket. Then stand up slowly." He did what she asked. Underneath it, one sleeve was rolled up, revealing a heavy bandage wrapped around his arm. "Looks like you lost a bit of blood there."

Spence gritted his teeth. "You know I did," he bit off. "You saw it, didn't you? You were supposed to."

Honor didn't correct him. Her smile was cold. "Can't wait to hear the story you have to spill. But before that . . ." She gestured to Vivian without taking her eyes of Spence. "Vivian here is going to make sure you're not packing any heat I should know about. If you move, I shoot you." She tossed off the words like they meant nothing. Spence shuddered. "Vivian?"

"Sure thing, boss," Vivian said, managing to match Honor's careless tone even as her heart raced. She slid her hands up and down Spence's legs, checked under his arms and in his waistband. Somehow she managed to be as cold and impersonal about it as Honor. Spence held so still she wondered if he was breathing, his eyes wide and fixed on Honor.

"Clean as a whistle," Vivian said, stepping back at last. She wished they had something with them to tie him up, but she didn't want to leave Honor alone to go look downstairs. She glared at Spence when he tried to smile at her. "For a snitch, anyway." He swallowed nervously, his face falling.

Honor grabbed one of the chairs in front of her desk and spun it around with one hand so that it was facing her. "Sit," she said, and he obeyed. "Now you spill."

"He just wanted me to get a slant on what you knew," Spence said quickly. "He knows Brown comes around here, because—"

"How?" Honor demanded. Vivian prayed silently that her boss wouldn't look at her. "I still don't know who this fella is, so what makes O'Keefe so sure I do?"

"One of his boys showed me a picture, and I recognized the face. He's a regular here," Spence muttered, his nervous eyes still on the gun. "Or he was. I hadn't seen him in a while, but then . . . He showed up. Right at the bar. I dropped the name, just to check, and he jumped like he'd been bit. He tried to shrug it off, but the look on his face . . . I knew right away it was him."

Vivian had never been so thankful that Spence was bad at his job. If he had been as good as Danny, he'd have remembered Leo's real name and everyone he talked to. But Spence didn't pay attention to details. And he'd left that night before he would have seen her and Leo dancing together.

Leo hadn't been around much the last few months. Not since things went south between him and Vivian. She wondered if their split might have saved his life—at least for the time being. Or maybe it had saved hers. She didn't want to think about what O'Keefe would have done to her if he thought she could connect him to Leo.

"And so you ran to O'Keefe that night and tipped him off?" Honor asked, almost conversationally.

"Of course I did. How do you think Silence ended up dead? O'Keefe offered him the same deal he offered me. Same deal he would have offered to Danny, but that went south for some reason. But Silence, stupid bruiser, tried to turn them down with his fists and got offed for his trouble." He shook his head. "I wasn't taking that risk. I didn't have another choice."

"Yes, you did," Honor said coldly. "You could have told me. You could have asked for help. Instead you turned snitch because you wanted to make a quick buck, and you didn't care who got hurt because of it."

"He was paying for information! Can you blame me for wanting a little something extra?"

"I can when it means ratting out my people."

"He ain't one of yours."

"The people who come to the Nightingale trust me the same way the people who work there do. How many secrets do you think are on that dance floor? For you to turn rat . . ." Honor shook her head, and the hard look in her eyes made Spence shrink into himself, fear written plain across his face. "It's a thing I can't forgive. Ever." She gestured to his arm. "Keep talking. What happened there?"

"O'Keefe came to my place with some of his fellas." Spence hunched his shoulders. "He was impatient, said it was taking too long for you to give him what he wanted. I told him you look after your people, that maybe if more of their lives were in danger, you'd hand over Brown. As soon as he said he liked that idea, one of his goons grabbed me, and O'Keefe pulled out a gun, and . . ." He shuddered.

Vivian shook her head. "I saw your place, Spence," she said. "That amount of blood didn't come from him shooting you in the arm."

"No, he decided it wasn't convincing enough." Spence's throat worked, and the look in his eyes almost made her feel sympathy for him. "There was another fella with them, from a different joint they were looking into. O'Keefe decided that I was still useful. But the other fella . . ." He swallowed. "They turned on him so fast. And then they dragged him outta there so you'd think it had been me."

"You dumb sap," Vivian whispered. "What the hell did you think you were getting into?"

"I realize that *now*," Spence whimpered. "But he'd seemed so . . . reasonable up until then. Said it was all business."

"And it was, I'm sure. To him." Honor shook her head. "And you were still stuck working for him."

"Well, I wasn't going to start telling him no, was I?" Spence said, his voice cracking. "Not after that."

"No," Honor said, her voice giving away none of her thoughts. Carefully, she de-cocked the hammer on the revolver and let her hand drop to her side. "I doubt that would have gone well for you."

"No." Spence shook his head. "Well, I guess—"

He jumped up, trying to dash past them toward the door. Vivian grabbed at him; she couldn't get her hands on him, but she managed to catch one of his feet with hers. He stumbled as he tried to avoid her, crashing to the floor. When he tried to rise, Honor was there, and she caught him across the temple with the butt of the gun.

He groaned and dropped again. Not unconscious—it wasn't a big gun, and Honor hadn't hit him as hard as she could have—but it was enough that he didn't try to stand up, just crouched on his hands and knees, whimpering.

Honor squatted down next to him, taking his chin in one hand and lifting it so he had to meet her eyes. "Here's what we're going to do," she said softly. Spence whimpered again. Vivian didn't blame him for being scared; the chill in Honor's voice was terrifying. "You're going to tell us where he's set up shop, and I might not re-create that scene from your living room."

"You think he'd have told someone like me?" Spence said, his voice cracking. "I'm just supposed to get him information here. That's all. Just information. He doesn't trust me enough for more than that, yet."

"Then you'd better come up with something else that I want to know," Honor suggested. "Real quick-like, if you want to walk out of here on your own two feet."

"I don't . . ." Spence tried to shake his head, but Honor's fingers were still tight around his chin. "I don't know anything, I swear."

Honor's smile was almost sympathetic. "That's a real shame, Spence," she said, dropping her hand and standing.

"Wait!" he squeaked, his eyes darting from the gun in her hand to Honor's face. "I do know . . . I don't know how much help it is. But I'm not the only new person on his payroll. He's been recruiting since he got back to the city."

Vivian couldn't imagine that sort of information would be any help to them at all, but Honor crouched down in front of him once more. "I'm listening," she said. "I hope for your sake that you can make it good."

Spence's gulp was loud in the quiet room. "He killed that one fella. But there were two new boys other than me. One of them I think might be a cop. And the other . . ."

The wind that morning was cold, and it cut sharply through Vivian's skimpy coat. She would have gone to the tradesman's entrance, as she usually did. But Honor strolled straight up to the front door and knocked.

"I hope you're planning to be a good boy," she murmured to Spence as they waited for the door to open.

He scowled at them both equally. "Do I have a choice?"

"If you don't, it's your own damn fault," Honor said, no sympathy in her voice. "Now try to make a good impression."

The maid who answered the door didn't bother to hide her shock, which might have been as much from the early hour as it was from the strange group on the doorstep. But something in Honor's manner seemed to stop her from sending them packing right away.

"Guessing you're here on a business matter?" she said a little nervously.

Apparently, some of the staff did have an inkling of what their employer did.

"Indeed we are," Honor said smoothly. "Trust me, she'll want to see us."

They weren't shown into the ladies' parlor this time; Vivian didn't know whether that was because of Spence's presence or because she wasn't there as the dressmaker's girl. The sitting room where the maid left them waiting was more opulent and less modern, with curtains still drawn against the morning sun and heavy, dark furniture. They didn't have long to wait.

"You know, I am growing tired of this," Hattie Wilson snapped as she strode into the room. "I told you both two days, so why have you dragged"—she gestured toward them, the barest flick of her hand—"all this into my home?" She eyed the strange trio: Vivian, looking disheveled in her clothes from the day before; Honor, her hand tight around Spence's arm and her face hard; and Spence himself, hunched and jumpy, with a bloody bruise on his temple where Honor had hit him with the butt of the gun.

Deliberately, Hattie Wilson took a seat in the room's largest and most comfortable chair, leaning back and crossing her legs. She didn't invite any of the rest of them to sit. "You look like you stepped straight out of the pictures. Or some melodramatic magazine story."

"Feeling a bit like it, the way this week is going," Vivian said. She took a deep breath and glanced at Honor. "Are you going to tell her, or am I?"

"Easy enough to put our cards on the table," Honor said, pushing Spence into a chair and standing so that she loomed over him.

Hattie Wilson's mouth tightened, but she didn't protest. She was too busy watching Spence. He pulled his shoulders up, looking frightened and miserable. Vivian couldn't find it in her to feel sorry for him.

"Harlan O'Keefe is recruiting. Found a little rat working at the Nightingale." Honor's grip was tight on Spence's shoulder as she gave him an unfriendly shake, and he flinched. "Lucky for him, he decided it was better to be a little singing bird once he got caught, and he had plenty of interesting things to say. Including the fact that you, Mrs. Wilson—" Honor's smile was cold. "You've got a rat of your own."

The room was silent. Hattie stared at them through narrow eyes. Then she crossed the room swiftly, gripping Spence's chin in one manicured hand and forcing it up so that he had to meet her eyes.

"Who?" she asked softly.

"Bruiser George," Spence stuttered, looking terrified. "There were four of us new since O'Keefe came back to New York, and he's one of them."

"And why should I believe that?"

"Haven't you noticed George looking a little more un-handsome than usual?" Vivian asked. "Fella's had a few too many bruises for a man whose boss has been keeping things quiet of late. Haven't you wondered why?"

"It's a rough city," Hattie said coldly, glancing her way. "And George likes to show off how tough he is. He'll go looking for a fight if work is too slow for his taste."

"Maybe," Vivian agreed. "Or maybe he's double-crossing you. Spence here just gave a pretty spot-on description of your bully-boy. Are you willing to take the chance that he's wrong?"

"And how do I know he's telling the truth?" Hattie asked, finally stepping away from Spence, who slumped into the chair, shaking with relief to have her attention off him. She turned to Vivian, her eyes glinting with fury. "How do I know you are?"

"How do I know you are?" Vivian countered. "You could have been playing me for a fool this whole time, with George acting on your orders. You know enough about the Nightingale that O'Keefe could make use of you." She was talking too fast, and she made herself take a deep breath, meeting Hattie's eyes. There was a hint of hesitation there, Vivian realized. Hattie Wilson was uncertain—perhaps even scared. "We might not be friends, Mrs. Wilson, but we've never really been enemies either. We've dealt with each other pretty honestly, all things said and done. So I'm going to trust you this time. Are you going to trust me?"

Hattie was silent so long that Vivian could hear the clock ticking. "O'Keefe's an old-fashioned tom. He doesn't make use of women unless he's got an itch to scratch," she said at last, her lip curling in distaste as she took her seat once more. "Out of all the people he could work with in this city, I'm probably one of the last he'd bother with." She turned to Spence. "You said there were four of you that O'Keefe had brought on new."

"Three now," Spence whispered, looking terrified. "One of 'em is dead."

"But everyone else is from his old operation in Chicago, you're sure about that?"

His head bobbed frantically up and down. "Positive. I promise. I swear. He plays things close to the chest, and he didn't—"

He swallowed whatever he had been about to say as Hattie raised one hand. "That's enough," she said, as though she were already bored with him. She glanced at Honor. "There's a good chance that he got sneaky with our boys in particular because he thought they'd be less loyal. Or that we'd be too dumb to notice."

Honor smiled. "His mistake," she said as she took her own seat at last. Vivian hesitantly copied her.

"Very much his mistake," Hattie said in a voice that made Vivian shiver. "And theirs," she added, smiling at Spence, who gulped audibly.

"If you're sure, Ms. Huxley, that you're willing to trust the word of a rat?"

"Oh, he'll be a good boy now, I'm sure," Honor said, reaching over to pat Spence's cheek. The former bartender flinched, glancing nervously between the three women. "He's got no choice but to throw in with me again. He knows if he goes back to O'Keefe after getting caught on the job, he's as good as dead."

"Then I'll borrow him, if you don't mind, for a few hours," Hattie Wilson said. "I happen to have a small chat planned with George and a few of my other boys this morning. I have a feeling they won't be too pleased to find out one of their colleagues is keeping his options open like that."

"What are you going to do?" Vivian asked nervously.

Hattie's smile was beautiful as a diamond and twice as hard. "We'll have a talk, of course, Miss Kelly. I'll see what George has to say for himself. And then, if I decide it's necessary, his former colleagues will take him for a little ride."

Vivian wished she were more surprised. "Never one to get your own hands dirty, are you?" she asked.

"A lady never does," Hattie said, flicking a speck of dust from her sleeve. Spence shuddered and hunched even farther into himself.

"As long as the talk and the ride are for your own boys," Honor said. She was still smiling, but there was a warning in her voice. "I want mine back in one piece."

Vivian wanted to ask what Honor was planning to do, but she kept her mouth shut. She told herself it was because she didn't want to put a foot wrong in this careful dance between Honor and Hattie Wilson. She didn't tell herself it was as much because she was afraid of the answer. She glanced at Spence, who met her eyes, his own wide with fear. Honor could be ruthless—she had to be—but Vivian didn't think she was as hard as Hattie Wilson.

She hoped not.

Hattie Wilson stood. "Do you two need to be on your way, then?" She looked them up and down, eyebrows rising. "Or should I offer you somewhere to freshen up?"

They took her up on the offer while Hattie Wilson continued to question Spence. The same nervous maid who had answered the door showed them to a guest room with an attached bathroom. Vivian couldn't help staring at the pale pink tile and gilded mirrors, the polished fixtures and towels so soft she could have wrapped herself in them and fallen asleep.

When she came back into the guest room, Honor was staring out the window, arms crossed and a calculating look on her face. It made Vivian shiver to see, and it took her nearly a minute to work up the nerve to walk toward her.

"What are you thinking about?" she asked. She stopped next to Honor, watching her out of the corner of her eyes.

Honor didn't look at her. "Spence."

Vivian thought of Hattie Wilson and her little drive. "What do you plan to do about him?"

Honor didn't answer for long enough that Vivian started to worry. "What do you think should happen to him?" she asked at last.

Vivian took a deep breath. "I don't think he knew what he was getting into with O'Keefe. He was stupid, and he was greedy, sure. But everyone messes up at some point, about something." She glanced at Honor. "Even me. Even you." Honor's expression was almost a smile. She didn't argue. "Give him enough money to get home and tell him to get out of the city. If he's smart, he'll hit the road. If he's not . . ." Vivian shrugged. "Then, he gets what comes his way."

"You're too sweet for this world of mine, you know," Honor said, shaking her head.

Vivian glanced nervously at her, then looked away. "Guess that's why I need to stay close to you," she said softly.

She let out a squeak of surprise as she found herself suddenly spun around, her back pressed against the wall and Honor's mouth on hers. Vivian's hands fisted in Honor's clothing without thought, trying to pull her as close as possible.

"Do you mean that?" Honor breathed in between kisses. "You don't regret what—"

"Never," Vivian said fiercely. *"Never."*

"What about"—Honor kissed her again—"your sister and—"

"It doesn't matter. I won't let it matter," Vivian insisted. She yanked Honor's shirt out of her waistband. She wanted to forget where they were and why. She wanted to feel Honor's skin under her hands.

But she couldn't forget, not entirely. When Honor stepped reluctantly back, Vivian didn't try to stop her. Out in the hall, they could hear two servants arguing about who had spilled something on the carpet.

Honor sighed as she straightened her clothing. "Well, let's just hope Mrs. Wilson keeps up her side of the bargain. Otherwise it'll be pretty hard to release Spence back into the wild."

"You're going to . . ." Vivian stared at her. "You mean you're not going to . . ."

Honor gave her a puzzled look. "I'm going to give him enough cash to get home and tell him to stay there. Isn't that what you just said?"

"But I didn't think you'd actually do it," Vivian protested.

"I told you last night, pet," Honor said softly. "If it's important to you, I'll do it."

"But why does what I want matter?"

"Why do you think I never wanted to let you close before?" Honor smiled wryly. "I don't do things halfway, pet. If we're in this together . . . we're in it together all the way."

"But it's your business, not mine. You're the boss."

"That's true," Honor said. "But I still care about what you think." She cupped her hand around Vivian's jaw, brushing her thumb back and forth. "And I could use a little more sweetness in my life."

"Oh." Vivian leaned into the touch. It was another step, another notch of trust between them.

Honor cocked her head to one side. "What are you thinking?"

The words were on the tip of her tongue. *Leo is Hugh Brown*. Vivian shook her head. "Nothing."

It wasn't her secret to tell.

Honor sighed. "Real world is waiting, pet. Let's go see what we've set in motion."

To Vivian's surprise, when they came downstairs, Mrs. Wilson had ordered her car and driver around to the front of the house, waiting to take them where they needed to go. Spence gave them a single, terrified look as they headed out.

"I want him back in one piece," Honor said, as if it were a pleasant reminder and not a warning.

Hattie shrugged. "He's not my business. One of my boys will bring him back to your Nightingale later today." She smiled. "And he'll let you know what we learn."

TWENTY-SEVEN

Danny was waiting for them when they stepped into the empty dance hall of the Nightingale. He didn't look happy.

"Where's my sister?" Vivian asked before he could say anything.

He glared at her. "She and Ruth are still at the restaurant. Lucky and his pals are keeping an eye on things. And she's pretty damn frantic, by the way, not knowing where you ended up or if you were all right. But I figured I'd find you here, if you weren't dead in an alley somewhere."

Vivian flinched. She should have let Florence know she was okay. "Well, you can go back and tell her I'm all right," she said. "We have to stay here to . . ." She glanced at Honor. "Wait for some news."

"Like hell I'm going," Danny snapped. "I'm staying right here, and you're going to tell me what's going on with you and Leo. I know you called him last night. And if I heard even half of that right . . ."

"It's noth—"

"Don't tell me 'nothing' again," he said, crossing his arms and glowering at her. "This is a hell of a time to be keeping secrets, so don't do it. What's going on?"

"Vivian?" That was Honor; when Vivian glanced at her, the wariness—the distance—was back in her eyes. It made Vivian's heart ache to see it.

She sighed. She couldn't quite look either of them in the eye as she admitted, "We're trying to find where O'Keefe is hiding out. Leo was working an angle with the coroner's office, and I was cashing in a favor from Mrs. Wilson." She glanced at Honor. "You knew about that part."

"And your Mr. Green is helping with this," Honor gave her a too-even look, "out of the goodness of his heart?"

They were going to put it together now, whether she told them or not. Danny had overheard too much last night. Vivian let out a slow breath. "He's helping because when Leo was in Chicago, he went by the name Hugh Brown."

The silence in the room was so loud it hurt her ears.

"When did you find out?" Honor asked at last.

Vivian didn't want to meet her eyes, but she made herself do it anyway. She owed Honor that much. "I thought it was Spence, at first. But then after he—" She shook her head. "After we *thought* Spence was dead, I figured it out."

"What do you mean, *thought*?" Danny demanded.

"He's alive and kicking, at least for now. He was our rat," Honor said shortly. Danny let out a stream of curses. "But I'm not so interested in him right now," Honor continued, her voice so steady it made Vivian flinch. But Honor wasn't looking at her. Her eyes were on Danny. "What are you going to do about it?"

"Me?" Danny stared at her. "I thought you were the ones with plans for the fella."

Honor shook her head. "I'm not handing him over to O'Keefe," she said quietly. "I made a promise." Vivian couldn't smile—not with everything else going on—but her entire body glowed with warmth.

Honor met her eyes for a long moment, then looked back at Danny. "Besides, with a man who plays the game like this, giving him what he wants isn't enough. Not anymore, at least, if it ever was."

"Danny-boy?" Vivian whispered.

He sighed. "I'd throw Leo to the wolves in a heartbeat if it meant keeping my girls safe," he said quietly. Vivian's heart could have broken for him; Danny and Leo had been friends for half their lives. "And I don't think he'd blame me for it, either. But if you two have a plan to send O'Keefe packing, I'd rather try that first."

"Not yet," Vivian said, glancing at Honor. "But we're hoping we will, soon."

"Swell." Danny took a seat at the bar, scrubbing his hands over his face. "We're hoping we will soon. That's just swell."

"Why does O'Keefe want him in the first place?" Honor asked. She took a seat next to Danny, but her eyes didn't leave Vivian. "Did he tell you?"

"He did." Vivian hesitated. She didn't know how Leo would feel about them knowing this corner of his past. But she wanted them to understand.

So she told them, starting with Nora Murphy and ending with Clyde Quinn. When she stopped talking, there was silence in the dance hall again. Danny let out a long breath.

"He never said anything," he said quietly. Vivian couldn't tell if he was hurt or not.

"We're a secretive lot around here," Honor pointed out. "It comes with the territory." She glanced at Vivian. "So what's this plan you two came up with, then? I hope it isn't something stupid."

"Probably pretty stupid," Vivian said with a weak smile. "We're going to find out where O'Keefe's holed up, and we're going to take it to the commissioner."

"To Leo's uncle?" Danny demanded. "That old bastard won't give him the time of day. What the hell makes you think he'll help?"

"Because he'll want to take credit for bringing O'Keefe in," Vivian said. "You're right, he turned us down when we had nothing to go on. He doesn't want anything vague. But if we can tell him where to find O'Keefe . . ."

Honor sighed. "And if they can find something to pin on him that sticks. From what I've heard, O'Keefe is a slippery bastard." She hesitated, then asked, "Leo's still hoping to find out what happened to his girl, isn't he?"

"He's hoping," Vivian said quietly. "But he'll take revenge if answers aren't on offer."

"We all take what we can get," Danny said. He rested his elbows on the bar, letting out a groan as he ran all his fingers through his hair at once. "So we're waiting now. Either of you want to share what we're waiting for?"

"Mrs. Wilson." Vivian slumped into her own seat at the bar. "I'll fill you in, but any chance we could make some coffee first?"

Honor stood up. "Coffee's upstairs. Telephone, too, if you want to call your sister. Let's go wait for some bad news, kids."

The call from Mrs. Wilson came sooner than they had been expecting, telling them to watch for a delivery at the front door. When it came, it was in the form of a thick-shouldered bruiser named Eddie. Vivian kept her distance as he hauled a terrified-looking Spence into the room behind him; she had encountered Eddie before, and she was wary of those big fists, even if he'd never taken a swing at her.

Eddie shoved Spence into the middle of the empty dance floor. "Boss lady said you wanted your rat back," he said. Vivian wasn't surprised by the grim look on his face. Eddie had been working with Bruiser George for a long time. She would have been willing to bet that he was even more stung by the betrayal than Mrs. Wilson had been.

Spence stumbled a few steps before he caught himself. When he finally looked up, he offered them a weak smile. "You know, I'm actually happy to see you," he said, shuddering a little. "Anyone's better than that harpy. Do you have any idea what she—"

He didn't get to finish. Danny had taken three quick steps forward and punched him in the face.

Spence shouted with pain, one hand clapped over his eye as he doubled over. No one rushed to his defense. But Danny didn't try to hit him again.

"Take a seat," he spat out. "And don't talk."

Eddie chuckled as Spence did what he was told, still groaning. "I remember that jab of yours," he said. "Got me in the eye too, first time we met."

"Wouldn't really call it meeting," Danny said shortly, shaking out his fist. "You and your pal jumped me."

"Still. Hell of a stinger. Beautiful." He sounded genuinely pleased by the memory, which made Vivian stare at him, since Eddie had ended that fight unconscious in a filthy alley. He saw her staring and shrugged. "A good fight's a good fight, even if you lose."

"I love reminiscing as much as the next person," Honor broke in. "But speaking of your pal, we were waiting on information. What've you got for us?"

"Sorry, lady. We got nothing."

It took a moment for his words to sink in. When they did, Vivian had to grab the edge of the bar to keep herself steady. *Nothing.*

"Boss lady was thorough with her questions, but Big Georgie had the same story as this joker"—Eddie jerked his thumb toward Spence, who flinched—"and they stuck to it. O'Keefe or his boys would get in touch with them, not the other way around. Only his old guard from Chicago knew where to find him."

Vivian pressed her fists against the bar's counter. She wanted to scream in frustration. Apparently, O'Keefe was too canny to trust any of his new men with that kind of information.

"I'd admire his business sense more under other circumstances," Honor said. "But right now, I'd prefer he take a few more wooden dimes." She sighed. "Well, tell your boss thanks for the help, anyway. Hope she has fun sorting out her own rat problem."

"She already did," Eddie said, giving the lapels of his suit a little snap to pull them straight. "And she told me not to linger around here. Said it wasn't the best place to be right now." He glanced around. "Shame. Always seemed like a fun spot. Oh well." He gave them each a nod, ignoring Spence, who was still whimpering as he felt gingerly around his fast-bruising eye. "See you around."

Danny watched him leave, then turned to Honor. "All right. What do we do now?"

She closed her eyes. Vivian could see the tight line where she was clenching her jaw. "We'll think of something."

Danny paced along the bar. "What if—"

Vivian didn't stay to listen. "I'll be right back," she said quietly, and went after Eddie while they were talking, hurrying up the stairs and into the hall so she could catch him just before he reached the door.

"Eddie!"

He turned, his surprise plain. "What?"

Vivian hesitated, then made herself ask, "What happened to your pal?"

She'd never thought of Eddie as a quick thinker; there was no doubt in her mind that Hattie Wilson kept him around for his muscle and his loyalty. But even he didn't have to ask who she meant. "Big Georgie has some regrets," he said, shaking his head. "Doesn't do to get greedy like that."

"But what—"

"Doesn't do to ask too many questions either," Eddie said, wagging his finger at her. "Boss lady has it handled." He squashed his hat onto his meaty head and nodded at her. "Done my job here," he rumbled as he turned toward the door, a mountain on the move. "Time for lunch."

Vivian stared after Eddie, picturing all her run-ins with Bruiser George, the number of times he had threatened or hurt her. The number of times she had seen him threaten or hurt someone else—sometimes people she cared about—with a smile on his weaselly face. There had never been a moment when he wasn't cruel, and she had hated him for it.

But she still shivered, thinking of what might have happened to him. She had been the one who recognized him from the description Spence gave; she had been the one who told Honor they could take that information to Hattie Wilson. Wherever—however—he had ended up, that was her responsibility as much as anyone else's.

Vivian stared that truth in the face, hating it almost as much as she had hated George.

She wouldn't have regretted it if it had gotten them what they needed. But it had all been for nothing. They hadn't learned a single damn—

Vivian froze in the middle of turning back toward the dance hall. O'Keefe might have been too smart to trust his new boys with too much information. But now she knew someone he did trust. Someone who had already tried his best to take her to his boss. She was pretty certain that if he had the chance, he'd try again.

This time, she'd let him.

Vivian glanced toward the curtains at the end of the hall, looped back now that the Nightingale was closed, so that she could see the top of the stairs. The sound of voices drifted up from the dance hall, though she couldn't make out what was being said.

Danny was worried enough about Florence and Mei that he might not try to stop her. But Honor would. She would be furious. But Vivian wasn't willing to waste time arguing or trying to convince her that it was a risk worth taking. She would just have to hope that Honor would understand.

They'd realize any moment that she hadn't returned and come to see what was keeping her. If she wanted to slip away, she couldn't afford to wait any longer. Before she could second-guess herself, Vivian followed Eddie out the door.

She had left her handbag downstairs. But she was still wearing her coat, and her coin purse was in the pocket. There was a subway stop just a few blocks away, but that would take too long, and Vivian knew that if she had to sit and watch the stops flash past, she might lose her nerve.

She couldn't let that happen. Vivian hailed the first cab she saw. Her hands were shaking as she told the driver the address, but they steadied as soon as the car pulled away from the curb and turned north.

Vivian settled back against the seat, watching the buildings slide by. There was no point planning, because she didn't know what would happen when she got there. All she could do was trust herself—and trust that the people she loved would understand when she needed them to.

Vivian paid the cabbie—she had just enough—and slammed the door behind her. She stared at the tidy row of houses, gathering her courage. It was just one more stupid idea. She was good at those. She took a deep breath.

Before she could take a step, she heard footsteps behind her. A hand closed tightly around her upper arm. It wasn't painful, but she couldn't have pulled away if she wanted to. She didn't try.

"Vivian." The voice in her ear was a low growl, but she could hear the surprise in it. "I thought you were smarter than this."

Vivian turned her chin so she could see him. "Hey there, Clyde," she said, her voice steady as her hands. "I was hoping we could talk."

"Sorry, baby girl," he said, shaking his head. She wondered whether his look of regret was all for show. "Talking's not in the cards anymore. Let's go."

"Where?" Vivian asked as he turned her back toward the street. There was an old flivver parked there; Vivian wasn't surprised when he yanked the door open. "I guess you're taking me to see O'Keefe?"

His hand tightened on her arm, and he pulled her around so he could see her face. "What do you know about Mr. O'Keefe?"

"Rumors spread," Vivian said softly. "Is that a yes?"

Her father sighed. "Do both of us a favor, all right?" he said as he pushed her into the car. "Don't make this too difficult."

TWENTY-EIGHT

When they pulled up behind the Ansonia Hotel, Vivian couldn't decide if she wanted to gape or laugh. Somehow, both happened.

"Here?" she demanded. "O'Keefe's been running things from here? He sure must like it fancy."

"Yes, now cool it." Clyde glared at her as he parked by the service entrance. "Right now, all Mr. O'Keefe wants is a word with you. That'll change if you make a scene or draw any kind of attention he doesn't like."

"I can keep it together," Vivian said, slouching back in her seat and crossing her arms. "I can be sweet as a daisy, if you answer one question."

His face was stony. "No promises, but sure. Ask away."

"When did you decide that being my father didn't matter as much as what he wanted?"

Clyde sighed. "Vivian, you'll learn soon enough. Nothing matters as much as what Mr. O'Keefe wants. Not if you want to keep your skin in one piece."

"But you've crossed him before," Vivian said without thinking.

She wanted to snatch the words back as soon as they were out of her mouth. Clyde's head snapped up, like an alley cat that heard footsteps too close for comfort. "What are you talking about?" he demanded.

She had been thinking of the bank truck robbery, the one that had sent Leo fleeing Chicago. But her father and Leo had been the only ones to leave that job alive. And if Harlan O'Keefe hadn't pieced together that she knew who Hugh Brown was, she sure as hell didn't want to tip him off now.

"Nothing," she said, slouching even farther down into her seat, trying to distract him with her sulkiness. If he was focused on getting her to be polite to O'Keefe, maybe he wouldn't have time to wonder too much about what she meant. "Let's just meet your boss and get it over with."

Clyde stared at her for long enough that she began to sweat, but she managed to meet his eyes without flinching. At last, he sighed and grabbed her arm again. "Come on," he said, hauling her across the seat. Vivian stumbled a little as her feet tried to find the ground, and he steadied her before she could lose her footing. "Mr. O'Keefe doesn't like to be kept waiting."

The suite Clyde took her to rivaled some of her richest clients' houses for elegance and comfort. Another time, Vivian would have stared at the crystal chandeliers and the soaring windows, modern wallpaper and plush upholstered furniture. But she only had eyes for the redheaded man, currently enjoying his lunch at a table set for one with white linen and silver flatware.

"I hope this was worth waiting for," Harlan O'Keefe said, wiping his mouth with a napkin before he rose.

His smile was handsome enough to belong on an actor beaming from a Lucky Strike ad. Silk tie around his neck, silk handkerchief in his pocket, shirt as crisp and starched as if the hotel had just delivered it from the laundry. Maybe they had. He looked like power and old money walking on two legs, and the only things marring the image were that twice-broken nose, the scar through his eyebrow, and the hard, shifty look in his eyes. Those things belonged to a bruiser from the streets, no matter how much he might be dressed in silk or slicked up with brilliantine.

"I was very disappointed not to meet your daughter yesterday," O'Keefe added. "And it's not like you, Quinn, to disappoint me."

Vivian tried not to flinch as he looked her up and down. Had it really only been yesterday?

"Turns out daughters can be a little slippery when they haven't had their pop around to teach them proper manners," Clyde said with a chuckle, but Vivian could hear the unease beneath it. "Don't worry, boss. She's come around. Decided to be a smart girl."

He was nervous; he might have even been scared. Vivian wanted to be glad—he deserved that and worse for what he'd done. But if he was scared, facing O'Keefe's displeasure, that meant her situation was even shakier than she had expected. And she had expected, when she snuck out of the Nightingale and went to find her father, that it would be pretty damn shaky.

"For her sake, I certainly hope so." O'Keefe paced slowly around the table. If her father had reminded her of a wary alley cat, Harlan O'Keefe was a far more dangerous sort of feline—a sleek, dark-eyed hunter who was only pretending to be civilized. Vivian didn't try to hide her own nervousness. She didn't want him to think she was a threat.

He glanced at her father. "Did I mention, Quinn, that I've met your daughter before? She's an excellent dancer."

Vivian saw the muscles clench in her father's jaw. But his voice was calm as he answered. "You didn't mention it, Mr. O'Keefe. I think that was before we knew she was my daughter."

"That's right, we didn't. And what a sweet family reunion it's been." O'Keefe turned back to Vivian. "How delightful to see you again, Vivian Kelly."

"If you say so," Vivian said, looking him up and down. She kept her voice pouty, even surly. "You know, you don't look like someone who has folks bumped off when they annoy him."

"Not when they annoy me, no." O'Keefe stepped closer to her and dropped his voice. "When they cross me."

He lifted his hand as he spoke, trailing the backs of his knuckles down her cheek, across her throat. The gesture wasn't flirtatious. It was a threat. Vivian felt her heart speed up as she stared at him, wide-eyed. She didn't try to hide that either. O'Keefe wanted her afraid, and she was going to give him what he wanted.

O'Keefe smiled. "Now that we understand each other, Vivian, do you want to ask what you're doing here?"

Vivian swallowed. "What am I doing here?" she asked, her voice trembling.

"I'm surprised you haven't guessed. You're here because I've been trying to persuade your boss to help me out with a little conundrum, a little search, for someone that I need to find." O'Keefe shook his head as if he were disappointed. "So far, your Honor Huxley hasn't chosen to be very helpful. I'm hoping you can give her a little call, persuade her to change her mind."

"Maybe she doesn't know where this someone is. Ever think of that?"

"Mm, but I know for a fact she can help me, you see. In fact, if what people say about her is true, I suspect that by now she knows exactly where to find him. But I'm worried that not only has she decided not to cooperate, she might even be trying to make things more difficult for me."

"I don't know how she could do that," Vivian said, hoping her face didn't give anything away. He was far too close to the truth. "Big fancy man like you. What could she possibly do?"

If she had hoped the compliment would placate him, she had misjudged. O'Keefe gave her a disappointed look. "Well, that's what I thought. But all of a sudden, one of my newest recruits didn't show up where I was expecting him last night. And another one seems to have gone missing this morning. Which makes a man in my position worry." He began to pace a slow circle around her, and Vivian felt all the hair stand up on the back of her neck. She wanted to turn with him, to keep her eyes on him, but she wouldn't give him that satisfaction. "Your whisper sister wouldn't have anything to do with that, would she?"

"What makes you think I know anything about what Ms. Huxley is up to?" she countered.

O'Keefe stopped in front of her. "Because before that fella disappeared last night, he let fall some curious tidbits about your Ms. Huxley."

"And how would your new recruits know anything about her?" Vivian asked, too innocently. "You working with rats, mister?"

He didn't rise to the bait. "I work with people who can get me what I want. And this one had all kinds of interesting information. Apparently, Ms. Huxley's got quite the taste for sweet little Janes like you. And apparently, you aren't the sort of girl to tell her no."

Vivian could feel her face growing hot under his stare. When she didn't deny it, O'Keefe's lip curled in disgust. "Unnatural," he spat out.

"Says the murderer," Vivian said, not bothering to hide her scorn. Out of the corner of her eyes, she saw Clyde gave his head a warning shake, glaring at her.

But to her surprise, that made O'Keefe laugh. "Murder is plenty natural, my dear. I'd lay odds human history's been shaped by it more than any other single thing." He flashed his handsome grin. "You might even say I'm just claiming my place in a long, proud tradition that stretches back to the dawn of time."

"Modest fella, aren't you?" Vivian asked, giving him a grumpy look. He wouldn't believe her if she'd tried to hide her dislike, but she could still do her best to make sure he didn't take her seriously.

"Careful now, little bunny," he said. His grin never wavered, but he grabbed her chin, forcing it up so he could stare into her eyes. "You stay quiet and do what I say, you get to go home at the end of the day. You make me angry and . . ." His fingers bit into her skin, and Vivian's stomach lurched. "There's no knowing what I might decide to do."

Just as quickly as he had laid his hands on her, he let go. Vivian stumbled backward, and the sight seemed to amuse him. He chuckled. "Now, are you going to be a good girl and make the call like I asked?"

Vivian swallowed, trying to work some moisture into her dry mouth. "Yes," she managed at last. She might be playing at being an empty-headed bird, but there was nothing pretend about her fear.

O'Keefe patted her cheek. "Smart choice, little bunny," he said, heading back toward his lunch. "You know how to reach her, I presume?" O'Keefe asked, a mockery of a polite question. He looked pleased when Vivian nodded. "Excellent. Now, let's get to it."

There was a telephone in the hotel room. Clyde gripped her upper arm again and steered her toward it. "No funny business," he warned under his breath. "Mr. O'Keefe is listening, and so am I."

Vivian glared at him. "I hope you know you're a bastard," she hissed.

To her surprise he flinched. "Just do what you're told," he growled as he marched her over to the telephone.

Vivian shook off his hand as soon as she could. "What am I telling her?" she asked, turning to O'Keefe and ignoring her father completely.

O'Keefe poured himself another cup of coffee, adding generous helpings of cream and sugar to it. "Tell her that, if she'd like to retrieve you, she can meet us by the pier at the south end of Riverside Park. I love a picturesque setting for an exchange of ideas, don't you?"

"Oh, always," Vivian said dryly.

His eyes narrowed at her tone, but he decided to ignore it. Or maybe he was just entertained by her small moments of defiance. "She should be there at eight o'clock tonight. Alone. Tell her not to bother with going to the police. I'll have someone watching her to make sure she doesn't. And not a word about where we are now. Understand?"

"Crystal clear, mister," Vivian said, reaching for the telephone.

"Oh, and Vivian?" When she turned back to meet his eyes, O'Keefe smiled. "I hate to tell people things they should already know. But please make it clear that if she's planning to show up without the information that I want . . ." He shook his head. "Well, it would be better for her not to show up at all."

Vivian tried to ignore her suddenly shaking hands. "What happens to me if she doesn't?"

O'Keefe glanced past her, toward Clyde. "That's an interesting question, isn't it, Quinn?" he said softly.

When Vivian looked at her father, his face was stony. But he said nothing. Vivian stared at him until he was forced to meet her eyes, and she waited until he looked away first. Then she calmly reached for the telephone receiver and waited for the operator to connect.

"Circle two-four-four-one," she said, her voice only shaking a little. That was all right; they'd assume she would be nervous. She tried to shift a few steps away from her father without his noticing, putting more distance between the two men and the sound of the voice on the other end of the line. Then she held her breath, praying that someone would be there to pick up.

"Hello?"

Vivian didn't try to hide her relief. "*Honor.* Thank God. It's me, it's Vivian. I'm so glad you answered."

"Viv! What—what's going on?"

"Just listen, okay? I need you to listen." She looked at O'Keefe as she spoke, trying to keep the words slow and even so she didn't forget anything. "Mr. O'Keefe wants to meet with you. About . . . about that fella he's been looking for. You understand?" There was a long enough silence on the end of the phone that Vivian could feel sweat start to gather at the back of her neck. "Honor, you there?" she pleaded.

"Yes, I'm here. I understand."

She let out a shaky breath. "I'm with my father and Mr. O'Keefe right now. Mr. O'Keefe wants you to come to the pier at the south end of Riverside Park at eight o'clock tonight. You have to come alone, Honor, do you understand? He wants . . ." She glanced at Harlan O'Keefe, who was sitting forward in his chair, his hands flat on the table and his eyes fixed on her. She swallowed, and another trickle of sweat made its way down her spine. "We have to give him what he wants."

"Viv, where are you right now? Where is he staying?"

"I can't tell you where I am," she whispered. "He's here with me, I can't tell you."

O'Keefe smiled at her. "Good girl," he said softly.

"And Honor—" She took another careful breath and spoke slowly, each word clear and precise. "Honor, *you can't go to anyone else.*" O'Keefe's smile grew. "He's going to have someone watching you. You just have to meet us there, okay?"

"I got it, Viv. I've got it. It's all going to be all right, I promise."

"This is our chance to talk to him, okay? If we give him what he wants—"

"That's enough, now," O'Keefe said suddenly, standing so abruptly that the dishes on the little table rattled. "End it."

A moment later, Clyde was at her side, yanking the receiver from her hand and slamming it down, hard enough that Vivian jumped back. She glanced nervously at her father, then at O'Keefe, wondering if she'd said too much. Had she raised their suspicions? Or was O'Keefe just worried that if she talked any longer, she'd let more slip than he wanted?

She waited, holding her breath, to find out what was next for her.

O'Keefe didn't actually need her anymore, now that his meeting with Honor was set. If he was as ruthless as he seemed . . .

"Poor little bunny, you look so nervous." O'Keefe's smile was all teeth. "You're safe for now, if that's what you're wondering. Your Ms. Huxley will want to see you before she tells me any of what I want to know. So as long as you do what you're told . . ." He checked his watch, then shrugged into the jacket that had been tossed over the chair. Vivian watched, heart in her throat, as he went to the desk and calmly pulled out a gun. He gave the chamber a quick spin to check it before tucking it in his pocket. "I have some business to attend to in the next few hours. Quinn, I'll see you downstairs in five minutes. Petrovski will be up to watch over your little girl for you." Harlan O'Keefe picked up his hat and smiled at them. "We wouldn't want anything to happen to her, after all."

When the door closed behind him, the room was silent. Vivian could hear the shouts of street vendors and the honk of car horns echoing up from Broadway half a dozen stories below them. Out in the hall, someone asked a bellhop for directions; Vivian turned toward the voices before she could stop herself.

"I wouldn't suggest it," Clyde said, sitting down and helping himself to the basket of pastries that O'Keefe hadn't touched. "I'd have to stop you, and that would get unpleasant."

"You'd choose to, you mean," Vivian said, dropping into one of the suite's plush, flower-patterned chairs. "I don't see anyone forcing you to do a single damn thing."

"Then you haven't been paying attention," he said, shaking his head. "Mr. O'Keefe—"

"Who you chose to work for," Vivian said, crossing her arms.

"Mighta looked that way from the outside, but for a fella in my line of work, there wasn't any choice about it. O'Keefe came out of nowhere, and he was making a hell of a name for himself. You were either on his payroll or in his way. And I sure as hell didn't want to be in his way."

"In your line of work?" Vivian asked scornfully, and she didn't look away as he glared at her. "You want to pretend like you didn't pick that line of work on purpose? I saw where you grew up, it's not like it was your only option. So you found the toughest big six you could after years of small-time. And now you're gonna pretend like none of it was your fault?"

"You been talking to Ruth, then," he said, shoving the chair back and standing suddenly. Vivian tried not to flinch, but she couldn't help it; he was twice her size. But he saw the motion and, to her surprise, took a deep breath. Slowly, the fists at his sides unclenched. "She don't know a thing about it."

Vivian hesitated only a moment. "And what did my mother think of it?"

They stared at each other, and her father looked away first. "Don't make it harder than it needs to be, baby girl," he said, sighing. "I want you to go home at the end of this."

"Do you?" Vivian laughed. "You got a funny way of showing that you care."

"Look, I've got a job to do," he snapped. "I didn't ask you to come barging into my life. O'Keefe would have picked you up, one way or another, once he found out about—" He grimaced. "About you and that Huxley woman. And anyway, if you knew I was working for him—if you got such a low opinion of me—why come waltzing up to my front door today, huh? No one made *you* do that either."

"Maybe I thought you'd want to help me instead of him," Vivian said. She hadn't, but she wasn't going to tell him that. And she didn't want him to think too closely about it, so she asked quietly, "Does he know about Florence?"

Another beat of silence, and then Clyde shook his head. "No," he said, just as softly. "Wasn't any need to tell him I had two daughters."

It wasn't much, but it was something. O'Keefe's men had ended up at the Chins' restaurant anyway. But Lucky's friends were keeping an eye on things now, and she was willing to bet that O'Keefe wouldn't be interested in the amount of trouble he'd stir up by messing with them. And if he didn't know to connect Florence to her and Clyde . . .

"Guess that's something, then," Vivian said, sighing. "Not much, but something. At least she won't end up like Nora Murphy."

She threw the name out like a lit match, wanting to see what would happen, willing to take the risk that he might say something to O'Keefe. She wasn't disappointed. Her father started badly enough that he knocked over the coffee carafe, and he stared at her as the dark stain spread across the tablecloth.

"What do you know about Nora Murphy?" he asked, his voice cold.

Vivian didn't look away. "More than I'd like."

Clyde stared at her, and Vivian could almost see the wheels turning in his head, trying to piece together what she might mean. But before he could ask anything else, there was a sharp rap on the door—three swift knocks, a pause, and then a fourth. When it swung open, a tall man strolled in, his face drawn into a smirk and wiry muscles standing out in his neck. Vivian thought she recognized him; when she glanced down, she could see tattoos of ivy leaves and roses on the backs of his hands.

"You're wanted downstairs, Quinn," the man—presumably Petrovski—said, jerking his head toward the door.

"I'm not leaving you alone with her," Clyde growled.

Petrovski chuckled. "Don't worry, pal. O'Keefe made it clear that it's worth my tripes to mess with her."

"What did he tell you?" Clyde demanded.

Petrovski shrugged. "I don't know from nothing. But the boss is smiling like he has something special planned for tonight. Now get downstairs, or he's going to come up here to find you. And you know he won't be pleased about it."

Clyde turned to Vivian like he wanted to say something else. But he just growled and strode out of the room, yanking the door shut behind him so hard the fussy chandelier above it trembled in a tinkling chorus of glass.

Petrovski chuckled again. “Emotional lump of muscle, that one.”

Vivian watched him warily as he turned toward her, ready to bolt if he tried anything. But all he did was pull a pack of cards from the inside pocket of his coat. “Up for a game, doll?”

Vivian took a deep breath. Three hours and, one way or another, it would all be over. “Sure,” she said. “Why the hell not?”

TWENTY-NINE

Dusk had enveloped the city when they hustled Vivian out of the hotel. She would have laughed if she hadn't thought she'd get smacked around for it. The glittering wealth of the Ansonia all around her: guests in dinner jackets and silk hats; whispering gowns and fur wraps. Gentle music drifting out of one room, the murmur of voices all around them. And her, still in yesterday's clothes and clunky shoes, with two criminals looming on either side of her, hustling down the back steps and toward the service entrance of the hotel.

They were a wrong note in the music, a jagged rip in the silk. They should have been stared at and whispered about. The manager should have come running. Everyone they passed should have noticed they didn't belong.

No one blinked an eye. People were usually pretty good at ignoring the things they didn't want to see.

There was a car waiting for them behind the hotel, O'Keefe in the back seat impatiently checking his watch, her father in the driver's seat. Vivian didn't protest as she was bundled inside, Petrovski climbing in after her. She could feel O'Keefe's eyes on her, cold and watchful and probably even amused, waiting to see whether she would try to pull something.

She met them once and then looked away, pressing her cheek against the window as she stared out at the twilight. She could ignore the things she didn't want to see, too.

It wasn't a long drive to the park. At first Vivian was surprised that O'Keefe had picked it as their meeting spot. But of course he had, she realized, glancing at him from the corner of her eye. It was there in the silk handkerchief peeking out of his breast pocket, the carefully polished inflections of his voice that couldn't quite hide the tough Bowery lilt. A low-class crook with ambitions of being more, the man clearly wanted to belong here, among the rows of elegant mansions that faced the park, marble façades looking toward the river. As darkness crept off the river, most of them had lit their windows. There was clearly a party happening across Riverside Drive, judging by the half dozen cars parked on the street. Vivian could see a few drivers dozing behind the wheels as they waited for their bosses to emerge, stumbling drunk and hopefully cheerful with it. Vivian could hear music drifting out of the house, floating toward the water.

There was always music, no matter what corner of the city you found yourself in these days. If they all had nothing else in common, they had that.

The car rumbled to a stop, the pier just barely visible. The line of trees that snaked through the park cast wavering shadows across the footpaths, and there were almost no streetlamps here. Maybe that was the real reason O'Keefe had picked it.

Vivian climbed out when they told her to and lifted her head to the sky. For a moment, she could smell the cool breath of the river, without the tang of garbage and smoke from the piers that lined it farther downtown. For a moment, when the clouds drifted apart, she could see the faint glow of stars.

A growl from O'Keefe, and her father grabbed her arm and urged her away from the street. O'Keefe was a step ahead of them, Petrovski two steps behind, his head loose on his neck as he looked around. Clyde was watching her, waiting to see what she would do.

But Vivian followed where they led her, not looking left or right, not wanting to see who might be there, or might not. There was nothing left to try, no reason to want to get away. Not yet. She had done what she could, told who she could, and she had to trust that it was enough.

There was a figure in a suit waiting just ahead, leaning against a tree by the end of the pier, arms crossed and face concealed by the tilted brim of a hat. O'Keefe raised a hand, and the four of them stopped, Clyde still gripping Vivian's arm in his. Petrovski took up a position a few steps away, watching everyone at once.

"You're early," O'Keefe said. Vivian couldn't tell if he was displeased or not.

Honor lifted her chin. "You've got my girl there, mister. I'm not going to drag my feet coming to get her back."

THIRTY

"You've got what I want, then?" O'Keefe asked, looking Honor up and down. Vivian could hear the sneer in his voice.

"That depends." Honor sounded unruffled as always—even unimpressed. Vivian couldn't help smiling, in spite of her nerves. O'Keefe wouldn't like that. He wouldn't like the way she looked past him either, as if he wasn't worth the effort of keeping an eye on him. "How're we doing, Vivian?"

"Oh, peachy, thanks for asking, boss," Vivian said, her voice as light and careless as Honor's own had been. Down by her side, she cupped her hand into the shape of a *c,* brows raised in a question. Honor gave her a quick, tight smile, one fist bobbing up and down by her hip. *Yes, yes.* Vivian kept talking. "Mr. O'Keefe's a swell host, if you ignore the whole kidnapping part."

O'Keefe snorted. "Well, aren't you two charming. Cool as cucumbers and twice as convincing. Let me see your hands."

Honor held them up, then, carefully, pulled her jacket open, showing off her empty waistband. "No heat on me, O'Keefe. And since you apparently had your boys watching me all evening, you know I didn't go to the cops either."

He laughed. "No, you barely left your little business, did you? And you know what that tells me, lady? That you—"

"That I knew where to find Hugh Brown all along?" Honor said, smiling.

She was deliberately trying to rile him up. Vivian thought it was working; his attention was sharp and focused. "That you could have saved yourself all kinds of grief if you weren't such a dumb bird," O'Keefe snapped, the Bowery rasp in his voice growing more pronounced the more irritated he got. He snapped his fingers at Vivian. "Come here."

Clyde's hand tightened on her arm, and the obvious reluctance in the gesture made Vivian turn toward him in surprise. But he didn't meet her eyes. "Be smart, baby girl," he whispered, soft enough that only she could hear as he released her arm. "Whoever Brown is to you, he's not worth crossing O'Keefe."

"Is anyone worth that to you?" Vivian whispered. She didn't expect an answer, and he didn't give her one, just pushed her forward.

Vivian took three careful steps toward O'Keefe, but her eyes were on Honor, waiting.

"All right, I've been patient. You can see she's just fine. Now it's time for you to start singing, or I'll—" O'Keefe broke off. "What are you doing?"

"Just seeing what kind of operation you're running," Honor said, strolling toward them with her hands in her pockets. She didn't get close to O'Keefe, but she kept her eyes on him as she walked in a wide half circle around him. "I've heard so much about the mysterious Harlan O'Keefe. Can you blame a woman for being curious?"

O'Keefe turned with her, keeping her in his sights. "Taking notes?"

"I'm an ambitious woman, O'Keefe. I'm always ready to learn from an expert."

He snorted, amused again. "And maybe you think that if you flatter me, I won't leave you and your girl in the river tonight? Tell me where to find Hugh Brown and I might consider it."

Honor stopped right where the light from a lone streetlamp could catch her face. She was beautiful, and cold, and in that moment, Vivian loved her more than anything in the world. Honor smiled. "He's right there."

Vivian had guessed what Honor was doing, as soon as she had started circling. She'd had to word her message so carefully in the hotel room, but they had understood. Honor had maneuvered O'Keefe easily, keeping him just annoyed enough that his attention stayed on her.

Now, he spun around, snarling, to find Leo emerging from the shadows of the trees, the gun in his hand trained on O'Keefe. He stopped a few feet away. Clyde didn't move, watching the unfolding scene through narrowed eyes, but Petrovski did. He didn't make it more than two steps before he was stopped by Honor, who raised the short, glinting length of Vivian's Fitz Special—its stubby length designed especially to be concealed by plainclothes cops—and pointed it at him.

"I'd stay where I was, if I were you," she suggested. Slowly, Petrovski put up his hands, glaring at her.

"Mr. O'Keefe," Leo said. The wind off the river was picking up; it pulled at the open sides of his coat and ruffled his hatless hair. Leo didn't move. "And here I thought you'd never leave your cozy little setup in Chicago. Must have been something particular to pull you away."

O'Keefe's laugh was short and angry. "Don't play games with me, Brown," he said, his voice flicking through the night like a whip. "You've got something of mine, and I'm here to get it back. Where's my money?"

"I'll tell you." Leo cocked the hammer back on his gun. Vivian, poised on her toes between O'Keefe and her father, held her breath as she watched them. "After you tell me what happened to Nora Murphy."

"Nora Murphy?" O'Keefe stared at him.

Leo's face became even harder. "I really hope you're not about to tell me you don't remember her," he bit off, "or it's not going to end well for you."

"Oh, I remember her." To Vivian's surprise, O'Keefe began to laugh. "Sweet little Nora and her idiot father. You're telling me you were her fella?"

"You killed her whole family," Leo said. Vivian could see his chest heaving, but his voice was clipped and controlled. "Connor and Agnes Murphy, and their son Daniel. On August seventh in 1920. Don't deny it."

"I won't." O'Keefe's smile was broad and delighted as he paced toward Leo. "That time, I even pulled the trigger myself. Not my preference, of course. But sometimes you have to get messy, when you need to make a statement. So now I've answered your question, it's time for you to answer mine. What happened to my money?"

"You didn't answer my question," Leo snapped, his chin lifting like an alley dog scenting a rat. "Nora wasn't there with the rest of them. What did you do with her?"

"Oh, you can guess, can't you?" O'Keefe tilted his head to one side, his voice slick and taunting. "Nora ended up just like the rest of her family . . ." He leaned forward until he was only inches away from Leo's gun. "Once my boys were done with her, of course."

Leo pressed the barrel of his gun against O'Keefe's chest. Vivian could see his hand shaking. She wanted to believe he wouldn't do it, but his face was in deep shadow and she couldn't see his eyes.

O'Keefe's voice was soft. "Do you have it in you to shoot me, Hugh Brown? For what I did to your girl?" He laughed softly. "I don't think you do. I think if you were going to, it would have already happened."

They stared at each other, and Vivian could have sworn the entire world around them was holding its breath. There wasn't even a breeze off the water to break the silence.

Slowly, Leo stepped back. A beam of a streetlight caught his face, and he smiled. "I don't need to, O'Keefe. I just wanted to make sure they heard your confession."

The stomp of boots echoed through the night as dark figures swarmed toward them from the shadows of the trees and pier. Vivian threw up her hands against a sudden flood of light as one of the idling cars across the drive turned on its headlights, pinning O'Keefe and his men in its beams.

Petrovski and Clyde reacted first, stepping toward each other and raising their hands skyward, making it clear they weren't interested in going down swinging. O'Keefe snarled and swore, backing up slowly as half a dozen cops, in a mix of suits and uniforms, surrounded them.

Leo smiled and lowered his gun. "You had a chance to meet our fine city's commissioner yet, O'Keefe? Seems like he's a fella you should know." He glanced over his shoulder. "You heard all that, Commissioner?"

"Every word." Leo's uncle stepped forward, crisp and polished as ever, looking over the small crowd in front of him as though he couldn't decide whether to be bored or disgusted. "Thank you, mister . . ." He gave Leo a raised-brow look. "Mr. Brown, was it? We will take it from here. Gentlemen. Bracelets for our guests, if you please."

"You got nothing to hold me on," O'Keefe snarled as three cops approached him and his men, tucking away their pistols so they could pull out handcuffs from their belts and jackets.

The commissioner made a tsking sound. "You confessed to murder, Mr. O'Keefe—several murders, in fact—in full earshot of multiple officers of the law. Names and dates included." He stroked his mustaches and smiled. "Harlan O'Keefe is a well-known name. It's going to be a pleasure to bring you in."

Vivian could see Leo shaking as he stepped out of his uncle's way, and she wanted to go to him, to wrap her arms around him and tell him that at least he had his answers now. At least he had justice. She wanted to throw herself at Honor, still standing just at the edge of the pool of light, her gun vanished as soon as the cops had appeared. She wanted to lie down on the ground, right there in the middle of the park, and sleep for a week. But she didn't move a muscle, not wanting to get in the way or draw any more attention to herself.

She watched, hardly able to believe how well the whole setup had gone, as one of the cops approached O'Keefe.

It happened before she realized it, before any of them could move a muscle. The cop stumbled as though he had caught his foot on something in the dark, one hand flinging out instinctively to catch himself before he fell. Lightning fast, O'Keefe moved, catching the man's arm and yanking, sending him catapulting toward the ground. Vivian wasn't sure who shouted, but she saw half the men around her surge forward at the same time she did, as if it would make an inch of difference. And then they all froze, and O'Keefe was standing there, the cop's gun in his hand while the man himself groaned in the dirt. In the silence, Vivian could hear the music from across the drive once again, low and thrumming.

"Where's my money, Brown?" O'Keefe demanded, his voice eerily steady as he pointed the weapon straight at Leo.

But Leo stared back at him with remarkable calm. "Wrong choice, O'Keefe. I'm no one to these men." Vivian couldn't believe how coolly he said it; Leo had spent years of his life wishing that he meant something to his uncle. Now, he smiled like it was a point of pride. "Shooting me won't stop them from arresting you. In fact, it'll make it easier to bring you in for murder."

"I'm not planning to shoot you, my friend," O'Keefe said, and the smile that spread across his face made Vivian's blood run cold. "I'm planning to punish you."

She knew what he meant as soon as the words were out of his mouth. Another lost girl, another Nora for Leo to grieve, and this one he would blame himself for. For a moment, everything was sharp as glass. She saw O'Keefe turning toward her, the light from the car glinting on the barrel of the gun, Honor starting forward with a look of horror on her face. Vivian tried to move toward her, but as slow as everything around her felt in that moment, she still wasn't fast enough. She heard the gun fire, someone yelling her name.

And then there was a shadow between her and O'Keefe, and Vivian was staring into her father's eyes as he staggered toward her. He reached for her—slow, it all felt so slow—and then he was on the ground and she didn't know how it had happened.

She could hear shouting, and suddenly everything seemed to be happening at twice its normal speed. Leo had thrown himself at O'Keefe, tackling him to the ground, and the two of them were swinging and kicking at each other with the ferocity of a street-corner brawl. The cops were hauling them apart, someone had O'Keefe by the arms, Petrovski was staring at her in horror while someone pushed him to his knees, and Honor . . .

Honor was by Vivian's side, hands shaking on her shoulders as she looked her over head to toe. "Are you all right?" she demanded. "Vivian, say something. Are you hurt?"

Vivian knew what had happened. But she couldn't make herself say the words, couldn't admit it even in her own mind.

"I'm fine," she whispered instead, her voice barely loud enough to be heard over the noise. But Honor saw her lips move, and she dragged Vivian into an embrace so tight it might have been the only thing in the world holding either of them together as the scuffle continued around them.

But Vivian still pulled away. Someone else needed her.

She dropped to her knees, and Honor followed her down, pulling off her coat and bunching it into a wad of fabric. She slipped it under Clyde as, together, they rolled him over so that he was facing the sky. In that position, Vivian couldn't see the sticky dampness that was slowly seeping across his back. But it was all over her hands, and she didn't know where to put them until he gathered them into his.

"Why did you do that?" she demanded. She would have hit him if his hands hadn't been cradling hers against his chest. "Why would you do a stupid thing like that?"

The taste of salt caught her by surprise. She was crying, which didn't make sense. She didn't care about him, didn't even like him. He reached up to brush the tears away, his hand already cold and shaking.

"I always knew your ma was right to leave me, you know," he rasped. The words made him cough, and a trickle of blood spilled over his lips, but he still smiled at her. "She was a hell of a mother—hell of a woman. Loved her to the moon, even if I didn't deserve her. Glad I could prove her wrong about me, in the end."

"We'll get you to a hospital," Honor said, half standing.

But Clyde shook his head. "I've shot enough folks to know when it's my turn. Listen, baby girl. You listening?" Vivian tried to tell him that she was, but her voice wouldn't come, and he didn't wait for her to respond anyway. "O'Keefe's a liar. He's one of us, you know. Irish Catholics got their code. Shooting a man . . . Shooting a man in cold blood is one thing, but . . ." He coughed again, gasped for air. "Tell Hugh . . ."

"Tell him what?" Vivian begged. "Clyde, please, we have to get you help."

"Florence," Clyde whispered, wincing at each word. "Night. The mission. You see? She had a baby girl." He coughed again. "Do something, Vivian?"

"What?" she choked out, her throat almost too tight to breathe.

"Call me Dad?"

Vivian swiped angrily at her tears with the back of one hand. "Thank you, Dad," she whispered. She didn't forgive him—not now, maybe not ever. But in that moment, it didn't matter. "Thank you for saving me."

"Don't cry," he mumbled, his eyes losing focus but his hand still tight on hers. "World don't need one more selfish bastard like me in it."

"What if I could have needed you?" Vivian didn't even try to hold back her tears anymore. There was a smile on his face, but he didn't answer her.

Vivian didn't move, her hands tangled with his, until after his breathing had stopped. She didn't move as the shouting died down into crisp orders, as she heard O'Keefe snarling while he was hauled away. Vivian could hear footsteps, but she didn't have it in her to look up. Honor did, though, and she stood quickly, putting herself between Vivian and whoever was approaching.

"She needs a minute," Honor said, cold and authoritative.

A pause. "A minute, then," the commissioner allowed. "But he was with O'Keefe. My men will need to take him to the coroner's office. Who was he?"

"His name was Clyde Quinn," Vivian said, her voice shaking. She didn't say that he was her father; she wouldn't give Leo's uncle that part of her life. Not unless she had to. But she couldn't hide the angry grief in her voice either, far more than a single encounter—even one that had ended with him dead—could have justified. "He's got a sister."

"Hmm." It was impossible to pick out a single emotion in the commissioner's voice. "Well, if you can provide her address, we will notify her of his death. And Harlan O'Keefe will be charged with his murder, as well as that of the Murphy family. And attacking an officer of the law. And various . . ." A note of satisfaction crept into his voice. "Other incidents."

"You sound pleased," Honor said dryly.

"What's not to be pleased by?" the commissioner asked, and Vivian glanced up in time to see his brows lift in surprise. "A dangerous criminal has been removed from the streets. Wasn't that the goal here tonight?"

"And of course you'll be the one taking the credit for his arrest," Honor said, as disinterested as if she were discussing the weather. "That's the sort of thing that can make a man mayor, if he plays his cards right."

"However my city would like me to serve," the commissioner said.

Vivian could hear the satisfaction in his voice. She clenched her hands in the fabric of her father's coat. She knew that was the way things worked; she didn't have any right to complain about it. She had been counting on it when she called Leo from O'Keefe's hotel room and told him exactly how they were going to set things up. But that didn't mean she had to like it.

"I'm afraid your minute is up, Miss Kelly." The commissioner's eyes were on her when Vivian looked up. For a moment, she thought he was going to offer her a hand up, but he was eyeing the blood on her palms, and his lip curled in distaste. "Here," he said, pulling a handkerchief from his pocket and handing it to her.

Vivian supposed she should have been grateful he didn't just toss it onto her father's body. She wanted to throw it back in his face. Instead, she took it and carefully wiped her hands.

"By the way," the commissioner added, "Mr. Green tells me I have you to thank for tracking down O'Keefe so that we could organize this little meeting. You can expect a payment for your work."

"I didn't do it because I wanted your cash," Vivian snapped. She wanted to take a deep breath, but her chest felt too tight. Honor held out her hand, and Vivian hauled herself to her feet. Honor didn't let go once she was standing.

"Nevertheless." The commissioner's eyes flicked down to their joined hands, and his mouth tightened for a moment before his eyes slid away. "Never let it be said that I don't pay my debts."

He stepped back as two of his officers came forward with a stretcher. Vivian watched, stone-faced, as they heaved Clyde's body onto it and carried him toward the waiting police cars. Honor's grip tightened on hers, and Vivian clung to her like a lifeline.

The commissioner straightened his hat, then glanced around the park and nodded. "A productive night, indeed," he said with undisguised satisfaction. "Levinsky, are you about finished?" he called.

Vivian glanced around, finally taking in the rest of what was happening. O'Keefe and Petrovski were already gone, along with half of the officers. The man whose gun O'Keefe had grabbed was just staggering to his knees, his nose bleeding and his face smeared with dirt; another cop grabbed his arm to steady him while he stood. Leo was sitting on the ground, slumped and exhausted, while a cop she recognized turned his head from side to side to examine his face.

"Just wrapping up, sir," Levinsky said, stepping back and nodding to the commissioner respectfully. "Mr. Green here should see a doctor."

"I'm fine," Leo grumbled, but Vivian could see the bloody lump on his temple. "Just need a good night's sleep."

"Suit yourself," the commissioner said, shrugging. "But you did satisfactory work. If there are any medical expenses, you may send the bill to my office. I'll be in touch when I have further need of your services."

"When?" Leo asked. "That's a change of tune from these last few months."

The commissioner gave him a stern look. "I can always change my mind again." He waited a moment to see if Leo had anything else to say, then nodded and began to follow his men toward the cars.

"Commissioner." Vivian waited until he turned back around. "You should know, our rat said he wasn't the only fresh face on O'Keefe's payroll since he came back to New York."

The look the commissioner gave her was sharp, but all he said was "Oh?" as if he were bored.

"According to him, one of those new boys was the sort to wear a uniform." Vivian nodded toward the cop who had been overpowered by

O'Keefe, still groaning as he staggered into a car, his arm over another officer's shoulders. "Looked like bad luck, O'Keefe getting the jump on that fella. But I was standing pretty close when he went down, and I didn't see anything for him to trip over."

"Interesting." The commissioner gave her a considering look. "I appreciate your observation, Miss Kelly. If there's anything to it—"

"I don't care about your money," she said, her voice shaking.

He smiled at her. "Everyone cares about money. You'll be glad for it when you've had time to calm down. And until then . . . Miss Kelly. Miss Huxley." He turned away once more, his voice drifting over his shoulder and back toward the water. "I hope I won't see you anytime soon."

THIRTY-ONE

The three of them were left alone in the park, battered and staring at each other, as the sound of the cars faded into the distance. In the silence, Vivian could hear the music from the party across the street.

Honor was the first one to pull herself together. "You okay?" she asked Leo.

He nodded, though he looked a little dazed. "I can't . . . I'm not sure what to think about it all. But at least it's done. At least he's . . ." Leo swallowed, glancing at both of them and then looking quickly away. "It's done."

"Vivian?" Honor asked quietly.

It took Vivian a moment to find her voice. "I think I'm okay," she whispered. "I'm in one piece, anyway, which is . . ." She had to take a deep breath before she could continue. "Anyway, Leo's right. It's done."

"Good." Honor's voice grew sharp. "That means I can ask you what the *hell* you were doing. Did you think your Quinn was suddenly going to lend us a hand just because you asked nicely?" She grabbed

Vivian by the shoulders and shook her, her voice rising. "Do you know what could have happened to you? What they could have—"

It might have been the most emotion Vivian had ever seen from Honor; any other time, she would have been thrilled. But her father had just died, and all she wanted was to go somewhere quiet and cry. She yanked out of Honor's grip without letting her finish.

"Of course I didn't think he was going to change his mind," she snapped. "But he wasn't going to hurt me."

"Because he was your father?" Honor asked, snide with worry.

"No, because he would have done that already if that had been the plan. He didn't come to my place yesterday to rough me up, Honor. He came to grab me. And he would have, if Florence—" She broke off, suddenly too overwhelmed to talk. He had mentioned Florence at the end there. She slumped to the ground without caring that she was sitting in the dirt. "Spence knew about you and me, Honor. He must have told O'Keefe, and that's why he sent my father to grab me. He wanted to force your hand."

"What if it had been because he wanted to force mine?" Leo asked quietly. "Spence could have seen us together. It was a stupid risk to take."

Vivian shook her head, looking back and forth between them. She wished they would sit too; she hated the feel of them looming over her. But standing back up felt like too much effort. "You haven't been around the Nightingale as much the last few months. Spence remembered you enough to finger you to O'Keefe, but not more than that. He didn't know about—"

Remarkably, Vivian felt her face growing hot. She would have thought she was beyond embarrassment in that moment. But every emotion inside her felt too close to the surface. She cleared her throat. "I figured he couldn't have been trying to get to Leo. Which meant if my father saw me turn up at his place, he'd haul me off to O'Keefe. And that seemed like the only way we were going to find out where he was. And I was right," she added defensively. "He told me to call you, Honor, and—"

"And you didn't," Honor broke in, and her voice shook as she said it, with fear or anger or both. She was hurt, Vivian realized—hurt that she hadn't been the one Vivian turned to.

"I had to tip off Leo to how to set things up," Vivian said quietly. "I didn't just need both of you to show up—I did, I needed you there too—but he had to know that it was time for Hugh Brown to confront O'Keefe. That was the only way I could think of giving the commissioner something . . ." Vivian reached for Honor's hand; to her relief, Honor let Vivian pull her down to sit next to her. Vivian held on tightly. "I couldn't risk any of that message being lost. And I knew I could count on you to show up anyway, even if you didn't have the full story. I knew I could trust you." She felt Honor go very still next to her; Vivian hesitated only a moment before she laid her head against Honor's shoulder. She glanced at Leo. "Both of you."

Leo's smile didn't quite meet his eyes; she couldn't blame him for that. They were all silent for a moment, then he held out both hands. "Come on, ladies. Let's get out of here."

It didn't take them long to find a cab; it was still early in the night, and they were in a ritzy enough part of the city. The cabdriver looked them over sourly; Honor looked put-together as ever, but Leo was a mess, and Vivian suspected that she looked pretty awful herself. But Honor had plenty of cash on her, and that was enough to convince the driver to shrug away his concerns.

They rode to the Nightingale in silence. Vivian leaned her head back against the seat and closed her eyes. Anytime a thought flickered into her mind, she pushed it away. She'd have to face it all, soon. But for the moment, she could just be glad everyone had made it through in one piece.

Almost everyone.

At last, the cab pulled up to the curb.

"Stick around; I'm just hopping out for a moment," Leo told the driver. The man grunted, still watching them uncertainly, but he didn't pull away once they had all climbed out.

Leo let out a long sigh. "Well, Viv, I can't say I was a fan of your pop. He pulled a real dirty one on me. But at least at the end . . ." He trailed off, as if he wasn't sure what to say.

Vivian wasn't sure either. He hadn't been her father—not really. But he had been excited to meet her. He had said he wanted to get to know her and Florence. He had told them about their mother and brought them pictures of his wedding day.

Then he had turned her over to his boss. He might have hesitated about it, but he had done it just the same, telling himself that he was just doing his job, knowing it might end up with her getting hurt or worse. And now he was gone, and she was an orphan once again.

She didn't know what to do with that. Maybe she never would. But she could tuck it away, very carefully, somewhere she could take it out and examine it from time to time until she had made her peace with it.

"And now I've got answers," Leo said, his voice shaking a little. "So that's something. And you . . ." His eyes flicked to Honor. "Well, I don't know about you two, but I think I could sleep for a week after all that excitement," he said. The jokiness in his voice was clearly forced, but Vivian appreciated the effort as he smiled at them. "We did good, didn't we?" he added. "All three of us."

"We did good," Vivian echoed. She didn't quite look at Honor as she said it.

She felt Honor's eyes on her anyway. "I'll give you two a moment," she said, cool as ever. "See you inside, Vivian?"

Vivian nodded. "See you inside."

She and Leo were silent once they were alone on the sidewalk. The streetlamps caught the angles of Leo's cheekbones and the shadows under his eyes. Vivian wondered if she looked as exhausted as he did.

"Are you sure you're okay?" she asked at last. "I know you've spent a lot of time thinking about Nora. Are you . . ." She trailed off, still not sure what she was trying to say or ask. But she remembered the look in his eyes when he confronted O'Keefe.

He had been hoping, even if he hadn't admitted it to himself until that moment. There had never been a body, so Leo had spent five years hoping that maybe, *maybe,* Nora was still alive.

She didn't say that out loud. She had a feeling he'd already figured it out for himself.

"I'd rather have an answer I hate than no answer at all," Leo said, and the heartbreak in his smile made her want to cry for him. "I'd rather be able to move on."

"And to know that O'Keefe is going to pay for what he did?" Vivian asked, wishing she could offer him something more.

"I'll take it if I can't get anything else." Leo glanced toward the corner where Honor had disappeared. "You going to be okay in there? Your Ms. Huxley didn't look so pleased with you."

Vivian bit her lip. "Leo, I—"

"You remember the first night we met?" he asked, fidgeting with his hat and not quite meeting her eyes.

"Hard to forget," Vivian said dryly. There had been a police raid at the Nightingale in the middle of their first dance together, and she had ended up in the drunk tank until Bea showed up to post her bail. Leo had been rounded up, too, and called Danny to bail him out.

"I asked you that morning, after we all had breakfast together, if your boss thought you were sweet." He looked up from his hat at last. "I think she does."

"Leo . . ." Vivian wasn't sure what she wanted to say.

But he seemed to understand anyway. He leaned forward to place a quick kiss on her cheek. "Thank you for what you did today, Viv." He set his hat on his head, tweaking the brim so it sat at just the right angle, and smiled at her. "See you soon, pal."

When Vivian made her way down to the empty dance hall, Honor was seated at the bar, waiting. Vivian slid onto the stool next to her.

"Are you angry with me?" she asked softly.

"For sneaking out of here without a word to me or Danny?" Honor asked. She stared straight ahead as she spoke. "Yes."

"You would have tried to stop me—"

"For handing yourself over to Quinn when you knew what he'd do? You bet I am. For putting yourself in danger? Absolutely. For nearly getting yourself shot today? Add that to the list."

Vivian sank farther into her chair with each icy statement. She wished Honor was the sort of person who yelled. But that careful, controlled expression was back.

"Honor—" Vivian whispered.

Honor held up a hand, turning toward her at last, and Vivian fell silent. "I'm angry because I was scared. I was so goddamn scared, Vivian, and if anything had happened to you, I couldn't have—"

Vivian threw herself at Honor, so forcefully she almost toppled off her stool, wrapping her arms around her and burying her face against Honor's shoulder. She breathed in the scent of her, the vanilla and vetiver of her perfume, the lingering starch on her shirt. Honor held her just as tightly.

Honor's laugh vibrated through both of them. "It's going to be a real education, loving you."

Vivian's head snapped up, and she stared at Honor as she tried to find her voice. "Do you mean that?" she managed at last.

"I do." Honor tilted her head to one side, watching Vivian closely. "Do you believe me?"

"Yes. No. I do. I mean, I hoped—"

Vivian was almost grateful when Honor laid a single finger against her lips, cutting off her stumbling words. Honor smiled, red lips tilting up slowly at the corners. "This is when you say it back, pet," she murmured, sliding her finger away.

"I . . ." Vivian met her eyes and took a deep breath. "I think you should take me upstairs. It's been a hell of a day, and I would like to stop thinking about it all." Honor stared at her in surprise, and Vivian leaned forward, letting her lips brush against Honor's ear. "And then I might have a few little words to say to you too."

Honor turned her head, just enough that her mouth hovered only inches away from Vivian's. "You're going to keep me on my toes, aren't you, pet?"

Vivian smiled. "Yes, Ms. Huxley. I think I am."

THIRTY-TWO

Florence didn't speak as Vivian stumbled her way through describing what had happened the night before, just held Mei against one shoulder and gently patted her back. Danny and Lucky were both there too, Danny with one arm around Florence and Lucky hovering at the door to the parlor. Florence didn't say anything after Vivian finished, either, just breathed slowly and deeply as she stared toward the window.

Ruth had enough questions for them both, and enough tears.

"I know he wasn't a good man, but he was my brother," she whispered as she wrapped her arms around herself. "I'm glad in the end—" She swallowed. "And I suppose I still have some family left. If you want me, that is."

Florence didn't answer; Vivian did her best to smile at her aunt. She wasn't sure how successful she was. "We've always wanted family," she said quietly. "I'm sorry about Clyde."

"Me too," Ruth whispered. "For a lot of reasons." She cleared her throat, glancing between the dry-eyed faces around the room. "I need to go fix my face," she muttered, standing and quickly heading toward the washroom.

Vivian didn't blame her for wanting a moment alone.

"Well," Lucky said, with a jarring degree of cheerfulness once Ruth was gone, "guess I can tell the boys to head home, if O'Keefe's going to prison. I would say let's hope they can make the charges stick, but it sounds like the commissioner won't let this one slip through his fingers."

"Not likely," Vivian said, but her attention wasn't on him. "Flo, are you okay?"

Florence glanced at Danny. "Do you think it's done?" she asked.

Danny squeezed her hand. "We'll see if it's in the papers later today. If the commissioner has already tipped them off, then Lucky's right. He's not going to let this one get away. I think we're probably in the clear."

"Good." Florence nodded sharply. "And good riddance."

"You mean to O'Keefe?" Vivian asked.

"Of course not," Florence said, meeting Vivian's eyes at last. "I mean Quinn."

Vivian felt as though someone had punched her in the stomach. "You don't mean that, do you?"

"Of course I do," Florence said, her voice chillingly calm. "Why wouldn't I?"

"He was our father."

"He made it clear that he wasn't," Florence replied, turning to Danny. "Don't you agree?"

Danny glanced between the two sisters. "Can't say I want to get in the middle of this one," he said slowly. "But if I'm going to agree with anyone, it's with Florence."

"Because she's your wife?" Vivian demanded. "Or because you think she's right?"

She wasn't sure why she felt so angry. She had hated him too, by the end. She had known with just as much certainty as Florence that he had thrown away the chance to be their father. But Florence hadn't been there. She hadn't held Clyde Quinn's hand as he died. He hadn't asked her to call him Dad.

"I don't want to listen to this anymore," Florence said abruptly, standing. "He was barely in our lives to begin with, I'm not going to fall apart because he's gone again. O'Keefe was who really mattered, anyway. If he's locked up, that's all I need to know." She turned to Danny. "Take the baby."

Startled by the abrupt demand, he held out his arms, and Florence handed him their daughter. Without another word, she walked into the bedroom and yanked the door closed behind her.

Lucky whistled. "Good luck with that." When Danny glared at him, he shrugged, holding up his hands defensively. "Okay, okay, don't have kittens. I'm off to help Auntie in the kitchen while you deal with your domestic squabbles."

"Lucky?" Vivian said quietly as he headed for the stairs. When he turned back, she gave him a tight smile. "Thank you for your help."

He shrugged. "It's what we do for family, yeah? And you're some kind of family now, Viv, even if it's not the normal kind." He grinned and glanced at Danny. "Better watch it, though, Danny. I don't think the little woman's going to be such a big fan of your job, after this."

Once he had disappeared downstairs, Vivian gave Danny a nervous look. He had settled Mei against his chest, and the baby was sucking her fist as she stared dreamily at her father through half-closed eyes.

"Are you going to go talk to her?" Vivian asked.

Danny shook his head. "You are," he said.

Vivian glanced nervously at the bedroom door. "I think she's upset with me."

"She's upset all right, but not with you. Unless she's angry at you for sneaking out on your own to get to O'Keefe. Which I am too," Danny added.

Vivian scowled. "Everyone wants to be angry about that, but no one seems to want to admit that I was right."

"You can be right, and we can still be angry," Danny said quietly. "But that's not the point right now. Quinn wasn't my dad. He was yours. And hers. So stop stalling and go talk to her."

She knew he was right. Vivian took a deep breath and knocked on the bedroom door. "Flo?" she called softly. "Can I come in?"

The pause was long enough that she started to worry. "Yes," Florence said at last.

When Vivian opened the door, she found Florence sitting cross-legged on the bed. They had all just been rising for the day when Vivian arrived to tell them the news, and Florence was still in her wrapper, hair falling out of the braid that she had worn overnight and cheeks flushed with emotion.

And she was emotional, Vivian could see now. Whatever composure Florence had managed in front of the others was gone now. She wasn't crying, but she was close. Scattered on the bed around her were the photographs Clyde Quinn had given them.

Vivian sat down next to her without speaking. Florence let her fingers drift over a photograph of her as a baby in her mother's arms; one of Mae Kelly—Mae *Quinn*—laughing in front of the house where they had found Ruth, one hand up to shade her eyes against the sun: one of Mae holding dark-haired baby Vivian while little Florence clutched at her knees, which they had been given by a near-stranger months ago, when they first began to piece together their mother's history. At last, Florence picked up the photograph of their parents on their wedding day.

"We're better off without him," she said.

"We are," Vivian agreed. "But it's still hard."

Florence nodded. "It's still hard," she echoed softly. "And there's still Ruth."

"She's glad we found her," Vivian said.

Florence sighed. "She is." They were quiet again for a moment.

"Danny told me about the money Clyde stole," Florence said. "Where do you think it ended up?"

With everything that had happened, Vivian had almost forgotten about the job that had started all Leo's trouble. "I don't know," she said at last. "I mean, I guess if he had it stashed anywhere, it was probably in Chicago." She laughed. "And I doubt it was in a bank. Or not most of it. But if it was . . . is it technically ours?"

Florence snorted. "Good luck trying to prove that. If it's in a bank somewhere, it's probably Ruth's. And if it's not . . ."

"Probably a nice surprise under a mattress for whoever empties out his home," Vivian said. "Can you imagine? Whatever rotten landlord he had goes in to toss his things down the stairs, and he pulls off the mattress, and he finds . . . he finds . . ." She was laughing too hard to finish.

Florence began laughing too, and soon they were both leaning against each other as they howled. Vivian couldn't tell if they were laughing or crying anymore. Probably both.

"Well, I'd have liked a pile of cash," Florence said at last, wiping her eyes. "But not one that was stolen."

"No, not that," Vivian agreed. "Maybe I'll ask Leo to tip off the commissioner. I'm sure he can ask the brass buttons in Chicago to track down where Clyde Quinn lived."

"Poor landlord," Florence said, her face not quite straight.

"Poor landlord," Vivian agreed. She glanced sideways at her sister, hesitating. "I think he was trying to talk about you, in the end. Clyde was."

"What do you mean?"

"He said your name." Vivian frowned, trying again to remember Clyde's final words. "It was so muddled. But he said your name, and he wanted me to call him Dad."

They were silent for another moment. Then, "I'd have liked a father better than a pile of cash," Florence said quietly.

Vivian sighed and leaned against her sister's shoulder. "Me too, Flo," she said softly. "Me too."

They sat like that until Vivian was late for work.

Vivian had worried what would happen when the Nightingale reopened, whether anyone would show up or whether word had gotten around that the sultry little back-alley dance hall had been shut down. Would anyone peek down the alley to see that the flickering light was lit once again? How many voices would whisper that they wanted to *dance 'til last call* and then find their way downstairs to do just that?

She shouldn't have worried. Whether it was because word had gotten around, or because enough people had missed the Nightingale's brief closing in the first place, there was no shortage of dancers on the floor that night, spinning and kicking for the Charleston or sliding cheek to cheek in a tango. There was no end to the calls for French champagne and Canadian whiskey and "gin, but the good kind if you have it." The band played sweeter and hotter than ever and still could barely keep up with Bea, who was so busy pouring her heart into every note that she barely seemed to stop for breath.

The Nightingale's staff seemed high on the energy of the night, running from table to table without complaining, sliding drinks across the bar without pause, barely waiting for their breaks to jump on the dance floor with their favorite regulars. Vivian even thought she saw Benny crack a smile as Bea began humming the opening bars of "Yes Sir, That's My Baby," though he quickly wiped the expression from his face and resumed his normal stoic scowl.

The lights were dimmed for the evening, as always, but they still caught on a thousand and more spangles, on the beads and jewels draped around the women's necks, the gem-colored gowns in silk and satin, the snowy linen of men's shirts already plastered to their shoulders with sweat. The air smelled of smoke and Barbasol and half a dozen perfumes. It smelled like home, and Vivian couldn't stop smiling as she breathed it in.

Spence was gone, of course. But there was a new bartender helping Danny out; Vivian shook her head when he turned to grin at her and she realized it was Lucky.

"Just filling in the gaps," he said as he deposited a batch of rum cocktails on her tray. "This isn't exactly my scene, but what's a favor between cousins?"

"It's not a favor if you get paid for it," Danny said, smacking Lucky affectionately on the back of the head as he reached past for a bottle of gin.

But Danny's smile didn't quite reach his eyes as he turned to the next round of customers crowding at the bar. Vivian wanted to stop and talk to him, to ask how Florence had been for the rest of the day, if he was okay too. But the night was too busy, the crowd too eager. She was pulled along with them, until she and Bea were slipping out to the alley for a breath of cold air and found him just coming down the stairs from Honor's office.

The heaviness of his expression pulled Vivian up short. "Danny, what's wrong?" she asked, a familiar jolt of fear in her chest as she glanced around to make sure no customers were close enough to hear them. "Was there some kind of news about O'Kee—"

"No, nothing like that," Danny said, the dejected look disappearing into a smile so quickly it might not have been there at all. "You girls on your break?"

"Heading out back for a nip and a rest," Bea said, patting her thigh where she'd tucked a little silver flask into her garter. "But just a short one. It's a wild crowd in there tonight, and they want the full show." She glanced toward the stairs. "Everything all right upstairs with the boss?"

"Swell," Danny said. "Just talking some business."

"New bartender," Bea guessed, nodding. She knew, by now, what had really happened to Spence. She had taken the news in stride, saying only that she was glad she could go back to disliking him now that she knew he wasn't dead. "Well, maybe you two can think about adding another singer to the roster too."

Danny gave her a sharp look. "A new singer?" he asked. "Any particular reason?"

Bea shrugged. "Even my pipes need a break sometimes," she said.

"Fair enough," Danny said, nodding. "All right, enjoy your break, girls."

He still didn't quite meet their eyes as he said it. Vivian stared after him as he disappeared into the dance hall until Bea called after her to hurry up, she wasn't going to hold the door forever.

"That was strange, wasn't it?" Vivian asked as Bea slid the brick into place to hold the door open. "I'm not imagining things."

Bea sighed as she slid the hem of her skirt just high enough to retrieve her flask. She took a quick drink and passed it to Vivian. "Hoo, should have asked for something higher quality than that. Burns as it goes down, so watch it." She shook her head. "I'm not too surprised. Figured it was only a matter of time, once he settled down with Florence."

"Figured what was only a matter of time?" Vivian asked before she took her own gulp.

"You can't guess?" Bea asked. "He's gonna quit."

Vivian stared at her. "Quit what?"

"Quit the Nightingale." Bea sighed as she leaned back against the wall, turning her face up toward the narrow patch of sky visible over the alley. "Bet you anything."

"But why?" Vivian demanded.

"Why?" Bea shook her head. "Viv, he's got a wife he's ga-ga over and a baby at home. You think he enjoys heading out every night, hoping he doesn't get picked up in a raid and have to call home for bail money? No, I think our Danny-boy is ready to settle down at last."

"But—" Vivian swallowed the tight feeling in her throat and shook her head. "But Danny loves the Nightingale."

Bea shrugged. "Of course he does. But he loves Florence and Mei more." Seeing the expression on Vivian's face, Bea gave her a wry smile. "You know, once I'd have expected a girl like you to do better with things changing. But you lose your head over it, every damn time."

"Bea—" Vivian stared at her in horror. "You're not leaving too, are you?"

Bea tried and failed to hold back a laugh. "Lord almighty, girl, the look on your face right now. No, I'm not planning on leaving." She shook her head. "If that producer had turned up and offered me a record deal, I wouldn't turn that down, though I think I missed my shot when things around here closed. But even then, the farthest I'd go would be moving my family into the nicest part of Harlem that would have us. And I'd still come back to sing at the Nightingale. Now come on." She hopped down from the stack of crates. "I have to get back, or Mr. Smith'll throw a fit."

Vivian followed her back inside; while Bea headed for the bandstand, Vivian looked immediately for Danny. But the night was too busy for her to corner him. It wasn't until after closing, once everyone else was gone, that she found him talking quietly with Honor at the bar. They fell silent when she came close, watching her with curious expressions.

"Is Bea right?" Vivian asked. "Are you leaving?"

Honor laughed. "That girl's smart as they come. I really should give her a raise."

"And a backup singer," Danny said, nudging his boss's shoulder. "She's right about that too. We don't want to risk losing her."

Honor shook her head. "I know. I'll look into it."

Danny gave Vivian a smile. "Kitten, don't look so down. I'm not going far. But the party has to end sometime. Mine's happening at home these days. Try not to be too sad about it, okay?" He tapped her nose playfully. "I'm not. And it's not like I won't see you around."

"And it's not like you won't still turn up here from time to time," Honor said, leaning her elbows back against the bar. "You'll just have your dancing shoes on when you do."

Danny pulled Vivian into a one-armed hug. "Don't get too bent out of shape over it," he said. "You couldn't get rid of me entirely if you wanted to."

"Considering you're married to my sister . . ."

He laughed as he went to grab his hat and jacket from the hook behind the bar. "See you tomorrow night, ladies," he said, heading for the basement door.

Vivian didn't know what to say once he was gone, but Honor did.

"Come on, pet," she said, her lips curving up in the soft smile that caught Vivian by surprise each time. She held out her hand. "You look like you could use some cheering up."

When Vivian arrived at the dress store the next morning, there were no boxes on the counter waiting for her. But Miss Ethel was on the telephone, her hands fluttery and apologetic as she tried to reassure whoever was on the other end.

"Of course, ma'am. Of course. I'll send someone over to deal with it right away," Miss Ethel simpered. "You have my sincere— Yes, that one, the delivery girl— No, not long—"

Miss Ethel broke off abruptly, staring at the telephone in her hands, her face twisted with anxiety and irritation. "Vivian," she snapped, scribbling an address on a slip of paper and shoving it across the counter. "This one first. Then head to the hat shop to see if they need more swatches."

"Of course, Miss Ethel," Vivian said, but she wasn't really listening.

She could guess exactly who was summoning her, and she glanced without surprise at the address on the piece of paper when she picked it up.

Mrs. Wilson, it seemed, had a few things to say.

"Well, Miss Kelly," Hattie Wilson greeted her from behind a newspaper, turning the pages with a snap. "You've certainly been busy."

There was something odd about the way she was speaking; it took Vivian a moment to realize that the usual impatience and condescension was gone from her voice.

"What do you mean?" she asked warily.

Hattie folded back the page she had been reading and tossed it onto the desk. It slid toward Vivian, who caught it with a quick smack of her hand. And there it was: *Criminal Ring Broken Up, Boss Behind Bars.* And next to a photograph of Harlan O'Keefe snarling at the camera, there was one of Leo's uncle seated at his desk, hands folded in front of him and wearing a sober, satisfied expression. Vivian studied the commissioner longer than she studied O'Keefe. That too-modest look on his face said he'd be announcing his bid for office soon, she had no doubt.

Vivian glanced up at Hattie Wilson. "What makes you think I—"

"Because I'm not an idiot," Hattie said dryly. "And because people like to talk."

"The police arrested O'Keefe," Vivian pointed out, crossing her arms. "You saying I'm a snitch?"

Hattie's smile had an edge. "I'm saying you and your Ms. Huxley know how to get things done. No one knows the full story yet, of course, and the commissioner is certainly going to be riding the coattails of his version for the foreseeable future. But word gets around. O'Keefe set his sights on an unimportant little place called the Nightingale, and all of a sudden he's behind bars for murder? Multiple murders?" She laughed, shaking her head. "Do you remember when we first met, Miss Kelly?"

"Sure," Vivian said warily. Mrs. Wilson had been wrapped in the protection of her new widowhood then, performing grief for the husband that she had come to despise. Even then, her eyes had been diamond-hard. "I figured out pretty quick you were dangerous."

"Because you're smarter than I gave you credit for." Hattie shook her head. "I'll admit it took me a little longer to realize you had sharp edges of your own."

"Hard to get by in this world if your edges are too soft," Vivian said. She leaned forward. "Speaking of, Mrs. Wilson, any chance of you sharing what happened to Bruiser George?"

"He learned his lesson," Hattie Wilson said, shrugging. "Best to leave it at that." Then she pursed her lips. "Though I can't quite leave it at that, can I? You found my rat before I did, Miss Kelly. I suppose that means I owe you another favor. Any chance you want to name your price now, instead of drawing this one out too?"

Vivian was caught off guard enough that she almost said no. She didn't trust Mrs. Wilson at the best of times; after everything with O'Keefe and Bruiser George, she was even more wary of the woman than usual.

Then she remembered her visit to Salon Doré, and she knew exactly what she was going to ask for.

"You know Ralph Peer, don't you? The record producer?"

Hattie Wilson's brows rose in surprise. "Noticing little thing, aren't you? Yes, I know him. Why do you ask?"

Vivian took a deep breath. "I want you to arrange for him to come to the Nightingale. He likes to scout new talent, right? And he likes jazz. Tell him there's a singer there who's worth listening to."

"You want him to spend an evening listening to your friend the Bluebird?" Hattie's lips pulled into a cynical smile. "You won't get far in this world using your favors like that, Miss Kelly. Take my advice and sit on this one for a while. Better to keep it for when you really need it."

"I've done okay so far," Vivian said, quiet but firm. "Bring him this Friday."

She could see that Mrs. Wilson was laughing at her, but she didn't care. She didn't want Bea to leave the Nightingale—didn't even want her to leave their corner of the city. But Vivian knew what an opportunity like this would mean to her friend. And she didn't want Bea to end up like Danny someday, with her family in danger because of where she worked.

A visit from a record producer wasn't a sure thing. Nothing was a sure thing. But Vivian knew beyond a doubt that Bea, with her voice like honey and smoke, and the sort of presence on stage that no one could look away from, had all the makings of a star.

Hattie Wilson shrugged. "All right then, if you say so. Doesn't matter much to me, one way or another. I'll make sure he's there on Friday. Will that be sufficient for you?"

"As long as you put in a good word about Beatrice Bluebird before you bring him over, that'll be swell," Vivian said.

"Lovely," Mrs. Wilson said, baring her teeth in a smile. "Out you go now."

Vivian intended to do what she was told. But she paused with her hand on the doorknob, and she was half turned back before she could think better of it. "You said word's going around that the Nightingale had something to do with O'Keefe's arrest. But Honor's kept things quiet. So how exactly is that word getting out?"

Hattie shrugged. "People talk, you know. And there are a lot of them working at your Nightingale."

"But not many of them who know O'Keefe's name, or what happened. In fact . . ." Vivian gave Mrs. Wilson a narrow-eyed look. "In fact, you're one of the few people who knew what was going on *and* that he had anything to do with it. So tell me again, how do you think word is getting out?"

Hattie Wilson's smile glinted like a knife. "I haven't the faintest idea," she said. "But you know what they're also saying? That O'Keefe had a few rats out there, including among my boys. And it ended as poorly for them as it did for him. Maybe worse. Who's to say for sure?" She settled back in her chair and picked up her newspaper again. "I expect that no one will want to bother your Ms. Huxley or her Nightingale for some time. Which I can't say I'm sad about, as it seems they'll also think twice, now, about interfering with me. And isn't it fun when people like us get the respect we deserve?"

"You've got a strange definition of fun, Mrs. Wilson," Vivian said softly.

Hattie smiled without looking up, folding back a new page of the newspaper. "Please remember to close the door on your way out, Miss Kelly. I have a busy day ahead of me, and I would hate to be interrupted."

Unnerved, Vivian was about to leave. But a story on the page Hattie Wilson had just turned caught her eye. She stared at it, then— "Sorry, just a moment, thanks," she said, crossing the room to yank it from Hattie's hands.

"I beg your pardon, Miss Kelly?" Hattie half rose from her seat, though she looked more surprised than outraged.

Vivian didn't answer, too busy scanning the headline that she had noticed. *Florence Night Mission, Bleecker Street Home for Unwed Mothers, Benefits from Anonymous Donation*. Her heart sped up, and she shoved the paper back at Hattie Wilson.

"Sorry, Mrs. Wilson, I have to go. Thanks again for arranging that visit from Mr. Peer."

Before Hattie Wilson could ask anything else, Vivian hurried from the room.

The building at 21 Bleecker Street wasn't that far from the Nightingale. But Vivian didn't often walk past there—no one she knew did, if they could help it. This stretch of Bleecker Street was dismal in the daytime, and at night, it turned downright hazardous.

The mission house itself made Vivian nervous as she stared up at it. She had spent plenty of days worried about ending up somewhere like this; it was one of the reasons she had, for most of her life, let romance sweep her away only so far and no farther. But there was no avoiding it today.

Vivian took a deep breath and walked in.

The woman behind the desk was polished and presentable, but there was an air of the previous century to her. Her deep brown hair was winged with gray and worn swept back in an old-fashioned chignon. Her clothing was clean and professional, covering her arms to the wrists and her neck to the chin. Vivian could guess that if she stood, her skirt would reach nearly down to her ankles.

But her expression as she greeted Vivian was soft. "How can I help you, my dear? Are you . . ." A quick flicker of the woman's eyes across Vivian's midsection. "Are you in need of assistance?"

Vivian took a deep breath. "Yes, but not the kind you're thinking of. I'm hoping to find someone."

THIRTY-THREE

"Tell me again where we're going?" Leo asked, glancing out the windows. "Am I being kidnapped?"

"Such a funny guy," Vivian said dryly, one leg bouncing nervously no matter how she tried to stop it. "Yes, you're being kidnapped, and this is my getaway train."

"Always knew you were a dangerous girl," Leo said, grinning. But even his cheerful jokes couldn't hide the fact that he was puzzled, maybe even a little worried. "You won't tell me more?"

"I think it's a seeing sort of situation," Vivian said. She stood abruptly as the train rattled into the station. "This is our stop."

Leo followed her off, and he didn't ask any more questions as she led him along the newly paved Bronx streets. It was quieter out here, though that was changing. As they walked, the nervous pit in Vivian's stomach seemed to grow. By the time they approached the large cluster of buildings, steeples pointing toward the sky and rows of windows watching them like eyes, she was suddenly afraid that she'd made a horrible mistake.

Leo glanced at the sign next to the drive. "The New York Catholic

Protectory," he read slowly, frowning. "Vivian, is this . . . is this where you grew up?"

She nodded, her mouth suddenly dry as sandpaper. "Maybe we should go back," she said abruptly, starting to turn around.

Leo caught her arm. "Vivian, what's going on?"

She swallowed, shaking as she met his eyes. "O'Keefe lied," she whispered. "I figured out what happened to Nora."

Leo stared at her, not understanding. Then, slowly, he turned to stare at the sign in front of them, the cluster of dormitories and school buildings, the church in the center of it all.

"Leo?" Vivian said, close to tears. "Say something, please. I'm sorry, I thought it would be . . . We can go back if you want. I'm sorry—"

He gripped her arm tightly, cutting her off. She could see his throat working, as though forming the words took more effort than usual. "I don't want to go back," he said at last, his hand dropping by his side. "What—who did you want to show me?"

Vivian took a deep breath. She wasn't relieved, not yet. It was too early for relief. But he knew, or he thought he knew, and he wasn't begging to leave. He didn't hate her for finding out. That was something. She took his hand and turned her face toward the once-familiar entryway. "This way. The Mother Superior is expecting us."

Leo didn't say anything more, but he didn't protest either as she led him up the drive. He didn't speak as they were greeted by the Mother Superior, just nodded stiffly when Vivian introduced him. The nun gave him a sympathetic look as she led them into her office, adorned only by a crucifix on the wall and, to Vivian's surprise, a vase of red and orange flowers on the windowsill.

The nun saw her glancing at them and smiled. "We all need a little beauty in our lives, do we not?" she said gently. Vivian, busy trying not to be overwhelmed with memories, nodded silently.

The Mother Superior glanced between them. Her eyes settled on

Leo, and she nodded, as if a puzzle piece had slotted into its appropriate place. "So, you are here about Mollie, I understand?"

Vivian heard Leo make a noise in the back of his throat; when she glanced at him, she could see the muscles standing out in his jaw from how tightly his teeth were clenched together. She swallowed. "Yes. When I spoke to Sister Mary Helen, she was able to help me piece together what had happened. But she said you could share some more information?"

"Certainly." The Mother Superior nodded, brisk and businesslike as she went to the cabinets that lined the walls. It took her only a few minutes of searching to find the file she was looking for. When she settled back at the desk, she cleared her throat, looking through the notes as she spoke. "Mollie came to us a little over four years ago. She was born at the Florence Night Mission, one of the Crittenton mission homes for unwed mothers. Her mother had been brought by a man who claimed to be her relative. He said the child's father was unknown and that he was unable to care for the mother, whose name he gave as Nora." She looked up from the papers. "The mission doctor who cared for her noted, when he brought Mollie to us, that Nora refused to say anything about herself, and that the man who brought her to the mission house never gave his name." She looked back down at the paper, then sighed and set the file aside. "Unfortunately, Nora contracted a fever after giving birth and passed into the hands of the Lord when her baby was only a few days old. Mollie has been with us ever since."

The room was silent as she examined them both. "I will give you a few minutes alone to decide what you wish to do," she said, a touch of sternness returning to her voice. "Mollie, of course, has not been told anything of your visit. And should you choose to leave here today, she never will." The nun's face softened. "I hope you will not, Mr. Green. She looks a great deal like you."

"Thank you, Mother Superior," Vivian said, standing politely. "We will have an answer for you in a few minutes."

She didn't look at Leo until the door had closed and they were alone again. He had retrieved the file from the nun's desk and was staring at the scant notes in it. There were tears in his eyes, and he didn't bother hiding them or wiping them away. "Nora had a baby," he whispered.

"O'Keefe lied," Vivian said, her own voice hoarse. "That's what my father was trying to tell me before he died. I thought he was talking about my sister, but he meant the Florence Night Mission. He said something about O'Keefe being Irish Catholic, and having some kind of code—"

Leo gave a laugh that was a half sob. "Figures. Bastard didn't flinch at killing the whole Murphy family. But I guess killing a pregnant girl was a step too far. No wonder he laughed when he asked if I had been Nora's fella," he added, wiping the heel of his hand against his eyes at last. He took a deep breath. "I didn't know she was—"

"I know," Vivian said. She gave his hand what was meant to be a quick squeeze, but Leo clung to her, and she didn't pull away. "And it's no wonder that she wouldn't say much to the mission workers. Not after what—" Vivian swallowed. "What she'd seen O'Keefe do."

"No," Leo said roughly. "All she'd have wanted to do was make sure the baby—" He broke off, as if finishing the sentence was too much. He closed the file quickly, pushing it back onto the desk like it would burn him if he held it any longer.

Vivian felt as if a rip had opened in her heart, one she thought she had closed long ago. But Clyde Quinn had begun pulling at the stitches that held it shut, and it tore open a little farther with each flicker of emotion across Leo's face.

"I know it's a lot," she said, trying not to let her own feelings enter her voice. She wasn't sure if she succeeded. "But what . . . what do you think you want to do?"

He gripped the arms of his straight-backed chair. "What would I need to do?"

"If you wanted her?" Vivian swallowed. "I don't know how the process works. They do like to keep families together, I know that. And they're always trying to get the children adopted or fostered. It just . . ." She shook her head. "It doesn't happen for a lot of them."

"And what will happen to her if she stays here?"

The office window looked out over the buildings beyond, the dormitory with its rows of windows and chimneys. Vivian turned her face toward it. "They'll raise her with as much kindness as they can when they have so many children to provide for. Schooling's important to them, so she'll learn to read and write and all the rest. And they'll teach her a trade. Sewing or secretary work if she's got a knack for one of them, factory work or something like it if she doesn't. She'll have to leave no older than eighteen, unless she decides to take vows. But they'll prepare her for that as best they can."

"Will it be a bad life?" Leo asked.

"No," Vivian said, surprised to find that she meant it. "Anyone's life can be bad, I suppose, but this one doesn't have to be. It will be hard. And it's lonely, to always wonder if there's someone—" She broke off. It wasn't fair to him to finish that sentence, any more than it was fair to Mollie that she might be left wondering, just as Vivian had for so long. "It can be lonely. But it doesn't have to be bad."

She waited, silently, while Leo stared straight ahead. At last he stood.

"All right," he said, his voice shaking. "Let's go see the Mother Superior."

There," the Mother Superior said, pointing at the line of children, none of them more than seven years old, all trooping together toward the school building. "They're just coming in from their morning exercise."

She waited until the group drew closer, then gestured to the sister at the head of the line, who held up her hand. The line stopped, and the children whispered and fidgeted and laughed, plucking at grass or sticking out their tongues at each other, while the two nuns conferred a few feet away from where Leo and Vivian waited. At last, the younger nun looked back at the children.

"Mollie," she called out. "Mother Superior wishes to speak to you."

A little girl trotted obediently out of the line—a girl who looked like Leo in miniature, with beautiful, dark curls tumbling down her shoulders, a nose just a little bit too big for her face.

"Jesus, Mary, and Joseph," Vivian whispered.

"Don't let the nuns hear you," Leo quipped beside her, trying to make a joke of it. But she could hear his voice shaking.

The little girl made a beeline for their group, stopping a few feet away and clasping her hands in front of her while she turned up her face toward them expectantly. "Yes, Mother?"

"Thank you, Sister Mary Helen," the Mother Superior said, nodding at the other nun. "You may return to the children." She gestured to Mollie as the line began its progress toward the school building once more. "Mollie, this gentleman and lady wish to meet you."

"Why?" Mollie asked in her piping voice, looking them over curiously.

The Mother Superior looked back at them, and Vivian followed her eyeline toward Leo. He was staring at the little girl as if he had seen a ghost. Mollie glanced between the three of them, a puzzled frown growing between her eyes.

Then Leo dropped to one knee and smiled at her, a broad grin that trembled across his face but stayed. "Well, Mollie, my name's Leo Green, and I thought I'd like to meet you because I heard you were a smart, tough little girl. But no one mentioned that you were covered in dirt."

The girl glanced down at her dress, which was indeed smudged with mud and grass, and giggled. "I'm not *always* covered in dirt," she said seriously. "We were spinning, and I got so dizzy I fell down, and

I got so dirty, and Sister Mary Helen gave me a great big scolding and said I have to scrub it clean and won't get any cookie on Sunday. Have you ever been scolded?"

"Lots of times," Leo said, his voice choked with something that could have been laughter or tears. Maybe it was both. "Are you fast when you spin?"

"Look!" Mollie ordered, and Leo stood quickly so that he could take a step back as his daughter began to demonstrate, laughing wildly.

Vivian watched them together, tears pricking at her eyes, able to feel every crack and splinter in her heart. But this time the ache was a good one, and she didn't mind it so much.

THIRTY-FOUR

The clouds were already edged with moonlight as Vivian left home that night; dark was coming earlier. She didn't mind as much as she would have a few days before. Slowly, the city traded one kind of noise for another, music drifting from an open window, a couple laughing as they climbed into a cab, a soft plea for help—a smoke, a nickel, a moment of your time—from the shadows. The impatient cars and shouting clerks had gone home for the night, the stores had locked their doors, and families were silhouetted against the glass of hundreds of glowing windows.

The Nightingale was waiting.

Mr. Smith would rule the bandstand, and Bea would have her eyes closed as she crooned a love song into the microphone, breaking hearts and mending them with every smoky note. Or maybe the trumpet would join her for a fast-scatting duet, dancers barely able to keep up. Ellie would bounce from table to table, and Alba would do her best not to scowl her way through her shift and maybe succeed this time while Benny and Saul loomed silently in their corners.

Miss Rose would be on the dance floor, never without a partner and making every single one of them look good. There would be a pair of baby vamps just out of school, giggling in the corner or kicking their heels up for the Charleston, red lipstick and flashing bangles and eyes only for each other. Pretty Jimmy Allen would ask her for a spin on her break, and old-fashioned Mr. Lawrence would stick to the dignified waltzes and foxtrots, though his eyes would always light up when he watched a really good quickstep.

Danny would be behind the bar, flirting and smiling while he mixed drinks with the flair of a magician. Every woman and plenty of the men who watched would fall in love with him, even if it was only for a heartbeat.

And Honor . . .

Honor would move through the world she had built like poetry and silk and the jazz that flowed from the bandstand. She would know who to greet with fanfare and who wanted to slide in unnoticed, who was there for a good time and who was waiting for a little cash slipped under the table. She would watch them all with a curve to her red lips, as if she was unknowable, as if nothing could ever touch her.

And Vivian would be one of the few people who knew that none of that was true, and the secret knowledge would carry her through the night like its own kind of music.

She was ready for the party, but she was no longer sure if she could call it an escape. Maybe it was just a home like any other, one that sometimes left you crying and sometimes set you free and always, always curled around your heart and into your bones and left its mark on you, whether you wanted it or not.

Vivian turned her feet toward home.

THIRTY-FIVE

The official reopening might have already happened, but Vivian had a feeling the regulars were still celebrating. Or maybe Hattie Wilson's whispers had gotten around and people wanted to get a glimpse of the mysterious Nightingale and its owner, because there were dozens of new faces there too. The dance floor was even more crowded than usual, and Danny and Lucky were so busy behind the bar that Vivian hadn't seen either of them take a breather by the time her first break rolled around.

"Vivian, baby doll, dust off those dancing shoes," a cheerful voice ordered as Bea began the opening lyrics of "Sister Kate." She turned to find Pretty Jimmy beaming at her, hand outstretched. "Don't say you can't, I beg you," he added, laying the other hand dramatically against his chest. "You wouldn't want to break my heart. And besides, I just heard that handsome bartender tell you to take ten."

Vivian laughed. "All right, you goof," she said, shaking her head. "But I expect to be wowed with your fancy footwork."

"I live to serve," Jimmy said solemnly, sliding a hand around her waist and wiggling them playfully backward toward the dance floor.

And then they were off, stomping and bouncing and sliding through the music with the rest of the crowd.

Mr. Lawrence introduced her to a friend of his after that, another dignified gentleman with gray in his hair and a face she thought she recognized from the society pages. Then there was a shy-looking girl hovering on the dance floor in black-and-gold spangles, who lit up like the sun when Vivian asked her to dance and held her own through the Charleston with a breathless determination that left them laughing as the song ended.

By the time she made her way back to the bar, she felt lighter than she had in days. She arrived just in time to hear the end of Danny's conversation with one of the other waitresses.

"—my last night," Danny was saying with a sad smile. "At least behind the bar. I'm sure I'll be back from time to time. But someone else will be taking over back here, I guess starting tomorrow."

Vivian's good mood came crashing down, and she stared at him in horror. "Tonight?" she demanded, though she had the presence of mind to keep her voice down. Any hint of distress could start a panic if the guests thought they were worried about something like a raid. "Tonight is your last night? You can't be serious."

"Well, we sure will miss you," the other waitress said, lifting a tray with two cups of coffee and a little decanter of whiskey. She was new enough that she looked disappointed but not devastated by the news. "Won't be the same without you behind the bar."

Danny gave Vivian a wry smile once they were left alone. "Dead serious, I'm afraid," he said, barely needing to watch his hands as he popped the cork on a new bottle of champagne. "I'll have to get you on the dance floor for a spin before the night is over to mark the occasion."

"But . . ." Vivian shook her head as she gestured toward the other end of the bar, where Lucky was holding court as he poured out fingers of whiskey. "We're not ready for you to leave. He can't take over."

Danny glanced toward Lucky and chuckled. "Ain't that the truth.

Lucky!" he shouted over the music, waiting until his cousin looked his way to add, "That one's for mixing, dummy. We don't need you giving any customers a heart attack." Without missing a beat in his story, Lucky pushed the glasses out of the way and began again. Danny laughed again as he turned back to Vivian. "Don't worry. You know Hux: she's always got a plan."

"But does it have to be so soon?" Vivian said, almost begging.

"It does," Danny said, his expression growing more serious. "There is no perfect time for change, there's just now. And right now, I want to be home with my girls." He glanced over her shoulder. "Cheer up, kitten. Someone you like is looking for you."

Vivian turned to find Honor coming around the dance floor, slow and purposeful as she surveyed the people around her with a half smile. She was wearing a jacket tonight, with a carnation at the buttonhole and a bow tie made of white lace at her neck. In the sweaty heat of the club, blond curls were making their escape to curl around her ears and neck, and Vivian wasn't surprised by the heads that craned around to follow her progress. Honor was in her element tonight.

She stopped a few steps away and crooked a finger at Vivian; when Vivian glanced back at Danny, he already had two coupes of champagne in his hands. As he handed them over, he winked and made a shooing motion with his hand. Puzzled, Vivian carried the glasses as Honor led her to a table for two in the corner near the bandstand.

Vivian looked around as she took a seat across from Honor. The last time they had sat in this spot, where the music would make it almost impossible for anyone to overhear what they were saying, had been the night Vivian decided she truly couldn't trust Honor. Now, it felt like a lifetime ago.

"What are the bubbles for?" she asked. Up on the bandstand, Bea began to sing a slow, sultry arrangement of "Brown Eyes, Why Are You Blue?" Vivian felt a shiver chase across her shoulders as the notes floated through the air.

"Well, that depends on you," Honor said. She set her own glass aside and reached into her jacket to retrieve a folded set of papers. When she set them down, she held them in place for a moment with the tips of her fingers, as though she were steeling herself for something uncertain. She met Vivian's eyes slowly. "All right, pet. Here we go," she murmured as she slid them across the table.

Vivian didn't feel any less puzzled as she unfolded the papers and began to read. With the music filling her head, it took her more than a minute to realize what she was seeing.

Vivian's eyes were wide as she stared at Honor. "What is this?" she demanded, her voice barely loud enough to be heard over the band.

"It's an offer," Honor said, and she didn't look hesitant at all anymore. "I need someone new now that Danny's leaving. A bartender. And a partner."

"But this is more than what you and Danny—" Vivian stared at the papers again. "Honor, this says I'd have a stake in the Nightingale."

"Yes."

"You can't offer me that!" Vivian insisted.

Honor looked almost amused by her protest, which would have been infuriating if Vivian hadn't been so confused. "It's my place, Vivian. I can do whatever I want with it. And if I'm looking for someone to run this place with me, I can't think of anyone better than you."

"Really?" Vivian shook her head. "Because I can think of plenty of people who would be better than me. I'm a seamstress. A waitress. I'm poor Irish trash who buys her dancing shoes out of a catalog. Just about anyone else— I can't—"

"You can," Honor said, cutting her off.

The band begin to pick up the tempo, the song shifting from melancholy to playful as the brassy notes of the trumpet joined the piano and Bea's voice rang out above them. The dancers caught the new rhythm eagerly as they spun across the floor.

Honor slid a glass of champagne toward her. "You've been behind the bar," she said. "You know the staff, you know the regulars. They know you. You don't have quite Danny's eye for spotting cops out of uniform, but you'll learn. And you're the person I trust the most to do this with me."

Vivian wanted to keep protesting, but her voice was tangled somewhere in her throat. She stared at Honor, still not quite able to believe what she was hearing.

"And it's something we can share." Honor turned her own glass in slow circles as she spoke. She didn't look away from Vivian. "It's a partnership, but it's also security. For you. Even if things fall apart between us, you can still cash in your share of the Nightingale. You'll still be okay."

"I don't want things to fall apart between us," Vivian said quickly.

Honor smiled. "Me neither, pet. And I'm not saying I expect them to. But there are some kinds of certainty I can't offer you. Not without more changing in this world than I ever expect to change. This, though . . . this I can offer you. If you want it."

Vivian could have kept arguing. But she could also say yes. There was nothing stopping her except herself.

"I do. Yes. I want this." She took a deep breath. "I choose this. I choose you."

The smile that spread across Honor's face wasn't like sunshine. She wasn't a sunshiny person. But it was like moonlight along the edges of clouds, like champagne bubbles and secrets, like adventure and freedom and home.

She lifted her glass, and Vivian, her hand shaking only a little, did the same. They couldn't hear the clink of the edges over the music, but Vivian could feel it in her body. "Cheers, then," Honor murmured, taking a sip. Then she set down her glass and stood, holding out her hand. "Dance with me?"

Vivian took a deep breath and stood up. For a heartbeat, she let her eyes close. She wasn't sure if it was the music or the champagne, the people around her or the woman in front of her. But in that moment, she could have sworn she was flying.

She opened her eyes and put her hand in Honor's.

"Yes," she whispered, smiling. "Let's dance."

ACKNOWLEDGMENTS

Writing the acknowledgments for the last book in a series is more than a little terrifying. So many people have made these books possible, in both tangible and intangible ways, that it's impossible for me to adequately thank them all. But I can try.

Nettie Finn was the first editor to decide that these books belonged on your shelf, and Hannah O'Grady was the editor who made sure the second half of the series got there, too. Both of them were expert guides who helped these stories reach heights I could never have managed on my own. I am indebted to both and so grateful for their hard work.

Five years ago, I told Whitney Ross I had an idea for a story set in the Jazz Age, and she told me I should definitely write it down. I could never have imagined that it would turn into four books and a series that would have the chance to touch so many people. Along the way, she provided everything from hands-on editing to creative encouragement to business advice. Every writer should have an agent like her.

The entire team at Minotaur and St. Martin's Publishing Group works around the clock to bring beautiful books to life, and I wish

I knew more of them than I do. I am grateful to my publicity and marketing team, especially Sara La Cotti and Allison Ziegler, for their endless creativity and the superhuman speed at which they respond to emails; to Maddie Alsup for keeping track of more details than any one human should be able to, in addition to having amazing editorial insights; to Christina MacDonald for her careful edits, and her patience when I wrote *further* instead of *farther* for the hundredth time; to David Baldeosingh Rotstein and Nikolaas Eickelbeck for my stunning covers; and to the many, many others who battle book piracy, correct printing errors, design ebook layouts, and so much more.

I'm grateful to the entire team at High Line Literary, who are so supportive of their authors, and particularly to Victoria Marini, who stepped in when Whitney couldn't be there for a few months.

Reagan, Yeneli, CeCe, Melissa, Charita, Samantha, Brice, and so many others have provided one of the greatest gifts a parent can get: time to work while knowing that my kids are safe, loved, learning, growing, and generally having a great time without their mom and dad around. I am more thankful to all of you than I can ever say.

Booksellers and librarians pour their hearts into making sure books end up in the right readers' hands, and I have been fortunate to know so many who have championed this series. I'm especially indebted to Flannery, Chelsea, Andi, and Kelly.

The Bluebird Writers are some of the most supportive people out there, and every one of them is an inspiration. I am so lucky to know all of you.

The friends and family who have supported and encouraged me as this series makes its way into the world are too many to list here. I hope you know how much I treasure every kind word, excited text, and book photo. (Also the cocktails, dinners, and offers of childcare.) Y'all are truly, truly the best.

I could spend pages of acknowledgments thanking Brian, but that would be really boring for everyone else to read. So I'll just send this wish out into the world: that everyone be fortunate enough to find someone who supports them as tirelessly as he supports me. I'm pretty sure I could get this all done without you, love, but it would be a lot more work and a lot less fun.

Finally, to everyone reading this, thank you. Thank you for loving these characters and their world. Thank you for your excitement for these stories. Thank you for letting me share a piece of my heart with you. It's been magical.

AUTHOR'S NOTE

Over the past few years, it has been a joy to write this series and an education to research it. It's become a running joke in my family to try to pick out the throwaway details that only appear in a single sentence but probably took a day or more to get just right.

Then there are the details that make up a much bigger part of the story but are still a challenge to track down because of the sparseness of the historical record. Adoption in the early part of the twentieth century is one such detail, for many reasons.

In the nineteenth and early twentieth centuries, like today, adoption policies were deeply entwined with public opinions on poverty, class, race, and gender. Children were not only placed in orphanages or put up for adoption after their parents had died. Many "orphans" had living parents who simply had too many children and too few resources to care for them all, similar to today's foster system. In other cases, mothers were discouraged or outright prevented from keeping children who were born out of wedlock.

In the 1920s, as in many other time periods, adoption proceedings were often shrouded in secrecy, with sealed records or, in some cases, no official records at all. But the places that Vivian visits in her search for the orphan Mollie were real locations in New York.

The Florence Crittenton Night Mission, which was located on Bleecker Street, was a mission home founded by Charles Crittenton in the late 1800s. It was named in memory of Crittenton's daughter, Florence, who died at age four. The mission's aim was to help women escape prostitution and poverty by offering lodging, food, assistance looking for work, and Gospel meetings. By the 1920s, it was one of nearly one hundred Crittenton Homes around the country that helped poor women and girls; during this time, Crittenton partnered with Dr. Kate Waller Barrett, who was instrumental in expanding the scope of the organization from preventing prostitution to serving unmarried mothers, as well as women and girls who were the victims of extreme poverty, domestic violence, homelessness, and other traumatic circumstances. Today, the national Crittenton organization operates as the Justice + Joy National Collaborative, with Crittenton chapters all around the United States.

The New York Catholic Protectory was a real orphanage that was in operation from 1865 until the 1930s. The Protectory was created to prevent the orphaned or neglected children of Catholic parents from being sent west by the Protestant Children's Aid Society, whose founder considered Irish Catholic immigrants to be "bad blood" and "dangerous." Many of the Catholic children sent away from New York on the Aid Society's "orphan trains" still had living parents or other relatives, but their parental rights were often terminated, and the children's names were changed when they were sent to new homes, making it nearly impossible for their families to track them down.

At the Protectory, children were housed, clothed, and educated, along with being taught a trade such as letterpress printing, carpentry, or shoemaking (for boys) and embroidery, cooking, or glove making (for girls). In 1938, the land that the Protectory was on was purchased by the Metropolitan Life Insurance Company, which razed the orphanage to make way for the construction of the Parkchester apartment house community. None of the original buildings remain. I'm indebted to Janet Butler Munch (CUNY Lehman College), Michelle Kahan (University of Massachusetts, Boston), and the Westchester Genealogical Society for their research into the Protectory and adoption policies of the early twentieth century.

ABOUT THE AUTHOR

Leah O'Connell

Katharine Schellman is an award-winning author of historical mysteries. Her novels, which reviewers have called "worthy of Rex Stout or Agatha Christie," have been named one of *Suspense Magazine*'s Best Books of the Year, a *Library Journal* Best Crime Fiction of the Year, and a *New York Times* Editor's Pick. A former actor, onetime political consultant, and graduate of the College of William & Mary, Katharine lives and writes in the mountains of Virginia with her husband, children, and the many houseplants she keeps accidentally murdering. You can learn more about her at www.katharineschellman.com.